I'm an Irish author who is addicted to writing romances featuring damaged, moody, book boyfriends searching for their happily ever after.

Visit K.A. Finn online:

www.kafinn.com
(trailers, excerpts, artwork, playlists etc)

Facebook: kafinnauthor

Instagram: kafinnauthor

Additional links: linktr.ee/kafinn

Also by K.A. Finn

Nomad Series (Space Opera)

Ares

Nemesis

Perses

Chaos

Mania

Cronus

Talos (TBA)

Blackjacks Series (Paranormal Romance)

Breaking Phoenix

Reviving Davyn

Defying Shep

Defending Rhain (2025)

Broken Chords (Rockstar Romance)

Broken Rock (Tate)

Fractured Rock (Gregg)

Split Rock (Tate & all band members)

Crushed Rock (Luke)

Shattered Rock (Dillon)

Damaged Rock (Gregg - TBA)

Twisted Legends (Folklore Retelling/Romance)

North Bound (Nick/Santa)

Shadow Bound (Damon/The Boogeyman - TBA)

TWISTED LEGENDS # 1

NORTH BOUND

K.A. FINN

Cover design by Get Covers
www.getcovers.com

Published by Cooper Publishing
www.cooperbookservices.com

ISBN: 978-1-914177-59-0

Coming next

TWISTED LEGENDS # 2

SHADOW BOUND

K.A. FINN

NORTH BOUND PLAYLIST

I'll be Waiting (Sad at Christmas) – Cian Ducrot
Storm – Anthony Gargiula
Christmas Lights – Coldplay
Naughty & Nice– Sia
Stay – Hurts
All I Want for Christmas is New Year's Day – Hurts
Brush it Off– Plan Three
The Great Unknown – Rob Thomas
It Won't Last – Matt Guillory
Nevermind – Deaf Havana
All For You – Cian Ducrot & Ella Henderson
Obsessed – Sam Riggs
Woke Up in Love (Acoustic) – Kygo, Gryffin, and Calum Scott
Where I Belong – Saint Chaos
Legends Are Made – Sam Tinnesz
Hope– Shinedown
Stay A While – Cemetery Sun
Closer To The Edge – Thirty Seconds To Mars
Make Believe – The Faim
Pretty Like the Sun – Prime Circle
Right Now – MASCOT
Life & Death – Blowsight
One I Wanna Be With – Trella
Northern Lights – Thirty Seconds To Mars
Don't Forget Me – Dermot Kennedy
Miss Me – Will Linley
Wish I Could Forget – SLANDER, blackbear, & Bring Me The Horizon
The Ghost – Charlie Scene
Take Me Home – Tape Machines, Zorro
Tonight, I Love You – Latency
Live Like Legends – Nathan Wagner, Rebecca Ray
Can't Forget You – My Darkest Day

Keep On Wanting – The Fray
Tonight, Together – The Goo Goo Dolls
I Could Be Stronger (Bit Only For You) – Gareth Emery
Power Over Me – Dermot Kennedy
Lose You Now – Lindsey Stirling, Mako
All I Need – Within Temptation
Never Stop – Safetysuit
Do Or Die – Thirty Seconds To Mars

Well, enough from me. I'll leave you in Santa's more than capable hands – have fun!

THE LEGENDS

NICK - SANTA

DAMON - THE BOOGEYMAN

COBH - TRITON

JOKUL - JACK FROST

HUNTER - CUPID

FLINT - THE HORSEMAN

REVE - THE SANDMAN

TALEN - KRAMPUS

This one is for everyone who still believes...

Scarlett climbs out of her car, wrapping her scarf around her neck, when the wind threatens to take it off her into the forest.

The predicted snow storm is already building, the wind howling through the trees, and around the cottage. It's rare to have a white Christmas in Ireland, but this year is to be an exception. But she doesn't mind. She's prepared for the worst. The shed out back has plenty of wood for the fire, she's got oil for the generator, in case the power goes, and the boot of her car is filled with enough food to last her a few weeks.

The quaint cottage sitting at the end of the cobbled path is as inviting as she remembers. The paint on the bright red door and white window frames could use a little attention, but it just adds to the character, in her opinion.

She carefully makes her way through the creaky gate, each footstep crunching on the freshly fallen snow. One whole week here. All. By. Herself. No interruptions. No visitors. No work stress. Just a lot of good food and great company.

Or maybe that last part is wishful thinking. She's spending Christmas with a pile of book boyfriends. When did her life reach such new and exciting levels? Then again, spending seven days with super sexy fictional men sounds like heaven.

She unlocks the door, giving it a good shove when it initially refuses to open. Before she does anything else, she lights a fire in the huge fireplace, then goes back outside to grab her bags and the groceries from her car.

She parks her car in the shed to the side of the house, closing and locking the shed doors to keep it secure. As she reaches the front door of the cottage, she turns around, taking in her neighbours for the next few days. Not neighbours exactly. The cottage is surrounded by trees. That's it. A lot of trees. And a lot of privacy. Just perfect.

Scarlett shakes the snow from her coat and shrugs it off, hanging it on the back of the door. She pulls off her gloves with her teeth, then throws them on the table next to the groceries. It takes a few minutes to unpack the food, then she helps herself to a large glass of wine, and drops into the overstuffed armchair by the fire.

One week until the big day, and this year, it's all about her. After missing another promotion at work, and her flatmate getting engaged, being around people was not on her to-do-list for the immediate future.

Or ever, if she had her way.

Her grandparents' old holiday cottage was left to her in their will. It's in the middle of nowhere, near Roundwood in Co. Wicklow, with a scattering of neighbours, the nearest about a mile away.

She goes into the cosy kitchen, takes a packet of crisps from the cupboard, and works her way through it, as she double checks the windows and doors are secured. They're predicting one impressive snowfall just in time for Christmas week. Bring it on!

Spending the holiday alone, with not even so much as a bauble anywhere in the cottage, might seem a little miserable to some, but she's fine with it. More than fine with it. Christmas was for families, and when her grandparents died, so did her family. She'll leave all the festive cheer to everyone else.

She doesn't begrudge anyone celebrating Christmas. Far from it. But decorating and going all out, just didn't make sense to her when she's up here all alone.

She smiles and takes another sip of her wine. Spending this time alone, with wine and her growing to-be-read book pile, sounds like heaven.

She opens the bag overflowing with books, takes the first from the top of the pile, then wraps up in a blanket by the fire.

One and a half book boyfriends later, Scarlett jumps when a loud bang sounds from outside, followed by a crash. She freezes, holding her breath as she listens. But there's nothing else. Just the wind howling through the trees surrounding the cottage.

She checks her watch. Three in the morning. She must have dozed off for a bit. The fire has gone out, her book is on her lap, and the moonlight is visible through the window. She jumps as another loud bang comes from outside.

Common sense is telling her to ignore it. She's read enough thrillers in her life to know you never head towards the suspicious sound. Especially when the sound is coming from a dark forest in a snow storm. Big no-no.

But two minutes later, she does the very thing she had decided not to do. She creeps over to the window, peering around the window frame into the darkness outside. Except it's not completely dark. There's a fire at the edge of the trees just beyond her property. 'Shit, shit, shit!'

Scarlett bundles into her coat and stuffs her feet into her winter boots, then grabs her torch. Having second thoughts, she stops by the door, picking up the axe resting against the log pile. Never can be too prepared.

With her head down against the driving snow, she slowly makes her way across the garden to the trees, using the moonlight to help her find her way.

By the time she gets to the fire, the snow has helped extinguish it. She guides her torchlight over what looks like some kind of vehicle wreckage. In the dark it's difficult to figure out what it is.

One end of the deep red vehicle is embedded in a tree, the trunk of the tree snapped in half by the impact and lying over the top of the vehicle.

As she examines it, she realises it's not a car. It doesn't have a roof for one, and she doubts you would take a convertible out in a snow storm. But it's also completely the wrong shape and doesn't have wheels. Two huge black runners sit in place of the wheels, stretching the full length of the wreckage.

Scarlett frowns, then shakes her head. As ridiculous as the notion is, she can't escape the fact it reminds her of a sleigh. A massive, deep red sleigh. But if it is a sleigh, what was pulling it?

Her attention falls on a huge footprint beside the sleigh and she swallows thickly. She's no wildlife expert, but she'd swear that's a reindeer footprint! And it's from the biggest reindeer ever, judging by the size of it.

'Shit...' she mutters to herself as she looks around the dark wood. The moon is casting strange shadows everywhere she looks. The thought of a mutant reindeer of some sort, potentially being out there, hiding in the forest has her firming her grip on the pick axe.

She tucks her chin in against her chest, as a gust of wind threatens to knock her over. The weather is deteriorating fast. She needs to stop worrying about giant reindeer and find the driver, or whoever was in the sleigh.

'Hello!'

Nothing.

Pulling her hat further over her ears, she cautiously makes her way around the wreckage, moving her torch in slow arcs across the deep snow. There are no footprints apart from her own, so where's the driver?

Scarlett pushes through the trees, scanning the darkness around her. 'This isn't creepy in the slightest,' she mutters to herself as the wind howls through the thick trees. 'Not one little bit. What the hell are you doing, Scarlett?'

Not finding anyone at the edge of the forest, she makes her way back to the clearing, turning in a slow circle, squinting against the falling snow. Then she spots something. There's a dark shape in the snow a few feet ahead of her.

'Shit!'

She trudges closer to the shape, half expecting whatever it is, to jump up and attack her at any minute. But it's not moving and is already covered in a thick layer of snow.

'There you are!' Scarlett crouches down beside the body and examines it. From the sheer size she'd guess it's a man. If he wasn't wearing a red coat, she seriously doubts she would have caught sight of him through the snow.

The poor guy is lying chest down in the snow after presumably being thrown from his... sleigh thing, or whatever it is? She slowly reaches out, pressing her fingers to his wrist to check for a pulse. It's strong and steady, much to her relief. 'Hello? Sir?'

But he's out cold. And he's cold. Really cold. She brushes the snow from the side of his face and hair. 'Hello?'

Still nothing.

She pulls her mobile out of her pocket and checks the screen. 'Of course there's no signal,' she mutters to herself. Even standing up and waving the phone in all directions doesn't help. Perfect! Now what is she supposed to do?

'Any ideas?' she asks him, but the man is utterly unhelpful, choosing to remain unconscious. She looks down at him and curses to herself. Not a lot she can do. She can't exactly leave him out here to die of exposure.

'Okay. So you stay put. I'll be back in a minute,' she says, before slowly picking her way through the snow back to her house.

'This was supposed to be a nice quiet break,' she says to herself as she searches around the back of the cottage for a sled, or anything she can use to drag him back to the house on. 'But no. Only you could have a random guy land on your doorstep.'

She moves some junk from the corner of the garage and smiles. 'Bingo!' Scarlett drags the sled from the bottom of the pile and brushes the years of cobwebs and dirt from it.

The bright pink sled came out every time they were lucky enough to have a white Christmas when she was growing up. It was designed to carry a child, not a grown man, but it will have to do.

She quickly replaces the flimsy string with some rope she finds hanging from the wall, before locking the shed behind her again.

With the sled trailing behind her, she makes her way back through the snow to the mysterious man. 'Is it too much to ask for a little peace and quiet? I just wanted to read a few books. Have quite a few glasses of wine. Eat myself into a stupor. Instead, I'm freezing my ass off, rescuing some random lost man that seems to have dropped from the sky.'

Unfortunately he's still out cold when she gets back to him. She places her hands on her hips and glares at him. 'You're just going to make me drag you back, aren't you?' She pulls the sled up beside him, then grabs the back of his heavy coat. 'I'm just rolling you over.'

It takes a hell of an effort to roll him onto his back, but she manages to get him onto the sled. His head and some of his upper body are on the sled, but that's the best she can do. He's a lot longer than his rescue vehicle.

She picks up the rope attached to the sled and digs her heels in.

'Right. Let's get you inside.'

The first few attempts to move him, end with her lying on her face or ass in the snow. He's one heavy guy. Cursing him for the umpteenth time, she tries again, nearly shouting aloud when the sled slides towards her.

She readjusts her feet, then goes again. Two steps down. Only a few dozen more to go.

Over half an hour, and a hell of a lot of cursing later, Scarlett braces her legs and gives one last heave, dragging the man into her living room. She's sweating and out of breath, but she's done it, and just in time too. The wind is now howling around the cottage as the storm worsens.

The man is still unconscious, sprawled out on top of her pink sled. She thought all the jostling would have brought him around, but unfortunately it didn't. It would have helped if he had woken up and was able to at least partly assist her getting him back to the house. He weighed a ton.

She hauls him over to the fire and positions him in front of the hearth to warm him up. His skin is pale and cold to the touch, but other than a wound on his head, he seems in good shape and he's breathing normally.

Scarlett would like nothing more than to leave the sled where it is, but she needs to remove it, or he'll wake up in serious pain from the uncomfortable position.

It takes another ten minutes to extract the sled from under him, but she finally succeeds. He's now lying on the wooden floor, but that's where he's going to have to stay. She's surprised she was able to get him as far as she did. Lifting him onto the couch is more than she's willing to attempt.

After stripping off her coat and boots, she adds more fuel to the fire, trying to get it going again. When the kindling catches, she drops onto the couch and looks at the man lying in front of her fire as she composes herself.

The entire situation is weird. Really, really weird. Things like this don't happen to her. Her life is remarkably uncomplicated. No drama.

She tucks her legs under her and stares down at the man lying at her feet. Clearly someone thought her life needed a little spicing up, so decided to send her a man.

She leans forward. A very nice man. Whoever he is, he's undoubtedly the most attractive man she's ever seen.

She brushes her wet hair back from her forehead, as she shuffles to the edge of the seat to get a closer look. Yeah, he's still stunning up close too. Even more so in fact.

She'd guess he's about five years older than her, probably in his early to mid-forties. His short light brown hair and tight beard are peppered with grey which she finds extremely sexy.

Stop staring at the man!

She sits back, but there's no way she can stop staring. It's impossible. He is so much taller than he appeared out in the wood. She knows the hearth is six foot wide and he's taller than that, maybe six-two. Definitely too tall for the low ceilings in the cottage.

What exactly is she supposed to do now? She can hardly sit here staring at him all night, however appealing that may sound.

She checks her phone screen again. Still no signal. There's no way she'll be able to get her car out either. She looks at the man as she considers her options.

Which right now aren't plentiful.

She's stuck here for the foreseeable with a strange man, who, now she sees him in the light, appears to be dressed a little like Santa.

The heavy red leather coat fits his broad chest and thick arms like a glove. The same with the red trousers. Teamed with the black combat boots he's certainly an edgier version of the typical Santa you'd usually see this time of year.

Maybe he was booked for a party? Could explain his mode of transportation too. Wherever he was going, she doubts it was to the local shopping centre for all the kids to swarm around. Certainly not to any centres she's ever been to.

She shakes herself out of her thoughts and gets back into serious mode. The least she can do is deal with his injuries, instead of leaving him bleeding on her floor, while she drools over him.

Scarlett gathers some first aid supplies, then fetches a bowl of warm water from the kitchen. Once she has everything she needs, she kneels on the floor beside him.

'Hey. Me again. I need to clean the cut on your head.' She pauses and narrows her eyes, waiting for a response. Still nothing at all. She shrugs and examines the wound. It's about the length of her thumb, but thankfully isn't too dirty.

Scarlett carefully moves his head to the side, so she can wash the blood from his forehead and side of his face. Not only is he handsome, he smells incredible. Just like the cinnamon cookies her grandmother used to bake. He certainly went all out with the outfit and the scent. He's Christmas in one seriously hot package.

And now she's drooling over an unconscious, injured man. Getting back to the first aid task, she fixes a plaster over the cut on his forehead, satisfied with her efforts. She sits back on her heels and frowns at his coat. One situation dealt with, and another presents itself. He's going to overheat if she leaves it on.

'I'm just going to open your coat. That's it. No funny business, I promise. I don't want you boiling on me.'

She waits for a second and, after getting no reaction, gingerly reaches over and unzips the heavy leather coat, opening it to each side.

She sits back on her heels and licks her suddenly dry lips, when she gets a better look at what was hidden under the coat.

A pair of black leather braces are attached to his trousers with a fitted long-sleeved white top underneath, which hugs his body in a seriously distracting way. The three buttons at the neck are open, showing a silver necklace with locket attached.

'Okay. Not too shabby at all.' She grimaces. 'I'm so sorry if you heard that. It was meant to stay in my head.'

Grimacing at her remark, Scarlett gets her duvet from her bed, then makes herself a cup of coffee and sits back on the chair by his feet. 'Sorry. Me again. If you can hear me I'd appreciate if you could let me know. Move your hand or something.'

But there's nothing. His breathing is steady and his colour returning to normal. The cut on his head isn't too bad. It doesn't look like that's the reason he is unconscious. It's nasty, but there's no bruising or swelling around it. Hopefully after some rest, he'll wake up.

She checks her phone again, but the signal is still non-existent. Scarlett picks up her book and looks at the model on the cover. 'What do you make of all this? Yeah. I agree. It's weird. Very weird indeed. Not an unpleasant weird, but certainly up there in the weird category. Are you getting a Santa vibe off him?'

The cover model chooses not to answer, but she's used to that. Having a conversation with a book can be a little one-sided.

'I mean it's not the typical Santa, but he's definitely giving off the vibe.' She glares at her book. 'Or I've read too many of these.' She places the book back on the nest of tables beside her chair. 'Yeah. Probably far too many fictional men.'

She shrugs to herself and wraps the duvet around her. There's no way she's going to go up to her room to sleep and leave a strange man in her house. She'll stay up and keep an eye on him until he wakes.

It's been a long time since he woke up with such a rotten fucking headache. Decades in fact. He also feels like he's going to throw up, which hasn't happened for decades either.

Groaning with the effort, he opens his eyes and winces, closing his eyes again. Fuck, he feels terrible. He rolls onto his side, feeling rough wood under his fingers. This isn't his bedroom floor. Not that he's spent a lot of time up close and personal with it. Where the fuck is he?

He pushes up to his elbow and winces as a ball bounces around his skull. Nope, not ready for that. His head is fucking killing him.

'Don't move.'

The female voice is unfamiliar, which immediately puts him on alert. He works with a lot of people, but he's sure he's never heard her voice before. He slowly turns his head towards the voice, blinking as he tries to get his vision to focus.

When it finally clears, he finds a woman sitting in an armchair next to him, her legs tucked up in front of her. She's peering at him over the rim of a large mug with steam coming out of it.

It's the wrong thing to think considering he hasn't got a clue where he is or what's wrong with him, but the woman looking strangely at him is one hell of a looker, whoever she is. Her pale skin is peppered with freckles and her green eyes have a hint of blue in the centre. She twirls the end of her long auburn hair as she peers down at him.

Who the fuck is she? She's definitely not someone from the workshop. He's sure he'd remember her.

She puts down the cup on the table beside her, and tucks her hands into the sleeves of the oversized Snoopy pyjamas she's wearing.

He leaves her staring at him as he takes in the rest of the room he's in. It's a cottage of some sort, with heavy wooden beams in the ceiling and walls. The open fire beside him fills the room with the scent of peat turf.

It's warm and homely, but doesn't help him figure out where he is.

'Where...' he groans, as his own voice echoes loudly in his head. 'Damn, that hurts.'

'I wouldn't move around too much if I were you. I found you in the forest a few hours ago. You were unconscious. There's a cut on your forehead but I don't think you've had a bang to your head. Well I hope not.'

He reaches up, quickly finding the cut she's talking about under a bandage. 'Ouch. You did this?'

'The cleaning and bandaging. Not the original cut. I promise that had nothing to do with me.'

She smiles and a little of the worry eases. So a pretty girl smiles at you and you trust her. Not the best move for someone in his position.

He convinces himself to stop staring and get his ass off the floor. He tries pushing upright again, but she joins him on the floor, gently guiding him onto his back. 'You really should take it easy. You've been out of it for about six hours. Go slow.'

He ignores her and drags himself to his feet, wobbling as the room shifts. Bracing against the wall, he just stops himself from crashing to the ground again. 'What date is it?'

'What?'

'The date? What is it?'

'The twenty-first of December. Why?'

The room sways again, but he forces himself to stand tall, cursing when he whacks his head on one of the very old, very solid ceiling beams.

The woman stands up, grimacing as she watches him rub the other side of his head. 'Ouch. That sounded like it hurt. You okay?'

'No I'm not okay!'

'At least you didn't hit the same side twice,' she replies, the small smile irritatingly attractive.

He glares at the beam, deciding he's going to have to stay stooped over, or risk continuously knocking himself out. 'Where am I?'

The woman examines his head, moving so close to him he can smell the coffee on her breath. 'Roundwood.'

'Where?'

'Wicklow. Ireland,' she adds, giving him a strange look. 'Do you remember how you got here?'

He knows full well how he got here. It's what happened after that, that's giving him problems. He can't remember anything. 'You said you found me. Where?'

She crosses her arms, probably irritated he's not answering her question, then nods to the front door. 'Outside. At the edge of the forest. I heard a loud crash. I went outside and there you were, lying in the snow.'

He stumbles over to the window and peers outside. Not that it does much good. That's one hell of a snow storm. 'Where exactly did you find me?'

She joins him at the window and points to the left. 'Over there.'

He opens the door and goes outside into the blizzard.

'Hey! What are you doing? Are you crazy? Come back inside.'

He scans the area, but it's near on impossible to make out the trees, let alone anything else. 'Was there anything with me,' he shouts back at her.

'A bit of wreckage from something, but I was kind of more focused on you.'

'Was anyone out here with me?'

She joins him on the path, wrapping a heavy coat around herself. 'What?'

'Was I alone?'

'Yes. Why? Should there be someone with you? I only found you. Have I missed someone else?'

He shakes his head. 'I was alone.'

'That's a relief. I thought there was someone else lying out there for a minute. Will you come back inside now? It's Baltic out here and you might have a head injury.'

He concentrates on his surroundings, ignoring her continuous efforts to get him indoors. There's something out there. Something he can't quite get a hold on. It's familiar, but he can't figure out where it's coming from.

He opens his eyes and looks over to the forest. He's got a niggling feeling they're not alone out here. He looks at the sky and whistles. Nothing. No surprise there. 'Did you see any animals around me?'

She frowns at him, clearly thinking he's lost his mind.

'Were there any animals?' he asks again, trying not to let his irritation show. Whoever was in the forest has moved away. If his head wasn't so sore he'd go after them. It's probably nothing. Maybe just a nosy neighbour. Maybe.

'Were there any animals?' he asks again. He understands why she's giving him strange looks, but right now, he couldn't give a fuck what she thinks about him.

'No, nothing. I did see a foot print from...'

'From what?'

'Okay so it might have looked like a reindeer print. But it was larger. I looked around, but couldn't see any actual reindeer - just the print.'

He checks his wrist and curses. The leather band with the tracking device is gone. He curses, reaching up to his neck. It's still there. The locket is still around his neck. Whatever else is going on right now, losing the last connection he has to them would be unbearable.

Losing his temper won't help him in the slightest, but he's seriously fucked off. He kicks the pile of logs, dislodging the wood, sending it tumbling to the ground. This is a fucking disaster. How the hell is he meant to get home? 'Shit, shit, shit!' He paces the driveway, stopping to punch the gate post, knocking the gate out of its catches.

'Whoa there! I get you're confused, but taking it out on my gate won't help. And it's flipping freezing out here. Your head is bleeding again too, so can you please come inside.'

She's right. It's not like he can see anything out here. He nods and turns back to the house, stumbling as a dizzy spell hits. She catches him before he falls, helping him back into the house.

Once inside, she shuts the door again and helps him over to the chair by the fire.

'Sit down and this time stay down. If you keep running around the place like a blue-arsed fly, your head will never heal and I have a finite first aid supply.'

He does as he's told, but only because his head is killing him. He's taken bumps to the head before, but this feels completely different. The pain encompasses his entire head, keeping his thoughts fuzzy.

'Stay there. I'll get you something to drink. Tea? Coffee? Chocolate?'

'What?'

'Would you like a drink?'

'Anything but tea, thanks.'

'You hungry?'

He nods absently.

'Okay, I'll sort that out. Can you please try not to hit anything while I'm gone.'

He smiles briefly and she winks, then goes into the kitchen.

This is a fucking nightmare. One week from Christmas and he's trapped in a snowstorm in Ireland, with no way of getting home. No ride. No tracker. No way for anyone to find him, even if they could, in the middle of a blizzard.

He gingerly prods his forehead, blood staining his fingers when he pulls them away. He can't remember what happened. Why can't he remember? Every time he tries, the pain ramps up a level. She mentioned a crash, which was presumably him, but that doesn't help in the slightest. He doesn't crash. It never happens. It's impossible. While he was travelling he was protected.

Something happened to disrupt that. It's the only explanation. But what?

He looks out the window at the snow swirling around the cottage. Until he can check out the crash site, he's just guessing at what might have happened.

And that's the part that's going to drive him crazy. Patience isn't his top quality. It isn't actually a quality of his, full stop. He's not so good at sitting around and doing nothing.

The cottage is small, barely enough head room for him to stand. There's nowhere to pace or run. He's stuck in this room, with a strange woman, until the storm blows over.

He turns his attention back to the kitchen when he hears the woman humming to herself. From what he can tell, she's alone out here, yet she took the time and effort to help him, even though she knows nothing about him. She could just as easily have ignored the sounds she heard outside and got on with her night.

That says something about her. Heading out there alone and dragging him back to the house would have taken one hell of an effort, and he appreciates that. There's no doubt he owes her his life.

She passes by the door and opens the fridge, taking out a bottle of milk. He's not one of those guys who claims to have a type. On the rare occasions he went out to meet someone, he tended to go for women who wanted the same thing from the night as he did. Sex. Nothing more. He can't have anything more than that. With his job, finding time to date came a distant last to everything else he has to do.

This woman hasn't said or done anything to even hint she wants something from him, but that just makes her all the more appealing. No make-up. No fancy clothes. No perfectly groomed hair. Just naturally stunning. And as for the Snoopy pyjamas... that's a new one, and he really likes it. He rests his head against the back of the chair, unable to take his eyes off her, as she butters a slice of toast.

His body isn't taking the headache into account. Potential head injury or not, he's turned on by her. He wants to see, to feel what's under her Snoopy pyjamas. He's never been more jealous of a cartoon dog before!

Being trapped here for the moment may not be ideal, given the time of year, but if he's going to be stuck with someone, he can think of worse people. In fact, spending a day or so with her sounds pretty fucking amazing.

He smirks, as she hums a little louder and he recognises the tune. *Santa Claus is Comin' to Town.*

Even though he's not in the best of situations, his smirk grows to a full smile. How would she react if she knew that, not only is Santa actually in town right now, but he's sitting in her armchair beside her fire, with one hell of a headache?

2

Scarlett peers into the living room at the strange man. He's slumped in the chair by the fire, one hand rubbing his head. He's acting so strangely, but for some reason she's not scared, or threatened by him. It makes no sense whatsoever, but she feels safe around him. She doesn't even know his name. He could be an axe murderer for all she knows.

Which isn't exactly a helpful thought.

He doesn't look like an axe murderer. She stops stirring their drinks and glances at him over her shoulder, then shakes her head. No, he definitely doesn't look like the axe murderer type.

But isn't that the point? If axe-murderers looked like axe-murderers, no one would let them in. She shakes her head again. No. He just crashed... something, was injured, and now needs help. That's it. Nothing suspicious, except the fact he's not really answering her questions.

He's hurt though, so maybe he's just dealing with that.

She peers around the doorway. If he is an axe-murderer, he's a seriously hot one. The whole outfit isn't helping either. Coming here was meant to help her avoid anything Christmas and man related. Now she'd ended up with someone who reminds her of a young, and irritatingly sexy Santa.

'Get your hormones under control, girl.'

'Sorry?'

She grimaces to herself, smiling at him through the doorway. 'Nothing. Just talking to myself.' She darts back behind the wall and leans against the counter. Perfect. She needs to keep her internal monologue internal.

She straightens her hair, then picks up the tray and goes back into the living room. The man is still in the chair, looking like he's got the weight of the world on his shoulders. She places the two drinks, and plate of toast on the table, then grabs her first aid kit. 'Are you going to take your coat off?'

He turns his head to look at her, clearly weighing up his options. Surely deciding to take off your coat or not isn't that big of a decision.

'We're in the middle of a snow storm. You're not going anywhere for the moment. And that's not a threat,' she adds quickly. 'It just might be a good idea to get comfortable. Besides, if I was going to hurt you, it would have been easier to leave you outside overnight. Not drag your heavy ass back here.'

Seemingly convinced, he pushes to his feet and shrugs off the coat before settling back in the chair, clutching his side.

'You're holding your side. Are you hurt there too?'

'Yeah, I think so. I'm sore all over, to be honest.'

'You crashed. I'm not surprised. Take off your top and I'll sort it out.'

He slowly pulls down his braces, then peels off the white top. Scarlett stares at what was under his top, struck dumb by this body. The vast expanse of solid muscle looks like it's been carved from stone. Her ex worked out every week, but he wouldn't get close to this, even if he worked out every day.

Then she notices his arm and her admiration turns to confusion. His right arm has a sleeve tattooed on it. But it's the theme that confuses her the most. His arm is covered in a mix of candy canes, nutcracker dolls, holly leaves, snow globes, all in glorious colour. If it's Christmas related, it's on his skin. Each image joins seamlessly to the next, to create one solid, stunning masterpiece.

She gets lost in the images, finding something new to admire everywhere she looks. She keeps her hands on her lap, forcing them to stay where they are. She wants to touch him, needs to run her hands over his chest and explore each perfectly defined muscle.

Before she can control herself, she drops her gaze to his crotch. He shifts in the seat, pushing his hips forward. She's sure he didn't do it on purpose. But the change in position brings that bulge in his perfectly fitted trousers closer to her.

Scarlett shakes herself out of her thoughts. 'Sorry, where else have you hurt?'

She meets his eyes and stops. His lips are parted, his eyes firmly on her. Oh God, did he realise she was staring at him like he's a piece of meat? His mouth curls into a small smile and he gestures down his body. 'Down there.'

'Excuse me?' Scarlett says, her voice a little higher than planned.

'Whopping great bruise on my side,' he adds, his grin still firmly in place.

She looks down and sees an impressive and colourful bruise, a thick gash sitting right in the middle surrounded by dried blood.

'Oh right. Sorry. I'll clean that for you.'

'I can do it.'

'Don't be silly. Just sit still and let me.' She passes him the plate of toast. 'Eat that while I'm seeing to the cuts. I'll start with the one on your head. If that stays down I'll make you something else.'

'Thank you.'

She kneels up, and carefully peels the plaster off the weeping cut on his forehead. He takes a bite of the toast, and Scarlett loses another few seconds watching his jaw muscles work as he chews. How can the man make eating toast look sexy? Damn, he even makes sitting in her old threadbare chair look sexy. This is going to be a fun.

'So,' she says, forcing herself to stop watching him eat. 'Do you remember what happened to you?'

'What sort of bang did you hear?' he asks, ignoring her question.

'You're not a fan of answering questions are you?'

His pale blue eyes shift to look up at her. They remind her of the storm outside. She could even swear there's white swirling in his irises, continuously moving in a hypnotic way. Then the corner of his mouth lifts a little into a smile. 'I can't answer if I don't know, can I?'

'I suppose not.' She takes another plaster from the box and fixes it over the cut, doing her best to hide the shiver that works through her when her fingers touch against his skin.

'So...'

'So what?' she asks, sitting back on her legs.

He licks his lips, then rests his head on his hand, as he peers at her with an amused expression on his face. 'What sort of bang?'

Scarlett hides her embarrassment by addressing the cut on his side. He smells incredible, the spiced cinnamon seriously addictive. 'It was kind of like a car backfiring. That's the best description. Louder though. Then there was a crash. The wreckage was on fire at first, but by the time I got to it, the fire had been extinguished by the heavy snowfall. I found you a few feet away.'

'And there was no one else around?'

Why does he keep asking her that? Thinking there could be someone else out there wandering around, isn't entirely settling. Especially if they were somehow involved in what happened to him. As soon as she's finished patching him up, she'll check all the doors and windows again. 'No. Not that I saw. And I did a fairly decent check of the area.'

'Are you sure you didn't see any animals near me?'

'Again with the animals? I only saw that one reindeer print. A really big print beside the bright red... car?'

He takes a long breath as his pale blue eyes turn to her. 'Why did you say it like that?'

She licks her lips, trying to stifle the smile. 'Okay, so don't laugh, but you are dressed sort of like Santa. Only sort of. Like a less cuddly version.'

He narrows his eyes and she wishes she hadn't said that. That's one way to make him think she's nuts.

'Less cuddly?'

'That's a compliment. Honestly.'

His frown eases, so she relaxes. 'Right. So, did you see any reindeer?'

She decides to play along for the moment. Talking to him is helping to distract her from his mouth-watering smell. 'No. I promise. Just the print, but I swear I didn't see any actual reindeer. It was just you in the middle of nowhere.'

'Damn it!'

He appears to be genuinely upset at that news. 'I'm sorry. I don't mean to make light of it. I've just never had a man drop out of nowhere before. The entire situation is a little bizarre.'

'Yeah. It's a first for me too. I'm sorry for being a bit short with you. I'm trying to figure out what happened, and my head fucking hurts,' he adds with a smile.

'I'm not surprised it hurts. You were a few feet from the wreckage. It looks like you were thrown clear.'

'That explains the raging headache then.'

'I'll get you some painkillers for that.' She grabs the box of paracetamol from the kitchen, leaving it on the table beside his chair. She holds out her hand to shake his. 'By the way. Hi! My name is Scarlett.'

He narrows his eyes as he looks down at her hand, then slowly reaches out to take it, his grip firm and strong. 'Nick.'

'Nice to meet you... Nick.' She smirks as she gets back to cleaning his side.

'What's so funny?'

'I'm sorry. The fact you're called Nick isn't helping to get the less cuddly Santa image from my head.'

He gives her a stunning lopsided grin. 'I guess it wouldn't, would it? So thank you for helping me, Scarlett. I really do appreciate all of this.'

'You're welcome, Nick. Besides, I could hardly leave you there all night now could I?'

Nick smiles, but doesn't say anything else, and she's all out of useful things to say. Talking helped distract her from being this close to him. She's never been so instantly attracted to someone before. Nick is getting to her on so many levels. How he looks, his deep voice, the intoxicating scent surrounding him.

It's not helping that his naked chest is inches from her face. 'So you're a fan of Christmas then.' It's a ridiculous statement, but she needs to talk to keep her mind off stripping him, and running her tongue over every inch of his body.

He moves his hips again and she holds her breath. She really wishes he'd stop doing that.

'You picked up on that, huh?' he replies, his voice laced with exhaustion.

'Picked up on what?' she asks, her mind still undressing him.

'That I'm a fan of Christmas.'

She doesn't miss the smirk before he responds. Why was he smirking like that? It was almost like he knew what she was thinking, which is ridiculous. 'It's a little obvious,' she says, nodding towards the sleeve tattooed on his arm. 'I mean that's a serious dedication to Christmas, getting something like that tattooed on your arm.'

He smirks at her. 'I guess you could say it's my time of year.'

Scarlett fixes the bandage over the cut and sits back on her heels, putting some distance between them. Nick is smiling at her again, that same seductive smile he's been giving her, since he took his top off. Maybe that's just his regular polite smile and she's turning it into something it's not. 'You're all done. I think you'll live.'

'Thank you, Scarlett.'

She packs away the first aid kit, then lifts herself onto the couch and passes him a cup of cocoa.

'I would offer you my phone so you can make a call, but the service is down. Your family must be worried about you.' She's positive there will be someone missing him. Possibly a girlfriend. Even if he is single, which she very much doubts, whoever he was dressed up for last night, would be missing him.

'No family.' He takes his locket in his hand, rubbing his thumb over it as he looks out the window. 'But my friends will be wondering where I am. I just have to wait. Hope they find me in time.'

His entire demeanour shifted when she mentioned family. Clearly it's a sensitive topic for him. 'Time for what?' she asks, trying to keep the conversation going.

'I just need to get home for Christmas.'

Nick clearly isn't one for explaining himself. His answers just lead to more questions, ones she knows he'll answer with more of the same. He's had a traumatic night and he's clearly tired. The last thing he needs is her firing questions at him like he's being interrogated. That's one sure way to make his headache worse.

This is her problem. Always has been.

She's not a fan of silences. Ever since she was a kid, she felt the need to fill any silence. Alone, it's not a problem. She doesn't spend hours talking to herself. For the most part, she's content with her own company. But as soon as you throw her in a room with even one other person, that's it. Verbal diarrhoea.

The poor guy crashed, has a head injury, and is stuck in the arse end of nowhere, with someone who is rabbiting on at him.

Her stomach growls and Nick turns towards her, one eyebrow raised, his hand still wrapped around his locket.

So, when she makes the decision to stop talking, her stomach takes over and does the talking for her. It's beyond mortifying. 'Sorry. I'm famished. I was about to make myself breakfast when you woke up. How's the toast settling in your stomach?'

'My stomach isn't making sounds like that, so I think it's fine.'

She smirks, still embarrassed by her unruly stomach. 'Glad to hear it. Do you fancy trying something more adventurous?'

'What exactly do you have in mind?'

His eyes do that swirling thing she swore she was imagining the first time. It's without a doubt the sexiest thing she's ever seen. She wishes he'd stop.

Or maybe not.

It's stunning and seriously distracting. What was she offering him? And why is he looking at her like that? And why is he still topless? He really needs to get some more clothes on. She needs him to put more clothes on.

Then he smiles and she barely suppresses the moan. If he keeps looking at her like that, she'll be offering him more than a fried breakfast.

She should turn away. But she can't or doesn't want to. Probably the second one.

And now she's burning up, the heat rising in her core, working through her body as his eyes keep her locked in their spell. He's not moving. Not doing a single thing to her physically, but tell that to her body. His gaze is like a physical thing.

Goosebumps scatter over her skin, like fingers brushing against her. Slowly tracing along her flesh, teasing her with the slightest of touches.

Her breath quickens as the sensation reaches the side of her neck, and she instinctively drops her head to the side to give him clear access. Not that it is him. He's still sitting in the chair, his intense gaze directed at her.

So why does she swear his lips brush against her skin, working up to her ear? Then he sucks on her earlobe, his teeth grazing against her skin as his warm breath sends a shiver through her.

His fingers comb through her hair, pulling her closer until his hard body presses against her. Scarlett groans, moving closer to his touch. It feels too good to resist. She wants so much more.

Then Nick blinks, the feeling sliding away from her, leaving her cold, embarrassed, and seriously turned on.

Scarlett licks her lips as she runs her clammy hands over her pyjamas. What the hell just happened? It felt like he was touching her. She could have sworn he was kissing her neck.

There's no way she could make something like that up. It was real. She knows it can't have been but, in that moment, it felt real.

Which is beyond ridiculous. She was watching him. He didn't move. Didn't even blink, which in itself is a little bizarre, but she'll just add it to the pot of everything else bizarre that's happened over the last day.

Clearly the excitement of finding this sexy man outside, is turning her into some horny teenager with a seriously overactive imagination.

'You okay?'

His deep voice sounds different to a few minutes ago. All thick and husky, which absolutely doesn't help her calm down. She needs a cold shower. Now.

'Scarlett?'

'Sorry?'

He leans forward, resting his arms on his legs, his hands clasped together. 'Are you okay? You're flushed.'

She licks her lips again, but it's a lost cause. Any moisture she had in her body is heading south. Whatever her imagination did to her, her body is on board with continuing. 'Yeah. Good. Great. I'm just a bit hot. Right, so breakfast.'

He nods, lying back in the chair, resting his chin on his hand. 'Yeah. Sounds good. Whatever you want, Scarlett.'

What she wants doesn't involve anything to do with food - especially when he says her name all low and sexy like that. 'Great. I'll just pop upstairs for a minute. Probably should get dressed. I can't laze around in my pyjamas all day. I'll get breakfast sorted in a minute.'

'I'll get it started.'

'No you will not. I'm not having you collapse on me again. Just stay. I'll only be a minute.'

Without waiting for a response, she hurries upstairs and shuts her bedroom door behind her, leaning back against it as she catches her breath.

'What the hell was that?'

She slides her hand under the waistband of her pyjamas. As she thought. Her panties are soaking wet. Horny teenager doesn't even come close.

How did the man get her so wet just by looking at her?

He wasn't touching her. He was sitting on the chair a few feet from her. No touching. No kissing. Whatever she thought was happening was entirely down to her sex deprived brain.

So why did it feel that way? Why did it feel like his hands, his seductive lips were on her?

'Because you clearly need to get out more,' she says to herself, pushing off the door. If Nick wasn't downstairs she'd lie back in her bed and continue what her brain had begun.

It's not happening though. No way. What she needs to do is calm down, get herself together, and stop drooling over a man she knows nothing about.

Scarlett checks her door is locked, then strips and gets into the shower, turning the water cooler than she'd usually prefer. She needs to stop whatever is going on with her body, before she goes back downstairs and cooks Nick breakfast. And then spends the rest of the day alone in a snug cottage with the sexy man.

She moans as her pussy clenches at the thought of spending more time with him. This doesn't happen to her. Ever. Of course she gets turned on from time to time, but this is so much more than just being turned on. She can't ever remember being this worked up during sex, never mind when she was alone.

But this is the first time she's had a ridiculously attractive man trapped with her. A seriously sexy, half naked Santa. She's only human after all.

Her fingers slide over her pussy, delving inside when the pressure becomes nearly unbearable.

She has no idea why the sexy Santa part is turning her on so much. It's all in her head. He's just a guy wearing red and white. He's not Santa.

Her hand braces against the shower wall. When did she slide two fingers inside? She doesn't do this either.

Scarlett closes her eyes, but that's the worst thing she could have done. Nick pops into her head, his solid body pressing against her back, as his arms wrap around her.

His fingers take over from hers, pushing deep into her aching pussy. She drops her head back against his chest as his thumb grazes against her clit, sending a shock through her body. His strong hand wraps around her jaw, holding her head to the side as he kisses down her neck, his fingers still driving her closer to the edge.

He shoves his knee between her legs, opening her up to him. Scarlett's legs buckle from under her, but Nick is right there, supporting her weight. He groans against her skin, his teeth and tongue nipping, licking, and sucking her neck.

'Are you ready to come for me, Scarlett?' His voice is low and commanding in her ear. She nods, not in any control of what her body is doing. His thumb swipes across her clit over and over again, his fingers plunging deep into her with each stroke. 'Now be a good girl and come for me.'

She bucks against him, the air rushing from her lungs as the orgasm rolls through her. His grip on her jaw tightens, then he turns her face towards his, kissing her, taking whatever oxygen was left in her body.

She moans against his lips, riding out the surge of pleasure taking over her body. 'You are so fucking sexy.' He slowly pulls his fingers out of her pussy, taking each one into his mouth as she watches. His tongue laps up her juices, his eyes never leaving hers as he sucks his fingers. 'Open your mouth.'

Scarlett has no idea what's going on right now, but it's the most intense fantasy she's ever had. And she doesn't want it to end. She opens her mouth, allowing Nick to slide his tongue in. Scarlett sucks his tongue, tasting herself and, for some reason, suddenly she can't get enough of her taste on his tongue.

He growls deep in his chest as she sucks his tongue like her life depends on it. Nick slides his tongue out of her mouth and, still gripping her jaw, runs his other hand slowly down her body. 'I thought you were nice,' he mutters in her ear, sending a shiver through her.

Then his hand is around the front of her neck, gripping her firmly. 'Who knew you'd be on my naughty list instead?'

She swallows, the pressure of his hand not helping the situation. Why did the way he said naughty sound so damn naughty? His voice is dangerous, all low and full of promise.

He nips her earlobe, pulling on it before he releases it from between his teeth. 'You have no idea of the fun I could have with you.'

Before she can respond to that delicious promise, his hands leave her body. She opens her eyes, bracing herself against the shower as the room spins for a few seconds. Once the disorientation disappears, she turns around slowly, checking the room. She's alone.

Scarlett shuts off the water and stands in the shower, just trying to catch her breath.

What the hell was that?

He made her come. That was real. Her pussy is still throbbing.

She opens the shower, examining the floor for wet footprints, but there's nothing.

Of course there's nothing. He wasn't in the shower with her. That's impossible.

After grabbing a towel from the radiator, she wanders into her bedroom, checking the door. It's still locked.

Okay, so she's going mad. There's no other explanation. Show her one good looking guy and she dreams up this massive sexual fantasy. The poor guy crashed, and now she's perving over him.

Scarlett flops back on her bed, reaching up to rub her jaw. It felt so real. His hand was around her jaw.

And it felt absolutely amazing.

Her previous sex life wasn't necessarily bad. It wasn't necessarily earth shattering either. And that's being kind. She wants more. Wants to be taken by surprise, to not know what's about to happen. She wants what her head created in the shower and so much more.

After what just happened in the shower, she knows without a doubt Nick could give her what she wants. What she craves.

Except there's one small problem with that.

It was all in her head.

He's one sick fuck.

There's no other way of putting it.

Nick lifts his head, facing his reflection in the mirror over the sink in the downstairs bathroom. His eyes are still white. It'll take another minute for them to go back to normal again.

She saved his life and he just did that to her! Okay, so he didn't actually touch her. All he did was give her one hell of an orgasm. He glances at his dick, still rock hard even though he'd come himself. It was a pretty intense orgasm for him too.

He slaps himself on the forehead, grimacing when he bumps against the cut. 'Sick, sick, fuck!'

He shoves his dick back in his boxers whether it's ready to calm down or not, then sits on the toilet lid, staring at the door.

That was a first. Part of being Santa means he can give people what they want, to a certain extent. But what just happened in the shower was a whole new experience. He's never done that before. Never felt like he was touching someone without actually touching them.

Something about Scarlett is messing with his magic. When she looks at him, he knows what she wants from him, and it goes beyond mere Christmas gifts. She's attracted to him. He's not being big-headed - he can feel it. He knows what she wants.

And she wants him.

No complaints there. He wants her too.

But it's not that easy. It never is with him, unfortunately. It's all part of the ups and downs of being Santa.

Ten minutes later, his eyes and dick have calmed, so he stops hiding in the bathroom. Scarlett is still upstairs. She's probably wondering what the fuck is going on.

That makes two of them.

He puts back on his t-shirt again. His side and head still hurt, but the pain is easing. He still doesn't have a clue what happened, and that's pissing him off. He looks up at the staircase as the door at the top unlocks, and Scarlett comes out of her bedroom.

She's not looking at him, her eyes focused on the steps as she comes downstairs. She's ditched her oversized pyjamas for a pair of jeans and a fluffy navy sweater. Pyjamas or sweater - she still looks hot as fuck.

Which is why he's in so much trouble.

When she finally looks at him she blushes, turning away to look out the window. 'Still snowing.'

He grins. 'Yeah. Appears to be. You okay?'

She nods and hurries into the kitchen. 'I'll get started on breakfast. Full Irish okay with you?'

'I'll have whatever you're having. Want a hand?'

She pokes her head around the door frame and smiles. 'I got it. You just relax. I'm good.' Then she disappears, the sound of cupboards and drawers banging loudly fills the slightly awkward and heated silence. Entirely his fault, but deep down he's not sorry. He probably should be. That would be a decent reaction, especially from Santa.

Not that he'd ever call himself a conventional Santa. He has reindeer and a sleigh, but that's about as far as it goes. Right now he'd like to get his hands on those fucking reindeer! They should have stayed with him. It's what they're trained to do.

Unfortunately, since he started, they've had more of a hate/hate relationship going on. The fleabags never warmed to him, preferring his predecessor to him.

They're part of the deal though, so, after a lot of bribery in the form of treats, he'd convinced them not to drop his ass off the sleigh every time he goes out with them. Or thought he had.

Something must have spooked them enough to have them take off. As much as they don't like him, they wouldn't have just left him. He just wishes he could remember what it was. Wishes he could remember anything after he left the workshop. But it's all a blank and that's pissing him off.

He doesn't believe in coincidences. Never has. He crashed because someone wanted him to crash. Which means they're either trying to kill him, or they want his magic. Neither reason is particularly fantastic.

Sure he has enemies. They all do. The problem is, he can't think of anyone who would benefit directly by trying to kill him. If Christmas didn't happen, he'd probably be out of a job. Maybe worse. He's not sure what the repercussions would be. No Santa has ever missed Christmas. He has no intention of being the first. Big talk from someone with no way of getting home.

But unless he finds a way to get back, whoever is out to get him, might just get their wish. The good news is that, whether the reindeer like him or not, they're trained to go home. Once they arrive back without him, a search party would be launched.

He looks down at his wrist. From the day he took the job as Santa, he hasn't taken off the cuff. Not for a second. And it doesn't come off easily. Someone took it off him. It's the only conclusion. Someone wanted him stranded, unable to be tracked.

Without the tracking cuff, his team will have a hard time finding him. There's a massive planet to search. Even with everyone looking, it'll still be touch and go whether or not they find him in time.

His Christmas magic might attract their attention, but that's not at its most powerful until Christmas Eve night. That leaves him trapped here with Scarlett for the next few days.

He smiles as he looks into the kitchen at her. She's twisted her long auburn hair into a messy bun at the back of her head, keeping it out of her way as she cooks. Why does she have to look so fucking adorable?

Thirty-five years as Santa, and he waits until he's injured and trapped, less than a week from Christmas, to find someone he's interested in. Talk about bad timing.

He needs to find a way to get home. He needs to figure out if someone ambushed him, and make sure they pay for their treachery. That should be his main focus.

So why is he still looking at her? Still thinking about what they did in the shower. Wishing he could do it for real.

He meant what he said to her. He could have so much fun with her. He could give her what she wants, what she yearns for.

He pushes to his feet and stands at the window, peering out at the snow. He can't do this again. Can't let someone get close to him. Besides, having sex with her would mean telling her who he is, and that's a sure fire way of killing off any attraction. She's not going to want to be with him if she knows who he is.

He looks over at Scarlett again, piling eggs and bacon onto two plates. The problem is, she might have to help him attract the attention of his search party, which would also mean he needs to tell her the truth.

She'd more than likely think he's off his fucking head. Of course she would. What else could she think if a strange bloke sits her down and says, 'Hey, so I forgot to mention that I am actually Santa. Want to help me get back to Lapland?'

Even saying the line in his head sounds fucking ridiculous. He's never had to tell someone the truth. Everyone he deals with on a daily basis knows who he is.

He's Nick. Santa. Leader of a group of mythical men who kill demons and monsters set on destroying the Earth. End of unbelievable story.

That part sounds even more ridiculous. The Santa part is a hard enough sell, without adding what he does for the other three hundred and sixty four days of the year. How do you even begin that conversation with someone outside of his world? It's impossible.

It doesn't help he's not exactly the image she'd have in her head of Santa. One of his predecessors went to town on the cookies and food left out by the children, and now they all get labelled as... what had Scarlett said, *cuddly*. Great image that had stuck through the generations.

'I hope you're hungry.'

He snaps out of his thoughts as Scarlett places the plates on the table. He lowers onto the chair opposite her, wincing as his ribs protests. Being thrown from the sleigh didn't agree with his body. 'Thanks. It smells amazing.'

'You're welcome. My culinary skills aren't the best, but I can whip up one impressive full Irish.'

He keeps his smirk to himself. She's still not making eye contact with him, focusing far too intently on her breakfast. 'Do you live out here alone?' he asks, tucking into one of the best breakfasts he's had in a long time.

She finishes chewing a mouthful of bacon, then takes a drink of coffee. 'I don't live here all the time. I was left the cabin by my grandparents. I come out here for holidays and every Christmas to get away from all the craziness. I just like the peace and quiet here.'

He takes a mouthful of coffee, while he gets his head around that. He noticed the very clear absence of anything Christmas related in the house. Could make things interesting if he does attempt to come clean about who he is. 'Not a fan of Christmas?'

She shrugs and wipes up her fried egg with a piece of toast. 'I used to be. It sort of lost its magic for me. That probably sounds a bit strange to someone who clearly loves it.'

He lowers his fork back to his plate. 'Why do you think I love it?'

'Your arm is covered in Christmas tattoos.' She leans across the table and lowers her voice. 'It was a bit of a hint. I'm clever like that.'

'Ah, fair point,' he admits, laughing. 'Yeah, I guess I do like it. What happened to make it lose its magic for you?' Her smile fades as soon as he asks the question. 'Sorry. None of my business.'

'No, it's fine.' She turns her cup on the table, not saying anything for a minute or so. 'It was life in general I guess. I lost my parents when I was young, and my grandparents took me in. Then they died a few years ago, and it was just me. There didn't seem much point in making all the fuss after that.'

'I'm sorry.'

'Don't be sorry. I love it out here. It's so quiet... usually,' she says winking at him.

'I can be sorry about that part.'

'Don't be. It's the most excitement I've had for a long time.' The adorable blush comes back and she looks away, clearing her throat. 'Anyway, you're welcome to hang around until the storm clears. If you want, of course. Then again, I don't really think you could leave, even if you wanted to. The roads are going to be impassable at the moment.'

'You don't mind if I stay?' He was hoping she'd say that. It's not like he has anywhere else to go, but he didn't want to invite himself to move in for a few days if she wasn't happy with that.

'Of course not. I was only planning on eating, drinking, and reading. So, how are you feeling? You don't look as pale now.'

'Bit tired, but yeah. Feeling more human.'

'Good. I'm glad.' She smiles at him and he can't resist smiling back.

He keeps the goofy grin on his face for a few seconds longer than he had planned, before he kicks himself. 'I'll clear this away.'

'There's no need.'

'I'm doing it,' he insists. He needs to put some distance between them, before he does something he probably shouldn't.

'Okay, thanks.' She takes her coffee into the living room, and sits on the couch, tucking her legs under her.

Nick tidies away the breakfast things and washes the dishes, taking his time to finish the job. He wants to spend time with her, but there are too many clothes on both of them for his liking.

He curses and angrily shakes his head. What the fuck is he doing? He needs to get his head out of the gutter.

But nope. Five minutes later, it's still there. Firmly wedged in the gutter, where it's going to stay as long as she's near him.

He glances over his shoulder, catching her looking at him at the same time. He doesn't turn away, doesn't back down. She must know he wants her. If it wasn't for the storm, he'd have made a move on her earlier, instead of giving her what she wanted from another room. But if he does try something and she rejects him, it'll make things so awkward for the rest of their time together.

This is her home. Of all the places she should feel safe, it's here. There's no way he's going to make things uncomfortable for her.

Besides, he doesn't have time to look at her the way he is. It's Christmas week! It's the most important time of year for him. If he doesn't get home for Christmas Eve, Christmas is fucked forever. There will be no recovering from that.

A tingle runs across his skin, sending a rash of goosebumps over his flesh. He clenches his right fist, as the tingle escalates to a sharp prickle as it moves down his arm to his hand. His magic is building in preparation for the Christmas run, and it's only going to get stronger as the big day draws closer.

He flexes his fingers, trying to ease the bizarre sensations. Something is wrong. The build up is usually pleasant. Like a warm pulse across his skin. This time it's sharper, almost painful. Thirty-five years doing this job and his magic has never hurt him before.

But this is the first time he's been away from the workshop for longer than a few hours, at this time of year. His Santa magic is stabilised by the workshop, and vice versa. They need that link to survive, but what he doesn't know is how his magic and the workshop will react to the separation.

And that's the part that's worrying him.

3

Damon materialises in the middle of the main workshop, bringing everyone to a stop. The humans stare over at him, the fear coming off them nearly bringing a smile to his face. He pulls his bat-like wings back into his body, rolling his shoulders as they settle inside him.

He hates coming here to Nick's house. The place makes his skin crawl. Always does. There are too many people. Too much chatter. Too many smiling faces. The constant churning out of Christmas music this time of year, like nails down a chalkboard. The whole sickeningly upbeat workshop goes against everything he does. Everything he is.

Nick's job is to bring people happiness. Damon's is the exact opposite. People celebrate Nick. They count down the days until he visits them - or at least their image of who Santa is. Damon isn't welcomed by anyone he meets.

No one in their right mind is going to roll out the red fucking carpet for the Boogeyman. But that's the contract he signed, and the burden he has carried for the last fifty odd years.

He could have travelled straight to the meeting room, but he wanted the extra time to walk through the workshop, to see if he could pick up on anything from the Christmas jumper clad, far-too-happy, workers.

But there's nothing out of the ordinary. Or at least the ordinary for this place.

He walks in to the meeting room and takes his seat next to the head of the table, stretching his legs out in front of him. The top seat is reserved for Nick, their leader. The lucky bastard assigned with keeping the rest of them in line.

Damon is second in command, but he only really takes charge around this time of year, when Nick is busy with all the Christmas shit he needs to deal with.

He brushes his jet black hair back from his face, and waits as everyone else arrives. He can travel faster than anyone else, so he usually arrives first.

It's not common for the team to meet like this, unless they were headed out on a mission. They each have very specific jobs and don't generally mix, unless something is wrong. They are a formidable team, but have little in common outside that.

Santa, the Boogeyman, the Sandman, the Horseman, Jack Frost, Triton, and Cupid. As diverse a group as you can get, with one common purpose - to keep the legends alive.

Their legends. It's got nothing to do with good or bad legends. Technically, he'd be on the bad side of the scale. The Horseman too, but what they do is so much more important than that.

It's about balance. Good and bad. Light and darkness. Downright evil bastards and slightly morally grey heroes. Without this team to keep the balance, the evil bastards would take over. And the regular humans of the world would have a serious issue with that.

He doubts they'd be thrilled about the whole *end of the world as they knew it* scenario. A part of him wouldn't be bothered, but for now, he's content with the side he's chosen.

'Did you make anyone shit their pants lately, Damon?'

He throws a withering look at Cobh as he takes his seat opposite him, with Hunter following right behind him. The merman has his legs, so presumably he hitched a ride with Hunter. 'Why don't you go talk to some dolphins, Ariel?'

Cobh grins widely and leans back in his chair. 'Do I look like a seriously hot mermaid. What?' he says looking at Hunter. 'Ariel is totally hot! And I reckon I'd be in with a chance there, being equipped with a tail and all.'

Hunter sucks in a long breath. 'Hell yeah. I would totally do Ariel. Work a bit of my Cupid charm on her. She'd be putty in my hands.'

'Who would?' Jokul asks, taking his seat.

'Ariel.'

Jokul grimaces. 'Eh, no! She's too young for you two bozos. That's seriously yuck! I, on the other hand, beat you two by a good decade. Better option all round.'

'Jack Frost and Ariel? No way!'

'Why not? You think you get first shot because you have a fucking tail? She fell for Prince Eric you idiot!' Jok smirks and nods towards Cobh. 'You get in the way and I'll freeze that tail right off you!'

'You'd have to catch me first, Frosty! I'm too fucking fast for you.'

Damon suppresses his groan. So much for insulting the merman. Trust Cobh to take things on a sordid tangent. Not that Hunter is much better. Or Jok for that matter. It's like working with a bunch of adolescents at times.

Thankfully the Sandman arrives next, moving the conversation away from who would do what, to a Disney mermaid. Reve rests his feet on the table and rubs his hands together, producing a small pile of sand in his palms. 'What are we talking about?'

'Don't ask!' Damon says, cutting off any further discussion. Being second in command has its perks. Ariel can thank him later for stopping these fuckers talking about her.

Eve, Santa's right hand woman, enters the room with Flint, the Horseman. Shadowing her, Nick's giant of a personal bodyguard, Kane, shuts the door behind her, silencing everyone in the room. He leans against the door, his massive arms crossed over his chest, glaring at the rest of them like they're disobedient school children.

Whether he's blocking them in, or stopping anyone from coming in, Damon doesn't know. And he's not going to argue. You don't mess with Kane. He's the Nutcracker for a reason. He's seen the man in action, and the name suits him right to the ground.

Kane glares over at him, his black eyes locking on Damon. He returns the look, only slightly relieved when Kane looks away first. Kane probably did it because he was bored, not intimidated. He's yet to find someone or something Kane is intimidated by.

Eve takes her seat next to Nick's chair and looks around the table, smiling at each of the occupants in turn. Or does, until she gets to him. Then the smile falters slightly. Whatever. After centuries of being avoided, he's well used to it.

Eve tolerates him…most of the time, but only because of Nick. And Damon tolerates her more than he does most people. The woman is slightly less irritating than the rest of the humans he's encountered. Slightly.

Her head is screwed on and, as heads go, hers isn't too bad. Her short blonde spiked hair is tipped with pink, both ears are pierced numerous times, and her figure hugging jeans hint at an impressive body underneath. Not that's he's thought about her like that.

But, as much as he tries to deny it, the woman has a personality, and an attitude, and he appreciates that.

'Thank you all for coming at such short notice,' she says, getting the meeting off to a start.

'Where's Nick?' Damon asks, cutting through the boring pleasantries. Eve doesn't take meetings without Nick. That's sending off alarm bells.

'Nick is missing,' Eve says quickly, glancing around the table to see everyone's reaction.

'How exactly do you lose Santa this close to Christmas?' Jokul asks as he traces his fingers over the desk, drawing an icicle on the wooden surface.

'We didn't lose him.'

'Where is he then?'

She visibly bristles at Damon's question. 'Okay, so maybe we've misplaced him... temporarily.'

'You lost Santa,' he repeats, getting a slight kick from the look on her face.

'Okay. Fine! Yes. We've lost Santa. He's gone. No sign of him whatsoever. There. Are you happy now?'

'Ecstatic,' he replies sarcastically. 'Of course I'm not fucking happy! Did he leave of his own accord or did he simply vanish?'

'He was doing his test run, as he always does before the big day. He doesn't like leaving anything to chance. But he didn't come back. Most of the reindeer did, but it's not like we can ask them what happened. One of them had blood on its back. Nick's blood. There was also no sleigh with them.'

The collective curse works through the room.

Flint sits up in his seat, his red eyes burning. Damon hopes he can keep his anger under control. Last time he was pissed off, he incinerated the table. 'Excuse me? No sleigh? Did it fall off or something?'

'The sleigh didn't fall off, as such. Some of it was still attached. It appears there was an explosion towards the front of the sleigh.'

'Where Nick sits.' Damon finishes her thought. 'Is there something on the sleigh that could explode?'

She shakes her head, visibly insulted by the question. 'Of course not. Why would we send him out with explosives?'

'I was just asking.' He turns to Kane. 'You're his bodyguard. Why weren't you with him.'

Kane slowly turns his head to look over at Damon. 'He does the run alone.'

'What use are you then?'

Eve holds up her hand, putting the brakes on Kane who takes a step towards Damon. 'No one but Nick can survive in the sleigh at the speeds it needs to reach, in order to complete the Christmas run. His magic protects him. Kane would have been torn to pieces within the first few seconds.'

'Not seeing the problem with that,' Damon responds, winking at Kane who chooses to ignore him. 'What did you mean most of the reindeer came back?'

'One is missing.'

'Presumably dead. She would have come back otherwise, right?'

Eve shrugs. 'I know as much as you do.'

'Someone must have seen him,' Cobh says quietly. 'You can't miss a giant of a man with Christmas tattoos. He kind of stands out.'

Eve shakes her head. 'I wish. We've had no reports from any of our contacts. He's vanished. And that's why I called you all in. Now, I know you all have your own roles to perform.' She throws a quick glance at Damon, before she continues. 'I'm asking for your help though. If he isn't here to do his run, that's the end of Christmas. It'll have a knock on effect on everything else. You all know that.'

Hunter speaks up. Cupid usually isn't so quiet, but Nick going missing has thrown them all. 'We fully understand how things work, Eve. What about his tracker? Is it malfunctioning?'

She takes the leather cuff out of her pocket and places it on the table. They each have a similar one, which is a constant irritation to Damon. But, he gets the importance of being able to track them, and so does Nick. As far as he knows, his friend has never taken his off. It hasn't left his wrist in nearly four decades. 'Where did you find that?'

'In his room.'

'But that doesn't make sense,' Jokul says.

'I know,' Eve says. 'He hasn't taken it off since he signed the contract.'

Damon drums his fingers on the table. Nick is solid. He doesn't do stuff like this. If one of the others pulled a vanishing act, fair enough. They may have to work as a team from time to time, but they're used to working alone.

Without Nick to keep them in line, there wouldn't be a team in the first place. He's their leader for a reason. He's genuinely decent, and you absolutely don't mess with him.

'What's the plan, Eve?' he asks, all joking aside. As ridiculous as it sounds, Nick is his best friend. Santa and the Boogeyman are best friends. And he will tear the fucking planet apart to find him. Which is probably why Eve called the whole team in, instead of just him. She knows how far he's willing to go when someone gets on his not so nice side.

'We need to find him. Without his wristband it'll be tricky, I know, but his magic will be growing in strength over the next few days. I'm hoping one of you will be able to pick up on that and use it to find him, or even just narrow down the search area.

'Myself and Kane will take out another sleigh with the reindeer. It will take us longer to cover ground as we won't be able to travel as fast as Nick, but I'm hoping the reindeer may be able to find him. You'll all be a faster option though.' She shrugs and rubs her forehead. 'I don't know. I'm making this up as I go. This has never happened before.'

Cobh leans on the table, clasping his hands together. 'We should be able to pick up on his magic as it grows, but he's going to have to use it in order for us to find him. It'll have to be something epic. We won't get a lock on him otherwise.'

Eve nods. 'Nick knows what to do. He'll be ready.'

Damon peers over at Eve, and she eventually meets his eyes. 'Don't mean to be gloomy and all, but—'

Cobh laughs. 'Yeah, the Boogeyman isn't known for the whole doom and gloom shit.'

Damon bares his fangs at him. 'You're assuming Nick's in a position to use his magic. His fucking sleigh exploded, Eve! He's a tough bastard, but...' He doesn't finish his thought. He doesn't need to.

Her attention drops to the table. She's genuinely worried about him - just like he is. 'We have to stay positive. Until we have definite proof otherwise, he's alive. We have to believe that. The fact the workshop is still functioning is a good sign. I'm sure if anything serious had happened to him, it would have a knock on effect here.'

Damon hopes she's right. Nick is the only friend he's got. Apart from the whole monumental disaster losing Santa would bring, he'd miss the guy.

'What about Krampus?' Reve asks. 'He's been quiet since Nick took over the contract. Every other Santa has been approached, except him. It's possible he got to Nick.'

Eve curses, mirroring the thoughts of everyone around the table. Krampus worked with Santa centuries ago, until it was decided by one of the Santas, that he was a little over the top. As in, sadistically so - even by Damon's standards. He was banished and, up until Nick, had approached each Santa, asking for his place on the team to be reinstated.

Nick wouldn't have allowed it. Damon is sure of that. He's got a vicious streak when he needs to, but working with someone like Krampus wasn't an option. 'Have there been any sightings recently?'

Eve shakes her head. 'Not a peep from what I know. I haven't heard his name since Nick first signed. I'm sure Nick would have told me if he'd been approached.'

'Reve is right,' Damon says. 'We can't rule him out.'

'We need to shake things up, Damon,' Reve says, leaning on the table. 'Someone knows where he is. Apply pressure and someone will talk.'

Damon shakes his head. 'No need for that yet.'

'Come on, Damon! You're the Boogeyman! Use that. Let all of us use what we are to track him down, however we can.'

A part of Damon would like nothing more, but that's not the way they do things. It's not Nick's way and, until he hears otherwise, this team will stick by his rules. 'You really think Nick would want that? If we spill any blood to find him, he's going to be pissed with us.'

'So we just politely ask around?'

'Try to track him through his dreams.'

'Oh so he'd be happy about that instead? Yeah right! He'll kill me.'

'If it helps to find him he'll accept it. Do it!'

Reve looks around the table, before focusing on Damon again. 'What? Now?'

'When would you prefer to try? After he's dead?'

Reve mutters under his breath, but lifts his hands out in front of him. His eyes turn yellow, as he spins his hands creating a ball of glowing golden sand. Everyone stays quiet as Reve stares into the ball for what feels like a fucking eternity.

Damon is itching to tell him to get a move on, but he'd be less than impressed if someone did that to him while he was working. In fact he'd probably kill them, or at least consider it, depending on his mood.

Finally Reve blinks and the ball of sand dissipates. 'Nothing.'

'What do you mean nothing?' Eve asks, getting there before him. 'How can there be nothing? Does that mean he's dead?'

Reve shakes his head. 'It just means I can't get a read on him. He's there, but I don't know where there is. Something is blocking him from me. Like there's a wall around him.'

'Which means what exactly?' Flint asks, surprising everyone. The Horseman isn't known for doing much talking.

'Which means he's alive, but that's all I know.'

'That's a great start though.' Eve looks over at Damon and smiles. 'What's your plan?'

Damon pulls his attention away from Eve's blue eyes, and looks along the length of the table. 'The plan is to find him before someone else does. Spread out. Search land, sea, and air. When he uses his magic, one of us should be able to trace him.'

She smiles a little, appearing somewhat relieved to hear him say that. They will be able to pick up on his magic. He knows that. But a lot depends on Nick being alive in the first place, and being strong enough to use the amount of magic it'll take for them to find him.

Another thought hits Damon as he stands and leaves the room. Whoever did this to Nick is still out there. Not only are they up against it time wise with Christmas and Nick's magic, they're also in a race to find him before the other party does, and finishes what they started, if they haven't done so already.

Nick stretches out on the couch, trying to get his body to relax. It's mostly down to his magic. He's buzzing, the surplus energy making him twitchy as hell, seriously uncomfortable, and more than a little horny. And Scarlett isn't helping the situation. Far from it.

She's curled up in the chair opposite him, buried in a book. He's been watching her read for the last hour, lost in the variety of expressions that run over her face, as she reads the romance novel.

She told him to get some rest after breakfast, but he's no more interested in rest, than he is in running around naked in the blizzard. Although, that might help cool his body down, so that is an option.

He turns on his side, concentrating on the fire instead of what his body is doing. Or wants to do. If he was at home he'd hit the gym, or go for a run. Here, he's trapped with all this sexual tension he's not used to. And it's driving him fucking crazy. Scarlett is driving him fucking crazy.

'Do you want a book to read?' Scarlett asks, drawing him out of his thoughts.

'Sorry?'

'You don't seem very settled. Reading relaxes me. It might help you.'

Not likely, and judging by the cover of the book she's reading, it's not going to help relax him at all. He's got enough steamy sex scenes in his head without adding more to it. 'Thanks, but I'm fine. Just restless.'

She lowers her book onto her lap. 'Is there anything I can do to help?'

Again, not likely. She's the reason he's so restless. 'Thanks, but I'm fine,' he repeats. He's far from fine, but there's not a lot he can do about it, unless he's going to act on some of the scenes going through his head.

Scarlett nods, then goes back to her book, leaving him staring at her again like some lovesick puppy. He turns to face the back of the couch and closes his eyes.

He manages to get his mind off Scarlett for a grand total of three minutes, before he feels her hands caressing his bare skin. He rolls over, expecting to see her in front of him, but she hasn't moved.

'Are you okay?'

He nods and smiles. 'Yeah. Sorry.'

He rolls back over and stares at the back of the couch. She's thinking about him. He tries to clear his mind of everything other than Scarlett, which isn't too difficult, considering he can't get his mind off her in the first place. Sure enough, her thoughts are occupied by him. Not only that, she's imagining him naked with her in her bed.

Nick licks his lips and swallows a groan as her hands move down to his dick. He closes his eyes and attempts to shut her out. It doesn't feel right getting in her head like that. But she makes it impossible.

He's never had this connection to someone before. Maybe it has to do with his magic? It's behaving differently away from the workshop.

He's always been able to tell what people want around this time of year. He's Santa. It's part of his job, but this is a whole other level of want. Sexual fantasies had never come in to the equation before. He doesn't even have to try with her. If anything, he needs to fight to keep her thoughts from his head.

He tucks his hands under his armpits. It's either that or he's going to touch himself, or ideally her, and that's just all levels of wrong.

Like not doing anything about it now will wipe out what he did to her earlier in the shower. He's already crossed a line that he had no right going near. He wants her naked under him, on top of him. Wants his hands on her smooth skin, but he can't.

Yes, she wants to touch him too, but fantasising about being with someone, is very different to doing the deed. She's holding back, stopping herself from acting on what she's thinking, so he's going to respect that. For now.

Her thoughts hit him again. He doesn't know how, but she's managed to put him in a scenario he'd have imagined himself. She wants him in charge, wants him to tell her what to do, wants him to praise her when she does what he wants.

And his dick is more than happy with that scenario too.

The idea of being with her again and again, bringing her from one orgasm to the next is an unbelievable turn on. He rolls onto his front and buries his face in the pillow.

He can do this. After all, he's been Santa for over three decades. He can control whatever is going on with his magic and how it's messing with his body.

Who is he kidding? This isn't working. He could easily lie here for the next few hours, his dick getting harder and his mood lower. Time to put some distance between them.

He pushes to his feet and takes his coat from the hook by the door.

'What are you doing?' Scarlett asks, lowering her book again. 'You heading out?'

Nick shrugs his coat on, ignoring the pain in his side as he zips it up. Going outside probably isn't his best idea, but fuck it. He's going with it. 'I just want to check out the crash site.'

'Are you crazy? It's snowing!'

'Is that what that white stuff is?' he says with a smirk, the smile she gives him in return lighting up her face.

'I just wanted to make sure you knew. No need to be all smart about it. Just promise you won't trip, or knock yourself out, or anything like that. I'd hate to have to drag you back in here again.'

'I promise. I'll be back in a few minutes.' He grins at her, before opening the door and escaping outside. Nick closes the door and takes a few seconds to calm down.

Going outside for some fresh, if not seriously freezing air, was the right decision. Some of the tingle from his magic has dulled too. He has no idea why, but it seems to be triggered by Scarlett.

Nick looks across the garden to the forest beyond. It's not far, but with the blizzard howling around him, it's going to be hard work to get even close to the crash site.

With his head down and his hands shoved into the pockets of his coat, he sets off. This is what he should be focusing on. His job. Keeping people safe from the creatures hiding in the shadows. Starting with whoever took down his sleigh.

So why is he still thinking about what he wants to do to Scarlett? Why can't he stop imagining every single detail of what he would do to her?

This is more than just wanting meaningless sex. He's attracted to her. It's distracting him from his job, which he's not thrilled about, but it's been decades since he felt that way about anyone.

Not since Emma.

He grips the locket in his hand, but instead of comforting him as it always does, the contact seems to release a flood of guilt that has him stopping in his tracks.

He's not doing anything wrong. Scarlett is single from what he can tell. And so is he. Has been for thirty-seven years. Even though the storm is raging around him, he opens the locket and smiles at the photo of his wife and daughter.

But calling himself single is like dismissing them. Like he's wiping them from his life. He was happily married with a beautiful daughter. Then he was a widower and a grieving father.

They died thirty-seven years ago in a car crash, and the grief nearly killed him. His entire life was torn apart in that moment, and he couldn't deal with it.

He'd lost his family, then his job, because he couldn't stay sober long enough to do it. Bankruptcy followed soon after, then he had to watch as the home they built together was repossessed, leaving him on the street.

If he hadn't been offered the Santa contract two years later, he would have drank himself to death in a back alley somewhere.

He's not over the loss by any means. Never will be, but it's not something he wants to get over. He needs to feel that loss every single day.

But that doesn't mean he can't find some semblance of happiness again with someone else. Does it? He's not going to age while he's Santa. That could mean a very long and very lonely life. Surely he can be Santa and have someone? Have Scarlett.

Emma would want him to be happy. He's just not sure he's ready for that. Ready to move on. To be happy with someone else.

But Scarlett O'Neill of all people! Part of his contract means he knows who everyone is - or at least those who believed at some stage of their lives. And she did, for a few years at least.

Until her life changed and he couldn't help her. Santa isn't all about spreading Christmas cheer. It's about breaking the hearts of too many kids who ask for the impossible.

He closes the locket and looks over at the remains of his sleigh. Who is he kidding? He has a job to do. A job that leaves little to no time for a relationship. And it's not like it's an easy job at that. He's lost count of the number of times someone has tried to kill him. It's nothing new.

No. The best thing he can do for Scarlett is keep away from her. As much as he wants to be with her, he'll just have to resist - for her safety more than anything.

It's a few days from Christmas and someone is clearly trying to take him out. Someone he needs to find and kill before they get to him. That's all that matters.

Scarlett stares at the same paragraph of text, the words still refusing to sink in, no matter how many times she reads them. She must be on the same page for the last ten minutes at least. She's surprised Nick didn't notice.

She lowers the book and walks over to the window. Through the snow, she can see his red silhouette near the trees. She doubts he'll be able to find out much from the crash site until the snow stops. The wreckage is no doubt buried under a few feet of snow by now. But having a break from him is a strangely welcome relief.

Not that being in the same room as him is a bad thing. Far from it - and that's the problem. They'd been together in the living room for about an hour before he left the cottage, and for that hour, she'd not read one single word of her book. Not one.

The whole time was spent stealing sneaky looks at him, before trying to focus on her book again. Which had been a total fail. Instead of reading, her mind had inserted Nick into some interesting scenes in her head. Mainly him naked on top of her, his impressive body against hers as he slides in to her pussy.

It was so wrong to have those thoughts, but she couldn't help herself. And it's not like he had been doing anything to distract her. He'd been stretched out on her couch, his legs hanging over the end. He's far too tall for the couch, but the cottage only has one bedroom.

When she stayed here with her grandparents she slept on a camp bed. It's still here in the store room, but would be much smaller than the couch. Maybe she should have offered him the bedroom? At least that way he would have been out of sight and out of mind.

She'd really tried not to stare at him, but she'd challenge anyone not to look at him. His red trousers, black braces, and white top is probably one of the sexiest outfits she's seen on a guy. Then you add Nick himself to the mix, and it's no wonder her book wasn't holding her attention.

She checks her watch and curses to herself. It's barely lunchtime. At this rate it's going to be a long, frustrating day. At least if he's out of the house for a while she can get a break from him. Having him here, feeling the way she does, it's like she can't breathe properly.

This is ridiculous! She goes back to her chair and focuses on her book again. Thinking like a hormonal teenager is just getting her all worked up.

Thinking about him is getting her all worked up.

Planning in detail how he'd walk over to her, all masculine and alpha male. How he'd strip her before she could argue... which she wouldn't, then make her orgasm more than she's ever done before.

She doesn't have thoughts like this. Years with her ex and she hadn't had one naughty dream, or even a sexy thought about him.

She'd never imagined him touching her the way Nick does in her mind. Never wanted him to take charge the way Nick is in her thoughts.

It's the wine. This is what she gets for going for the cheap stuff.

She glances over at her cup of coffee. Okay, so maybe it's not the wine. She hasn't had any today. It's probably the books. Damn things are putting ideas in her head and Nick is sliding in to the fantasies.

Why can't he slide in to her?

She grimaces as that thought pops into her mind. When did she turn into a horny, sex mad woman, thinking about having all kinds of dirty sex with a man she barely knows?

A seriously attractive, insanely built man.

And it's not even like he's shown any interest in her. She doubts she's his type.

She'd only ever had sex with men she was in a relationship with. As in a long term relationship. If she had sex with Nick, it would be what? A one night stand? Maybe a two night stand?

Maybe they'd spend the next few days naked and sweaty in her bed going from orgasm to orgasm.

She shuffles around in the chair, glaring at the words on the page of her book. Like that's a helpful thought.

Why couldn't he have packed a pair of unflattering flannel pyjamas? Anything other than sleeping on her couch dressed like he is, looking all hot. It's not fair. And not helping her calm down in the slightest.

He really is quite a sight, all hard muscle and tattoos. He's so far out of her league. And he's injured. Not badly, but she doubts he'd be up for anything physical.

But she could... what exactly?

March over to the couch and throw herself at him? She's not like that. As much as she'd love to have the confidence to do that, she can't.

She also can't sit here and stare at the same page of her book all day. Maybe she'll get lunch ready. Anything is better than sitting and lusting over him. As she passes the window, she stops and tries to see where Nick is. But there's nothing visible through the snow.

Maybe he left? Maybe he took this as his chance to escape from the woman who is quite clearly leering at him.

She's just dishing up lunch when he comes back inside, shaking the snow off his coat. At least he came back, but, with the snow storm outside, there aren't many places he can go.

'You must have a fantastic sense of smell. Lunch is just ready.'

He leans against the front door, staring over at the fire, lost in his thoughts as he takes off his snow covered boots.

'Nick?'

He lifts his head and she could swear his eyes are changing colour. 'Sorry?'

'Is everything okay?'

He seems to shake himself out of his thoughts and smiles at her. 'Yeah. Sorry, I was miles away.'

'I've made lunch. It's just soup and bread. Hope that's okay?'

'That sounds amazing. Thanks.'

He pours them both a coffee then sits down, his attention on the view out the window behind her. 'Did you find anything?'

He shakes his head as he takes a bite of bread.

'I'm sorry.' She has no idea what she's apologising for. He just looks so lost, she wanted to say something.

Nick shakes his head again and smiles. 'No, Scarlett. I'm sorry. I'm being rude. I didn't find anything. I'll have to wait until the snow stops. I can barely see my fucking hand in front of my face. I don't know what I was expecting to find in the first place.

'I just... I wish I knew what happened. One minute I was minding my own business and the next...' He lifts his hand, holding it level then swoops down slamming it on to the table. 'Boom!'

'You were flying?'

He gives her a strange look, then smiles. 'Just being dramatic. Of course I wasn't flying.'

'Can I ask you a ridiculous question?'

He hits her with those magical eyes again and smiles. 'Peaked my interest now. What ridiculous question do you want to ask?'

'What exactly crashed? I mean I'm no car expert, but that doesn't look like a car out there embedded in a tree. Is it like one of those trike things?'

'Something like that,' he answers, focusing on his soup again.

That's the end of that topic. This man is equally as infuriating as he is captivating.

'How's your book?'

He flashes her a strange look and, when he grins, she can feel her cheeks reddening. 'My book?'

'Yeah. You seemed to really be getting in to it before I went outside.'

She nods and spoons some soup into her mouth. She doubts she even turned a page in the damn thing. She glances at him and he's still giving her the same look. Then he winks and takes a sip of his coffee.

What the hell was he winking at? Did he notice she was paying him more attention than the book? She's sure he didn't. So why is he looking at her like he knows something she doesn't?

'Yeah. It's good, thanks. Are you done with your soup?' she asks, desperate to stop whatever is going on. The way he's looking at her is unnerving. And really turning her on.

'Yeah. I'll get those.'

'No! Sorry. That was a bit loud. I just meant you're my guest. You sit and relax. I insist.' Scarlett quickly gathers the plates and hurries into the kitchen before he can argue. What the hell is going on? And why is she so turned on?

She fills a glass with water and drinks it. It's a little after midday. She's got the whole day with him. If he keeps winking and looking at her the way he is, it's going to be a long and incredibly frustrating day.

'Why do you keep blushing?'

Scarlett faces Nick. He's still leaning back in the chair, his legs spread and his head tilted slightly to the side as he stares over at her.

'What?' She clears her throat and attempts that again. 'What?'

'When I asked about your book, you blushed.'

'No I didn't.'

He pauses and frowns, then looks at her again. 'You weren't thinking about me, Scarlett, were you?'

Whatever about blushing before, she's going as bright as a tomato right now. His presence is filling her small cottage, sending her heart fluttering, and quickening her breath. And that's before she even begins to think about the effect his words are having on her.

Nick leans forward, resting his arms on his legs, his intense gaze sending shivers down her. 'Were you thinking about me?'

'What? Of course not!' Her response sounds weak as soon as she says the words, but she doesn't want to admit the truth.

He leans back in his chair, his legs spread and one hand draped over his thigh. He knows she wants him. She has no idea how, but he knows. 'Now that was a lie, Scarlett.' He stands up and walks towards her, stopping at the entrance to the kitchen. His cinnamon scent hits her. 'I wasn't going to do this Scarlett, I really wasn't, I swear. But you're making it impossible for me.'

'I'm making what impossible?'

He looks down at the ground for a moment and takes a long breath, almost like he's deciding if he should continue. And she wants him to. Whatever he's about to say she needs to hear it.

'You're making it impossible not to think about what I could do to you, with you.'

She nods before she can stop herself. 'I see.'

'You can feel it too, can't you? This thing between us.'

She nods again, then swallows, as Nick takes another step closer to her.

'I'm attracted to you Scarlett, and I'm fairly sure you're attracted to me.'

And there she goes, nodding again.

Nick smiles and his eyes lighten. The light must be playing tricks on her. 'I thought so. I guess that leaves us with two choices.'

'What choices?'

Another step brings him right in front of her. He places a hand to either side of her, pinning her against the counter between his arms and his body. Scarlett keeps her attention on his chest right in front of her. She can't look at his face. Having him this close to her is intense enough.

'We can either keep our clothes on, and my hands off you. Continue being polite and seriously frustrated, as we have been, until I can go home. Or, we could forget all that, and you can let me show you how very grateful I am for your hospitality.'

He still hasn't touched her, but she's already wet, and the thought of how he could show his gratitude is only making her situation all the more precarious.

'Are you wet for me, Scarlett? Are you imagining what I can do to you, if you let me?'

She groans, instantly hating herself for being so transparent.

Nick laughs, a deep rumble that hits right between her legs. Her body is doing a great job of screwing her at the moment. It's too busy thinking about what it would be like, if he screwed her instead.

'I'll take that as a yes. Do you want my hands on, or off you Scarlett? You decide. All you need to do is tell me what you want. I promise, if you don't want this I'll leave you alone.'

She watches his chest rise and fall as he breathes. She's not reckless. Never has been. Not until she found Nick outside and took him into her house. Agreeing to do this with him is far beyond anything she's ever done. It won't come to anything long term. Nick will leave in a few days.

So what's the harm in enjoying each other until then? They're both consenting adults. They wouldn't be doing anything wrong.

'On.'

She could swear he holds his breath for a second. 'Look at me.'

Scarlett looks up at him. Why do his eyes have to be so hypnotic? As soon as she looks into them she could swear she's floating.

'I'm going to need a full sentence Scarlett. Tell me what you want?'

'I want your hands on me.'

He lifts his hand, his strong fingers gripping her jaw firmly, holding her in place as he kisses her.

The first thought that hits her is that this kiss feels the same as the one in the shower. The one she imagined. Which is impossible.

Then his body presses against her and she stops thinking.

'You didn't answer my question,' he says, finally letting her up for air.

'What question?'

'Are you wet for me?'

'Why don't you check for yourself?' She has no idea where those words came from, and right now she couldn't care less. The only thing she wants is Nick and what she knows he can give her.

'Mmm, definitely on the naughty list.' The tips of his fingers slide under the waistband of her jeans. His nose traces along the side of her neck, as his fingers glide gently over her pussy, through her panties. He purrs against her neck.

'Tell me who you're wet for, Scarlett.'

Instead of answering, she moves slightly, pushing against his hand, but he pulls away.

'Not until you tell me.'

'You're really going to make me say it?'

He grabs a fistful of her hair, gently tilting her head back. 'If you want this to play out the way I know you do, you'll behave and answer me.'

The feel of his strong fingers gripping her is so good. She wants more of whatever he wants to do. 'I'm wet for you.'

'Again, and say my name this time.'

Scarlett swallows before speaking. 'I'm wet for you, Nick.'

His fingers slip under her panties, caressing her pussy. 'Mmm, you are wet, aren't you?'

He removes her jeans and panties remarkably quickly, before lifting her onto the counter. Nick spreads her legs, then drops to his knees, his hands holding her legs apart.

'You look so sexy with your legs spread, ready for me to play with you.'

He looks up at her, then slowly swipes his tongue along her pussy.

Scarlett arches back and moans. 'Oh God!'

'You taste incredible, Scarlett.'

She nods, barely able to form any intelligent words, let alone string them into anything resembling a sentence. Nick's firm hands are keeping her in place as his tongue laps and licks at her pussy, gliding deeper with every stroke.

She's already so close to coming and he knows it. He massages her clit with his tongue, the pressure continuing to build when he sucks it.

'You're going to come for me.'

It's a command rather than a question, but she nods anyway, gripping onto the edge of the counter. Nick concentrates on her clit, sucking on it until she's pulsing, gasping for breath and trembling. But he doesn't give her a break, his tongue and mouth drawing her orgasm out.

Then Nick stands and presses his mouth to hers, his tongue sliding between her lips.

He tastes of her, which is such a turn on.

'You taste good, don't you?'

'Yes!' His tongue is relentless, the possessiveness of the kiss stealing the air from her lungs.

'I want you naked on your bed, spread out for me to play with.'

She groans at the low, husky way he said that last part. It is entirely unintentional, but it's out there and he hears it.

Nick helps her off the counter and takes her hand, pulling her through the living room and up the stairs to her bedroom.

Scarlett stares up at the wooden beams in the ceiling over her bed. She's about to have sex with Nick. Hot sex, if what happened in the kitchen is anything to go by. The bed dips as Nick lies down, his body pressing against hers when he leans over her.

Why can't she look at him? Why is she focusing on the ceiling instead of the gorgeous man leaning over her? Maybe because she's about to freak out, and is trying to remain calm.

He straightens his arms so he can look at her properly. 'You sure about this? I'm getting funny vibes from you. Do you want me to stop?'

'No, I am sure! I'm sorry Nick. I'm having a stupid moment. I'm just not used to doing things like this.'

'Things like what?'

'Sleeping with people I barely know.'

Nick lowers, his body barely a hair's breadth from hers. 'Believe it or not, neither do I.'

She's surprised to hear that. 'Really?'

He smirks. 'Don't believe me?'

'I do. Oh, I don't know. Just ignore me. I'm over-thinking.'

He slides to the side, lying beside her, instead of leaning over her. 'First, I'm not going to ignore you. Second, we can take this at your pace, if you want to continue. Believe it or not, I'm actually a really nice guy. I'm not going to force you to do anything you don't want to do.'

She turns on her side to face him. 'I appreciate that. And I believe that you're a nice guy.'

'A really nice guy,' he corrects her, his gorgeous smile lighting up his face.

'A really nice guy then. I want this Nick. I really do. It's just been a while since I've been with someone like this.'

'How about I take it really slowly? Prove you can trust me.'

Scarlett couldn't be more relieved. She wants this. Wants Nick, but it's been so long since she did anything like this with anyone.

He props his head up on his hand, then looks down at her, his breath warm on the side of her face. 'Do you want me, Scarlett?'

She nods. His pale eyes meet hers and she can't look away. She's never seen eyes like his before.

'That's a good place to start.' He takes a deep breath and groans. 'And I want you, Scarlett.'

She shudders as a shiver works through her. 'Hang on! I don't have anything with me. I wasn't planning to do anything like this. I mean I'm on birth control but...'

'I'm clean, Scarlett.'

'Really? Sorry. I'm killing the mood.'

He nuzzles the side of her neck with his nose. 'I swear you have nothing to worry about. And as for killing the mood? That's not possible. Can I kiss you now?'

'Yes.' She doesn't even have to think about it.

As soon as Nick kisses her, any reservations she may have had disappear. It feels right being with him.

His lips trace down the side of her neck while his hand runs up her bare legs, sliding under her jumper to her waist.

He keeps his word, taking things slowly, but she's not so sure she wants him to go slow anymore.

As if reading her mind, his hand moves further up her body to cup her breast. Scarlett moans and reaches up to run her hand through his thick hair.

What started slow, builds to something more, as Scarlett lets go and gets carried away by the feeling of his hands on her body.

But she wants to feel him. Wants to know what it's like to touch him. He's pressing against her leg, his arousal long and thick through his trousers.

Nick reaches down to unfasten his trousers. She doesn't know how he does it. How he seems to be in her head. Scarlett doesn't even try to avert her gaze as he lifts his hips, sliding his trousers and boxers down his long, seriously toned legs. It takes her a few seconds to stop drooling over his legs and focus on the main attraction.

Nick rubs his hand over his dick, drawing her attention to where it should be.

Her first thought is that there isn't a hope in hell that will fit in her. His dick is long and thick, reaching past his belly button. Then he wraps his hand around it, stroking his dick as he looks at her. If that's not one of the sexiest things she's seen she doesn't know what is.

His head moves closer, his breath caressing her ear. 'Touch me.'

She slowly places her hand over his, groaning when he slides his hand out, leaving her gripping his dick. Nick squeezes her hand, forcing her to hold him tighter. Nick sucks in a breath and shifts his hips. 'I like that, Scarlett.'

The groan comes out before she can stop it. She wants him. No question, but she can't get any words out. Thankfully, Nick is on the case.

He grips the back of her head, crushing his lips to hers. Scarlett groans and opens her mouth to kiss him back. Nick's tongue fills her mouth, exploring and tasting, leaving her breathless from the kiss alone.

He's possessive.

The way he touches her, kisses her, it's like she's his, and he's making sure she knows.

Okay, so maybe some of her books are playing up the image in her head, but she can't escape that thought. She can't stop her imagination from wondering how possessive and controlling he could be with her.

He grips the hem of her top and she raises her arms so he can take it off. Her bra follows and he captures one nipple in his mouth, sucking hard, before moving to the other side.

Nick covers her with his body, just like she had imagined. His eyes meet hers as he presses against her pussy, grinding against her slowly, teasing her with what's to come.

Scarlett gasps when he pushes inside her briefly before pulling out again.

'Oh Nick...' Seems her body wants him as much as her mind does. Scarlett moves her hips, guiding Nick inside.

He sucks in a breath and stills. 'You okay?'

'Just go slow, but yeah. I'm really good.'

Nick kisses her again, his tongue exploring her mouth as he slowly fills her, one inch at a time, until he's buried deep inside her.

Restraining himself is proving more difficult than he thought it would be. Scarlett is so tight it's taking all his self control to hold back and take it easy. For now. He knows she wants him to be a little more forceful, to have him take over, but not yet. The last thing he wants to do is freak her out, by going in all heavy handed first time.

But if this happens again, he will show her how controlling he can be.

It would help if she knew who he really was. If she did, he could use his magic to push the limits, give her everything she craves and more. If he starts reacting to every thought she has, she'll what? Put two and two together and guess he's Santa? No chance, but stranger things have happened to him since he signed his contract. He's not going to take the risk.

Unable to hold himself back any longer, he pulls back, watching his dick slide out of her. He could get used to that image. Get used to her body reacting to his dick inside her. He pushes back in, loving the groan she releases, the way her breasts heave as she takes a long breath. Her auburn hair is spread out on the pillow, her lips parted as she closes her eyes. She is simply stunning.

He keeps the pace slow for another minute, then decides she's ready. And he's more than ready. Nick wants her to look at him while he fucks her, but he knows his eyes have whitened. Seeing his scary eyes will put an untimely end to this.

To keep his eyes hidden, he kisses her, his tongue matching the thrust of his hips. She wants him to go harder, wants more from him, and he's only too happy to oblige. He takes both her arms, stretching them over her head, before holding her wrists in his hand.

Her pleasure hits him almost immediately, like a wave ending in his balls. He's never experienced an intensity like this before. Never felt such immediate pleasure from anyone he's been with. It could be due to the time of year. Maybe being away from the workshop is messing with what he's picking up on. Maybe it's Scarlett. Whatever it is, the blur of thoughts and needs coming from her, are doing nothing to calm him down.

For now, he'll fuck her hard, just like she wants. He uses his free hand to lift her right leg up, spreading her wide so he can get as deep as possible. Her eyes are closed, her head turned to the side, but he keeps his own head down to hide his eyes. Not like the view down there is bad in any way.

His dick pumps into her, stretching her wide as his balls slap against her ass. Having sex as Nick is so much more difficult than he thought it would be with her. His magic is so strong this time of year, holding it back is nearly as difficult as holding himself back with her.

Something he's not going to be able to do much longer.

But she's close, her thoughts swirling as she nears. He lets go of her leg, using his thumb to massage her clit. Her stomach tenses, her back arching off the bed. He wants to tell her how hot she is, to praise her for just being so incredible, but he can't risk her looking at him, so he clamps his mouth closed.

His balls are aching, desperate to unload into her, but not yet. He'll keep her on the edge a little longer. She writhes under him when he slows down, bringing her back, holding her there for a minute. Waiting until she comes back from the edge, loving the small whimper she makes.

She wants to come but he leaves her waiting, his strokes slow and deep.

Then he stops holding back, his dick driving deep into her tight pussy as he massages and presses against her clit until she arches off the bed, screaming as she orgasms. As soon as her pussy grips him he can't hold back. He comes a few seconds after her, his whole body trembling with the release.

It takes a ridiculous length of time for his dick to calm down, but Scarlett doesn't seem to be in any hurry for him to pull out. And he's in no hurry to pull out either. She feels so good. He releases her wrists then slowly slides out of her and sits back on his legs.

With her legs spread, her wet pussy on show, Scarlett is incredible. He lies down beside her, closing his eyes and concentrating on calming down. Hopefully his eyes will go back to normal. If not, he's going to be having an awkward conversation in the next few minutes.

'You okay?'

He grunts. 'Oh yeah. You?'

'I think the correct term is fucked.'

Nick laughs. 'Good word. I'm fucked too.' The tingle associated with his magic dissipates, so he opens his eyes, then looks at her. 'Do you have any idea how utterly breathtaking you are?'

She blushes, and it's unbelievably adorable. 'You are fucked, aren't you?'

'Yes, but it's the truth. Watching my dick sliding in and out of your pussy was the single hottest thing I've seen.'

She pushes him in the arm and blushes even more. 'Nick!'

'Take the compliment!' He pulls her close to him. 'Now, how about a shower, then some more food?'

'Why did you grin when you said shower?'

'Because you won't be in there alone.'

Nick leans on the window sill, watching the snow fall outside. He can't sleep. Even after being with Scarlett for hours, he's still wound up. Behind him, she stirs in her bed and sighs before turning over, hugging the pillow to her. The covers have slipped down her body, leaving her stunning ass visible. She's so beautiful he could just look at her for hours.

In his thirty-five years as Santa, he has never been so instantly attracted to someone, like he is to Scarlett. He's seen it happen to other people over the decades. Seen it so many times he's lost count.

But never to him.

He's all about the job. All about the contract he signed. Apart from one night stands, he's never allowed himself to even consider something more. It never entered his mind. As soon as he signed the contract, he'd put dating, or a relationship of any kind, to the back of his mind.

He opens the locket on the chain around his neck, and looks at the picture of his wife and daughter. Every time he sees their faces it's like someone rips out his heart all over again.

He closes the locket, holding it in his hand. He needs to keep away from Scarlett, but he doesn't want to. Even if there was even the slightest chance of a relationship with Scarlett, there's a huge obstacle in their way.

How exactly do you tell someone you're Santa Claus?

Okay, so telling them wouldn't be too difficult. You just say the words. It's the aftermath of saying those words that worries him. He has no doubts she'd think he'd lost his mind. He'd had the exact same thoughts when he was offered the contract.

He absently rubs his wrist, missing the cuff he's worn there for the last three decades. And that's another part of the complicated situation he's managed to find himself in.

He's more sure than ever, that someone took it off him and left him to die. He has magic, but he's still human. He's far stronger than your average human and his magic does protects him to a certain degree, but he can still be killed. Not easily, but he's not immortal.

Nothing is making sense and he's driving himself crazy trying to figure it out. The fucking headache isn't helping his mood. He remembers leaving the workshop. Everything was as it had been every other time he left. He knows he was flying high enough that there wouldn't be anything to crash into. Not that Santa crashes.

So if he didn't crash into something, how had he ended up where he did? And why the fuck can't he remember? He seriously doubts his minor head injury would have messed with his memory. He's strong and healthy, so he wouldn't have passed out, or fainted, or anything like that.

'Nick? Are you okay?'

He smiles at her as she joins him at the window. 'Yeah. Just thinking. Did I wake you?'

'No. I just rolled over and you weren't there.' She looks out at the snow. 'You seem tense.'

Tense is a massive understatement. 'Yeah. I'm fine. Just not good at being cooped up like this.'

'You probably shouldn't have ventured out when there was a storm due.'

He wasn't planning on being anywhere near a storm when he went out. Then again, he hadn't planned on anything that happened. Hadn't planned on crashing. Hadn't planned on finding Scarlett. Hadn't planned on being stranded. He smiles, not sure how to answer that one, without giving her more questions.

She kisses his arm then slips into her strangely appealing Snoopy pyjamas, hiding her body from him until he unwraps it again later. 'I'm thirsty. Do you want something to drink?'

'I'll give you a hand.'

He quickly throws on his boxers, trousers and top, then follows her downstairs. Nick sees to the fire as she fixes them a hot drink. Scarlett sits on the armchair by the fire, tucking her legs under her, while he lowers onto the couch and does his best to relax.

His magic is messing with him again. While he was having sex with Scarlett, the sensations flowing through his body were bearable. Now he's wired. It's a mix of his magic and the intense need to bury his dick in Scarlett as many times as he can.

She wraps her hands around her mug and hits him with a quizzical look. 'That's a fairly intense frown. What are you thinking about?'

I desperately want to hear you scream my name when you come, over and over again. 'Sorry. Miles away,' he lies.

She nods, but he knows she doesn't believe him. Being economical with the truth is necessary, but he knows he's not fooling her for one second.

'So, Nick. I don't know anything about you. What exactly do you do? For a living I mean.'

And so it begins. He knew it would only be a matter of time before curiosity got the better of her. 'Manufacturing,' he answers truthfully.

'Oh. What do you manufacture?'

He flexes his fingers, the tingle spreading like the worst case of pins and needles. 'Whatever I'm asked for mostly.' She nods, sipping her drink as she tries to hide a smirk. 'What's with that look?'

'I was just thinking about how you were dressed, your name, and what you just said.'

'I don't follow.' Of course he follows. He knows exactly what she's getting at.

'Your name is Nick, you were dressed like Santa, and you make what people ask you to make. Surely you can see the connection?'

For the briefest of moments, he considers telling her she's right. That he is actually Santa. Then good old common sense comes back into play again. 'Back to the Santa thing again? I'm wearing red and white. I'm sure I'm not the only guy in the world who does that.'

Scarlett nods, then smiles at him. 'I suppose you're right. That might just be my imagination and the time of year, I guess.'

'And your book,' Nick says with a grin, as he clenches his fists under his armpits. The tingling is turning to cramps. Both arms are aching. He's getting worse, and has no idea how to ease it. He's never had this discomfort before, but he's never been away from home at this time of year. If it wasn't dangerous, he'd go for a fucking long run outside.

'You might have a point there.' She gives him a long look and frowns. 'Are you all right? You look like you're in pain.'

How to answer that one without sending her screaming out into the storm to get away from the madman? 'I'm usually at home this time of year, and I'm worried I won't get back in time.'

It's weak as anything, but her face softens. She's bought it. Or does, until she leans closer to look at something. Nick realises far too late what's caught her attention.

'Nick?' She points to his arm as her eyes widen. 'Is your tattoo moving?'

He glances down at his arm even though he knows his tattoo is doing exactly what she said it is. It may look like a regular, if not highly detailed tattoo, but it's not. He didn't have it before he took this job. As soon as he signed the contract, the tattoo appeared. And the images don't move as such, they shift on his skin. It's part of the build up. Once he's done the Christmas run and expelled all the energy, they'll go back to normal.

He should have kept his sleeves rolled down, but he didn't think. He's not used to being around people who don't know him, don't know how his body reacts to this time of year.

She stands up and backs away from him, her attention still on the shifting ink on his arm. His stupid mistake has landed him in a shit situation. There's no choice now. He has to tell her. Has to somehow convince her he's not losing his mind. Or that she's not losing hers.

'Fuck!' He didn't mean to shout and it does nothing to calm the situation. He stands and takes a step towards her. 'Please don't back away from me like that. I'm not going to hurt you, Scarlett.'

She points to his arm. 'Why are your tattoos moving, Nick? What's wrong with you? What the hell is going on!'

'Can you please sit down. I can explain, but it's not a quick story.'

She shakes her head, moving behind the couch. 'What's not a quick story? You're freaking me out now!'

'That's the last thing I want to do. Please, Scarlett. Just sit and I'll explain everything. I promise.

She shakes her head. 'I'm quite happy where I am, thank you.'

This isn't how he wanted to do this. He wasn't even sure he wanted to do this, full stop. But he's got no choice. He might as well tell her everything and take the backlash. Or the laughs. And then figure out what to do, when she kicks his ass out the door.

He wants to sit down but she's not, so he leans against the window sill, trying to keep as much distance from her in case he spooks her even more than he already has. 'Okay. I've never had to tell anyone what I'm about to tell you, so I'm winging this.'

'Tell anyone what?'

He leans against the window sill and crosses his arms to stop himself fidgeting. He needs to get this out fast, so he can go lock himself in the bathroom, or in the pantry, and do something, anything to ease the cramps.

'Right. Okay. I'm just going to launch into this, so bear with me until I'm finished, no matter how crazy it sounds. I actually am Santa. I live in Lapland and every Christmas Eve I travel all over the world. It uses a massive amount of energy, and my body kind of stores it up for the few days before I head out. This is the first time I've been away from home this time of year. It feels different here. Really fucking horrible actually. My tattoos are linked to me being Santa, which is why they shift.'

He gives up on the window sill and goes for pacing instead. He doesn't want to look at her. Can't bring himself to look at her. There isn't a hope in hell she'll believe a word he's saying.

'I took my sleigh out for a test run. I do it every year. Have for ages. But something went wrong this time, and I woke up here instead. I don't remember what happened. No idea at all. I need to get back home before Christmas Eve... somehow and ... yeah. That's it, I guess.'

After a good minute or two of silence, he forces himself to look over at her. She's frowning at him. Not laughing, which is a good start, but the frown is fairly intense.

'Are you on medication? And I don't mean that in a cruel way. It's a genuine question.'

He shakes his head. 'No Scarlett. I'm not. Everything I just told you is the truth, I swear. Don't believe me, huh?'

'Strangely enough, no. You know this isn't funny, Nick? You realise I could have left you out in the woods to die? I could have just gone upstairs to bed and forgotten all about the bang and gone to sleep.

But no, instead, I dragged your extremely heavy ass back here, through a goddamn blizzard, then looked after you. All I'm asking for is the truth. Instead, you make fun of me. Nice! Thanks for that!'

'I'm not making fun of you. I swear. I can prove it, Scarlett.'

She crosses her arms and fixes him with a bemused look. 'Oh you can prove you're Santa? As in the Santa? Hard proof?'

'Yes.' He sounds convincing, but he's not so sure. His magic should work, but he's not feeling himself. A lot also depends on how open she is to what he's suggesting. He needs her to believe, which is going to be the hard part. Not many, if any, adults believe in him. All he can do is hope, deep down somewhere, she believes. Or is at least willing to believe.

She narrows her gaze again. 'How can you prove it?'

'This is the tricky part. I'll need you to take my hand, close your eyes, and trust me. Can you do that?'

Scarlett examines Nick, waiting for the smile to break out, or for him to slap his knee and confess it's all a big joke. Something, anything to give her even the smallest hint that he's taking the piss out of her. But he doesn't do anything. In fact, he's as sombre as she's seen him since he woke up.

He believes what he's saying to her, which absolutely should put her on alert. But, as with everything to do with Nick, he's not scaring her. Whatever is happening with his tattoos is freaking the hell out of her, not him. And that is nearly more laughable than what he's saying to her.

He genuinely believes he's the Santa and that he can prove it to her. She doesn't know if she should laugh at his suggestion, or give him a sympathetic hug.

Nick holds out his hand. 'Please, Scarlett. Trust me, and I'll prove to you I'm not losing my mind. I swear. It'll take a minute at the most.'

And there he goes chipping away at whatever resolve she had left. 'What are you going to do?'

'Just hold your hand. That's it.'

'And you honestly believe you can prove to me you...' She shakes her head and laughs nervously. 'You really believe you can prove it?'

'I do. But I swear I'll leave if I can't. Please Scarlett. You've got nothing to lose.'

She looks down at his outstretched hand and sighs. 'What the hell! It's not like I've anything else to do.' She moves from behind the couch, and gingerly takes his hand.

He smiles, clearly relieved she's giving him a chance. To do what exactly, she doesn't know. It's not like there's any chance he's telling the truth. Perhaps the bump on his head was more severe than she initially thought.

'Now, I'm not in top form thanks to being away from home, but this should still work.'

'You hope.'

He flashes her a tight smile. 'Yeah. Okay, close your eyes and concentrate on something Christmas related.'

'Like what? The real Santa?'

Nick grins and, even though the entire situation is beyond bizarre, she can't help but smile back.

'Funny. No I mean like the tree, or maybe decorations. I don't know. Something that reminds you of Christmas. Anything at all. Just make it big.'

'Then when?'

'Just keep thinking about it. I'll do the rest.'

She gives him one last look, then closes her eyes. Nick has had a rough time. Might as well humour him, before she has to say goodbye.

Initially Scarlett holds back, trying to think about anything except Christmas, but when she takes a breath, Nick's scent disrupts that. He smells of everything that reminds her of her childhood. Of Christmas in this very cottage with her grandparents. In that instant, her mind drifts back to everything that Christmas meant to her. Waking up early to open her presents. Helping her granny make Christmas dinner. Eating roasted chestnuts her granddad prepared, over the open fire. Decorating the tree and hanging tinsel along the mantle. Memory after memory come back to her, as she holds Nick's hand.

She has no idea how long she's holding his hand, but when he let's go, it's like she's woken from a dream. One she doesn't want to wake up from. She misses those early Christmas holidays.

'Okay. You're done. You can open your eyes now.'

Scarlett opens her eyes, fully expecting nothing to have changed. Why would it? It's not like he's Santa or anything.

But what she sees is far from nothing.

She rubs her eyes, convinced she's still lost in the dream he somehow brought to mind. But she's very much awake. She turns around, her eyes open wide as she takes it all in.

The cottage is exactly as it looked in her memory. It's like he pulled the images directly from her memories.

She smiles widely as she breathes in the scent from the enormous tree, laughs when she runs her hand along the tinsel resting on the mantle, her mouth watering at the smell of roasted chestnuts.

'How... what the hell?' Scarlett spins and looks at Nick, standing at the side of the room. 'I don't understand. Where did this come from? How did you... this is... How?'

He shrugs, suddenly appearing less confident. 'You created all this yourself. I just brought it out. It's kind of my thing. I make Christmas wishes come true.'

'But how? I mean how did you do this?' She looks around the room, the tears coming before she knows what's happening. 'This is my childhood, Nick. All of this. I haven't thought about...' She wipes her face and turns to face him again. 'How?'

'I can't explain how I do it. I just do it. I know it's probably impossible to believe, but I'm telling you the truth, Scarlett. I am Santa. As mad as this is going to sound, I have magic to help me do my job. I used it to tap in to what you were imagining and bring it to life. I didn't want to make you cry though.'

She sniffs and wipes her eyes again. 'These aren't sad tears. Really. I love it, Nick. I...' She frowns and walks over to him, taking a few minutes just to look at him. Try to find some logical reason or explanation for what she's just witnessed. But there's nothing. No special effect or trickery. 'You're not making this up.'

'I didn't pull a full sized decorated tree from my ass, Scarlett. It was magic.' He holds out his hand. 'You can leave your eyes open this time. I just wanted to make sure you were concentrating last time.'

She takes his hand and Nick pulls her close. He lifts her other hand and positions it in front of her. 'Something small this time and look in my eyes.'

As she focuses, Nick's eyes lighten, white swirling with the light blue. She grins widely as the bright red bauble takes form on her hand.

'Oh my God! You are freaking Santa!'

Damon storms through the workshop, ignoring all the humans, as they busy themselves with last minute preparations. No fucking point, unless they get the main man himself back.

With Nick missing, there's no Christmas. Big disaster all round.

There's still no sign of Nick, and that worries him. Everyone is on edge. He can feel it. The Boogeyman in him is enjoying it.

He stops at the meeting room door and listens. Eve and Kane are inside, arguing. He hears Nick's name being mentioned a few times, but can't make out anything else. He melts into the shadows as the door bursts open and Kane steps out. Damon waits until he has disappeared, then grabs Eve as she rounds the corner, covering her mouth with his hand to stifle her shout of surprise.

When she sees who it is, she relaxes to a small degree, but is still terrified. He can feel it and it's too damn good. 'I'm going to take my hand away and you're going to be quiet.'

She nods, so he lowers his hand.

Eve attempts to knee him in the balls, but he sidesteps, blocking the hit. 'What the hell are you playing at, Damon? You scared me!'

He shoves her back into the meeting room, holding her at arm's length so she can't aim for his groin again. 'What was that about?'

'It was a private workshop meeting. Nothing to do with you. You shouldn't even be here. You're not allowed here unless it's for a meeting. Shouldn't you be looking for Nick?'

'I go where I want to go. It's my thing. What were you talking about with Kane? And also, Kane can talk?'

She rolls her eyes at him. 'You know he can. And it's still none of your business, Damon.'

He bares his teeth and his fangs slide down from his gums. He's still in control of himself, mostly. But Eve doesn't know that. 'Oh you should know better than to lie to me, of all people. I feed off lies, Eve. Feed off your fear. Now, the Nutcracker predates Nick. He's watched over the last three Santas. If he's got his knickers in a twist, I want to know why.'

'Nick is missing, in case you've forgotten. We've all got our knickers in a twist. It's a freaking big deal!'

'I'm not buying it's just that. Talk to me, or I'll let my not so friendly side out.'

She tries to push him away, but he's too strong. 'You're an asshole!'

'So I've been told. Mainly by you. The fastest way to get rid of me, is to talk.'

She focuses on the ground for a minute, before looking up at him again. 'This can't go any further.'

'Who the fuck am I going to tell? The only people who talk to me are you and Nick.'

Something crosses her face but he's not sure what it is. Whatever it was, she composes herself again, before he can comment. 'It's Nick. We need to find him. Urgently.'

Damon is sorely tempted to let his dark side out, just to scare her into talking. Not that he's so sure it would work on her. He takes a controlled breath and pulls himself back. 'You're testing my patience, Eve.'

'I wasn't aware you had any.'

'What little I have then. Answer the question.'

'You know, manners don't hurt.'

Damon convinces himself to keep quiet. Eve would just continue the back and forth to irritate him. Thankfully, she gets the message.

'Fine. Nick's magic is at its strongest at Christmas. He needs all the energy to make the Christmas run.'

'Yeah. And?'

'If he's not here, his magic is unstable.'

'Unstable how?'

She looks around, then lowers her voice even though they're alone. 'He needs the workshop to stabilise his powers, until he does the Christmas Eve run. If he's not here on Christmas Eve night, the power overload could kill him, Damon. He'll have surges leading up to Christmas Eve, then, if he's not back, he'll lose the connection and the magic will leave him.'

'So you're saying he'll be human again?'

'No, he needs it to survive. As soon as he signed the contract he was bound to the magic. Without it, he will die. Besides, when I said the magic will leave him, I meant violently. It could tear him apart, Damon.'

'Fuck! Does he know?'

'Of course not. Do you think he would have signed if he did?'

'So you lied to him.'

'Hey, this has nothing to do with me. I just found out myself. Kane knew, but didn't think Nick needed to be made aware.' She pauses and her face hardens. 'Apparently, protecting Nick also means keeping things like that from him. And just for the record, I don't agree with that. He should have known. A lot of us are only here because of Nick. We actually care about him as a person, not just because he's the current Santa.'

Damon's anger ebbs away a little. He knows when people are lying to him. What she just said was the truth.

'Who else knows about this minor detail?'

'Just Kane and the previous Santas. I've been Nick's assistant since I arrived, and I didn't know. I get why no one wanted it to be common knowledge, that Santa can be killed by keeping him away from the workshop at Christmas.'

'Yeah well, someone else knows.'

She looks him in the eye and, for some irritating reason, it unnerves him. People don't usually look him in the eye. 'Why do you say that?'

'Nick has disappeared just before Christmas. Do you not think that maybe someone is taking advantage of what you just told me? Nick is dedicated to his job. You know he is. There isn't a chance he'd disappear just before Christmas. Someone, or something, has either taken him, lured him away, or is keeping him away.'

'But why? What would they gain by doing this?'

'Power. Nick's magic tops all of the rest of ours put together.'

'Yes, for one day a year. And if he dies without passing it on to someone else, by having them sign the contract, the magic is lost. There's no way of taking it.'

'You so sure about that? Because right now that's the biggest gain, by taking him out of the equation. And his power is at its peak this time of year.'

'What about the team? Maybe they want to take it over?'

Damon laughs at that. 'Do you honestly think anyone in their right or wrong mind would want to lead us? I'm surprised Nick does. And there's no chance we'd answer to anyone except Nick.'

She grins at that. 'Yeah. You're right. I wouldn't wish the team leader job on anyone.' She pauses and looks at him. 'I don't suppose... I mean can you pick up on any thoughts?'

'What do you mean?'

'Can you sense if anyone has negative thoughts about Nick? I don't know exactly what you can do.'

He steps closer to her, resting one hand against the wall, trapping her. 'My contract means I can tell if someone means to do wrong.'

'How do you do that?'

She's nervous, but he gets the impression she's genuinely curious. Apart from Nick, no one has ever been interested in his abilities. Hearing about all the inventive ways he has of inducing fear, isn't something that comes up in conversation.

Damon takes a deep breath, suppressing the smile that wants to break free. The peppermint scent surrounding Eve is far too intoxicating. Too addictive.

Too distracting.

He's here for Nick, not Eve. He's the fucking Boogeyman! He can't afford to let his mind get carried away. Time to stop being weak.

Damon grabs her by the throat and peers into her eyes. She squirms under his gaze but he's more powerful.

'You want to know how I do it? I'll show you.'

'Damon!'

'Stop struggling. Let me in.'

'Get off—'

Ignoring her, he pushes into her mind, searching for anything that raises alarms with him. He's usually shit hot at being able to tell if someone is up to no good, but there's nothing suspicious with Eve. He releases her and she coughs, clutching her throat.

'Damon! What the hell was that? I asked you how you do it - not for a demonstration!'

'There's no darkness in you. No jealousy, no greed. Nothing. You're boring as hell, to be honest.'

'Oh well thanks for that.' She wipes blood from her nose. 'You invade my thoughts like that again and I'll tear off your dick and make you eat it. Do you understand me?'

He licks his lips and smiles at her. 'For someone who thrives on pain, that's one hell of a tease.'

She shoves him back, wiping her bloody hand on his black t-shirt. 'I really hate you!'

He sucks in a breath and she groans.

'Oh lay off! I hate that I can't insult you, without you getting pleasure from it. You're an asshole, but you're an asshole who is close to Nick. I am too. I don't want him to die,' she says, wiping the last of the blood from her nose.

Whatever trace of guilt he may have felt about what he did to her, doesn't hang around for long. He can't afford human traits like guilt and remorse. There's no way he could do his job, if he regretted everything he did to people.

'I know. That's why I haven't killed you.'

She crosses her arms and glares at him. 'Oh wow! That's nice to know! So I don't suppose you have had any bright ideas? We've only got a few days to find him.'

'Get me a list of everyone who has access to the workshop. Someone put his cuff in his bedroom. I know it's going to be a long list, but it's a starting point. Someone took it off him, and left it here so we couldn't track him.'

'Do you think that's what happened?'

Damon leans back against the wall, crossing his arms as another thought hits him. 'Can you see Nick just handing it over?'

'Of course not!' She pauses, then frowns at him. 'So you're saying he wasn't physically able to stop someone taking it off him? Or, do you think he took it off and left?'

'As in left the job?' He runs his tongue over his fangs. That thought never crossed his mind. 'You think he'd leave? Walk away from his contract?'

'No.'

'You answered fast.'

'It's Nick.'

'Yeah. No way he'd call it quits. Nick is sickeningly devoted to his job. Can I check his room?'

Eve surprises him by nodding. 'Of course. We should talk to Kane too.'

'Does the asshole talk?'

Eve actually grins at that and, for some reason, he likes it. 'He's not here to talk, but yes, he can. You just heard him speak, so stop being an ass. He spends a lot of time with Nick. We can trust him.'

Damon licks his lips. 'I'll be the judge of that.'

'Seriously? You want to do that mind probe thing on Kane?'

'I'm not trusting him until I do.'

She gives him a long look, then shakes her head. 'It's your funeral. I trust you can get into Nick's room without needing something like the code for the door?'

'You know I can.'

'Fine. Just please don't let anyone see you do that mist disappearing thing you do. I'll get Kane and meet you there in a bit.'

Damon watches her walk away. She's a strange woman. He dematerialises, melting into the shadows, moving through the workshop completely invisible to everyone. He reforms inside Nick's room and looks around the vast suite. Being Santa certainly has its perks. Damon was given a derelict house as part of his contract. Lucky him!

Damon paces the wooden floor, opening and closing his hands as he walks. He's struggling to control his darkness. Nick is doing this to him. He never had a problem until that man took over. He hadn't expected to be accepted, but Nick treated him just like everyone else. He'll never admit it to Nick, but he's hands down the best Santa he's worked with.

And the team needs him.

He pulls off his coat, tossing it on the chair by the fireplace. 'Right Nick. Let's find out what the fuck is going on.'

6

Nick finishes his third glass of water and focuses on the fire again. Creating the Christmas scene for Scarlett has taken the edge off. For now. But, it's not going to go back to normal unless he gets home.

Scarlett groans as she eats another chestnut from the fire. 'Seriously,' she says around a mouthful of food. 'These are freaking amazing. You got to try one.'

'Don't hate me, but I really can't stand the things.'

'How can you say that? What sort of a Santa are you, if you don't even like chestnuts?' She grins and takes another bite as she looks at him.

'Clearly a terrible one.'

'Clearly,' she replies jokingly. Scarlett takes another bite and closes her eyes, groaning to herself.

The expression on her face is priceless. And absolutely beautiful. He's not big headed by any means, but there's something about that childlike wonder related to Christmas, that gets him every single time. It always did, but it increased tenfold when he signed the contract. His need to protect, to make sure everyone around him is safe, underpins everything he does, on both sides of his job.

Scarlett is so happy at this moment and it's seriously rubbing off on him. Being able to do this for her, means more to him than he expected it would. He's granted Christmas wishes before, far too many to begin counting. This time is so different.

Helping to bring her childhood Christmas' back to life, has not only made her Christmas, but his too. Instead of being something he felt compelled to do because he's Santa, the look on her face made him truly happy for the first time in far too long. Out of everything he's going to do this Christmas, her face, when she saw what he'd brought to life, will be the highlight of his year.

Scarlett sits on the couch beside him and sips her coffee. 'So, should I call you Nick or Santa?'

'I prefer Nick.'

'Is that your real name, or just what they call you because you're... you know... Santa? Sorry. That still sounds so strange.'

'Believe it or not, it's my real name. Just a crazy coincidence.'

She turns to face him, tucking her legs under her. 'Your eyes. I presume that's something Santa related?'

'Yeah. When I use my magic my eyes change. It doesn't freak you out, does it?'

'Are you serious? I actually think they're pretty stunning actually.'

He's surprised to hear that. Over the years a few of the workers had commented that his white eyes freak them out. He'd kind of assumed everyone would think the same thing.

She takes another chestnut from the bowl. 'Okay, I'm going to apologise in advance here, because there will be a lot of questions heading your way. I mean like lots, so be prepared.'

He slouches back in the couch, stretching his legs out in front of him. He gets the impression this might take some time and he can't blame her. So far, she's taking this a hell of a lot better than he expected. 'Go for it.'

'How did you become Santa? I mean was there an application process or something? Advert in the local paper? Something like that?'

He laughs. 'Now that would be one hell of an interview process, wouldn't it? No, I just sort of fell into it.'

'You can't leave it at that. How do you fall into being Santa?'

'My family...' He winces, then shakes his head. He can't go there with her. Not yet. 'I hit rock bottom and took up drinking. Then drugs. A while later I was homeless, and heading towards either drinking myself to death, or overdosing. Maybe both. It was Christmas Eve morning, and I was sprawled out in some doorway, when a guy came up to me and asked if I wanted a job.

'I said yes. Not because I wanted a job. I was more interested in getting some money for my next fix or bottle. He brought me to a cafe around the corner, and bought me breakfast. Not exactly what I was looking for, but I hadn't eaten for days. While I ate, he asked if I would be interested in bringing happiness to people over Christmas. I could do that while having a roof over my head, home cooked meals, safety. The job would be mine as long as I wanted it.'

Nick pauses and rests his head against the back of the couch. Fuck he feels rough. 'Even though I was half drunk and high, I listened to what he was saying. I'd hated Christmas for years. It was the single most painful day of the year for me. For a lot of people. The thought, no matter how crazy, that I could bring happiness to even one person at that time of year, struck a chord with me. I wanted to do that. So I agreed.

'Next thing I know, I'm not in the cafe anymore. I'm in this stunning, absolutely massive log cabin. My new home apparently.'

Nick shrugs. 'To be honest, I didn't have a clue where I was, or what was going on. It took a couple of weeks for me to get clean. I don't remember a lot of that time, but it was far from fun. When I finally got through it, and was able to go outside with a clear head, I knew where I was. I knew I was in Lapland. Sounds fucking ridiculous I know, but there was something in the air. It just felt like home. And no, I promise I was clean and still am.'

'I wasn't going to suggest otherwise.'

'I saw the look on your face,' he says with a grin. 'And I don't blame you. Anyway, even though I knew where I was, the whole Santa thing was a bit of a stretch. The guy who helped me, was Santa at the time, but he was ready to pass the job on to someone else. Don't have a clue why I was chosen, but I was. May have been a shortage of applications that year,' he adds, grinning.

'Cutting a seriously long and completely unbelievable story short, I was eventually convinced I could do the job, so I agreed to sign the contract.'

'Contract?'

'Yeah. It just details what the job entails and what's expected of me. As soon as I signed, the tattoo appeared and I felt... I don't know, I guess stronger, more sure of myself. I honestly haven't got a fucking clue how to explain it. Each contract adds something to the person signing it. Some trait associated with the job they're signing up for. I think Santa is one of the easier contracts.'

'What other ones are there?'

He rests his hand on her leg, slowly rubbing it as he buys for time. He's not sure if he should go there with her. But part of the reason he came clean with her, was so she could help him. If she's going to do that, he needs to tell her everything. 'Okay, this might push the whole unbelievable part to a new level. I work with a group of men who have each signed a different contract. We each have very different jobs to do individually, but outside our contracts we work together to keep the legends alive as much as possible.'

'Yep - now you're talking gibberish. What legends?'

'I lead the Boogeyman, the Sandman, Cupid, Jack Frost, the Horseman, and Triton.' The expression on her face is priceless, and exactly what he was expecting. 'I've gone too far now, haven't I?'

'Did you say the Boogeyman?'

'Yeah. His name is Damon. He's a decent guy... most of the time. Probably one of my closest friends.'

'Hang on there one second. Are you telling me Santa is friends with the Boogeyman?'

'Yes I am.'

'And with Cupid? As in the cute cherub?'

'Hunter isn't a cute cherub.'

'Who's Hunter?'

'It's his name. We're all human men, Scarlett. But when we take the job we get traits of that particular role.'

'Oh. So no flying cherub?'

He laughs and shakes his head. 'No. He's taller than me with a beard and black wings.'

'This is going to take a while to get my head around. Knowing Santa is real is one thing, but when you add the Boogeyman and all the others, my brain hurts. So how long have you been Santa for?'

'This Christmas will by my thirty-fifth one.'

'What! But that doesn't make sense. You don't look that old.'

'Another perk. When I signed the contract I stopped ageing. I'm eternally forty-one until I quit the job. When I decide to go back to my old life, such that it was, I'll begin ageing again.'

'Are you... I mean do you live there all alone?'

'No. All the workers are human who, like me, had nothing and no one. Now we belong somewhere. Now we're safe.'

'So no elves?'

'Afraid not. That would just be ridiculous, wouldn't it?' He winks at her, then looks back at the fire.

'And no Mrs. Claus? I mean there isn't one... is there? It's probably a little late in the game for me to ask you that.'

He instinctively reaches for the locket around his neck. 'No, there's no Mrs Claus. I wouldn't have done anything with you if there was. There are single women working for me, but I'm kind of out of bounds. You look surprised?'

'I just find it difficult to believe you're single, that's all.'

'I could say the same thing about you.' The way she blushes is so adorable. It also does nothing to ease his need to take her upstairs. Or down here.

'What do you mean you're out of bounds?'

He rolls his head to the side again to look at her. 'I'm Santa Claus, Scarlett. The whole Santa legend has been around for centuries. The jolly, cuddly man who delivers presents to children. That image is a difficult one to move past. I could walk around there butt naked, and no one would come near me.'

'Are you being serious?'

'Deadly fucking serious.' Not that he'd get with anyone from the workshop. He's the boss there. It's never a good idea to mix business and pleasure. Being Santa is something he has taken seriously from the second he signed the contract. Everyone in the workshop is depending on him to do his job, so they can do theirs.

'I never thought about it like that.'

'The second I signed that contract, I made myself untouchable. I'm wrapped in cotton wool all the time. I have a damn bodyguard who follows me around the place in case I get a fucking splinter or something. It's infuriating!'

'A bodyguard? Was he in the sleigh with you?'

He shakes his head. 'Thank goodness, no. I'm the only one who can travel in the sleigh when it's going at top speed. Anyone else would get torn to pieces. Literally. My magic protects me.'

'How did you end up outside my house?'

'I'd love to be able to tell you, but I honestly can't remember. I always head out for a test run a few days before Christmas. Have for decades, but I guess something went wrong this time. I'm hoping it'll come back to me at some stage, but who knows?'

She nibbles on a chestnut as she processes that. 'I take it you need to leave before Christmas Eve?'

He nods. 'I'm kind of on a tight schedule. I need to go home, but I don't know how.'

'What do you mean?'

'I'm stuck here, Scarlett. And I don't mean that in a bad way, honestly. But I can't get home by myself. I had a wristband on that held a tracker in it, but someone kindly removed that, or it somehow came off when I crashed or fell, then my ride up and left without me. Bastards!'

She lowers the chestnut from her mouth and licks her lips. He hates chestnuts, but he'd tolerate the taste, if he can suck on her bottom lip. It's full, and moist. Damn he needs to kiss her.

'Your ride? Do you mean the reindeer?'

He blinks, unlocking his gaze from her lips. 'Reindeer? Sorry. Yeah. Downright ungrateful, vile, moody bastards.' He props himself up on his elbow to look at her, as she laughs. 'What are you laughing at?'

'You seriously have reindeer? Like the ones with antlers?'

'Of course I do. What the hell is so funny?'

'You with reindeer. I mean I know Santa has reindeer and a sleigh and all that, but I didn't match that part of it with you, until just now.'

He remembers having the same reaction when he first signed the contract and was faced with his new ride. Santa used reindeer - everyone knows that. It still sounds fucking ridiculous though - especially saying it out loud. 'It's not like I can catch the bus or drive myself. I need to use them to get around. I've got a pretty massive distance to cover in one night.'

'So you have Dancer and the gang?'

'Fuck no! They died centuries ago. These are relatives I think. I try not to have too much to do with them, to be honest. We don't get on.'

'Santa doesn't get on with his reindeer! I wish I was writing this stuff down.'

'It's not funny. They say you should never work with children and animals. I'm screwed from the start. The kids aren't so bad, but the reindeer...' He grimaces at the thought of the vile creatures. 'Let's just say we don't see eye to eye. They should have stayed with me. Instead, I get thrown from the sleigh or whatever happened, and they just fuck off and leave me. If I ever get back, I'll kick their asses. Not literally,' he adds when he notices the look on her face. 'Probably not.'

'And you're wondering why they left you behind?'

'Oh ha ha.'

'Seriously, you're genuinely stuck?'

'Genuinely. I need the sleigh to get around or, worse case, one of the team to find me and bring me back. We all have different ways of getting around. I drew the short straw with the reindeer.'

'Right. That's all going to take time to process. Can you not wish yourself home?'

'No. It doesn't work like that. I can only grant Christmas wishes for others - not myself. My magic is at its strongest on Christmas Eve night so I can do the run. I'm hoping if I wait until then, maybe they'll be able to pick up on me. It's all I can think of.'

'Can I wish you home?'

'Unfortunately no.'

'Oh God...'

'What is it?'

Scarlett suddenly gets to her feet, her mouth open and a strange expression on her face. 'Oh my God! I had sex with Santa. I mean, oh God! We had sex!'

'Yes. We had hot, sweaty, very amazing, sex. And I licked you out.'

'Santa licked me out on my counter!'

'And in your bed,' he adds but she's not listening to him. Nick slouches back in the chair, smiling as she completely freaks out. About time. He thought she'd freak out about some aspect of who he is sooner or later. Bringing up that she had sex with Santa, wasn't what he thought she'd go to first, but it's not like there are rules when it comes to something like this.

'Oh this is bad. Really bad.'

'Care to tell me why?'

'Were you not listening? Santa, Nick. You're freaking Santa! I'm going to hell. Oh I am so going to hell!'

He laughs, then stops himself. She's seriously freaking out. 'No hell for having sex with me. I promise.'

'How are you so relaxed? How can you just sit there like nothing's happened?'

He pushes to his feet and slowly walks over to her. Nick captures her chin in his hand, tilting her head back. 'Breathe.'

She takes a long breath.

'I'm the same person I was before.'

'You're Santa Claus.'

'Yeah, but it's just a job.'

'Is it? You brought all this out of my head, Nick,' she says, gesturing at the room full of Christmas decorations. 'That's more than just a job. It's magic! And you're Santa! And you work with the Boogeyman! This is big. I mean huge. And now I'm freaking out!'

'Look at me.' His commanding tone does the trick.

When she does as she's told, he smiles. 'I know I've thrown a lot at you, but you don't need to freak out. I wasn't always Santa. It's my job, that's it. What I'm trying to say is that under it all, I'm just a regular guy.' He shuffles a little closer, relieved when she doesn't move away. Her cheeks flush and his cock twitches at the sight.

He wants her more than he's wanted anyone before. It has to be on her terms though. He's thrown enough at her tonight. If she wants him again, she can have him. No question. He'll be hers as often and in as many ways as possible. But not like this. Not when she's trying to get her head around his world - or at least the small part of it he's shared with her.

94

'What do you do?'

She frowns at him, thrown by his random question. 'What?'

'For a job. What do you do?'

'I'm a recruitment officer. What's your point?'

'My point is that you're Scarlett and you're a recruitment officer. I'm Nick and I'm Santa. It's my job. It's not who I am.'

'You can hardly compare the two jobs.'

'Why not? I wasn't born Santa, and I don't plan on dying as Santa. At least not by choice. I fully intend on passing on the sleigh at some stage, and going back to being plain old Nick. But for now, it is what it is. Nothing has changed. I'm still the same man who had his tongue buried deep in your pussy an hour ago.'

He smiles when she blushes. 'Yeah. I haven't forgotten.'

'I'm relieved to hear that.'

'I don't know, Nick. This is all so... bizarre.'

'Of course it is, but all I'm asking is that you try to see past the whole Santa thing. It's just a job. A title. That's it. But, if you've changed your mind about me, I'll accept it. I'm hoping you haven't. I'm hoping you can see me the same way you did before I told you.' He gestures towards the stairs. 'I'll give you some space.'

He's blown it. One look at her face, and that much is obvious. No one wants to fuck Santa. Hell, no one wants to even date him.

Scarlett takes a few seconds to process what Nick just said to her. What Santa just said to her. Nick is Santa.

She believes him. Absolutely believes every single word he spoke. How can she not, when he produced her childhood, bringing it out of her head with his... magic? She presumes it's magic. So much of what is happening still confuses her.

Reindeer. Magic. A sleigh. It shouldn't make sense, but it does. She looks over at him. Of course she's attracted to him. How could she not be. He's gorgeous. But that doesn't take away from the fact he is who he is. He turns towards the stairs. If he leaves the room, the connection will be broken. If she lets him walk away, he'll always think his job had come between them.

'Nick...'

He stops and turns to face her. Santa or not, this larger than life, stunning man wants her. She can't for the life of her figure out why. But he does. Maybe it's a case of her being the only option available at the moment.

'Don't do that.'

'Do what?' she asks, not sure exactly what she was doing.

'Put yourself down. I want you because you're beautiful. Absolutely gorgeous actually. I want you because I'm attracted to you. I don't sleep around, Scarlett. I was with you last night because I wanted to be with you. To feel you, touch you, hear you.'

'Are you in my head?'

'Not all the time. Why did you stop me from going upstairs?'

'What?'

'You stopped me. Why? I'm going to keep asking you, so you might as well stop skirting the question and answer it honestly.'

'I guess I didn't want you to leave. I didn't want you to think I couldn't get over what you've just told me. Even though I'm not sure how to let it all sink in. It's a big info dump, Nick. You're Santa. The Santa.'

'Fine. You win.' He walks back over to the couch and sits down, one arm resting on the armrest and the other on his leg. He pats one of his legs with his hand. 'Come here.'

'Excuse me?'

'Santa is asking you to sit on his lap and tell him what you want for Christmas.'

Scarlett laughs loudly. This is getting more and more bizarre by the second. 'Are you being serious?'

'Deadly serious. I'm Santa. It's what I do... apparently. So, come on. Humour me.'

'Can you still sit on Santa's lap when you're an adult?'

'Oh would you just shut up and sit on my fucking knee! I'm not going to do anything sordid, I promise. Not unless you want me to.' He grins, then pats his knee again.

She doesn't have a clue why he wants her to sit on his knee, but she does know she wants to. She wants to straddle him to be precise. Her brain is stuck on the fact he's Santa, but her body is craving his touch again. The two sides of herself are at war with each other, and right now, sense is winning over everything else, as it should.

Or will, until she sits on his knee. She knows as soon as she makes contact with him, she'll be a lost cause. So why is she delaying?

She meets his steady gaze and moves towards him, suddenly drawn to him like a moth to a flame. As soon as she gets close enough, he grabs her around the waist, resting her on his firm leg. 'Nick!'

'I was just speeding up the process. Stop complaining and look at me.'

'What?'

'Do you have to answer everything with a what? Please Scarlett. Look at me.'

After sighing again, just to make it seem like she's not desperate to do anything and everything he wants, she turns and look at his eyes. 'Now what?'

'You've got a serious fucking attitude problem, you know that? I really like it,' he adds with a mischievous grin. 'Okay, so keep looking in my eyes.'

'I'm looking,' she says with a bored tone. Bored doesn't even come close to how she's feeling. Turned on and horny would probably be a better description. Especially when his blue eyes swirl with white. God she could look at his eyes forever and never get tired of it. He slowly traces the side of her face with the back of his hand. Now she's horny and wet. When he speaks again, his voice sounds like it's coming from inside her head. 'What do you want for Christmas? And I swear if you respond with what I'll spank you.' He winks, and she can't help but smile at the thought of him doing just that.

'Do you want me to ask for a doll or something?' She's doing a lousy job of distracting herself, but she'll give herself full marks for effort.

'I'll give you anything you ask for Scarlett, but in this case just think about what you want for Christmas. From me.'

She keeps looking at him, her heart racing at what he just said. She can do this. She can absolutely remain calm and composed around this unbelievably sexy man. No problem at all.

Focusing, she thinks about perfume and other trivial items. But then she takes a breath and his scent hits her. One minute she's thinking about her favourite perfume and the next she's naked and so is Nick. Her treacherous mind paints a vivid picture of the two of them on the couch, his hands and mouth on her skin.

He groans, a satisfied look on his face. 'Yeah... you're definitely on the naughty list, Scarlett.'

'What?'

He brushes his long fingers through her hair, then taps her forehead. 'I can feel what you want.'

She cringes at his words. 'Oh God! You can read my mind? I thought that was a one off with the decorations?'

His eyes drop to her lips, giving them far too much attention. Or just the right amount. 'I make Christmas wishes come true... for the most part. Not everyone can write me a letter. I need to be able to know what kids who believe in me want. It's a perk of the job.'

'So you saw or heard or...'

'More like felt or sensed it. It's difficult to explain.'

Then she realises something that sends a blush straight to her face. 'If I say the word shower, what would it mean to you?'

'My fingers in your soaking pussy, and you coming on command.'

Totally humiliated, she buries her face in her hands. 'Oh God. I'm so sorry, Nick. I didn't mean to.'

He gently pulls her hands away. 'Look at me.' She lifts her head and looks into his eyes. 'What are you apologising for? I should be apologising to you.'

'You didn't actually touch me though... did you? You didn't, right? I mean you just made me think that... didn't you?'

'No. I'd never touch you unless you wanted me to. Or begged me to.'

'Nick... That's really not helping.'

'I'm sorry. Like I said earlier - you make it impossible for me.' He takes her chin in his hand, turning her face to his. 'I'm attracted to you, Scarlett. As in constant, hard-on attraction. And I'll let you in on a little secret,' he says moving his lips closer to her ear. 'I want what you want. You want someone to worship you. To make you come so many times, you can't scream any more. To keep you guessing about what they'll do to you next, where they'll touch you next. Someone to make you forget everything, except the sensations flooding your body.'

Scarlett is trapped in some freaky alternative universe. She's turned on by the buff version of Santa, and he's turned on by her. And she wants him.

'I was holding back last night.'

She groans before she can stop herself. 'You were?'

He nods, his nose tracing down the side of her face to her throat. 'Hell yeah! Now you know who I am, I don't have to hold back.'

Why is she hesitating? Last night was... she swallows the lump in her throat. God, it was so good, and hearing him say he can do more to her... It's not every day she's going to get an offer like this. If he is actually offering and she's not having a moment, imagining the whole thing?

'Yeah, I'm offering. You can have my body to do with as you please.'

'You know, being in my head isn't exactly helping.'

'Sorry. It's not really something I can shut off. And your thoughts aren't quiet. Far from it. I'm not holding a gun to your head, and I won't lay a hand on you unless you want it. You have my word.'

'Your hand is on my waist.'

'Do you want me to remove it?'

'Remove what?' she asks, unsure if he's referring to his hand or something else. This is what he does to her, confuses things. Makes rational thinking nearly impossible.

His breath tickles the side of her neck as he moves closer still. 'I'm going to ask you one more time and this time, I'd like an answer. What do you want for Christmas Scarlett?'

'I want you, Nick.'

'Right answer.'

This is going to be a lot of fun.

He's never been with someone who knows he's Santa. Never been able to be with someone and use his magic on them, the way he wants to with Scarlett.

The possibilities are enough to wake his dick up. Not that it's ever asleep when Scarlett is around.

He lifts her, then places her back on his knees so she's straddling him. "What do you want me to do to you, Scarlett? Deep down, what do you really want. Right here. Right now.'

Her mind instantly brings up an image of him naked, his body pressed tight against hers as he fucks her from behind.

His smile grows and he licks his lips again. 'If you could see inside my head, it would be a carbon copy of what's in yours right now.'

'Get out of my head!'

He grins wickedly. 'Stop wanting me and I will.'

Scarlett stares at his chest and her thoughts wander again. She thinks his body was designed with sex in mind.

'I'll take that as a compliment.'

'I said stop that.'

'What do you expect me to do when you keep undressing and fucking me in your mind?'

Her mouth drops open and she blushes, which is adorable. 'I do not!'

'You want me to take you from behind on the couch.'

She closes her mouth and her eyes drop to his crotch before she snaps out of it and looks over at the fire. 'Whatever.'

He laughs loudly and runs his hands over her arms. 'God you're stubborn. You say you want me. Your thoughts say you want me. Why are you still holding back?'

'Eh, Santa, remember?'

'No! Nick.' He leans back against the couch and looks at her. 'I'm Nick and I can honestly say I've never been more turned on by someone wearing a pair of Snoopy pyjamas.'

She glances at her outfit then crosses her arms, blushing again. 'It's not like I packed for company. It was just going to be me and my books for the week.'

'You know I can always fix the Snoopy situation for you.'

'What do you mean?'

He leans forward, bringing his face close to hers. 'I could take them off.'

She swallows thickly as that image does the rounds in her mind. 'You could?'

'Absolutely. I could quickly remove Snoopy from the situation. Three's a crowd and all that.'

He winks but she doesn't laugh. She's too turned on to make light of what he just said. 'Interesting proposition.'

'It is, isn't it? And it's not like it would be the first time, Scarlett. I'll let you in to a little secret. We've already had sex. I've already seen you naked. I've already licked that tasty pussy.'

She squirms on his knee, her breath quickening.

'My dick has already been buried deep inside you.'

His dick twitches when she thinks about him undressing her and pushing her down on the couch.

Nick grips the bottom of the pyjama top and lifts it up. Scarlett raises her arms, allowing him to remove Snoopy.

'Stand up.'

It takes less than a minute to remove the bottoms, leaving her standing naked in front of him. Nick drops to his knees, kissing his way up her thighs to her pussy. He laps at her, and groans. She's already wet for him.

He swirls his tongue over her clit and she bucks against him, her hands dropping to his head to grip his hair.

'Tighter, Scarlett!'

Her hands tighten on his hair, pulling him tighter against her. Scarlett's soft moans of pleasure are so hot, and mixed with her grinding her pussy against his face while she holds him in place, has him desperate to come himself.

But her first. He wants her to use him to get herself off. Then he'll fuck her the way she wants. Her fingers pull at his hair as she comes, the delicious dart of pain travelling straight to his dick. God, he wants to fuck her so badly.

'Oh fuck, Nick!'

She releases her grip on his hair and shudders as she comes down. Scarlett peers down at him, her eyes glassy and her cheeks flushed. She is so beautiful.

He pushes to his feet, then sits her on the edge of the couch, while he pulls off his clothes. He fists his dick, turned on by the way she's looking at him.

'Get on all fours.'

He can feel her excitement as she positions herself on the couch, leaning on the armrest, her stunning ass in the air for him to play with.

Nick takes a few steady breaths to calm down. Her mind is going full speed, the images assaulting him, as though he's experiencing the sensations himself.

To give himself a second to rein himself in, he takes her arms, pulling them behind her, so her chest is resting on the padded arm of the couch. He grips her wrists in one hand, holding her firmly so she can't move.

He can't tell if her groan of pleasure is in her head, or out loud. Everything is blurring for him, twisting reality with her fantasy.

'Push back your hips. I want to see your pussy.'

She does, and this time the groan is him. She's soaking wet, ready for him to slide in. He wants to taste her again, but not now. Now he needs to be inside her.

He presses the head of his cock against her pussy and it slides in, the pressure so fucking amazing as she takes him all. He'll never get tired of the sight of his dick disappearing into her pussy.

Scarlett whimpers and pulls her arms back. But she's playing with him. She likes that he's restraining her like this. He tightens his hold on her wrists, fighting against her fake struggles. The wave of excitement hits him. She's far from what he expected. The fact she's on the same page as him is the cherry on a delicious cake.

A cake he plans on enjoying as many times as he can.

Time to see how much she can take.

He smacks her ass, not hard, but enough to have her jolting away from him. Less than half a second later, she pushes back against him, her mind begging him to do it again. So he does, this time a little harder. Scarlett gasps, then pushes back again, driving him deeper into her tight pussy. He digs his fingers into her ass, grabbing her firm flesh as he fucks her harder.

Knowing that she's enjoying everything he's doing is such a new thing for him. Not only is he hearing and seeing her reactions to him, he can also experience it from her viewpoint, which is such a turn on.

As he pounds into her, he smacks or squeezes her flesh, turning her stunning ass a delicious shade of pink.

Scarlett is about to come, so he slows, which is easier said than done. The last thing he wants to do it slow down. But the whimper of frustration is so worth it. He draws in and out of her, keeping to long, slow strokes, as she moans and tries to grind against him, speeding things up again.

'You want me to go harder?'

'Yes...'

'Beg me.'

Scarlett doesn't pause for a moment. 'More, Nick. Please!'

'What do you want me to do, Scarlett?'

It takes all his willpower to keep things slow. He's on the verge of coming himself.

'Harder Nick!'

'Do what harder?'

'Fuck me, Nick! Please just fuck me!'

Unable to restrain himself any longer, he does exactly what she demanded.

Scarlett rolls over and comes face to face with a very sexy Santa. Nick is still asleep on his front, his face turned towards her. How the hell did she manage to find herself in this situation? This gorgeous man landed outside her house, turned out to be Santa, and made her orgasm more times in one night, than she probably had over the full span of her last relationship.

The man is unbelievable. She's never been touched the way he touched her. He was so sure of himself and what he was doing. Being with someone with that confidence is such a turn on. He knows what he wants, and she has no problem giving it to him.

What began on the couch, moved to her bed, where it continued for the next few hours, until exhaustion finally forced them to get some rest.

Scarlett shuffles a little closer to him, putting her face right in front of his. His scent is so good. Everything about him is.

The snow storm is due to last for another day or so, and she couldn't be more grateful. More time with Nick, possibly means more of what happened over the last few hours. She reaches out to touch his face, but pulls her hand back. She doesn't want to wake him. He's more than earned his rest.

Her attention is drawn to his tattoo. The images are still shifting on his skin, almost as if she's looking at them through moving water. It's hypnotic and absolutely beautiful. As she watches the images, the realisation of exactly who he is, hits again. It's not something she can just accept. It's not that easy.

At least it explains her initial thoughts on him. What she had put down to an overactive imagination, or seeing something that wasn't there, was the truth. She had somehow recognised him for who he really is.

Her eyes travel down his naked body. He's a seriously sexy Santa at that. And she had sex with this seriously sexy Santa. A lot of sex with him.

But what if that was it? What if it was just a one night thing, and now it's finished?

She moves back to the other side of the bed, or at least tries to. A heavy arm reaches across and wraps around her waist, pulling her close to him again. Nick smiles without opening his eyes. 'I liked it. A lot. And I'm really hoping that wasn't it.' He opens his eyes and hits her with a look that sends a shiver right to her core. 'You were really, really good and I want it to happen again, and again.'

Scarlett stares dumbstruck at him, blinking a few times as she replays what he just said. 'Hang on! You could hear what I was thinking? I thought you could only do that if you were looking at me?'

'My powers are getting stronger. Why would you think I wouldn't want to be with you again? You were there, right?'

'Yes. I was definitely there. It's just... I'm not used to this sort of thing. I don't do this.'

'Have sex?' he asks with a grin.

'Funny. Yes I have had sex before, thank you. But, not like that. This is just so surreal. I had sex with Santa.'

'You had sex with Nick. And he's really hoping we can do it again. And again.'

'He is?'

'Oh yeah. In fact, I'm really hoping we get to spend the next two days in this bed, naked. Or maybe downstairs. Kitchen too. And the shower.' He tucks his hand under his head. 'There's so much more I want to do to you.'

Scarlett licks her lips, then laughs. 'You see? Surreal. That's exactly what I'm talking about. Things like this don't happen to me. I don't get hot guys dropping out of the sky and doing things to me like you did. It doesn't happen.'

'It's real, Scarlett. I did drop out of the sky and thanks for calling me hot. And as for what I did to you... That's only the beginning.'

She stares dumbfounded at him for a minute before blinking. 'Like I said, totally surreal.'

'What's surreal about me wanting to fuck you as many times as I possibly can?'

She buries her head under her hands. 'Oh stop it!'

He lifts one of her hands up and peers down at her. 'If you really want me to stop I will. Do you want me to stop?'

She snorts loudly. 'No! Of course not. Just give me a minute to get my head around this.'

Nick turns her over so she's facing him again. 'Listen, I don't know what's going to happen on Christmas Eve. I don't know if Damon and the others will find me in time. I don't know what will happen if they don't. What I do know is that, for the next two days, I can't imagine anywhere I'd rather be, than here with you. Preferably naked with my dick and tongue buried deep inside you. But that part is not a deal breaker.'

'You are actually trying to give me heart attack, aren't you?'

'The plan is to give you a lot of orgasms actually.'

'You're on a roll so far.'

'I damn well hope so!' He licks his lips in that seriously sexy way he does, and pauses briefly. 'I'm going to let you in to a little secret. The whole knowing if someone is bad or good, is true.'

'It is?' She has no idea where he's going with this, but she absolutely wants him to continue.

'I know you're a good person, Scarlett. I know you've been a good girl and I know you want to be treated that way... mostly.'

And just like that, her pussy clenches. Nick lifts his hand and slowly wraps it under her chin, forcing her head back. 'Between you and me, what you want, what I feel you want, it gets me seriously turned on.'

'It does?'

'Yes. In the interest of being fair. I'll give you an insight into me. I take my job very seriously, but that doesn't mean I'm all jolly and sweet like they make out. I enjoy being in charge and calling the shots. And I'd seriously love to show you what it's like to be with someone who knows exactly what you want, and how to give it to you. Again, and again, and again.'

She can barely hear his words over the rapid beating of her heart. 'What I want?'

He nods, rubbing his nose along her neck. 'You want heat, passion, you want to be fucked so hard you can't think straight, and just get lost in the sensations over and over again. You want someone to take control, to dominate, to fill your throat and pussy with their dick, coming in, and on you, as many times as possible.'

She didn't think it was possible, but Scarlett could swear she's ridiculously close to having one of those orgasms right now.

'How... I mean... what?'

'I told you; I know what you want.'

'You really should come with a health warning or something. There's a strong chance I'm going to have a heart attack.'

He laughs, drawing his finger down the side of her neck. 'I'll take it slow if you want. Can't have you keeling over on me.'

The whimper isn't planned, and Nick's grin at her response is sexy as hell. 'Sorry. Not sure what happened there.'

His hand slides between her legs, his deep groan sexy a hell. 'I have a fair idea.'

'Yeah,' she admits, struggling to keep her thoughts in order.

'Spread your legs for me.'

She does, no longer in control of her body. It's doing its own thing right now. 'Good girl.'

This time the whimper is loud. Nick kisses her, his tongue invading her mouth, owning it, leaving her breathless, as his fingers tease her with just the right amount of pressure.

'You're a little flushed, Scarlett.'

She swallows again in a vain attempt to get some moisture back in her mouth. 'I wonder why?'

'I want you to be mine for the next two days. I want my cock inside you as often as possible. I want it in your pussy. I want it in your mouth.' He leans down and presses his lips to hers again, kissing her deep, leaving her with no doubt he's going to make the next two days the best of her life. 'You going to let me?'

'Yeah,' she whispers, finding it difficult to concentrate, while his hand is still caressing her. 'I'm definitely going to let you.'

'I know you are.'

Nick throws the duvet off them, then positions himself between her legs. He pushes her knees up, then his mouth covers her, his tongue swirling over her clit. Scarlett gasps, bucking her hips when his thumb slips into her pussy, slowing fucking her, as he continues to lick and suck her.

She loves seeing him between her legs. Loves when his white eyes target her, like they are right now, as his tongue drives her crazy. She wants to taste him too.

Nick stops what he's doing and gets to his knees, a sly smile on his face. He fists his dick, slowly moving his hand as he looks at her. 'You want it? You can have it. But on one condition.'

It takes her a second to realise he picked up on what she was thinking. 'I'll have to watch what's going through my mind when I'm around you. What condition?'

'I get to lick you out at the same time. I'm only just getting started with you. I want my dick in your mouth when you come. And I really want my dick in your mouth when I come.'

Nick lies down beside her, his hand still around his dick. 'Sit on my face, Scarlett. I want your pussy. Now!'

She climbs on top of him and Nick grabs her hips, pulling her down, his tongue immediately getting back to work. Faced with his cock, Scarlett hesitates briefly.

But Nick isn't prepared to wait. Leaving one hand holding her tight against his face, his other massages his dick and balls, his hips rotating as he plays with himself. Scarlett joins in, running her tongue along the tip when he holds it upright. Nick groans against her and lifts his hips, sliding his dick into her mouth.

As soon as she sucks him, he goes into a frenzy, his tongue laps at her clit then pushes deep into her pussy, over and over again, the rhythm matching his hips as he drives himself deep into her mouth.

There's no more thinking at that point. Nothing to distract her from what he's doing to her and his thick dick fucking her mouth hard. When his hand drops to the back of her head, Scarlett moans loudly. He takes hold of her ponytail, holding her steady, keeping her where he wants her as his hips pump rapidly. He's close to coming, his stomach clenching, the muscles rolling under her.

Nick sucks on her clit hard, the sensation running through her body, taking the breath from her. She comes, her whole body tensing as his tongue continues to massage her, drawing it out. All the time he keeps up the pace, using her mouth in the best way possible. His body tenses under her, then he groans against her pussy as he comes down the back of her throat.

He releases his hold on her hair, but Scarlett isn't finished. His dick is still twitching and feels too good, and she's not ready to let him go yet. He swipes his tongue along her, the slow laps helping to bring her down from her orgasm.

When she releases him, she flops onto the bed, lying beside him as she tries to catch her breath. The bed moves under her as Nick joins her. He kisses her, his tongue possessively driving into her mouth.

'I love tasting me on you.'

She couldn't agree more. 'I love tasting me on you.'

He chuckles, giving her one last deep kiss before he lies down and drops his arms across his face. 'I really like eating that delicious pussy. That's going to happen a lot. Just advance warning.'

'Thanks for the warning, but go for it.'

He rolls over to face her and smirks. 'I was giving you a heads up, not asking for permission.'

There's no doubt he's in her head. She doesn't want him to ask - just to take. She barely knows this man, but she knows she trusts him. But it's foolish to trust someone she doesn't know. Even more foolish to do anything like this with him. But there's something about him that makes her want to do things with him she's never contemplated doing with anyone else.

'Just say stop.'

'I'm sorry?'

'You can trust me. I know that means nothing. I could just be saying it, but I swear I'm not going to do anything you don't want me to. I'll know if I go too far.' He taps the side of her head. 'You won't be able to hide it from me, but just in case, tell me to stop. I want you to enjoy this, enjoy me.'

'I have to admit, you're off to a good start, Santa.'

He grins, his eyes whitening again. 'You call me that while I'm fucking you, and you'll be in trouble.'

'Good trouble or bad trouble?'

'You're going to make this fun, aren't you?'

Scarlett smiles when she walks down the stairs and finds Nick in the kitchen, making dinner. They'd spent the last few hours in bed, and only took a break because they were both hungry. She stumbles to a stop when she sees what he's wearing. 'Dear God! What exactly are you trying to do to me?'

He spins around and flashes her a smile, when he realises what grabbed her attention. 'What? You don't mind me borrowing this, do you?'

Never in her life could she have imagined her Snoopy apron could look so damn good. 'No! Go for it! Do you want me to wash your clothes for you?'

'I've got a wash on. Hope that's okay. I didn't exactly pack a lot of outfits. I wasn't planning on staying overnight anywhere.'

She stands in her living room and watches as he turns back to the cooker, exposing his naked ass to her. 'No. I don't mind in the slightest. That's one image of Santa I never thought I'd have in my head!'

'I can take it off and give you another image?'

'I wouldn't want you to do yourself an injury while you're cooking. Best to stay covered... for now!'

She sets the table, while Nick finishes their dinner. This is so much worse than any crush she's ever had. It's more than a simple crush on a random guy. She wants Nick like she's never wanted anyone before, and it's driving her to distraction.

She fills a glass with water and goes back into the living room, trying to put some distance between them.

Which lasts two minutes until Nick joins her, two plates of stir-fry in his hands. He nods at her and his smile widens. 'Nice pyjamas.'

Scarlett looks in horror at her choice of nightwear, and grimaces. She'd just grabbed the first thing she saw when she got out of bed. Going for her comfortable, baggy Snoopy pyjamas wasn't her best move. 'I wasn't exactly planning on anyone seeing my Snoopy pyjamas. And you can talk!' Although she's not complaining. Nick in just an apron, is certainly not something anyone in their right mind should complain about.

'Maybe next time you should pack an overnight bag in the sleigh? And, I can't believe I just said that. It sounds so ridiculous!'

He laughs, and then rubs his hand over the bandage on his side. 'Ouch! Don't make me laugh. And yeah - it does sound ridiculous. I talk about this stuff every day at home, and it sounds normal. How come it all sounds like complete gibberish when I'm here with you?'

'I'm sure if I was talking to you in your home about recruitment stuff it would sound weird too.'

He sits down and takes a sip of water. 'You'd be surprised. Recruitment is a big issue for us. Do you have any idea how difficult it is to find people to work for Santa?'

Scarlett laughs at the thought. 'I can imagine it must be a nightmare!'

'Too fucking right! But if it helps, I swear the first thing I'll do when I get back, is pack an overnight bag and put it in my sleigh.'

'That would probably be a good idea. You don't want to damage your image by dressing like that.'

'My image? People think I'm a cuddly, jolly, old guy with a massive beard. I've pretty much screwed all that up already.'

'You might be right. I don't think people would mind if they found out the truth. I'd hardly call you a disappointment.'

He smiles over at her. 'Thank you, Scarlett.'

They finish their dinner and move to the chairs by the fire to digest. Much to her disappointment, Nick exchanges the apron for a towel, but she has no doubts he'll be naked before long. She'll make sure of it.

Scarlett wraps her hand around her mug of cocoa and looks over at the tall, superbly built man staring into the fire, and laughs out loud.

'What's so funny?'

'This. I'm just thinking of every single image there is of Santa. Of you. You're a lot less... cuddly than you're portrayed. I mean, look at you! You look more like—' She stops herself before she finishes her thought. But she was a bit too late.

He tilts his head and smirks at her. 'I look like what?'

'Let's just say you don't look like Santa, and leave it at that. I don't mean that in a bad way. Honestly.'

The smirk turns to a grin. 'I'll let you off. Won't add you to my naughty list for that.'

He winks, and she feels her cheeks redden. The way he says naughty hits her straight to her core every time. Nick holds her gaze for a few seconds, his pale eyes mischievous. Eventually he looks away, and she takes a breath.

'I get what you're saying though. My predecessors took advantage of all the milk and cookies and other shit the kids leave out. I decided not to.' He shrugs and smiles again. 'I'm also really good at keeping hidden. Don't want to ruin the image for the kids. The cuddly version is all they know. I doubt this version would have the same sort of appeal to them.'

She nods. This version may not appeal to the kids, but it absolutely appeals to her.

'Then again, you've sort of ruined my track record,' he adds with a smile. 'The secret is out. I'm just going to have to persuade you to keep me to yourself.'

Her core clenches at his words. Stop drooling over Santa.

He rests his arm across the back of the couch and hits her with a serious look. 'Can I persuade you to keep me all to yourself, Scarlett?'

'Of course. No one would believe me if I told them Santa is six foot tall and built like you are.'

'I'm six two actually.'

She swallows heavily. 'Six-two then. And if I knew Santa looked like you, I might have convinced myself to keep believing.'

'There aren't many adults who believe in me.'

'Can I ask you something?'

He turns his head to her and nods. 'Sure.'

'What's it like?'

'What's what like?'

'Lapland. Sorry, is that what you call it?'

He nods, pushing himself onto one elbow so he can look at her properly. 'We just call it the workshop. It's kind of hard to explain. I guess in some ways it's like what you see in films. Lots of wood and stuff like that. But that's just an area of it. It's been expanded over the years to accommodate extra staff as they were brought in.'

'How many people work there?'

'Forty-two including me.'

'Forty-one people live with you? Seriously?'

'I'm lucky to have a great team supporting me and what I do. Eve looks after things for me for the most part, leaving me to do all the Santa stuff. She's been my assistant since the start. I'd be lost without her. It's a bit much sometimes having that many people living in the same building. That's why we expanded a few years ago. Everyone has their own space. There's a cafeteria, gym, games room, cinema.

Everything they need to live a normal life.'

'A normal life, working for Santa,' she says with a smile.

'You know all this sounded normal to me, before I met you. Now everything I say about it sounds fucking ridiculous!'

She laughs at the entirely fake hurt look on his face. 'So sorry, Santa.'

'Yeah and you can stop that too. It's Nick. Not Santa. That's just my job title.'

'But I love the way you go all defensive when I call you that.'

'Keep it up and I won't keep you up until the early hours.' She peers at him over the rim of her cup, as she takes a sip. The way Nick has been with her so far, means there isn't a chance he'll be able to stick to that.

'How haven't you been found? It can't be easy to hide all those people.'

'The entire workshop is underground,' he mutters, before reaching out to take his own cup off the floor.

'Are you serious?'

He nods. 'There's the house on the surface, with everything else underground. It's all hidden. While we're there, we're all safe. No one can find us.'

'How did you find so many people to work with you. I've been in recruitment for a while. I can't say I've seen anything mentioning working in Santa's workshop.'

He places his cup back on the ground and grins at her. 'Yeah, funnily enough we try to stay out of the spotlight whenever we can. Everyone there is just like me. Taken off the streets and given somewhere to call home.'

'Really?'

He nods. 'The way I see it, the workshop gave me a second chance. I wasn't going to survive much longer the way I was going. If I hadn't taken this job, I'd be dead. If I can offer the same chance to other people who have nothing, people who have no family, no money, no way to save themselves, then it's a good thing.'

'That sounds amazing, Nick. You've done an amazing thing.'

He shrugs, trying to brush it off.

'I'm being serious, so take the compliment. What you do, who you are, it's really special, Nick. There aren't many people who manage to bring joy to millions of kids all over the world. That's a great thing.'

He gives her a sad smile. 'I couldn't help you though.'

'Me? What do you mean?'

'I remember getting a letter from Scarlett O'Neill asking Santa to bring your parents back to life.'

Scarlett stares at Nick for a long time, not quite believing what he just said to her. After her parents died, she'd written one last letter to Santa, pleading for him to bring them back to her. She never told anyone about that letter. Not even her grandparents.

'How... you got my letter? You read it? Really? You?'

'Of course. I get every letter that's written to me. And I came to visit you that year.'

Nick gives her a few minutes to get her head around what he just said, before he speaks again. He wasn't sure about telling her that he remembers her from all those years ago, but he's being honest about his role, and this is part of it. Holding back at this stage is a waste of time. He'd prefer she knows as much as she can about him, and what he does.

Okay, so maybe some of the demon hunting part of his job can be kept from her for another while. No need to put that dark cloud on everything for her yet.

'But how do you remember that? Remember me?'

'You'd just lost your parents. You asked me for what a lot of kids ask for. You wanted your parents back.' He looks away from her, focusing on the fire again. 'I hold on to all those letters. It keeps me grounded, if that makes sense. People get so carried away with the expensive gifts and the fancy food, but others just want loved ones back, or even a basic meal. They don't care about all the expense or greed, that goes hand in hand with Christmas.'

When Nick looks at her, he could swear she's holding back tears. 'My daughter and wife were killed in a car crash on Christmas Eve. They were killed on the same road your parents were killed on.'

'Oh my God.'

'I was meant to finish work early so I could take them to a Christmas concert at the school. But I got tied up, so I contacted my wife and told her I'd be late, and I'd meet them there. They didn't make it.'

'I'm so sorry Nick. I'm sorry.'

He nods as he focuses on the fire. It's his fault they died. Entirely his fault. If he'd left work when he said he was going to, if he'd kept his promise to them, they wouldn't have been involved in the car crash. The guilt just loaded onto the unbearable loss, driving him to drink, then drugs, bankruptcy, and homelessness.

He didn't want to live, but was too much of a coward to do anything about it. Instead he went for the slow, pathetic, painful route. He's just lucky the old Santa found him when he did.

'Yeah. Me too. That's why this Santa gig seemed like a good idea. Gave me something to do, that didn't involve slowly killing myself too. I can't bring people back from the dead, Scarlett, as much as I want to.' And he would give anything for that not to be true - for himself and for everyone else who has asked him. 'I couldn't give you back your parents. I wanted to, believe me, but that's way beyond even my magic.'

'Thank you.'

He frowns as he looks at her again. 'For what?'

'For reading the letter. Leaving aside this bizarre situation, knowing that Santa... that you read my letter, it's comforting in a way.

I can't explain it. I think just knowing that you received it, that you receive all the letters kids send you, it's... yeah, it's really comforting. Thank you.'

'I couldn't help you though. I guess that's the hardest part of what I do. I can't make everyone happy as much as I want to.'

'Of course you can't, Nick. No one expects you to.'

He laughs, sitting up and scrubbing a hand over his face. He hadn't planned on telling her about his family. It's not something he really ever speaks about. It hurts too damn much. 'Oh believe me, kids are funny creatures. They put something on paper to Santa, they expect it to happen, or I'm the worst guy in the world.'

'Yes, okay. You might have a point there.'

'And you blamed me for not giving you what you wished for.'

'What?'

'I kept an eye on you that year. I don't know why. I just felt I needed to. You were living with your grandparents and they'd gone to town on the decorations and stuff.'

'You were there?'

'I was on my way home, but I couldn't leave. I detoured past your place. I've never been physically affected when someone stops believing. I mean it happens all the time. They either don't get what they want, or grow up and stop believing. But when you came down that morning and your parents weren't there...' He pauses and looks back at the fire. 'When you stopped believing, it was like a punch to the gut. I mean like someone had physically hit me. I was stuck outside your grandparents house, watching the kid whose heart I'd broken.'

Scarlett reaches out and takes his hand. 'Nick. I can't believe you did that for me.'

'Why wouldn't I?'

'I don't know. I mean it's like you said, there are billions of children you have to look after. Surely there were others who needed you to check on them more than I did?'

'Yeah, like I said, your situation struck a chord with me. And it kind of ruined the whole Christmas thing for you. After that I never got another letter from you. You were just a kid, and you stopped believing in the magic of Christmas.'

'Until you came back.'

He looks down at her hand, tightly holding his. 'Look around you, Nick. You've helped me believe again. You've helped a sceptical adult woman believe in the magic of Christmas. Believe in Santa again. I'd call that a pretty amazing Christmas miracle, wouldn't you?'

Scarlett takes Nick's hand as he guides her through the knee deep snow. The blizzard has finally stopped, the sky was clear for the first time in days. She grips his hand firmly, making sure each foot is on solid ground, before putting her weight on it.

His hand feels so right in hers. Strong and steady, supporting her. He'd kept her up all night, those hands of his doing things to her she never thought possible. Even with little to no sleep, she isn't in the slightest bit tired. In fact she can't remember feeling this good before. Being with Nick is energising in so many ways. The thought of losing him tomorrow doesn't bear thinking about.

He stops at the sleigh, brushing the snow off the surface, uncovering the damaged red paint. 'Stand back.'

He grips the edge of the metal and pulls, dragging it away from the tree and out into the open. Now she can see it clearly, Scarlett realises she's looking at the front of the sleigh. Part of the hitch the reindeer connect to, is still attached to a piece of the seat. She crouches down, running her gloved hand along the charred, torn metal. 'You're lucky this didn't kill you.'

Nick nods, but doesn't reply, as he examines what's left of his sleigh. Any follow up questions are kept to herself, when she catches a flash of anger on his face. This isn't the time to irritate him. He flips the sleigh over and rests his hand over the scorch mark underneath. His eyes whiten, the air around him crackling. 'It was one of us.'

His voice sounds like it's coming from far away.

'One of us?'

'Someone with magic. A legend.'

'Any idea who?'

He blinks, his eyes returning to normal. 'No. This isn't good.' He holds out his hand and she takes it without question. Nick leads her through the trees, his eyes searching for anything she might have missed. Not that he could find much through the thick snow.

'How many bad legends are there?'

'No one knows. Any folklore or fairy tale creature you've heard of, exists in some form or other. And there aren't bad and good legends as such. The world needs a balance. Flint and Damon aren't your typical good guys, but they're an important part of my team.'

'Flint?'

'The Horseman. What separates us is the end goal. What we're fighting for. We're fighting for humanity. Others want humanity kneeling at their feet. Whatever cause we're fighting for, we're supposed to remain hidden as much as possible, but the two worlds cross from time to time.'

'Like when Santa drops on my doorstep.'

He turns and grins at her. 'Like that. Typically dropping in on people is frowned on.'

'By whom? I mean, who regulates you guys?'

Nick laughs, gripping her hand tighter. 'I wish someone did. It would make my life easier. We're left to our own devices. Which is what causes the problems. Some would prefer they had a little more airtime. A larger hold on the human world. Others are happy with the way things are. Which is where my team comes into it. We try to keep that balance.'

'What do you do?'

The look he gives her is dark. 'We convince them to back off.'

She doesn't ask him to explain. She's not so sure she wants to know. Scarlett pulls him to a stop when she notices something on the snow beside her. 'Nick... is that blood?'

He keeps her behind him as he changes direction. Broken branches hang from the trees. Something big came this way, tearing through the trees. As they move through the forest a huge dark shape in the snow comes into view.

'Oh fuck!' Nick lets go of her hand, and pushes through the snow towards it. As she nears the shape, Scarlett realises it's an animal, but it's not like any animal she's seen before. It must be the size of a pick-up truck, its massive body covered in dark brown fur.

Then she notices the antlers. It's a huge reindeer.

Nick walks around the fallen reindeer, kneeling in the snow at the head of the animal. Scarlett walks closer to the reindeer, not wanting to disturb Nick, but needing to see for herself.

He runs his hand over the reindeer's face, his look dark and full of anger. 'She's one of mine,' he explains before Scarlett can ask the question. She takes a few seconds to really look at the reindeer. It must easily be the size of a moose, with huge fierce looking, razor sharp antlers. This isn't a typical Santa's reindeer. But then again, it's not like Nick is your typical Santa.

'Is she...'

He nods. 'She's gone.'

'I'm so sorry, Nick.'

He pushes to his feet and stares down at his reindeer. 'I need to bury her. If someone finds her it'll be an epic disaster. You got a shovel at the house?'

'Yeah, of course. I'll help you.'

He shakes his head, taking Scarlett's hand again. 'I really do appreciate the offer, but I need to take care of her myself, if that's okay. She's my responsibility. It's my fault this happened to her. I need to do this alone.'

'Of course. I understand.' He's pulling back from her and it hurts, but she's not going to push him as much as she wants to.

The trudge back to the house takes place in stony silence. He's furious and she understands why. This is so much worse than she could have imagined. This is more than Nick crashing. Someone tried to kill him, killed one of his reindeer.

'There's no one around,' he says, startling her. 'You'll be safe at the house. It's just us, but keep the door locked until I get back.'

She brings him around the back of the house and unlocks the tool shed. Nick takes a large shovel and gestures to the house. 'Get inside and thaw out. You're freezing.'

'Are you sure you'll be okay alone? I can help.'

He rests his forehead against hers, closing his eyes for a moment. 'I appreciate the offer, but I have to do this alone. I'll be back in a bit.'

Scarlett nods and watches as Nick walks back into the forest.

Nick stops at the edge of the forest and looks over his shoulder. He can't shake the feeling someone is watching him. His fingers tighten around the handle of the shovel. Given the choice he'd prefer his sword or guns but it'll do. He turns slowly, scanning the trees for anything out of place.

He waits a few minutes before lowering the shovel and setting off again. It's probably just his magic messing with him. He's been on edge since he woke up here. Being away from the workshop is throwing him off balance.

He's faced some shit since he signed his contract thirty-five years ago. He's been shot, stabbed, burned, and kicked around more times than he can count. There was also one time he was nearly strangled by a Banshee he pissed off. Every member of the team had been hit in one way or another. It was bound to happen given the creatures they go up against.

But no matter how bloody, broken, or bruised they were, each member of the team had made it back, every single time. As much as they don't get on, he considers his stubborn reindeer part of the team.

The hulking form of his reindeer appears through the trees, and that rage builds in him again. He crouches down beside her, then carefully lifts her heavy head off the snow, exposing the deep red stain under her. The bastard had slit her throat and left her bleed out in the snow, alone.

Losing her in this way, burns in his gut like no anger he's felt before. He's livid, and wants to spill some blood himself. His reindeer are trained to protect him. She must have tried to help him, or stop whoever was trying to kill him. She died out here alone, doing what she's supposed to do.

For the first time since he signed his contract, he's helpless. In that moment, it doesn't matter that he's Santa, or the leader of the team. He's just Nick, and unfortunately for him, Nick doesn't have the first clue what to do, or how to get home.

The frustration of the whole messed up situation hits him. The tree beside him takes the brunt of the attack, his blows and kicks shake snow free from its branches, landing on top of him. Two bloody fists later, he actually feels a little better. Scarlett will be pissed that he'll be digging into her first aid kit again.

He smiles as that thought hits him. Everything is going to shit around him, but in a way he can't help but be thankful he met her. Yeah, so crashing and having one of his reindeer murdered is something he deeply wishes didn't happen, but it led him to her. Silver lining on all the other dark and gloomy crap surrounding him.

He hangs his coat on the nearest tree, rolls up his sleeves and brushes some snow aside with his boot. It's as good a spot as any to bury the reindeer. Digging into frozen ground won't be easy but he'll stay here all fucking day if he has to. His magic makes him stronger, so he should be able to dig a deep enough hole to bury her.

It takes him about an hour of solid digging to get down deep enough to cover her massive body. He pulls himself out of the hole and rests the shovel against a tree. He's worn out, but the uncomfortable spike in his magic actually came in useful. The extra energy helped him dig through the frozen ground quickly.

Nick crouches down beside his reindeer and strokes her face. 'I'm so sorry this happened to you. I promise I'll find whoever did this and kill them. You have my word.'

He rolls her over, dropping her body into the hole, grateful that it's big enough to accommodate her. He grabs the shovel again and begins the task of covering her body. By the time he's finished his hands are killing him. Serves him right for having a fight with a tree.

There's not a lot he can do to hide the grave. Even covering it with snow it's still obvious someone was digging here. Hopefully she'll remain hidden. He doubts many people wander around this deep in the woods.

After making sure he's hidden the grave as much as he can, he picks up the shovel and trudges through the snow, back to Scarlett.

As much as he loves being here with Scarlett, he needs to get home. It's Christmas Eve tomorrow. If Santa isn't in Lapland on Christmas Eve the whole holiday is potentially destroyed forever. Him too probably, but that's another issue. The priority is making sure Santa does what's he's meant to do, on the one day of the year he's meant to do it. All the demon and monster fighting stuff is part of it, but not what the kids of the world are concerned with. His entire contract revolves around tomorrow night. One day to get it right.

It's not looking good for this year.

A blown up sleigh, dead reindeer, and a raging headache that's refusing to give him even a minute of peace. Not a happy Christmas so far for him. Then again, he hasn't had a truly happy Christmas since he lost his family. Since he became Santa, Christmas day was spent asleep, recovering from the Christmas run. And that suited him just fine. He may be Santa, but celebrating the actual day didn't appeal to him.

Or didn't, until Scarlett.

It's just a shame he can't be with her. He doesn't have a place in her world, especially with all this shit going on. And she doesn't belong in his.

If he can't figure out who's after him, the best place for her is far away from him.

He can take care of himself. Just because he's been gone for over two hours doesn't mean something's happened to him. It was a massive reindeer. Burying the animal could easily take hours. She just wishes he had let her go with him, but she understands why he wanted to do it alone. He was heartbroken over what happened. Furious too. Under the grief, his anger burned. She wouldn't want to be on the receiving end of that when he unleashed it.

She slides her bookmark into the book, marking the same page she took it out of a few hours ago. Reading is a lost cause with Nick around. Maybe she'll have a glass of wine to steady her nerves. But then if he doesn't come back, she'll need all her brain cells in the right order so she can go and find him.

But all her worrying was for nothing. When she walks up to the window, she spots him, standing at the end of her driveway, looking out over the snow covered landscape. The man is simply spectacular. His heavy coat is blowing in the wind as he leans on the gate, lost in thought. As much as she wants to go out to him, she leaves him to his thoughts for a while, just watching him from the living room window.

When he's still out there ten minutes later, she bundles into her coat and makes her way through the deep snow to join him. 'Are you all right?'

'Yeah. Just thinking. Trying to figure out what the hell is going on.'

'And?'

He shakes his head. 'Nothing. Still haven't got a fucking clue.' He taps the side of his head. 'There's something in here blocking me from remembering. I'm convinced of it.'

'You mean like magic or something like that?'

He nods. 'I remember leaving the workshop, then waking up here. I was gone for a good few hours before I would have reached here. So why can't I remember that time? There's a damn wall around the memories and I can't get through. And I can't shake this damn headache. I've had it since I woke up and it's not budging.'

'Are there any people like you who could do that? Block memories from you?'

'Too many unfortunately. We all have magic to a certain degree. I barely understand my own, without having the first clue about any of the thousands of creatures on Earth with magic of their own.'

'Have you got on anyone's wrong side lately?'

He looks sideways at her and grins. 'How long have you got, cause that's a hefty list?'

'Aren't people meant to get on your naughty list, not the other way around?'

He shrugs and smirks. 'I'm not one for sticking to the rules. Seriously though, it could be any number of creatures. Putting an end to Christmas won't bode well for me. Kids will stop believing in me. Between you and me, I don't want to know what that'll mean for me.'

She shivers, so he wraps his coat around both of them. He pulls her tight against his body and rests his chin on top of her head.

'I'm so sorry about your reindeer.'

'Thanks. I'll get revenge for her when I find out who's behind whatever happened to my sleigh.' He gasps, then tightens his grip on her as his whole body tenses.

'Nick?'

He pauses and hugs her closer. 'Sorry. Just my magic. It's sort of hitting in waves. It's getting stronger though. I'll have to try and get home tomorrow. My magic will be at its peak in a few hours, but we'll need to get to higher ground. I'm depending on one of my team picking up on my magic. High open ground will make that easier. Is there somewhere nearby we can go? Ideally with a large body of water.'

'Water? Why?'

'Depending on how my magic is behaving I might need all the help I can get. Water can sometimes amplify magic. And I'll need all my team to be able to perform at their best. Cobh can fight on land as well as anyone else, but if he can get into water, he's fucking lethal.'

'The nearby reservoir. High ground and lots of water. It's the nearest place accessible by car. It's about ten minutes drive from here.'

'That'll work.'

'I'm absolutely not trying to get rid of you sooner, but why can't you try to attract their attention now?'

'My magic is too unstable right now. It will peak on Christmas Eve. I need that extra surge to compensate for the fact I can't quite control it right now. Do you have the keys to your car?'

She pulls them from her coat pocket, then takes his hand as he leads her around the side of the house. Nick checks her 4X4 before walking down the driveway to the track leading from the house. 'I'll have to dig some of the track clear, but we should be able to get it out.'

'We?'

Nick leans against the bonnet of her car, drawing her into his arms again. 'I'll need your help Scarlett. I can't use my magic unless someone makes a Christmas wish. Santa is selfless, apparently,' he adds with a smirk. 'My magic exists to make others happy. I'll need you to help me attract the attention of my team.'

Now he's spelled it out for her, she understands what he's talking about, but it doesn't help ease her worry about having such a vital part in his plan to get home.

'Hey,' he says, lifting her chin so she's looking at him. 'It'll be fine. I promise.'

'Has anyone ever told you you're a strangely optimistic person?'

'Part of the Santa thing I guess. I know everything is up in the air at the moment. Someone clearly doesn't want me to do my job. I'm trapped here and my magic is seriously screwing with me. I should want to get away from here as fast as I can.' He meets her eyes, and they swirl with white. 'But I'm kind of glad I found my way here.'

'You are? Why?'

He pulls her closer. 'Because I met you.'

Scarlett's breath catches in her throat at his words. She feels the same about Nick. No question, but not for one minute did she imagine he'd feel the same. He's trapped here, thousands of miles from home with a lot on the line. She never thought he'd be happy about that. 'Me too. I mean I hate that there's this big load of doom and gloom hanging over us, and I hate that one of your reindeer was killed, but I'm glad you crashed outside my house.'

'Just for the record, I didn't crash,' he says, smirking at her. 'Santa doesn't crash. That would just be ridiculous now, wouldn't it?'

'Yeah. I guess it would be. I apologise for misspeaking, Santa.'

'As you should be. And stop calling me Santa.'

Scarlett grins mischievously. 'I apologise again... Santa.'

He laughs and pulls her close. 'Brat!'

Scarlett snuggles in against his chest. While she couldn't be happier about Nick bursting into her life, the fact he is potentially being targeted by someone or something, scares her. Downright terrifies her. After seeing the wreckage of his sleigh, it's clear they want him dead, not just to incapacitate him. Not that the second option would be great either, but she's not so sure she wants to be part of a world where someone is trying to kill Santa.

But even with all that craziness and the potential unknown threat hanging over them, she doesn't want him to leave. He's thrown everything in her relatively normal, but boring life, upside down, and she likes it. Life had become predictable of late. Work, home, repeat. Nothing about Nick is predictable. Nothing about being with him is predictable, and she's going to deeply miss that. And him.

'Nick?'

'Why am I sensing one of your deep questions?'

'Because you can read my mind.'

'Only when it comes to what you want. I can't read your thoughts, I swear. So, what do you want to ask?'

She wants to ask what happens when he is found and brought home. Will they ever see each other again or is this just a really enjoyable holiday romance? But she can't ask the question. Probably because she doesn't want to hear the answer.

He'll leave and go back to his weird and wonderful life. He has to. And she'll be left missing him.

'I was going to ask if we can go back inside. I'm freezing.' She can feel his body tense against her. He doesn't buy that for a second, but he keeps quiet and unwraps her from his coat so she can walk inside with him.

'You going to let me warm you up?' he asks as he closes the door behind them. 'We have a few hours to occupy before we need to leave.'

'That depends. What did you have in mind?'

Nick grins and points to the stairs. 'After you. I think it's time to see just how good you can be for me.'

Scarlett sits on the end of her bed, waiting for Nick. He's taking a few minutes to make sure everything is secure downstairs, before he joins her. And she's already wet thinking about what he's going to do.

He doesn't leave her waiting long. Nick closes the bedroom door behind him and points to the far side of the room. 'I want you over there. Stand facing the chair.'

She does as she's told while Nick pulls down his braces and takes off his top. He lounges back in the chair at the end of her bed, his legs stretched out in front of him, spread wide. He rests his head on his hand and levels his pale eyes on her. 'Take off your clothes.'

She laughs, nerves taking hold under his intense scrutiny. 'What?'

'Take off your clothes, Scarlett.'

'You mean like a striptease?'

He shakes his head. 'No. It's what's underneath that I care about. It doesn't matter how you take off your clothes. I want to see you naked in front of me. Now.' His lips curl into a slight smile, before he returns to being serious. 'Don't make me ask you again.'

She swallows as her body responds to what he's doing. Or not doing. Just talking to her is turning her to putty. She quickly takes off her clothes, instinctively wrapping her arms around herself.

'Don't ever hide yourself from me. Arms down. I want to see your stunning body.'

She lowers her arms, the goosebumps rising on her skin having nothing to do with being cold. Nick's eyes are taking in every inch of her body, his intense gaze full of promise. And she can't wait to find out what he's going to do.

'Kneel.'

She drops to her knees, her heart racing in her chest. Nick doesn't move. His massive body laid out in the chair in front of her like some god, and she's powerless to disobey. Not that she wants to. She wants so much more.

His eyes whiten, the blue swirling hypnotically. 'Crawl to me. Slowly.'

Scarlett moves towards him, excitement gripping her as she nears. He spreads his legs wider, giving her room to crawl between them. He unfastens the top button on his trousers, then rests his hands on the arms of the chair. 'It's all yours. No hands. Just use your mouth.'

Scarlett leans over him, nuzzling her face against his crotch. She grips the zipper in her teeth and pulls it down. Nick groans as she frees his cock. He lifts his hips, pushing his trousers down a little. He grips her chin, forcing her head back.

'You hesitated when I asked you to take off your clothes. I'm going to have to punish you now.' He fists his cock, slowly drawing his hand over it. 'I'm not going to let you come until you've made it up to me.' He draws her closer, guiding her mouth towards his dick. 'Open.' She opens her mouth, groaning when he pushes inside, the tip hitting the back of her throat.

'Look me in the eyes as you suck my dick.'

She lifts her eyes, the pure and intense lust in his eyes adding fuel to the situation. This is so much better than anything she could have imagined. And she had imagined quite a lot over the years. He's using her to get himself off and she is in a whole other world of ecstasy. She's giving Santa a blowjob.

His fingers dig into the arms of the chair, his abs clenching as she sucks, taking him as deep as she can.

But not deep enough.

'Take it all. I want to see you choke on my dick.'

She won't have a problem doing that. He's barely half way in and stretching her mouth to its limits. Not satisfied she's taking him deep enough, Nick grips the back of her head, then slowly pushes into her, hitting further down her throat.

He holds her head in place, thrusting his hips. She closes her eyes, but he taps her on the cheek, reminding her to keep them open and on him. She relaxes as much as she can, pushing down the gag reflex as his dick presses against the back of her throat.

'That's it. You're so fucking naughty, Scarlett. Your mouth feels so good wrapped around me.'

She swallows and he curses, his hips rising off the chair.

'Fuck! Do that again.'

She does, loving the way his body reacts.

'So close...' He grips her jaw, holding her head in place as he moves his hips, driving his dick deeper into her mouth. He suddenly pulls out, pumping his dick in his fist. 'Tongue out,' he says, his body trembling as the orgasm builds. He comes on her tongue, squirting into her mouth and down the back of her throat.

He lifts her off the ground, and places her on his knees, facing him.

He grabs her hands, holding them behind her back. 'Use me Scarlett. Use my magic. Just like you did downstairs.'

She knows exactly what she wants, so doesn't waste any time thinking about it.

'Glad to see we're on the same page,' he says, as he wraps a length of tinsel around her wrists, pinning them together. Nick lifts her up, positioning her above his dick. He slowly lowers her, sliding into her.

'Oh God...'

He wraps his hand around her neck as his other hand tightens on the makeshift restraints. 'The only sound I want to hear is groaning, screaming, or my name. That's it.' He pulls out then pushes back in and she groans. 'Better. Now you're going to be a good girl and come when I tell you. Not a moment before.'

She nods, lost in the haze of sensations flooding her body. Nick fills her, his hands moving to her hips to keep her in place as he thrusts into her. She's so close to coming and he knows it. Nick slows down, her orgasm fading away.

'Not yet. You'll have to work for it.'

She'll do whatever she needs to do. Anything and everything he tells her to. His hand slides from her waist to her pussy, his fingers tracing over her clit as he moves painfully slowly.

'I'd never tire of fucking you, Scarlett. Never.' His fingers trace down her back to her ass. He grips her ass cheeks in his hands, his finger swiping over her hole sending a shiver through her. 'Mmmm. Another thing to explore later maybe.'

She'd never been touched there by anyone.

'Would you let me fuck you in the ass, Scarlett?'

She nods, the slow, steady movement of his dick driving her insane.

He pulls on her restraints sharply. 'I didn't hear you.'

'Yes, Nick.' She can't believe she just said that, but she honestly thinks she would let him.

His eyes are white, faint blue still visible through the storm. 'I'll keep that in mind. You're a dark horse, Scarlett.'

He grips her by the hips, holding her above him as he drives into her. Her orgasm builds again, each thrust pushing her closer to the edge.

'Nick...'

He smiles as she says his name. 'I'd never tire of that either. I love hearing you say my name while I'm fucking you.'

And she loves hearing him talking like that to her.

'I'm going to use my magic on you now, okay?'

She nods, no idea exactly what she's agreeing to. Then she finds out, as his fingers tease her nipples even though his hands are still on her hips.

'Oh God...'

Nick smiles as his touch takes on a life of its own. Just like in the shower, Nick's hands and mouth are on her, kissing, touching, feeling, teasing her everywhere at once. It's all consuming, her senses going into overload.

He caresses the side of her face, but she's so lost in the moment she has no idea whether it's his actual hand, or his magic. 'You're so beautiful, Scarlett.'

His breath comes harder and faster as his pace increases. His body tensing under her, his hands caressing her flesh in all the right places at the same time.

'Come now, Scarlett. And I want to hear my name loud.'

As soon as his fingers massage her clit, Scarlett jerks back, screaming his name. The orgasm grips her, the only thing keeping her upright is Nick, who continues to pump into her. She's still coming down when he arches back in the chair. His dick pulses deep inside her, his hard body going rigid as he comes. 'Fuck, Scarlett!

Scarlett collapses, Nick's arms around her stopping her from sliding off his legs onto the floor. He unfastens the restraints with one hand, hugging her to his chest when she's free.

She lies against him, listening to the steady beat of his heart, as she comes down from the intense orgasm he just gave her. Not that she really wants to come down. He strokes his fingers through her hair, then kisses the top of her head. 'Still with me?'

She nods lazily. 'I think so.'

'Too much?'

She shakes her head, pushing herself upright so she can look at him. 'Absolutely not.'

He grins and runs his hands down the side of her face. 'You're seriously dirty you know that? I love it.'

'I wasn't until I met you.'

'That's a lie. It was there. You just hadn't let it out.'

'I'm worried it won't go back in again.'

Nick flashes her a devious smile. 'Good. It shouldn't.' He rubs her arms. 'You're getting cold.' He picks her up and carries her over to the bed, tucking the duvet around them then pulling her against his chest again.

'Nick?'

'Yeah?'

'What happens if you don't get back home in time for Christmas?'

He doesn't answer her immediately, which sets alarm bells ringing. 'To be honest, I don't know. Christmas won't happen for starters. First time ever, so I'd prefer not to know what happens if I mess it up.'

'This is hardly you messing it up.'

'It's not going to matter whose fault it is. I'm kind of the one tasked with making sure it happens.' He holds her closer, running his fingers through her hair. 'I'd imagine my popularity will take a nosedive too. If no one believes in me I'm kind of obsolete.'

'That doesn't sound good. But what about you yourself? You mentioned something about your magic and how it alters around this time of year.'

'I'll be fine.'

She pushes back from him and waits until he looks at her. 'Nick.

Don't do that.'

'Do what?'

'You're brushing me off.'

He rests his head on his hand and smiles at her. 'No I'm not.'

'Yes you are. That might pass in the workshop where you're the boss, but not here.'

'I thought you liked me being the boss?'

She shoves him in the arm. 'I didn't mean like that. And yes, I really do like it. But can you please answer my question, Nick. I'm worried for you.'

He nods and runs his hand down her cheek. 'I'm sorry. I just don't want to add to all the shit I've already landed on your plate.'

'I'm in this far. No stopping now.'

'Okay, the answer is I don't know. I honestly don't know what will happen to my magic, or to me, as a result of that.' He holds out his hand and she can see the trembling. 'My magic is stabilised by the workshop. I don't know what will happen if I'm away for too long - especially this time of year. My magic is increasing. I feel odd, Scarlett. Like my skin is charged. It's the only way I can describe it.'

He runs his fingers through her hair. 'Being with you takes the edge off. And I seriously don't mean that as blunt as it sounded. It's just the magic seems more controlled when I'm with you like this. And no, that's not the reason I want to be with you, so don't even suggest that.'

She lies back down beside him, tracing the ink on his arm. Nothing he just said is putting her at ease. His entire world is so different to what she's used to. It's like he's speaking of a fairytale or something like that. But the part that's scaring her is what happens to him if his team can't find him in time.

He rolls over to face her and brushes her hair back from her face. 'Hey. It'll all be fine, I promise.'

'How exactly can you promise that?'

He winks and smirks at her. 'Because I'm Santa.'

10

Nick climbs back into bed beside Scarlett and takes her in his arms. He'd spent the last hour clearing the snow from the driveway and along the track to the main road. His power is increasing, and the painful vibrations made digging the snow more difficult, but they're running out of time. They'll have to leave soon.

He runs his fingers along Scarlett's face. Her soft body fits so perfectly with his. She groans in her sleep, and hugs his arm closer to her chest.

He hadn't slept with anyone since he lost his wife. Sex yes, but nothing personal like this. He hadn't been interested in anything like this. Not until now.

But it's not as easy as finding someone and dating them. Not with his job being so completely abnormal. Scarlett has a life here. She has friends, a job. All he can give her is a massive dose of the bizarre. There's no way he's going to drag her back to the workshop and lock her away there for the rest of her life. They have two very different separate lives. Two lives that don't mix.

All that can happen is a hell of a lot of heartache in the future for both of them.

'What are you thinking?'

He smiles and kisses her shoulder. 'I thought you were asleep.'

'With Santa beside me? No way.'

'Try to get some sleep. I promise you'll need all your energy in the morning. I plan on keeping you in bed all day.'

She groans and cuddles up against him. 'I'll hold you to that,' she mutters sleepily.

'You won't have to.'

He lies awake, holding her as she falls asleep again. Time is running out - not just for them, but for him too. No way he's going to worry her by talking about his concerns.

No Santa means no Christmas. Does that mean he won't be Santa anymore? Does it mean he won't be alive anymore? He's no idiot. He feels far from right. There is something seriously wrong, and that's freaking him out. He lifts his right arm. The tattoo is fading. The ink is linked to his magic and to the workshop. The fact the damn thing is fading isn't a good sign.

He clenches his fist, watching the sparks of magic travel over his skin.

It's nearly time. Another few hours and his magic will be at its peak. He holds Scarlett tighter, breathing in her scent as he stares at the wall opposite him.

They'll try to stop him. Whoever blew up his sleigh is far from finished. If they wanted to keep him away from the workshop, they've only been temporarily successful. Clearly they know how things work. They know he'll make a run for it. Try to get home. Damn it! What if it's someone from the workshop itself?

That thought doesn't sit well with him. The place is like Fort Knox. You either had to know someone in the workshop, or work there yourself to be allowed in. Whoever it is will no doubt know he'll make a bid to get home in a few hours.

It won't be a case of walking outside and getting into her car. Someone or something will be waiting to stop him. He looks over to the window. They're probably out there right now, hiding in the shadows, waiting.

As much as he needs to get home, he has another concern. And that's Scarlett. He needs her help to alert his team, but that means dragging her through who knows what. He'll be putting her in direct danger, and that's not sitting well with him. He'll protect her. He'll fight and kill without hesitation to protect her. But he's not thrilled about her seeing that side of him.

It's one thing telling her he fights monsters, but it's another witnessing him actually doing the deed. Seeing him actually gutting the bastards.

There's a chance it won't come to that. But he's not going to get complacent. He's been doing this job long enough to know that he's trapped here for a reason. There's no such thing as a coincidence - especially in their line of work.

An hour later, he's still wide awake, and twitchy as fuck. His skin is tingling so badly it's driving him insane. Something feels off. More than just his magic kicking his ass. There's something... not right. He can't explain what it is.

He slowly climbs out of bed, careful not to disturb Scarlett, and grabs his boxers. She stirs when the bedroom door creaks, but doesn't wake up. Nick goes downstairs and stands at the window, peering into the dark forest outside.

He curses when his magic ripples through him, sending pain spearing through his limbs. He can't take much more of this. Being with Scarlett eases the discomfort a little, but it's getting worse. Fast.

Then he sees movement outside. He steps back from the window, watching more intently. He sees it again, the briefest flash of grey against the total darkness.

'Fuck!' That explains why he's so uneasy. He could feel the demons outside.

He quickly checks the doors are locked, then hurries upstairs and gently shakes Scarlett. 'Wake up.'

'What is it?'

'You need to get up now. We have to go.'

He throws on his clothes, sitting on the end of the bed to lace his boots. 'What? Why?'

'It's time.'

That spurs her on. Scarlett jumps out of bed and quickly dresses. 'Now? But I thought you said you had a few more hours?'

'I was wrong,' he says, moving over to the window and peering out. More movement. There's more than one visitor.

'What is it?'

'We've got company.'

She freezes with her head stuck in the neck of her jumper. 'What!'

'They know.'

She shoves on her boots then goes over to the window, but he holds her back behind him. 'Who knows what?'

'Whoever blew up the sleigh. They're either outside or sent some mates. They want to keep me here.' Or kill him. Blowing up the sleigh isn't exactly a friendly gesture. More of the shadows come closer to the house and he curses. 'Púca.'

'You what? As in shape-shifting fairy tale Púca? Are you freaking serious?'

'We're surrounded by black horses. I've come across them before. They're not here to talk.'

She shouts when a loud thump sounds from downstairs. 'What was that?'

'We've got to move! They're going to break in.'

'In here? What will they do if they get us?'

He doesn't tell her the Púca would tear them to pieces if they got them, but the look he gives her convinces her to dress faster.

Nick doubles over when his gut twists. 'Fuck. I'm running out of time. I need to get home.'

'But how can we get through them?'

He straightens, then takes her hand to lead her downstairs. 'By force.'

Scarlett stares at him like he's lost his mind, as he passes her a coat, before slipping on his own one. 'But how?'

'You'll need to drive and I'll take care of them.' He grabs the poker from beside the fire, then goes into the kitchen and stuffs his pockets with a few of her sharpest knives.

'Take care of them how? Hang on. Are you going to kill them?'

He tests the poker, twirling it in his hand. It's not great but it should take down a few of them.

'Nick?'

'Yes, Scarlett. I wasn't going to get into this with you, but they're not here to make friends with us. They're here to make sure I don't make it home. I'm going to do what I have to, in order to stop them.'

'Fight them?'

'Kill them.' He takes the keys for her truck from the drawer, and holds out his hand. 'Ready?'

'What? Now?'

'My magic will peak soon. It needs to be now. That's why they're here.' She looks at the door, the fear of what they're about to do written all over her face. She shouldn't be in this situation. It's his fight — not hers. But she's part of it now, and he'll protect her. If he has to kill every single one of them, he will, to keep her safe. 'I won't let anything happen to you. I swear.'

She hesitates briefly, then takes his hand in hers. 'Ready.'

Nick kisses her, crushing his lips to hers like they're not about to go up against demon shape-shifters. 'Now run for the truck and don't stop, no matter what happens. Got it?'

She nods, so he opens the door and steps outside.

Scarlett has been to so many Halloween events over the years. She's seen interpretations of the various Irish spirits and read their stories. But what she sees when they go outside her cottage, is a whole different world.

Dozens of black horses surround the property. But as she watches, some of them shift into demonic type creatures with tails and long ears. These ones climb onto the horses, getting ready to take chase. 'Nick...'

He grips her hand. 'I've got this.'

She has no idea how he thinks he has this, but she's so completely out of her depth, all she can do is nod. The Púca turn to look at them, their grins sending chills down her spine.

'Scarlett.'

'Yes?'

'Run!' He shoves her towards the car at the same time the horses at the front leap over the fence, moving towards Nick. Even though she doesn't want to leave him, she races to her truck, hitting the remote as she runs. She pulls open the door, climbs inside and slams the door shut. It takes a few attempts to get the key in the ignition, her hands are shaking so badly, but it finally fits and she starts the engine.

When she looks up to see where Nick is, she can't believe the scene in front of her. Púca are crowding him, attacking from all sides, but he's still standing. He slashes at them with the poker and a knife, cutting and striking with deadly accuracy. He's not randomly lashing out. He's controlled and methodical.

Nick swings the poker against the head of one of the riders and Scarlett grimaces as it falls to the ground. He races towards her car, wrenching the door open and climbs inside. 'Go!'

She screeches out the gate and along the track to the main road. 'Are you okay?' she shouts over the roar of the engine.

Nick wipes purple blood off his face, smearing it across his skin. 'Yeah. Put your foot down!' He turns around, peering over his shoulder.

'What the hell was that?'

'What was what?'

'You were fighting them.'

He shrugs out of his coat, dumping it on the back seat. 'They're not usually fans of sitting down and having a chat.'

'But you were fighting. I mean like you'd done it before.'

He nods as he meets her eyes. His own are pure white, giving him a seriously dangerous look. 'I told you that's what we do.'

'Yeah, but I thought... actually scrap that. I haven't got a clue what I thought. I just wasn't expecting that.' Scarlett screeches when something heavy lands on the roof of the car.

'Hold that thought.' Nick opens the car door and stands on the edge of the seat. A high-pitched scream comes from above the car, then one of the Púca slides down the windscreen, it's throat gaping open, spilling bright purple blood onto her car. Nick grabs it by the leg, throwing it away from the car, before dropping back into the seat.

She manoeuvres the car off the track onto the single lane road, pushing it faster now she's on a smooth surface.

Nick cleans her kitchen knife on his trousers and glances over at her again. 'What were you saying?'

'I have no idea. I don't even know what's going on right now.'

Nick squeezes his eyes shut and sucks in a breath.

'Are you hurt?'

He shakes his head. 'Just my magic. Are we nearly there?'

She checks their surroundings, recognising some of the landscape, even in the dark. 'About five minutes. Can you last that long?'

'No problem.' He curses, then grabs the wheel, ploughing the car into a large black horse that steps out in front of them. Scarlett lets go of the wheel, screaming as it crashes over the car, landing on the road behind them.

'Goddammit! How the hell are you so calm?' she asks, taking the wheel from him again.

'I told you. It's my job.'

'You're fucking Santa, Nick! You give presents to kids.'

'And fight the bad guys. I only deliver gifts one day a year. I don't sit around on my arse for the other three hundred and sixty four days. We fight.'

'So Santa, Triton, and whoever else, are actually what? Soldiers or something?'

'We're a team of men who make sure dicks like that,' he says, gesturing over his shoulder, 'don't take over the fucking planet. They want to run the show. We can't let them, so yeah, we fight. It's not all the time, but the bastards are getting braver.'

'I can't process this.'

He squeezes her leg which doesn't put her at ease, thanks to the fact it's covered in purple blood. 'I'm afraid you're going to have to. They'll know where we're going.'

'Are you saying they'll be waiting for you?'

But Nick doesn't answer. Scarlett looks across at him. His eyes are squeezed shut and he's breathing strangely.

She leaves him to it. There's not a lot she can do for him while running away from those creatures. And he needs to save his strength. They're still behind her. Every now and again she catches the glow from their eyes in the rear view mirror, spurring her on. She's terrified, but with Nick out of action, she can't afford to let it take over. It's up to her to help him now, and she's not going to let him down.

Scarlett sees the turn she's looking for, but doesn't slow down, taking the exit at the same speed. Her poor pick-up is beaten up as it is. It's not like she can make it much worse. The change in direction jostles Nick awake again.

'Nearly there, Nick. Hang on, okay.'

'Hanging on.' His voice is weak and laced with exhaustion. He's deteriorating... fast. If those creatures are waiting for them at the top, they're in serious trouble. There's no way she can fight them off alone.

11

The last three minutes of her drive up to the reservoir are the longest three minutes of her life. Scarlett keeps her eyes on the track ahead of her. There's no point constantly checking how close the Púca are. It's not going to make her car go any faster.

Beside her, Nick is drifting in and out of consciousness, his breathing coming in shallow rasps. She knew he was playing down his condition. This is so much more than his magic going a bit crazy. He's dying in the car beside her, and she honestly can't see what she can do to help him.

Finally, she reaches the top, the black water of the reservoir stretching out in front of her. Scarlett unfastens her seat belt then nudges Nick on the arm. 'We're here.'

He opens his eyes and looks around. 'Any company?'

She gets out of the car, hurrying around the front to help him. 'I think they're still following us, but I don't know how much of a lead we have on them.'

He struggles to stand unaided, taking the support offered by Scarlett. 'I'm sorry about this.'

'Don't be silly. Where do you want to go?'

He glances around, then nods towards the trees to the side of the reservoir. 'That's perfect.'

It takes a good few minutes to drag him from the car to the spot he chose. Once they reach the location, Nick drops onto his knees, unable to support himself any longer. Through the trees she can hear the screeches of the creatures moving towards them.

He hears them too, using the blood stained poker to shove himself to his feet again. Covered in blood and who knows what else, white eyes blazing, Nick is downright terrifying. This is a version of Santa she could never have imagined no matter how hard she tried.

'Now what?'

His white eyes turn to her. 'Now I need you. You know what I did in the house. With the decorations?'

'Yeah.'

He wavers slightly, his legs clearly about to give under him, but he stays standing. 'We need bigger. I need you to think bigger. This should be the peak of my power. Use it. Go nuts.'

'Out here?'

He nods. 'I need you to do this. I can't do it without you. It needs to be now, Scarlett.'

She takes his outstretched hand and looks into his eyes. For a few seconds nothing happens, then one by one, the trees surrounding the water, brighten. She doesn't want to look away from him until she's finished, but his white eyes are nearly painful.

Then he drops to his knees, his eyes fluttering closed. 'Nick! Keep looking at me. Come on. Please.'

She kneels beside him and takes his hand in hers, holding his chin steady with her other hand. He opens his eyes again and she smiles at him, ignoring the sound of the approaching demons. 'You're doing great, Nick. Nearly there.'

'Sorry I dragged... you into... this.'

'This is the most fun I've ever had. Leaving the scary demons aside of course.'

He looks around the clearing, smiling sleepily. 'Great work.'

'Big enough? Do you think your friends will notice?'

His reply is cut off when he slumps to the ground, his body trembling like he's having a fit before it stills.

'Nick? Nick! Wake up. Please...'

But he doesn't. She picks up the poker from beside him and faces the trees. Instead of darkness surrounding her, with Nick's help, she's covered every single tree with white lights, as far as she can see. The light is dazzling, easily visible for miles around. Unfortunately, it also helps to highlight the dark shapes moving closer to them. They're not in any rush. Maybe they know something she doesn't.

She looks down at Nick's still body, but pushes those thoughts from her mind. He's still breathing. As long as he's breathing there's still time. She hopes.

She grips the poker firmly in her hand as one of the horses moves out of the trees. She can do this. She's never even squished a bug in her life, but she can totally take down an army of demon shape-shifters, single-handed. No problem.

Then she hears something that not only freaks her out, but the Púca standing in front of her too. It's a horse, but the sound is straight out of hell. She turns towards it, not quite believing what she sees charging towards them through the trees. It's a rider on a monstrous black horse. But the rider's head is engulfed in flames.

More importantly, the demons seem to be terrified of him. Or it. Whatever. The rider thunders through the trees, sending the Púca scattering, screaming as their flesh ignites. To her left, one of the Púca races from the trees, turning to ice, as it's hit from behind.

Another screams to her right, tearing around the clearing clutching it's head, a black mist circling him.

Scarlett moves closer to Nick, guarding him against whatever the hell she's in the middle of. She screams, as a large Púca horse drops behind her, unconscious. She ducks as an arrow whistles over her head, hitting a Púca creeping up from the other side.

She covers Nick with her body, shielding him as the world goes crazy around her. Focusing on his face, she blocks out the screams, and shouts, feeling each shallow breath he takes. He's growing weaker, his skin greying in front of her eyes.

Then the world goes cold, a cool mist covering her body. Scarlett opens her eyes and barely believes what she sees. A solid wall of water separates Nick and herself from the fighting. She looks around, seeing the barrier surrounding them on all sides. Scarlett watches in horror as the barrier moves outward, capturing any Púca close enough, trapping them in the wall of water, drowning them.

She has no idea how long they are behind the wall of water. Beyond it, she can make out small details of the raging battle, but it's difficult to tell what's going on. Or who is winning.

'We're just chasing down any stragglers.' She turns and gasps. Suspended in the water behind her, is who she can only assume is Cobh. Triton smiles at her as she stares at him. 'It's the tail right? You're impressed.'

And she is. The black and silver tail must be at least ten foot in length, reaching from his waist and ending in an impressive silver fin. The gills to either side of his body pulse as he watches her. 'How is he?'

'I don't know. Not good. He's unconscious.'

Cobh's eyes glow and he lowers his arms, dropping the wall a little. 'Hey! We good?'

'Clear!'

Cobh looks back at her. 'You're safe now.' Then with a flick of his tail, he disappears under the surface of the reservoir, the wall of water following him.

Scarlett slowly lifts her head and faces the most intimidating group of men she's ever seen. The five men are solely focused on her and Nick, bodies of fallen Púca all around them.

'Hey Cobh! Cover up.' One of them throws something towards the water and a minute later Cobh joins them, adjusting a pair of boxers on his wet skin. None of them make a move to introduce themselves, but by looking at them she can guess who each of them are. Like Nick, they each show subtle traits of who they are in their appearance.

There's someone missing though.

As one, they look towards the trees. A tall man appears, but instead of the lights highlighting him, the shadow seems to follow, covering him as he walks over to her. The rest of the men look back to Nick as the shadowy figure joins them. The shadows disappear and Scarlett gets her first proper look at the Boogeyman. He's easily as tall as Nick, with jet black hair and eyes, every inch of visible skin covered in black tattoos. But it's the thick horns and massive wings that hold her attention. She has no doubts meeting him on a dark night would be truly terrifying.

'You're Damon.'

He frowns, then smiles, or at least she think he does. It was either a smile or a snarl. Whatever it was, it lasted just long enough to give her a good look at his enormous fangs. 'Nick told you about us.'

His heavy Spanish accent surprises her, but he doesn't give her a chance to dwell on it. Damon turns to the others. 'Hunter and Jok, head upwards. Make sure we're alone. Everyone else, secure the area while Flint takes care of the bodies. Move!'

They walk or fly away, leaving Scarlett alone with Damon. He shudders once, his wings and horns disappearing. He crouches beside his friend and feels for a pulse.

'How long has he been unconscious?' he asks.

'About ten minutes I think. I lost track of time when those things attacked us. Is he going to be okay?'

Damon stands, brushing snow from his black jeans. 'I don't know. We need to get him home. The workshop will stabilise his magic.' He holds out his hand to help her up, smiling when she hesitates. 'Don't believe all the stories. I'm one of the good guys... most of the time.'

She takes his hand, surprised that his flesh is warm. For some reason she assumed it would be cold.

'What's your name.'

'Scarlett.'

'You better come with us. Nick would kill me if I just left you here. We're heading back!' he shouts to the others, startling Scarlett.

'I'm sorry. What?'

'Lapland. We need to get him back. You're coming too.'

'Púca are taken care of, Damon,' the Horseman says, the flames surrounding him extinguished.

'Anything else heading our way?'

Scarlett squeals as a huge man drops out of the sky, his black feathered wings folding neatly behind him when he lands. He fastens the bow to his belt and grins at her. 'What? You were expecting me to be a short round dude wearing undies, right?'

If the situation wasn't so precarious she would laugh at the real life Cupid, but Damon isn't in the mood for joking around.

'Hunter! Anything else?'

Cupid shakes his head. 'Clear. We're good to get him home. And can we make it quick. I'm not a fan of you being in charge. No offence.'

Damon snarls at him, then grabs Scarlett's arm, dragging her over to Cupid. 'This is Hunter. He's a dick, but he'll get you back safely. If he doesn't, Nick will hang his fucking wings on the wall as trophies.'

'Fuck's sake, Damon. Ease up on the Boogeyman shit before you terrify the poor girl.'

Scarlett isn't keen on going anywhere with any of these guys without knowing Nick will be okay. But it's not like she can fight them off.

Damon releases his wings again and crouches down beside Nick. 'What are you all standing around for? We're on the clock here!'

Scarlett watches as Damon wraps his massive wings around Nick's body, then disappears, taking Nick with him.

'Where did they go?'

'Home,' Hunter explains as he holds out his arms. 'Come on. Time we get out of here before more of those assholes come back to finish the job.'

She allows Hunter to pick her up, hanging on to his neck as he lifts them off the ground and away from the mountain.

Scarlett hasn't got a clue how they managed it, but Hunter transported them all the way from Ireland to Lapland in less than a minute.

But not only that. When they landed and she was led through the workshop by Hunter, Damon was already there with Nick and some other members of the team.

A woman with pink hair hurries past Scarlett and Hunter, rushing over to Damon.

'How is he?'

'Weak,' Damon says, as he lifts Nick off the ground. The woman pulls off his coat, before Damon lies him back on the ground. 'He needs to connect again. Should be okay then.' He tears Nick's t-shirt off him, pulling the remains of it out from under him.

'Who helped him?'

Damon nods over at Scarlett. 'That's Scarlett. She knows everything.'

The woman gets up, and smiles as she holds out her hand. 'I'm Eve.

Nick's assistant.'

'He told me about you.'

Eve laughs and goes back over to Nick. 'Yeah well, don't believe everything the Boss tells you. How bad did he get before he lost consciousness?'

Scarlett takes a few seconds to realise everyone is looking at her. 'Oh sorry. He was up and down a lot over the last day. It was like he was getting cramps in his arms. He tried to hide it but it wasn't entirely successful.'

Damon and Eve manoeuvre Nick on the ground, placing him under a heavy chandelier type light hanging from the ceiling.

'What are you doing?' Scarlett asks. Surely they should be trying to help Nick instead of putting him on the floor. It doesn't make sense.

'This is the heart of the original workshop,' Eve explains. 'It's where the magic lives. Nick's Christmas magic is stabilised by the workshop and vice versa. One can't survive without the other. All I know is that being away this time of year has broken the link between Nick and the workshop. If they can't connect to each other... Let's just say we need them to connect.'

Scarlett doesn't need to ask Eve to explain. Her face says it all.

'All we can do now is wait, and hope he comes through.' She stuffs her hands into her pockets and looks over at Damon, leaning against the railing. 'So,' Eve says. 'Did Damon make the introductions?'

He turns his head towards Eve, eyebrows raised.

'Stupid question. Of course not. Damon is our delightful Boogeyman. This is Reve, the Sandman, Flint, the Horseman, Jokul or Jok, is Jack Frost, Hunter is Cupid, and Cobh is Triton.'

'I'm a seriously kick-ass merman, but you already saw me in action.' Cobh holds out his hand, smiling when Scarlett shakes it.

'Thank you, Cobh.' Eve faces Scarlett and rolls her eyes. 'And these seven men are the reason I drink far too much coffee for my own good. Bunch of egos on legs this lot.'

'I'll get some chairs. We'll stay until he comes around.'

'Thanks, Jok.' Eve crouches down beside Nick and rubs his arm. 'Come on Boss. I'm not running this place without you.'

Scarlett looks from Eve to the team, then to everyone gathered around here. She can see the same thing on all their faces. They're worried. Nick said they work for him, but looking around the room, she knows it's so much more than that. Nick saved each of them, gave them a second chance. They care about him and, from the little she knows of him after a few short days, he cares about them too. They're a big family.

She thanks Jokul as he gestures to a chair he brought out for her. 'Actually do you want to get cleaned up first?' he asks, frowning at the purple blood on her clothes.

'I'd like to stay with him if that's okay.'

He nods. 'Of course. Make yourself comfortable. We could be here for a few hours.'

Eve glances at the workers watching everything happening below them. 'Back to work everyone. He doesn't need any onlookers. I'll keep everyone posted.'

Scarlett hears a few grumbles, but the room empties, leaving her and the other members of his team.

'I'll get everything ready to go for him and have a new uniform brought to his room. I'll make sure this level is sealed off. Kane, no one gets near him without going through one of the team or you. Got me?'

The silent bodyguard nods, so Eve leaves to get things ready for Nick.

She tenses as Damon puts a chair next to hers and sits down. His black eyes lock on her. 'You really give a fuck about him, don't you?'

'Yes, I do. I'm guessing you do too.'

He shrugs and looks back at Nick. 'I'm the Boogeyman. I don't have friends. Except for him. Santa and the Bogeyman. Who'd believe that story?'

'He speaks highly of you.'

That seems to surprise Damon. 'He does? He spoke of me?'

'Yes. He mentioned you quite a few times. Will he be able to... reconnect?'

'I don't know. Eve seems confident, so I'm going with that. But he's never been away from the workshop at Christmas. Never had to deal with the power surge without the protection this place offers. They are linked though. This is the only way to save him.' He leans back in the chair and crosses his arms. 'All we can do is wait, and hope for the best.'

12

One minute Nick is lost, deep in a dream, and the next a surge of power hits his body, sending his muscles into spasm. Seriously painful spasms that drag him from his dreams.

He opens his eyes, shouting as the pain intensifies, then somehow manages to scramble to his feet. The wall he bangs in to stops him from landing on his ass, but also adds a sore back to everything else wrong with him.

His body is buzzing, the power racing through his limbs. He slams his palm against his chest. His heart is pounding! The damn thing is beating against his rib cage like crazy. His world tilts to the side, doubling him over as the sensation of falling increases. Someone holds him up, keeping him in place, until everything stops spinning.

Suddenly, he is thrown back against the wall when someone launches themselves at him. As soon as her arms wrap around him, he buries his face in Scarlett's hair, her scent instantly comforting him. He can't believe she's here! Maybe he's still dreaming.

'Welcome back, Santa. You scared the hell out of me!'

He moves back so he can look at her properly. Her pale skin is covered in Púca blood, as is her top, and her hair is a tangled mess. 'Are you okay? Were you hurt?'

'Your team came to the rescue just in time. I'm fine. But, how are you feeling? Have you reconnected with your magic? Is that what you had to do? I'm sorry. I'm still trying to get my head around all the terminology.'

He scrubs his hand over his hair and nods, finally in control of his body again. 'Yeah, I'm good. My magic is buzzing, but it's the way it should feel. Not like it was a few hours ago.' He steadies himself against the wall, when the room tilts again. 'Maybe it's buzzing a bit too much. I just need a minute.'

Nick doesn't resist when Damon pushes him back onto a chair. Scarlett sits beside him, rubbing her hand along his leg, as he gives his body a chance to recover.

Damon crouches down in front of him and frowns. 'That was close, Nick. Even for you.'

'Yeah. It wasn't planned. What happened with the Púca?'

'You and Scarlett put on one impressive display! No chance we'd miss something that powerful! We all picked up on it and came to your rescue, just in time. You were unconscious, and Scarlett was about to take on a hoard of Púca with a poker. By the way, I'm impressed,' he adds, glancing over at her.

'I'm just glad you arrived when you did. Thank you, Damon.'

He nods and pushes to his feet. 'Glad you're back with us, Nick. Hunter and Cobh are irritating assholes!'

Nick laughs. 'I know!' Then he turns to look up at the clock on the wall, and the laugh dies. 'Fuck! Cut that close, didn't I?'

'Yeah,' Damon says, holding out his hand to help him up. 'Being dramatic as usual. Will you be okay to leave in a few hours? You look rough.'

'Fuck off!' he replies with a grin. Damon stands beside him, until he's sure Nick isn't going to fall on his ass. 'I'm fine. It's all settled again, thank fuck. Is everything sorted for the run?'

'Of course,' Eve says, walking down the stairs to join them. She hurries over and gives him a tight hug. 'Glad you're back, Boss. You had us all a smidge worried there for a bit.'

'Sorry about that. We all set?'

Eve nods. 'Everything is ready whenever you are.'

He reaches out and takes Scarlett's hand. 'Damon, are the rest of the team here?'

'Around, yes.'

'I want a meeting now.'

'You need to get ready for the run.'

'Meeting first.' He glances down at his arms and clothes. 'Actually, give me ten minutes. I stink of Púca.'

Eve grumbles to herself, then nods. 'You're the boss. I'll let everyone know.'

The Boogeyman falls into step with him, as he leads Scarlett through the workshop. It's amazing having her here with him like this. He had never thought about bringing her back to the workshop. Didn't even contemplate it. His concern was getting himself back. But walking through his home with her beside him, is better than he could have imagined. And at least if she's here while he does the run, he'll know she's safe.

He just wishes her introduction to the workshop hadn't been so crazy. Having to sit in the heart of the workshop, waiting for him to reconnect with his magic wasn't the best way to show her his home for the first time. It's such an amazing, magical place. He'd love to show her around properly, but time is against them. Again.

He glances over at her and smiles. Her eyes are darting all over the place, taking in everything around her. The workshop isn't like it's depicted in the dozens of Santa films. But you would absolutely know it's Santa's workshop. No doubt. He knew the minute he was brought here. Even drunk and on drugs he knew exactly where he was that first night.

But it really comes alive this time of year. From the decorations hanging out of the vast wooden beams, to the constant playing of Christmas music, to the huge Christmas trees scattered throughout the workshop to his amazing team of workers, hurrying around in brightly coloured Christmas jumpers. This was their time - his, Eve's, all the workers - and they absolutely owned it.

'Are you all right?'

Scarlett nods. 'Oh yeah.' She smiles up at him. 'I'm in Santa's freaking workshop! With Santa! This is your workshop! It's so—'

'Sickeningly Christmassy.' Damon finishes. 'What the fuck is it with the music?'

'Blame Eve,' Nick says, still unable to take his eyes off Scarlett. 'The music and jumpers are down to her. She suggested the tradition a while back and it stuck.'

'Figures!'

As much as Nick doesn't want to bring up other business with Scarlett around, he's against the clock. 'Is the workshop secure?'

Damon nods, his black eyes scanning their surroundings. He's never at ease. Never settled. 'Of course. Has been since your reindeer came back with a piece of the sleigh and no Santa. Any idea who attacked you?'

'No.'

Damon steps into the elevator with the two of them and leans against the wall. 'Someone is trying to kill you, Nick. You do understand that, right?'

Nick feels Scarlett's hand grip his a little tighter, so he squeezes back. Damon tended to say it as it is. It's part of the reason they get on so well. 'Yes, Damon. I understand that. The fact my sleigh blew up was a bit of a hint. I'm only here because of Scarlett.'

Damon nods. 'I heard. That'll put a target on her too.'

Nick's warning glare comes a little too late.

'Me! Why?'

'Ignore him,' Nick says, but the damage is done. Fucking Damon! 'Okay, so if someone wants to put a stop to Christmas, they'll be looking at me, and anyone close to me. That may include you now.'

'Oh, yay for me!' She smiles, but she's worried, and she's not the only one.

He'd prefer she wasn't included on that particular list. Damon is right though. He brought her into his world and helped put that target on her. 'You'll be safe here,' he says as they step out of the elevator and walk down the corridor to his suite. 'I can protect you. I don't work with elves, and we don't play with tinsel all day,' he says, smirking.

'You realise you've just killed all remaining images of Santa I had in my head?'

He unlocks his door and smirks down at her. 'I think I did that with the whole less cuddly thing?' Damon snorts behind him, but he ignores his friend. 'You will be safe here, I swear. We're all trained to look after ourselves.'

'Oh, I sort of got that impression when you took down an army of those things, with only my fire poker and a kitchen knife.'

Damon smiles, his fangs appearing as that image goes through his head. He gets seriously turned on by fighting and blood of any kind. 'Kitchen knife? I like that, Nick. I might be a little impressed.'

'You would, you sick fuck! Like you didn't sweep in and take care of the leftovers!'

Damon shrugs as he sits on the arm of the couch. 'I may have enjoyed tearing a few of the stragglers to pieces. By the way, Eve found your cuff beside your bed,' Damon says, getting back on track again. 'I'm presuming you didn't take it off and leave it there.'

'No. I didn't. So, it was someone from the team, or the workshop?

I suspected as much.'

'We, as in myself and Eve, think someone is after your magic. It can be taken from you if you're away from the workshop when Christmas Eve hits. It would have killed you, Nick. No more Santa.'

'Someone on your team is trying to kill you?'

He shrugs, wishing he could give her a definite answer. 'Someone wants my magic. That's all we know for sure. Damon, are you picking up on any negativity from anyone on the team?'

Damon shakes his head. 'Everyone fucking loves you! It's irritating. But we all have powerful magic, Nick. If someone wanted to block me or throw me off, they could probably do it too. Reve mentioned Krampus as a possibility?'

Nick hadn't thought about Krampus, but it would make sense. They're very similar, and so is their magic. 'He couldn't get into the workshop.'

'Unless he's working with someone on the inside?'

That's certainly a possibility. 'Damn it! Okay, I need you to keep a close eye on everyone. You, Eve, and Scarlett are the only ones I trust without question. If it is someone on the team, I'd prefer to get to them first, before they have a chance to take another shot at me.'

Scarlett ignores Damon and Nick as they talk about things she can't get her head around right now. A few hours ago she was convinced both Nick and herself would be killed by the Púca. Now she's in Santa's workshop having a conversation with the Boogeyman.

She's still struggling with the fact she's in Santa's workshop, before you even bring Damon into the equation. She's in freaking Lapland! The house or workshop is hands down the most beautiful building she's ever seen. Nick was right, from the outside, it's just a house. A stunning house, but there was nothing to suggest to anyone looking at it, that Santa and his reindeer lived here.

Where they are right now may be buried deep under the ground, but it doesn't feel that way at all. If she didn't know otherwise, she'd swear they were in a log cabin at a fancy ski resort. There's wood everywhere. Vast beams and tall ceilings help make the space feel spacious and homely.

And that's before she saw Nick's personal suite.

Everything about the room matches Nick perfectly. From the huge four poster bed that she can see through the door at the far side of the room, covered with dark green throws and blankets, to the deep brown leather couches surrounding the huge fireplace, and the tall bookcases against the far wall, packed with an assortment of leather bound books.

It's him. And it smells like him. The entire workshop does. She thought it was a cologne he was wearing but now she's not so sure. Maybe it's Nick himself, or this place. Whatever it's from, she loves it.

Eve joins them, carrying a tray of food. She places it on the table behind the couch, then hands Scarlett a bag. 'Fresh clothes. I scrounged them from some of the other women here. Hopefully something will fit you and keep you going for the moment.'

'Thanks, Eve. I appreciate that.'

'Don't mention it. So, Boss,' she says turning her attention to Nick. 'Everything is ready for you. I left a clean uniform in your bedroom. The reindeer will be hitched up in a bit. We've checked the sleigh a dozen times. It's clear. We will go over it again, just before you leave.'

'Thanks. Don't fancy having my ass blown to pieces again. I'll just grab a quick shower then head to the meeting room.'

Eve grimaces as she looks at the pair of them. 'Might I suggest thirty minutes? You've got time. There is quite a lot of blood on the two of you and, if I'm not mistaken, you have Púca guts or something similar in your hair. It's not a good look, Boss. Especially not for

Santa. And no offence, you both stink of rotting Púca too. There is no chance in hell I'm sitting in an enclosed space with you for a meeting.'

Scarlett sniffs her arms and gags. The blood smells like rotten eggs. 'Oh God. That's foul!'

Eve nods to the clean clothes. 'That was my subtle way of telling you. I'll leave you to get cleaned up. We'll be in the meeting room in thirty minutes. Scarlett, just throw your clothes in the chute in the bathroom. We'll disinfect them for you. We're well used to that with this one,' she adds, nodding to Nick.

She smiles at Scarlett again, then leaves.

'I'll leave you to it,' Damon says, moving towards the door. 'I've got things to do. People to scare and all that fun stuff.'

'Do not scare any of my staff!'

Damon's smile is less than reassuring as he fades into a cloud of smoke and disappears.

'Fucker never listens to me.' Nick locks his door, then turns around and smiles. 'Hi.'

'Hi again.'

'You okay? You've had a lot thrown at you the last few hours. Over the last few days actually. Do you need to freak out? Scream? Anything like that?'

She absolutely should be freaking out. Or even screaming as he suggested. Any normal person would, given everything she's seen the last few days. But that couldn't be further from her mind.

Everything is so bizarre and unbelievable, but with him here, it somehow makes sense. Even Damon and the rest of the team makes sense now she's here. She understands what Nick meant when he spoke of his first days here. There's a feel about the place. Something instantly comforting and calming. 'I think I should be able to restrain myself for the moment.'

He wraps his arms around her and kisses her. 'I can't believe how great you're being about all this.'

'You're Santa and your best friend is the Boogeyman. Oh, and

Cupid flew me back to Lapland, after none other than Triton himself put a protective water wall around us. What's not to be great about? It's all perfectly normal.'

He laughs loudly. 'When you say it like that, I barely believe it myself.' He goes over to the table and pours himself a coffee from the pot Eve left. 'Want one?'

'I'm good, thanks.' She goes to sit on one of the chairs, having second thoughts when she gets a whiff of the Púca blood on her clothes.

Nick drinks his coffee, his light blue eyes peering at her over the rim of his mug. 'Come on. Out with it.'

'Out with what?'

'You're thinking about something. And that's coming from Nick - not Santa. What is it?'

'Was Damon right? About someone targeting you.'

He grimaces, then places his cup back on the table so he can wrap his arms around her. 'I'm the leader of the group, so I'll always have a slightly larger target on my back. It's not the first time I've been attacked, and it probably won't be the last. But I can handle myself, and so can everyone here. We train a hell of a lot. We're really fucking good at what we do. I promise it's nothing to worry about.'

'So why is Damon worried? Because it's obvious he is, and I doubt much could unsettle the Boogeyman.'

'He's being cautious. It's what he does. We've been fighting for centuries and I've led the team for a little over three decades. I can look after myself. We all can.'

'Oh I know that. I witnessed all of you in action first hand. Who knew Santa and Cupid could be so vicious.'

'Only when we're provoked. The rest of the time we're reasonably nice.' His grin is mischievous as his hands run up her back. 'Most of the time.'

He's trying to distract her, and she won't fight him. Going over how worried she is for him and the others won't help. All she can do is trust

166

him. And it's not as if she has any say in his life.

'Stop thinking about it,' he says, tracing his fingers along her skin.

'Can you move back a little? You stink.'

He moves closer, and runs his nose up the side of her neck. 'You don't want me to move back. And just for the record, you stink too.' She shrieks when he picks her up, throwing her over his shoulder. Nick kicks open a door to the side of his bedroom and carries her inside. He sits her on the edge of the huge black sink, and quickly turns on the shower, before he begins stripping her.

'I can undress myself.'

'Where's the fun in that?' Her jumper, t-shirt, and bra get dumped down the chute in the wall, then he stands her up, so he can deal with her boots, jeans, and underwear. 'Fuck, even covered in blood you're ridiculously hot!'

'And you're ridiculously messed up.'

'You have no idea.' He strips in record speed then lifts her again, putting her on her feet in the shower. The bruises from the crash have a few new friends thanks to the fight with the Púca. 'You're hurt.'

'Fuck that! I'm horny.'

He captures her mouth with his, shutting off any further talk of injuries. Nick grabs a bottle of shower gel from the stand and lathers it in his hands. She moans when his hands glide over her body, washing away the blood and grime from the fight, as he kisses her.

He turns her around to face the wall, bending her over and placing her hands against the tiles.

He gets down on his knees behind her and Scarlett groans as his tongue swipes from her clit to her ass. 'Oh God, Nick.'

He slaps her ass and she pulls away. 'Push back. I want to see that pussy.'

She does as she's told, and his tongue slides inside her in one stroke. His fingers dig into her cheeks, holding her wide so he can get as deep as possible. The combination of him sucking, licking, and fucking her with his tongue has her breathless.

She jerks as his thumb presses against her ass.

'Nick...'

'Trust me.'

His thumb presses against her hole again, and this time she moans. She's never been touched there before, and having Nick do it while he's licking her is an unexpected turn on.

'You like that, huh?'

She can't answer. All her energy is going into the simple task of breathing. Then his thumb is replaced by his tongue and she whimpers loudly. 'Oh God...'

It shouldn't feel this good. But it does. Scarlett cries out as Nick slides a finger into her pussy, his tongue swiping over her tight hole over and over, pushing into her a little more each time, teasing her.

She pushes back against him, suddenly desperate to have so much more of that tongue inside her. Nick slides a second finger into her pussy as his tongue pushes deeper into her ass. 'Nick!'

He slaps her ass, the sudden sting delicious against her wet skin.

'Push back. I want you to fuck my face.'

She sticks her ass out, forcing Nick's fingers and tongue deeper when she grinds against his face.

The orgasm grows, building in the base of her stomach. She moves faster, pushing back against him. Nick's tongue and fingers match her pace, pushing her to new levels of pleasure she'd never dreamt of. Desperate to come, she reaches behind her, grabbing a handful of Nick's hair, pulling him tight against her. When he realises what she's doing, he groans loudly against her ass, his own movements becoming frantic.

Scarlett only needs a light brush against her clit, before she's screaming loudly into her arm. Nick's fingers and tongue continue fucking her, drawing out the orgasm or adding more to it. She's not sure which one, and she honestly doesn't care. She's lost to the sensations. Lost to his fingers and tongue and what they're doing to her.

While she's still recovering, he slides his dick into her, driving all the way in, with one thrust of his hips. He pumps into her, his hand gripping her shoulder, holding her in place. He slaps her again, the sting driving her crazy. His other hand caresses her ass, massaging the tender flesh, brushing against her hole, as his balls slap against her.

'You ready to come again?' he asks breathlessly.

'Oh my God, Nick!'

'I'll take that as a yes.' He pulls her upright, wrapping his hand around her neck and the other arm around her waist to keep her in place. 'Scream my name when you come, Scarlett.'

And she does. His name tears out of her along with another orgasm. While she's still riding it out, he curses loudly, his dick pulsing deep inside her as he comes.

Scarlett loses track of time. With Nick supporting her, she hangs in a blissful limbo, the warm water hitting her skin, his throbbing dick buried deep in her. He releases his hold on her neck, his rough fingers tracing down the side of her face. His lips follow in the path of his fingers, his warm breath sending a shiver through her body. 'You are stunning, Scarlett.'

In hindsight, replying with anything other than a grunt would have been great. But she's surprised she even got the grunt out. Her body and mind are completely fucked by this amazing man.

Nick's chest rises and falls against her back, his deep breaths against her neck doing nothing to calm her down. She's never wanted to have sex over and over again with someone before. She'd have sex and that would be it. Job done. With Nick, they come, and she wants to come all over again. And again.

'I'm with you there, Scarlett. I'd love to go again,' he says, his breath warm on her ear. 'But I'll be late to my own meeting.'

'Get out of my head.'

His slips out of her, turning her around and taking her in his arms again. 'I told you - I'm not in your head. It's not my fault you're mentally fucking me every minute. It's my magic. I can't help but pick up on it.'

She slaps him playfully on the stomach. 'I do not. And it's got nothing to do with your magic. You're insatiable.'

'Eh yeah. You do actually. You're doing it right now.'

'I think if you did that to me again right now, you'd kill me.'

'Whatever, and I'm only insatiable because I've got you to play with.'

'You can play with me whenever you want.'

He kisses her, his hard wet body feeling so good against hers. 'Like I said, I'd keep you in my room for the next few days, but I'd never hear the end of it if I miss my own meeting. You going to fall, or are you good?'

'Fifty fifty at the moment.'

Without another word, he gathers her in his arms and carries her into the bedroom, tucking her into the monstrous bed. It could easily fit five or six people without any problems.

'You couldn't get a bigger bed?'

He slides in beside her, gathering her in his arms again. 'It's fucking ridiculous, right? I remember seeing this room for the first time. I'd been sleeping in doorways for about a year, then get brought to Lapland of all places, and was handed this. Don't know why he picked me, but I'm damn grateful he did. It's been a crazy thirty-five years.'

'I just realised something,' she says moving back from him so she can look at his face. 'You're in your seventies.'

He grins and winks at her. 'Yep. Seventy six to be exact. That's freaked you out.'

'Not at all. With everything else I've had to process over the last few days, the fact I'm sleeping with a guy in his mid seventies isn't a big deal. And you look really good for someone your age.'

'I'm going to take the compliment from all that, and say thank you. The age thing is a bit of a strange one though. I've been alive for seventy six years but technically I'm still forty one.'

'Was that not weird for you? Everyone else is ageing and you're not.'

He smiles briefly. 'I didn't have anyone left. It was just me so not ageing wasn't an issue for me. The rest of my team are locked in time too. As are the workers here. It's a perk and, for some, not so much. I guess it depends on what we're leaving behind.' He takes a hold of the locket around his neck so she decides to ask the question. 'Can I see them? Would you mind?'

'You want to?'

'Of course.'

He pauses for a moment, before opening it and showing her the picture of his wife and daughter. 'They're beautiful, Nick. Your daughter is the image of you.'

He nods. 'Yeah. I know.'

'What were their names?'

'Emma and Bethany. I bumped into Emma outside a coffee shop. Literally. Covered her in coffee. But my clumsiness paid off. We were married a few years later, then Bethany arrived.' He frowns deeply, closing the locket again. She leaves him to his thoughts. Losing his entire family like that is heart breaking.

He pushes upright, lying back against the headboard. 'You're coming with me to the meeting,' he says, back to business again. 'I want you to know everything. It's only fair since I dragged you into this fight. I'll have to go on the Christmas run after that. I'll be gone for about a day once I get around to everyone. When I get back I'll be out of it for a bit.'

'What do you mean out of it?'

'Travelling at that speed around the world and delivering all the gifts takes a massive amount of energy. That's why my magic increases this time of year. I need it to survive the job. But it takes it out of me. I'll get back and, after loading up on a serious amount of calories, I'll hit the bed for a few days.'

'A few days?'

He nods, running his hands through her hair hypnotically. 'I'm usually unconscious anywhere from a week to ten days. My body crashes and I need to sleep to get back on track.'

'But how can you survive that long without food or water?'

He gestures around them. 'The workshop keeps me alive.'

'I don't get any of this,' she admits. The more she hears, the more bizarre and unbelievable it all sounds.

'I'd like you to stay here until I get the run out of the way. After that, I'll make sure you're brought home. Once I've completed the run you'll be safe. But just to be sure, the team can take it in turns to watch over you while I'm asleep. I promise nothing will happen to you. You have my word.'

Scarlett nods, curling into him when he pulls her close to his chest. Until he mentioned her leaving, she hadn't thought about that. It makes sense that he'd go back to his world and she'd go back to hers. He's Santa. He fights demons or whatever those things were. This is his life. It's here with his team and Eve.

Staying with him would mean leaving so much behind, and after only knowing him for a few days, that's hardly a sensible or reasonable thing to consider.

His arms tighten around her. Is he picking up on her thoughts? She thinks it's only her desires he can feel, but she's not sure. She doesn't want to ask. It's unfair to put either of them in that situation.

'We'd better get dressed.'

She nods against his solid chest, but doesn't move. Breathing in his scent, listening to his heartbeat, it's all so right.

'It would put too much of a target on you, Scarlett. I won't put you at risk like that.' He kisses the top of her head, then pulls away to look at her. His eyes are white again. God she desperately loves when they do that. He smiles and she knows he heard that.

'You'll be late for the meeting.'

He nods. 'Yeah.' He gets out of bed and offers her his hand. 'Come on. Shouldn't keep them waiting.'

13

Nick slips on his t-shirt, his eyes never leaving Scarlett as she gets dressed at the other side of the bed. He loves seeing her in his room like this. She belongs here. Belongs with him. A few days with her and she's managed to captivate him like no one has before. It's beyond ridiculous, but he's going with it. When you know someone is right for you, you know.

He picks up the leather cuff, then fastens it around his wrist where it belongs. He still hasn't got a clue how it separated from his wrist and then found its way back to his room.

He still doesn't know who tried to kill him.

Still doesn't know who sent the Púca after him.

And that's why he can't keep Scarlett. Not that she's a possession.

But that's how he feels about her. She is his. End of story.

The thought of anyone else touching her, or being with her, is enough to have him reaching for his sword and drawing blood.

But he has to let her go.

He meant what he said. He doesn't want to risk her life by keeping her close to him. The bastard got into the workshop. They breached the one place on the planet where he should be safe. Unless he's planning on having a member of his team here all the time, it's just not feasible.

If he can't keep her safe here...

Putting distance between them will take her off their radar - whoever they happen to be. When he finds them and kills them, he might change his mind about having her in his life.

'Are you okay?'

He smiles at her, so unbelievably grateful she can't get into his head. 'Just thinking.'

'About what?'

'What's going on. Who's behind this.' Seriously regretting the fact I have to let you go. 'You ready?'

She takes his hand which feels so right. His magic must be messing with him. He's not usually so sentimental. Scarlett's hand tightens in his, as he guides her through the workshop. Nick glares at a few of the workers, as they give Scarlett a little too much attention. This over-protective streak is throwing him off balance.

Everyone is already seated when they get to the meeting room. Just the way he likes it. Eve has moved down a seat, leaving the one next to him for Scarlett.

'Everyone good?' Nick asks, as he settles into his seat at the head of the table. One by one, his team nod. 'Good. I'm sure you've already made your introductions, but this is Scarlett. She found me unconscious in the snow. Saved my ass. Scarlett, this is Eve, Damon, Reve, Flint, Jok, Cobh, and Hunter.'

She nods at them and Hunter opens his mouth to speak, but Nick holds up his hand, silencing him. 'Don't even go there.'

Hunter grins and winks at Scarlett, before smiling at Nick. Hunter's dick tended to control his mouth. Even the way he's looking at Scarlett is grating on Nick's nerves.

'Do you know what happened to you?' Jok asks, getting the meeting back on track.

'No. Whatever happened knocked me out. One minute I was in the sleigh, and the next in Scarlett's house. Nothing in between.'

'Did you see anything?' Flint asks Scarlett.

'Just Nick and some of the sleigh. I mean I didn't know it was a sleigh at the time. But I looked around really well in case there was someone else with him. I didn't see anything. There was a big bang and then there he was.'

'Not many can control the Púca,' Damon says. 'And those bastards rarely act alone.'

Nick agrees. 'They're not ones for following orders. Anything out of the ordinary here? Any of the workers acting weird?'

'No one was skipping around the joint all happy that you were missing,' Cobh says. 'No one who works here would be so stupid. You don't take on someone like you, with the backing you have from us. It would be the last stupid thing they do.'

'So do we have any ideas? Cause I've been thinking non stop since I woke up, and I'm hitting a brick wall.'

Flint taps on the table. 'I examined the wreckage we brought back. Nothing to trace the explosives back to whoever tried to kill you. It wasn't magic.'

'Can we stop saying that someone is trying to kill me. We don't know the motives.' He wants Scarlett to know what's going on, but would prefer the word kill wasn't mentioned in relation to him.

'Someone attached explosives to your sleigh. What the fuck do you think they wanted to do to you? Give you a hug or something?'

'Thank you, Damon. I kind of got that part.'

Eve clears her throat and points to the clock on the wall. 'Time,

Boss.'

'Damn it! Okay, so I have to do the Christmas run. I want you all to contact everyone you know. We need to find out who is after my neck. I'd like to twist theirs, before they get another go at mine.'

He catches Damon's attention as the others file out of the room. Damon hangs back and Nick waits until the room is clear before he speaks. 'Damon, I want you to watch Scarlett while I'm gone. Until we find out who is doing all this, she sticks by you or me.'

'I can do that.'

'Thanks. I'd better get ready to go. We'll have time to figure this out once I'm back.'

He takes Scarlett's hand again, as they walk out of the meeting room and enter the lift to the bottom level. He's a little reassured to know that Damon has her back. He trusts his friend more than anyone else on the planet.

As long as he makes it back in one piece, he'll find the bastards responsible, and kill them. At least that way he knows she'll be safe.

He's exhausted and desperately needs to go to bed, but for the first time in his thirty-five years in this job, he's not in any rush to go home. Scarlett is there and he wants to see her, but as soon as he gets back, he'll have to bring her home.

It's for the best though. Best for her.

He forces himself to smile as he brings the sleigh down, landing just inside the huge double doors of the workshop. Nick climbs down from the sleigh and smiles at Eve who, as always, is waiting for him.

'You made good time.'

'Wanted to get back.'

She smirks as she glances over to Scarlett. 'I'll bet.' She steps aside and Nick walks over to Scarlett, wrapping his arms around her. 'Hey. You okay?'

'I know you're Santa, but when you do things like that, it hits me again.'

'It's the sleigh right?'

Scarlett laughs, looking over his shoulder at the downright intimidating reindeer. 'Among other things.'

His smile drops as he takes her hand. 'You ready to head?' Her nod is as enthusiastic as he feels. But this is the only way. He's going to be out of it for a few days. The rest of the team will watch over her while she goes back to her life. Now Christmas is over for another year, she won't be in any danger. 'We'd better go. These grumpy fleabags will need a break in a bit,' he says pointing at the reindeer.

'You know that's not really a good way to make friends with them. And I'd want to be friends with them if you depend on them to do your job.'

Nick walks over to the two reindeer at the front. They're the same height as him, before you take their fierce antlers into account.

'We're mates aren't we?' He holds out his hand and one of them sniffs it before turning away. He glares at the animal, barely resisting cursing at it. Scarlett is right. If he's going to get them on side maybe he should make more of an effort with them. He'll worry about it later.

'Looks like you're great friends,' she says, laughing at him.

'It's only been thirty-five years. You can't rush these things.'

She joins him at the head of the nearest reindeer and holds out her hand.

'If she bites you don't blame me,' Nick says, as she moves her hand closer.

But instead of biting her, the reindeer sniffs her hands then licks it, before nuzzling its nose against her arm. Scarlett rubs the animal's neck, laughing when it rests its head on her shoulder.

'What the fuck!'

Scarlett hugs the neck of the reindeer, laughing again when it nibbles on her hair. 'Stop! That tickles.'

Nick takes a step back and crosses his arms as he glares over at them. 'Thirty-five fucking years, and I get a snort on a good day. Why do you get a hug?'

'Because I don't call them fleabags or...what was the other term? Oh yeah. Fuckers. I don't think I'd warm to you if you called me that.'

He may be pissed his relationship with the reindeer isn't the best, but watching them behave this way with Scarlett warms his heart in a way he wasn't expecting. His moody, stubborn reindeer are acting like a bunch of cute and cuddle reindeer around this magnificent woman. Seems they all have a soft spot for her.

He stifles a yawn behind his hand. Fucking exhaustion is creeping up on him already. But there's no way he's letting anyone else take Scarlett home. 'Has Flint left?' he asks Eve, as another reindeer moves in to give Scarlett a hug.

Eve nods. 'He left for Scarlett's about an hour ago. He wanted to make sure everything is clear.'

Sounds like everything is sorted. No reason to delay the inevitable. 'If you've all finished being pals with each other, I probably should get you home.'

As one, the reindeer turn to glare at him over their shoulder. For the first time in decades, he's on the exact same page as them. He doesn't want her to leave any more than they do.

Scarlett stops to gives each of the eight reindeer a scratch on the neck, before joining Nick at the sleigh. He lifts her in, placing her on the seat beside him.

'Back in a bit, Eve.'

'Sure thing Boss.'

Scarlett waves at Eve, then settles back in the seat, cuddling against Nick's side. Neither of them say anything as he guides the reindeer back out the door and over the workshop. There's nothing to say.

Scarlett opens her front door and looks around the small living room. So much had happened in the last few days. So much she's still trying to process. It feels like a lot longer than three days since Nick crashed into her life and turned her world upside down.

The man himself ducks through the door and joins her in the living room. 'I arranged for a new car to be delivered. It's in the garage. Key is on the table.'

'Nick, you didn't have to do that!'

'Your car was destroyed helping me. Shut up and take it. You don't have a choice.'

'Thank you. I really appreciate it.'

'I'll just make sure the house is secure.'

She nods, not sure what to say. She doesn't want this. She wants him to stay. Or for her to stay with him. Either option would suit her just fine. Even after a few short days, she can't imagine her life without him in it.

But her life is in Dublin. His in Lapland. This was a holiday fling. Fair enough, having a Christmas fling with Santa himself is a new one, but she's romanticising what was, in essence, just a bit of fun. With a few life and death situations thrown in on top, but mostly fun.

He comes back downstairs, looking like no man has any right to. Even exhausted after his run, with black rings under his eyes, he's incredible.

He sits on the arm of her couch and clasps his hands on his knee. 'You're secure. Flint will stay with you while you pack up. There's no rush. So, you heading back to Dublin?'

'Yep. Back to normal I guess. Although that sounds boring after the adventure I've just had.'

He laughs. 'Yeah, it was a bit more than I'm used to. I'm hoping things will settle down now.'

'So, do you plan on passing this way again next year?' She hates the desperation she hears in her own voice.

'If I do, I'm not planning on crashing. I'm not keen on making that a new Christmas tradition. It also depends on one small detail.'

'What?'

'It depends on whether you still believe in me next year.' He winks and grins. 'And how good you've been.'

Scarlett walks over to him, tucking in between his legs. 'I thought you preferred me naughty?'

He shrugs then wraps his arms around her. 'I'll be naughty and you can be nice. That work for you?'

'I think so.'

They fall silent again. She has to let him go, but she doesn't want to. They both turn around as Flint opens the front door and looks over at him, not in the least bit bothered that he might be interrupting something. 'You should go, Boss. Sun is coming up.'

'Thanks, Flint. Now get the fuck out of here!'

Flint nods and goes back outside. Nick smiles at her, brushing some hair behind her ear. 'I don't regret crashing here. I mean that.'

'Me neither. I'm going to miss you.'

He rests his forehead against hers and takes a deep breath. 'I'm going to miss your Snoopy pyjamas.' They both laugh in spite of the depressing situation. Nick kisses her, then stands up and takes a step back. 'Look after yourself, Scarlett.'

'You too, Nick.'

He kisses her forehead then walks over to the door and goes outside. Scarlett waits by the door, watching as he talks to Flint, then climbs onto his sleigh. His eyes meet hers and he winks. She keeps the tears back as the reindeer take off and Nick disappears. Scarlett glances over at Flint, sitting on his horse. He nods once, then turns his back to her.

She goes back inside and closes the door, then lets the tears out.

Nick sits on the edge of the bed. He's utterly shattered. Downright miserable too. He needs to sleep. Needs to let his body get over the run.

Flint is looking out for Scarlett, taking point for the next few hours as she packs up the cottage and goes back to Dublin and her life.

It's the right thing to do. He knows it, but that doesn't mean he's happy about it.

'I brought you some food.'

He nods at Eve, as she places the tray on the table at the end of his bed. His bed probably still smells of Scarlett. He's not usually so sentimental, but she's got to him, and he hasn't got a clue how to get over her. Or even if he wants to.

'Do you need anything else?' she asks, sitting on the bed beside him.

'No, thanks, Eve. Just keep an eye on things while I'm out of it.'

'We'll watch her, Nick. I promise she's safe.'

'I meant the workshop.'

'Of course you did.'

He flops back on the bed, exhaustion going over him in waves. The extra trip to Ireland had used whatever reserves of energy he had left. He doesn't even want to eat and that's not usual. 'There's no reason for anyone to go after her now.'

He doesn't fight back when Eve takes off his boots. She taps him on the leg. 'Lift up your ass.'

When he does, she untucks the duvet from under him and lays it over him, still fully dressed. He honestly doesn't care. The thought of even moving a finger is too much for him.

Eve sits back against the headboard. She always stays with him until he's asleep. It's a tradition that's stuck since his very first run. The exhaustion and weakness had scared the hell out of him first time. He hadn't been prepared for the severity of it. So she'd stayed, talking to him until he dropped off.

And right now, he's so grateful for her company. He doesn't want to be alone with his thoughts.

'Do you want to eat something before you sleep?'

He shakes his head once. 'Tired.'

'Just sleep then. You can eat when you wake up.'

He nods, rolling onto his side. His head is still killing him. The headache has refused to budge since he woke up on Scarlett's cottage floor. He thought it would be gone by now. It's probably exhaustion, but as he's drifting off, he can't shake the feeling his headache has something to do with whatever is going on. But he can't figure out what. Something about it doesn't feel right, but also, in a way, it's familiar.

He can hear Eve talking about general workshop gossip that never interests him. It's what she does to help him sleep, but this time the distraction isn't helping. He needs his mind clear, needs to concentrate on whatever that niggling thought is.

But it's a lost cause. He's so far beyond exhausted, so he allows his body the rest it needs, his last thought of Scarlett, as he falls asleep.

14

Scarlett packs the last of her clothes into her bag and looks around the bedroom. She had planned on staying here for another few days, but without Nick, the place just feels too empty. She'll spend the day as planned, watching crappy Christmas TV, then head back to her flat in Dublin in the morning.

She'll still be alone there, but it's better than being alone here with all the memories.

She's being absolutely ridiculous, she knows that. She was with Nick for a grand total of three days. Of course nothing else was going to come of it. How could it when he's Santa? It kind of puts up a slight barrier between them. Scarlett wanders back downstairs again and stands in the middle of the living room, looking at the pile of books she brought with her to read. She had a crazy holiday fling with Santa himself. There's nothing in those books that could possibly come close to that.

'Get a grip girl. It was three days of hot, steamy, fucking amazing sex, followed by a terrifying demon fight. Move on.'

She grabs a bottle of wine and a glass from the kitchen, and slumps back on the couch, staring at the fireplace. A knock at the door a few minutes later has her jumping to her feet and rushing over to open it. 'Oh. Reve. It's only you.'

The Sandman grins at her, stepping inside when she moves aside. 'Wow! That's one way to bruise a guy's ego. Thanks.'

'I'm sorry. I didn't mean that the way it sounded. I just thought...Never mind. My imagination is running away with me.'

He sits on the arm of the chair and brushes a hand over his close shaved hair. 'I'm sorry, Scarlett. He's not coming back. He'll be asleep by now.'

She shrugs and sits back on the couch. 'I know. Ignore me. So, is everything okay outside?'

He nods. 'All good. I've taken over from Flint. You've got me for the next few hours. Just shout if you need anything.'

'Thanks Reve. I think this is all overkill though. I'm sure I don't need you guys to babysit me.'

'You don't say no to Nick when he decides something. He tells me to be here, I'll be here. Same goes for the others.' He gets up and stretches. 'I'll leave you to it.'

'Stay in here. Please. I don't want you freezing your ass off outside. You might as well keep me company. You can protect me even better from in here.'

'If you're sure?'

'Sit. Please. Wine?'

He shakes his head. 'I'm on guard. Drinking won't help me look after you.'

'Good point. Do you mind?'

'Go for it. After the few days you've had, you could probably do with a drink.'

'You can say that again.'

Reve takes the couch, stretching his legs out in front of him the same way Nick did when he sat there.

Cursing herself, she picks up the TV remote, flicking through the channels for something to fill the silence. She may want company but she's not in the mood for conversation. All she wants to do is drink her wine while watching something that will, hopefully, distract her from thoughts of Nick.

Whether thanks to the drink, or the old comedy she found to watch, Scarlett drops off to sleep, thoughts of Nick entering her dreams. Then he's suddenly replaced by Reve.

I'm sorry for crashing your dreams but you need to wake up.'

'I do? Why?'

'The Púca are here.'

'But Nick isn't here. Why are they back?'

'Who the fuck knows how their minds work. All I know is that the place is surrounded. I'm going to wake you up but you need to stay quiet. Do you understand?'

She nods, then the next second she's awake with Reve staring at her.

'Go upstairs to your room. I'll try to knock them out, buy us some time.' She moves towards the stairs, pausing as Reve's eyes glow gold. He turns his hands in a circle in front of him, a spinning ball of sand appearing between his palms.

'I said go upstairs. Now! And lock the door behind you. Don't come out no matter what you hear.'

She turns away from him, racing up the stairs and locking the door behind her. She checks her window is locked, but instead of turning away, she pulls the curtains aside and looks out. There's nothing out there. The last time the black horses surrounded the cottage. Reve said the same thing was happening now, so why can't she see any of them?

Scarlett jumps when she hears shouts coming from downstairs. The Púca must have changed their tactics. This time they're in the house and Reve is dealing with them alone. She backs away from the door as some of his sand blows through the gap. She doesn't know much about him, but she's guessing if she breathes in his sand, she'll go to sleep and that's the last thing she needs with Púca in the house.

But more and more of it comes under the door, creating a swirling dust cloud she can't hide from. She hears him shouting and more Púca screaming. The air is thick with Reve's sand by now, but there's too much of it. Her eyelids droop as some of his magic hits her. The last thing she sees before losing consciousness, is her door being broken off its hinges by a terrifying Púca.

Damon is all about giving people bad feelings. Thrives on doing what he can to put them on edge. But the tables have turned in this instance. Now he's the one with the really bad fucking feeling, and he doesn't like it.

He's been summoned to the workshop more times over the last few days than he has over the previous year. Either Nick is in trouble, or his woman is. There's no other reason to request his presence. As Nick should be unconscious by now, he'll bet his woman has found herself in trouble. Just like he knew she would.

Damn Nick!

He should have kept her with him.

But as usual, he put being Santa, before being Nick. It's what he does. Always has. He distances himself from anything that reminds him of his old life. Damon knows what happened to his family. He'd never had a wife or child, so has no idea what Nick went through, but he can imagine. His imagination is dark. It needs to be, if he's to do his job right.

And that's another thing that's giving him a bad feeling. His job is losing its attraction. He loves being the Boogeyman... most of the time. He thrives on fear, on pain. But lately it's a chore. It's work.

He hasn't told Nick about this. Doesn't plan on telling him either. It's probably just a phase he's going through. A bump he needs to get over. And sooner rather than later.

He materialises in the meeting room, scaring the living hell out of Eve, which improves his mood greatly. She's an entertaining woman. He shuts down that thought as soon as it surfaces. He can't afford to find anyone entertaining. It goes against his job.

Eve thumps him on the chest, something that nearly has him breaking out in a smile. Nearly.

'I wish you'd stop doing that! You can't just pop up like that and scare people.'

Damon crosses his arms and peers down at her. 'Did you honestly just hear what you said? I'm the fucking Boogeyman!'

She sneers at him. 'Yes. I have heard, but thanks for reminding me. Anyway, we have a problem. I need you to come to the infirmary with me.'

He follows her down the corridor, then curses when he sees Reve sitting on one of the gurneys, blood pouring out of a wound on his head. 'What the fuck happened to you?'

'Púca. They attacked her house. Damon, they took Scarlett.'

'Fuck!'

'There's more. I saw Krampus.'

'You what? Are you sure?'

'Like I'm not going to recognise that monstrous bastard! It was him, Damon. No doubt.'

Eve sits on the end of Reve's bed and looks at Damon. 'Do you think Krampus is controlling the Púca?'

He wouldn't be surprised. Krampus is one powerful demon. Controlling such a large group of Púca would need a hell of a lot of power. Or incentive. The Púca don't tend to attack in those numbers unless they have a serious reason. And Krampus could no doubt offer them something that would get their attention. 'Okay. Back up. Who exactly did you see taking Scarlett? Krampus or the Púca?'

'Krampus. I saw him taking her before I was knocked out.' Reve passes Damon a piece of paper. 'I found that on the ground outside the cottage. It's got coordinates on it. I'm presuming it's where Krampus wants to meet Nick.'

'What can we do?' Eve asks.

Damon knows exactly what they have to do, but it's not something he's particularly keen on doing. He doesn't even know if it's possible, but they have no choice. 'We've got to wake Nick.'

Damon leans against the wall at the head of Nick's bed and looks down at the sleeping Santa. Eve paces beside him, her blonde and pink spikes ruffled, as she runs her hand over her hair again and again, as she walks.

'We've never done this before. And I mean in the history of the workshop. Santa goes to sleep and we leave him to it. I don't even know if waking him early will hurt him. This is a whole new thing for me.'

'It's the level of hurt he'll inflict on us if we don't wake him, that I'm thinking about. We have to try.'

Five minutes later Nick is still out for the count. They've tried shaking him, shouting at him, shouting louder, but he's completely unresponsive to everything.

'Any other bright ideas?' Eve asks, sitting on the bed next to Nick.

Damon hasn't got a clue. It's not like a normal sleep. It's more like a coma. And how the hell do you wake someone from a coma? 'We need Reve.'

Even frowns at him. 'Reve? He gives people dreams. What good is that?'

'Sleep is his area. I know Nick isn't technically asleep, but I'm out of other ideas.'

Eve gets up and nods. 'I'll bring him in.' Damon paces Nick's room, his attention on his friend, as he waits for Eve to come back.

He's itching for the fight that's coming their way. His other side is begging to be released.

If they do manage to rouse Nick, he has no doubts Santa is going to go fucking ballistic. That's why Damon likes him so much. Nick does everything Santa is meant to do. But he's got a vicious side to him. Which is probably why he's so good at leading their group.

Eve is back a few minutes later with Reve, who isn't looking thrilled about what he's being asked to do.

'Are you strong enough to do this?'

'It's not my head I'm worried about, Damon. It's his. I could seriously damage him if I do this. I don't even know what I'm going to do.'

'Damage him how?' Damon asks.

'I don't know. I've never forced someone to wake up. I usually do the opposite. I have no idea how he'll react.'

'If we don't wake him and Krampus hurts Scarlett, how do you think he'll react?'

Reve nods slowly. 'He'll kill us. Fine, I take your point. But you two better step up and protect me if he comes after me.'

'Fine. Whatever. Just get on with it.'

He rolls his eyes at Damon, before standing beside the head of the bed and placing his hands to either side of Nick's forehead. 'I apologise about this, Nick,' he mutters before he closes his eyes.

Damon understands the apology less than a minute later, when Nick's whole body jolts in the bed and tears pour from his eyes.

'Damn it, Reve! He's crying,' Eve says, moving towards the bed to stop him, but Damon holds her back.

'We need to wake him up. Let him finish.'

Nick's breathing increases. He's visibly suffering, his face contorted as the tears continue to flow. But Damon doesn't stop Reve. He wouldn't do this to Nick unless it was the only option.

They all jump as Nick roars. Damon has heard people roaring in despair many times, but never like this.

Nick's eyes open and his hand clamps around Reve's neck before any of them can react. Nick throws him over his shoulder onto the bed and straddles him, squeezing his neck in his hands. Damon snaps out of it and tries to pull Nick off Reve, but he's in a rage. Damon gives up on persuading him to stop, going for a punch to the side of the face instead.

Which works.

Momentarily distracted, Nick releases his grip on Reve's neck, giving the Sandman time to scramble away.

Damon pushes Nick back onto the bed before he can lash out again. 'Hey! Calm the fuck down, Nick! Just look at me and breathe for a few minutes. You're safe, okay.'

Nick looks up at Damon as he gets himself together. Whatever the hell Reve did to wake him worked, but it was far from easy. Tears are still pouring from his eyes and he looks downright terrified.

'What the hell was that?' Eve asks, slapping Reve on the shoulder.

'The workshop had too good a hold on him. I had to forcefully separate them so he could wake up.'

'Forcefully how? He's freaking out.'

'Nightmares. Really bad ones.'

Damon places his palm against Nick's forehead, trying to soothe some of his pain. He'll take it from him without question. At least he can deal with it, harness it, use it in their favour when they fight. Reve had used memories of Nick's family to jolt him out of the sleep. Harsh but necessary.

'It's okay, Nick. Just keep looking at me.'

Nick eventually calms down, so Damon removes his hand. He was able to push the memories back a little to give him a chance to recover, but not deep enough that he won't remember if he wants to. 'You good?'

Nick swallows and nods quickly. 'Yeah. I'm good. Thanks.'

'I'm sorry, Nick,' Reve says, 'I didn't know how else to get you to wake up.'

Nick closes his eyes and nods. 'Sorry... for choking... you,' he says, still trying to catch his breath.

'I deserved it.'

'Why did you wake me? What's wrong?' His eyes have cleared, but he's still shaking under Damon.

'Krampus took Scarlett before she could get back to the city.'

15

Scarlett groans, the sickening headache hitting her as soon as she wakes up. 'Move slowly. Take your time.'

She doesn't recognise the voice, but at that moment, she can't do anything other than as it says. Her head is killing her.

'I have water. Open your mouth.'

It tastes incredible, helping to moisten her dry throat. Her head is still killing her, so much worse than the worst hangover she's ever had. 'Nick?'

The low rumble of a laugh isn't Nick's. But why would it be? He had left and gone home. 'I'm not Nick, I'm afraid.'

She opens her eyes, wincing, even though the room is in shadow. Even her eyes hurt. 'Who are you?'

A light turns on behind her, casting a little light in the otherwise dark room. The hooded person beside the bed stands up. 'You should move slowly until you recover. Reve's powers take a while to recover from.'

'Where is he?'

The man moves over to the fireplace, adding more wood to the embers. His face is still hidden under the hood, but the voice clearly belongs to a man. A giant of a man, unless her perspective is all wrong. He's incredibly tall.

'I do not know. I presume he went back to the workshop. You're going to be my guest for a while, so get comfortable.'

'Who are you?'

He sighs and shrugs off his coat. Scarlett's breath catches in her throat when she sees the creature in front of her. He has to be at least seven foot tall, with long braided black hair, two massive twisted horns, and grey skin. His ears are pointed and pierced, a black plug in each lobe. His wide chest is bare, the leather trousers and boots the only clothes he's wearing. Whatever he is, he appears to be at least partly human. The shape of his body is human... mostly.

He crosses his arms and smiles at her, showing pointed teeth. 'You have no idea who I am, do you?'

She shakes her head. 'This world is still new to me.'

He nods, his yellow eyes examining her. 'You could be part of this world for centuries and still not be familiar with all the details.' He sits on the chair beside the fire and looks over at her. 'My name is Talen. You probably know me better as Krampus.'

'Oh God...'

He smiles again, his long tongue flicking out of his mouth. 'Funny how that reaction still bothers me. But I suppose centuries of being accused of hunting children will have a detrimental impact on my popularity. I would have thought after meeting Santa, you would not be so quick to believe all the stories you've heard.'

'So you don't? You know. Do what they say you do?'

'Oh I do. Or at least I did,' he says, stretching his legs out in front of the fire. 'I'm sure your boyfriend has explained the basics at least. We all have our roles to play in this world. Whether on the side of light or darkness, we are all pieces in the bigger picture. Unfortunately, I took things a little further than most. Not recently, but I doubt that makes much of a difference to you.'

'What do you want with me?'

'You've managed to get yourself in the middle of something I don't fully understand.' He gestures to the chair opposite him. 'I don't ever have guests. Will you join me?'

Sitting anywhere near him isn't appealing, but the last thing she wants to do is piss him off. She slowly gets to her feet, her head throbbing when she stands upright. Scarlett lowers into the chair opposite him. Being a little closer to Krampus, she realises he has more human features than she originally thought. His eyes may be yellow, but she could swear he's sad.

'Why did you take me?'

He massages his forehead as he looks at the fire. 'Someone has big plans for Nick, and I don't mean that in a positive way. He wasn't supposed to get back to Lapland in time for Christmas. You found him, and not only brought him back to your house, also helped him reconnect with his team. You, Scarlett, saved Christmas, which is quite impressive. I'll give you credit for that. Not many humans would have done what you did.' He turns his head to look at her. 'But that has placed you in danger, Scarlett.'

'You tried to kill Nick?'

He shakes his head. 'Of course you'd assume that. Of all the men to take up that role, Nick is the one I have the least issues with. What reason would I have to kill him?'

It's a fair enough question. She had just assumed he was the one behind everything. 'I suppose the stories I have heard about you, and you have captured me.'

Talen laughs and rests his chin on his hand. 'Granted the stories don't exactly help my position. As for capturing you, did I do that? Or did I rescue you?'

'Rescue me? From who?'

'The real creature behind all of this. Look around you Scarlett. You're not tied up. I'm not stopping you from leaving. I haven't hurt you and don't plan to.'

'I just—'

'Because of my appearance you assumed I'm not to be trusted.' He looks into the fire and shrugs. 'That was true once, but not now. We all began our lives as human men. But when we sign our contracts...' he pauses and sighs, lost in thought for a few minutes.

It's easy to jump to conclusions given the horns and grey skin, but seeing him like this, staring into the fire, she realises he's not as scary as she originally thought. He could even be attractive, or perhaps once was, before he was altered the way he is.

'The creatures we become are powerful. I'm sure you found that out with Nick and his magic. But some are more powerful than others. And I'm not talking about magic power. Krampus has been around for a long time. That's a lot of history, a lot of legends and stories to overcome.' Talen looks back at her. 'At the time, I couldn't control that side of the creature and here I am.'

'I'm so sorry.'

He looks surprised by that. 'For what?'

'Just for everything you said. It must be horrible having to fight yourself.'

He nods and the smile he gives her this time is less scary. 'Thank you. It's been a long time since someone listened, let alone understood. I have control of Krampus now, but it took too long and at a great cost to myself. I have made many mistakes over the centuries, but I can assure you, as of now, I am not a threat to you, to Nick, or to anyone.' He smiles a little. Or at least she thinks it's a smile. It's difficult to tell when he's got impressive fangs that keep making an appearance. 'From what I have heard of Nick, he's is quite the character. I have never heard of a more... unconventional Santa.'

Scarlett can't help but laugh at that. 'I agree. He's far from what I expected too. Is that why someone is trying to kill him?'

'Perhaps, but I believe it has more to do with his magic. He's the most powerful of the legends. If his power could be harnessed and used by someone else, we'd all be in a lot of trouble.'

'And that's why they tried to keep him away from the workshop?'

Talen nods. 'But it's far from over.' He gets up and goes into the next room, peering around the corner when she doesn't follow. 'I need to show you something.'

She gets to her feet and follows him into a large room, lined with shelves of books. 'The internet signal out here is less than reliable, so I'm forced to study the old fashioned way.' He pulls a book down from the shelf and opens it, laying it on the table. Talen points to a paragraph of text. 'It says here that his power can be harvested at certain times of the year, not just Christmas.'

'Why don't I like the sound of harvesting his power?'

'Because it will kill him. You can harvest his power by taking it at Christmas if he's not in the workshop. You stopped that plan by getting him home.'

'And the other way?'

Talen sits on the edge of the desk and turns his glowing yellow eyes towards her. 'If he is stabbed with his own sword, it will drain his power.'

'His sword?'

'Nick fights with a long sword.'

'Of course he does! Why wouldn't Santa have a sword!'

Talen smiles. 'I am impressed at how accepting you are of all of this.'

'I didn't really have much of a choice when Santa crashed outside my house. I don't know him for long, but I can't see Nick leaving his sword lying around - especially if he knows it can be used against him.'

Talen nods in agreement. 'True. Nick is cautious and would not take a risk like that. But I don't believe he knows about this potential issue. I have never heard mention of it before. I do think his attacker will attempt to use his sword against him imminently. Nick only brings his sword out of its secure housing when he goes to fight. And this will only work if he is stabbed while in a weakened state.'

'Which he is right now after the Christmas run,' she finishes. 'But he's asleep. No one will be able to get to him.'

'He won't be asleep. Reve saw the Púca take you. Unfortunately he also saw me with you. I saved you from the Púca, but Reve did not witness that part.'

'Oh. So why didn't you give me to Reve?'

'He was too far away. If I had left you, the Púca would have you now. I had no choice but to leave with you. Reve will have gone straight back and the rest of the team will be figuring out of way of waking Nick. It will be difficult, but possible. Then I have no doubt Nick will come for you. And me too unfortunately.'

'But whoever is behind this doesn't have me. How are they going to get Nick to come to them?'

'Nick isn't aware the true culprit doesn't have you. That's all that matters. He'll go to them to get you, and then they'll try to harvest his magic. I must find a way to get you back to Nick, before they capture him. I have no doubt once he knows you are safe, he will react, and we've both seen him in action.'

'Hang on? You've been watching us? That's how you know my name.'

Talen grins sheepishly and nods. 'I apologise. Santa and Krampus were linked a long, long time ago. The connection still exists for me as my bond to Krampus is so strong. I felt Nick was in distress and came to assist. I miss being part of the team. I am embarrassed to admit I was hoping that if I helped him, perhaps he would...' He stops talking and takes a deep breath.

Scarlett is struggling trying to match the creature she's heard so many stories about with this torn... man in front of her. He may look like a monster, but he's far from that. Under it all, he's a lonely man.

Scarlett straightens and nods her head. 'Fine. So what do we do?'

'This isn't your fight, Scarlett.'

'They're going to harvest his power. This is my fight. Do you know who is behind this?'

'I believe it is a member of his team. No one else has access to him as they do. And no one but a legend could take his power.'

'Do you know which member?'

'Unfortunately not. I can still feel Nick's presence. As far as I can tell, he's still in Lapland. I would imagine they are attempting to wake him. When he arrives I'll know. I'll bring you to him.'

'Why are you doing this? Why are you helping, after you've been cut off the way you have?'

'Redemption perhaps. I don't expect to be allowed in Nick's team. Not at all. But being allowed to live, without hiding from them would be a pleasant change. I am tired of looking over my shoulder.'

Nick paces his bedroom, trying to get his messed up head in the game. The nightmare Reve gave him was awful. He gets why he had to do it. There was no other way of waking him, but reliving his wife and daughter's crash was something he never wanted to do again.

And now Krampus has Scarlett.

This wasn't supposed to happen. Christmas is done for another year. Killing him now would mean nothing. There was no reason to take her. All that gets Krampus is a seriously pissed off Santa coming after him with two loaded barrels.

Krampus has history with Santa over the years. He'd heard the stories from the workers and the previous Santa. It was assumed Krampus would make an appearance when Nick signed his contract, but he never showed up. To be honest, he thought Krampus had slithered under a rock decades ago and given up.

Historically, he'd approached every Santa, bargaining for his place among the group to be reinstated. Nick's predecessors had turned him down. Nick would have too, had Krampus tried. There's no way anyone in their right mind would agree to work side by side with someone who wanted to punish the naughty kids, like he used to centuries ago.

If he hurts Scarlett, Nick will tear the bastard's head from his shoulders. He falls against the wall, bracing himself before he whacks his head. Less than a day of sleep had done nothing for his body. He still feels as crap as he did when he collapsed into bed after the run. The sickening headache is turning his stomach every time he moves.

How the fuck is he going to fight Krampus and whoever else he's convinced to join him? He's going to get his whole team killed. Scarlett too.

Damon suddenly appears by his side, helping to hold him up, as his legs go from under him. 'Thanks. Is everyone here?'

'They're on the way. You need to sit down.'

Nick pushes Damon off him. 'I'm fine. I need to find her, Damon. I have to find her. He has her, because of me. I've done this.'

Damon shoves Nick against the wall, harder this time. 'You need to take a second. You're exhausted.'

'I don't have time to take a second.'

'You can barely stand. This is me, Nick. I know you. How long can you keep going before you collapse?'

'As long as I need to.'

'Stubborn fucker.' Damon grabs his face in his hands and looks him in the eyes. 'Don't move.'

'What—'

'Shut up and let me help you before you drop.'

Nick tries to shut his eyes, but Damon is stronger than he is at that moment, keeping them open and focused on him. The dark cloud in Damon's eyes moves towards him and he fights to get out of Damon's grip.

'Stop fighting, Nick. I swear I won't hurt you.'

He doesn't have much of a choice, bracing, as the cloud consumes him. When it fades, Nick blinks, then shoves Damon off him. 'What is it with people forcing themselves into my head today?'

'Did it work?'

Nick holds his hands out in front of him. No trembling. He's strong, the exhaustion that accompanies the run, suddenly gone. 'What did you do?'

'I transferred some of my power to you. It should keep you going until we get Scarlett back. You'll hit the ground hard afterwards, but it'll get you through.'

'Thanks, Damon.'

'You okay after what Reve did?'

'Yeah. I'm fine.' He's far from okay about any of this. The flashes of memories are distracting. His brain is foggy and that's not going to help Scarlett. He has to be focused. It's one thing his body being recharged by Damon, but his mind is a mess.

'Listen, I need to talk to you before the others get here. I keep getting this... feeling I guess. I know the person who blew up my sleigh.'

'You remember?'

He shakes his head. 'Not like a clear thought. More like a memory that's stuck. I can't get the fucking thing out.'

'You want me to try?'

'You think you can?'

He shrugs. 'Won't know until I get in there. The thing is, I can only access your fears, all the bad shit in your head.'

'If I do know who it was, I guarantee the memory will be in there with all the bad shit.'

'Lie down.'

Nick stretches out on his bed and tries to steady his stomach. He's seriously off kilter and it's messing with his body. Letting Damon into his head probably won't help get him straight, but he has to try.

'Now keep eye contact.'

'Will do.'

Damon rests his hands on either side of Nick's forehead and focuses on his eyes. Less than a minute later Damon curses and lets him go.

'What's wrong?'

'Something is blocking the memory from me. It's like there's a fucking wall around it.'

Nick sits up and leans back against the headboard. 'Fuck it! This isn't done, Damon. This is about my magic. I'm absolutely convinced of it. Can you get Eve to check all the records for every Santa before me?'

'Check for what?'

'I have a horrible feeling there's another way of taking my magic. There's no other reason to keep coming at me like this. No other reason to push me like this by taking Scarlett. One of the team wants my magic, Damon.'

The Boogeyman crosses his arms and looks at him without saying anything for a few minutes. 'You meet the team. I'll talk to Eve.'

'You don't think I'm overreacting?'

'You don't overreact when it comes to the contracts and the team. Other parts of your life maybe,' he adds with a quick smile. 'But no. You might be right. Don't know who, but I'm sure they'll make themselves known soon enough.'

Nick can't wait for that moment. He just hopes he gets to Scarlett first. If anything happens to her he'll never forgive himself.

16

Scarlett tucks her legs under her, then flicks through the pages of the book Talen showed her. Learning about the history of Nick and his team is bizarre. Everyone knows the stories of Santa and the others, but the fact these were all regular men, before they signed a contract, is the part she can't quite get her head around. Talen passes her a glass of water and sits back beside the fire.

The more time she spends with him, the more of the man she sees behind the monster. She really does feel sorry for him. She can't imagine what it would be like to have a monster like that fighting for control every day. Is it that way for all the men?

Does Nick struggle with whatever the Santa contract brings? She hadn't noticed anything unusual about him like Damon and Talen, but that doesn't mean it's not there, under the surface.

She shivers and pulls the chair closer to the fire. Talen's home is freezing, the only warmth coming from the fire in one of the rooms. The entire dwelling is barely standing. She very much doubts he has the means to repair it. It's not like he can find regular employment looking as he does.

In spite of his lack of funding, Talen is clearly making the most of his situation. In the equally dilapidated barn to the back of the cottage, he has a cow and some chickens, supplying him with eggs and fresh milk, while the small garden is providing him with the vegetables he needs. He hunts for anything else, such as rabbit which is on the menu for tonight. The smell coming from the kitchen is heavenly.

She can't imagine what it would be like to live as he has been for decades - perhaps longer. Having to hide away from the world because of how he looks would be difficult enough. When you add the threat of Nick and his team to that, she has no idea how he has managed to survive so long.

No doubt the demon inside gives him strength.

She turns the page and faces yet another creature from legends she's heard about over the years. All real. All creatures Nick has faced at some stage since he signed his contract.

'You appear more confused than you were when you first began reading.' Talen sits in the chair opposite her, manoeuvring until his tail can slide through the hole he carved in the back. It must be a nuisance to live with that feature more than any of the others.

'It's a lot to take in. I can't believe these creatures are real. I've heard about all of you from a young age, but this,' she says, tapping her hand against the book, 'this is...'

'Unbelievable,' he finishes with a grin.

'To put it mildly. How have you... I mean legends like you, not been seen?'

'Of course we've been seen. That's where the tales you were told originate. Some humans have even tried to capture us.'

'Really?'

He nods. 'The Tooth Fairy especially is one who must be careful. Many have come close to capturing him.'

She slowly lifts her head. 'Excuse me? The Tooth Fairy is a guy?'

'The last I heard, yes, but I'm not exactly up to date with the contracts. That may have changed.'

'I suppose it's not that hard to believe considering Cupid is a huge guy with tattoos.'

'It would make it too easy to identify, and potentially capture us, if we were what people expect. Hunter is as far from the image of Cupid as you can get.'

Scarlett laughs loudly. 'You can say that again! Okay, so you may have a point there. None of you are what I expected.'

When he smiles, she sees so much of the man hidden under the demon. 'That's appreciated.'

'Can I ask you something personal?'

He glances over to her and nods. 'I haven't had anyone ask me anything for a long time.'

'I've just been reading about the contracts. Can you not... I don't know, get out of yours? I apologise if that sounds a bit stupid. I'm still trying to get my head around all of this.'

'I wish it were that simple. First, you need to find someone willing to take over your contract. Santa isn't too hard a sell. Krampus is. The fact I look as I do, won't help me persuade anyone to take over. And second, Krampus has too strong a hold on me. I can't separate myself. It will take years of ignoring his pull for my human appearance to return. Until then, I am what I am.'

'I'm sorry.'

'The blame is with me and me alone. And my situation is improving. A few centuries ago I had cloven hooves. My legs are human now. Hopefully, over time, I will earn my human appearance. I'd especially like to lose the tail next. I can't tell you how uncomfortable it is to sit with it. I have had to cut holes in everything I sit on.'

He smiles and Scarlett can't help but laugh. 'You're absolutely not what I expected.'

'And that's a very welcome compliment.'

'I wish there was something I could do to help you.'

He stands up and stretches. 'If you could persuade your boyfriend not to kill me when we next meet, that would be appreciated. I'll check on our food. We need to be ready to leave as soon as I feel Nick's magic.'

'Talen?'

He stops and looks over his shoulder at her.

'Do you want to be part of the team again?'

He turns to face her as he thinks about that one. She can imagine Nick and Talen fighting side by side with little difficulty. He may come across as gentle, but in some ways so does Nick, and that couldn't be further from the truth when he's pushed too far.

'If I am being honest, yes. I would like that very much, but Nick is no fool. He won't welcome me back with open arms, and I wouldn't expect him to. Realistically, the best I can hope for is to be left alone.'

He smiles and goes back to the kitchen, leaving her staring after him. How many more people like Talen are out in the world, stuck in contracts they are unable to escape from? How many of these people are being targeted by Nick and his team? How many would be different, less of a threat, if they could control whatever legends they are linked to?

She closes the book and stares into the fire. After reading what she has, and spending the few hours with Talen, what Nick and his team do is becoming less clear cut. Are they fighting against people like Talen? People who are misunderstood and have no chance to make up for past mistakes.

Nick storms through the stables, ignoring the reindeer he uses to pull his sleigh. Like him, they need rest, need to recover after the run, so he leaves them to their sleep, only slightly envious they can still rest. But he can't rest right now. Scarlett needs him, and this situation calls for someone with a little more attitude than his less-than-regular reindeer.

He stops at the final stable and faces the massive reindeer. Atlas only comes out on special occasions, just like this one. Bringing a sleigh into a battle tended to be cumbersome, which is where this brute comes into play. 'You ready to fight?'

Nick opens the stall and rubs the black reindeer on the neck. Unlike the other reindeer, his relationship with Atlas is good. The two just saw eye-to-eye from the first moment. He quickly saddles the reindeer, leading him out of the stall, back towards the workshop and the rest of the team.

'Shit! You're bringing out the big guns, huh?' Cobh says when Nick appears with Atlas by his side.

'I'm fucking pissed, so yeah. I'm going in with both barrels. We all ready to go?'

'We're ready, Boss.'

'Where's Damon.'

'He's on the way,' Flint says, climbing onto his own horse.

Nick pulls himself into the saddle, steadying himself against Atlas' neck when his head spins.

'You okay?' Reve asks from beside him.

'Just tired. I'll be fine once we get out there.'

Eve and Damon arrive with Kane, the latter kitted up with every weapon imaginable. Kane thrives in a battle situation. He usually doesn't let him join them on missions, leaving him looking after the workshop while he's gone.

The Nutcracker is tasked with protecting him, and it's a job he takes fucking seriously. But it's impossible to fight with his bodyguard getting in the way to protect him.

He reaches down, taking his sword from Eve, and slipping it into its sheath. 'We good?'

She nods, stepping back when Damon joins them. His friend nods at him so he takes the reins in his hands. 'You all know the plan. Scarlett is the priority. You hear me Kane?'

'I got it.'

'Good. I want whoever took her. It's my kill.'

They all nod so he turns Atlas towards the door. 'Let's go.'

Less than a minute later Atlas lands at the coordinates beside the others, stamping his hooves impatiently on the ground, as Nick closes his eyes and tries to get himself together. He doesn't feel right.

'What's wrong?' Damon asks as he joins Nick.

'I don't know. My head is all over the place.'

'It's the way I had to wake you,' Reve says, keeping his attention on their surroundings. 'I told him it could mess with your head.' Reve glares over at Damon.

'We didn't have a choice,' Damon says.

'Enough!' Nick doesn't care who did what. He just wants to find Scarlett and get back to bed - ideally with her beside him. He checks his guns and sword are in place, then takes a deep breath. He's fought in worse physical condition, but the exhaustion is a whole other issue. He can ignore pain. Has done too many times to count. But he's never fought the day after his Christmas run. It's going to make things interesting.

Nick glances around at his team. He's not thrilled at the concern he sees in their faces. It's his job to look out for them, not the other way around. 'We ready?'

'Always,' Jokul replies. 'How about you, Boss?'

'I'm fine. Let's do this.'

Before anyone else can ask if he's up to doing his job, he gestures for them to spread out. Flint takes up the rear on his own horse with Nick and Atlas at the front. When they step out of the clearing, Nick curses. He was expecting Krampus, a few dozen Púca, and Scarlett. Instead there must be at least a hundred of the bastards. No Krampus.

And no Scarlett.

'What now?' Reve asks from beside him.

'We're not going to get much conversation from these assholes.'

Damon's laugh from his other side is downright scary. 'I guess we're heading into a bloodbath then.' He twirls his blades in his hands as he releases his wings. 'I'm looking forward to this.'

Nick would prefer not to lead his team into the bloodbath that Damon is so excited about. No choice though. Especially when the Púca slowly circle them, closing them in.

They stand facing the Púca, waiting for someone to make the first move. Something is off about this whole thing. The Púca should have attacked by now, but apart from a lot of serious staring, no one moves.

Jok spins his staff in his hand. 'If this were a scene in a movie, you'd be screaming *it's a trap* at the screen, wondering what the fuck the good guys are still standing around for.'

Nick couldn't agree more. 'Time to get this moving so we can figure out how much shit we're actually in.'

But he doesn't get a chance to open his mouth to give the command. The Púca move as one, launching themselves at the team.

17

Atlas charges through the Púca, crushing the bastards under his hooves, his antlers spearing through any close enough to get in his way. Nick swings his sword, taking out the stragglers who don't fall, coating himself and the reindeer in bright purple blood.

Still no sign of Scarlett and that's worrying him.

He grunts as a Púca gets in a lucky shot, scraping its talons across his back as it brushes past him on the back of a black horse. He spins, decapitating the bastard, the purple blood spraying over his face as it falls to the ground. Ignoring the blood dripping down his face, he targets the next one, raising his sword over his head.

He turns Atlas around, ready to take another run at them, but the reindeer rears back, then crashes to the ground. Nick pulls his leg free from under the fallen reindeer, checking the animal for wounds, but there's nothing he can see.

'He's just asleep.' Nick freezes as the tip of a blade digs into his side, under his ribs. 'Don't move. I don't want to kill you... yet.'

He looks over his shoulder, not quite believing who's holding the knife. 'Reve? What the hell do you think you're doing?'

'Give me your sword. I'm not fucking around, Nick. Give me your sword.'

He lowers his weapon, passing it back to Reve. 'Now what?'

'We're going for a walk.' He nods ahead of them to the trees. 'Walk, or I'll have to ask my friends to tear Scarlett to pieces.'

Nick tenses, but Reve pushes the knife into his side, drawing blood. 'I know you probably don't give a damn about your own life, but you care about her. You've hardly been subtle about it. Do you really want to be responsible for the death of someone else you care about? Now walk.'

Nick does as he's told, his mind racing as they disappear into the thick forest, leaving the fight behind them. 'This has all been you?'

Reve laughs from behind him. 'Bravo, Santa. Now shut up and keep walking.'

Nick's head spins and he stumbles into a tree.

'Having a bit of trouble, huh?'

Nick straightens, throwing a hard look at Reve. 'Your fault too I'm guessing?'

Reve shrugs. 'You can blame Damon for that. He's the one who wanted me to get into your head to wake you. I guess I couldn't resist temptation. Once I was in there, I had to mess with you a little.'

'Mess how?'

Reve shoves him in the back. If he was in control of his own body he'd kick Reve to the other side of the fucking planet, but he's not. Whatever Reve did to him is making putting one foot in front of the other a challenge. 'When you're tired, it plays with your mind, with your body. I just made sure that effect was exaggerated.'

Reve slams Nick against a tree trunk, reaching up to pull some chains down from the branches. Bastard has everything all ready to go. After chaining Nick's arms over his head, he stands back, Nick's sword in his hand.

'You planning on killing me now?'

Reve shrugs. 'Not directly. If I kill you, your magic dies too. I need to take it from you which means, unfortunately, that you have to live. For now at least. But I wouldn't get too comfortable. I do plan to take your power and we both know what that'll mean for you.'

'So you're going to leave me here until next Christmas? Not sure that's your best idea.'

'It's actually tragic how little you know about what you are. You were so drunk and high, you didn't bother to read the small print of your contract. I, on the other hand, took the time to find out about our new leader. I wanted to figure out what was so special about this drunken lout who was put in charge.'

'You trying to hurt my feelings or something?'

Reve paces in front of him, keeping Nick's sword in his hand. 'You honestly haven't got a fucking clue what's going on, do you? I tracked down your predecessor. He was privy to some information you weren't. Apparently it was decided it would be best to lose this information between his signing and yours. Before I drove him to suicide, he was quite vocal about another way to strip you of your power.'

'You killed him?'

'Technically he killed himself, but yes, I may have had a hand in it. So,' he continues, not in the least bit bothered by what he just said. Reve lifts Nick's sword, examining the blade in his hand. 'According to what he said, if I stab you with this while you're weak, as you are right now after the run, it will drain you of your magic, and I can take it.'

Nick laughs to himself, desperately trying to get his body to cooperate, but holding himself upright is hard enough work, without

212

trying to fight back. 'So that's it. Fucking clichéd isn't it?'

'What is?'

'Bad guy wanting all the power. You couldn't have come up with something more original? I'm insulted.'

Reve slaps Nick, jerking his head to the side.

'And then you bitch slap me? C'mon, Reve! Make this exciting. You're boring me right now.'

'You honestly don't comprehend what's going on.'

Nick tests the chains, but he's locked good and tight. 'I'm not an idiot, Reve. I comprehend exactly what's going on. You don't think being the Sandman is good enough for you. Compared to everyone else, you what? Give people dreams? I'm guessing you believe I'm the most powerful of the legends, which I probably am for one fucking day a year. So you're going to kill me and drain my power. Then what? You want to be Santa and the Sandman? Bit greedy Reve.'

Reve jams the tip of the sword against Nick's neck, forcing his chin up. 'You have no idea what I can do. Who do you think messed with your head the day of the crash?'

Nick swallows as the metal digs into this neck. 'You? You can mess with memories?'

Reve nods. 'Yes, Nick. I rigged the sleigh so it would crash. I was following your tracker so I reached you seconds after the impact. The plan was that you would die in the crash, your power would be up for grabs, and I'd take it. But, not only were you not dead, you were beginning to come around. You saw me.'

'I did?'

'Oh yeah. I won't repeat what you said to me, but needless to say, you put two and two together. So I made sure you wouldn't remember anything. Meddled around in your memories, which knocked you out. I might have pushed a little too hard but I'm still getting to grips with what I can really do.

'I removed your tracker so you wouldn't be found for a while. Sent the rest of the team into panic mode when you went missing. I had planned on killing you, but one of your filthy reindeer attacked me. By the time I slit her throat and moved her into the woods, that bitch Scarlett had saved your ass. I was going to kill her and take you, but someone else was watching. I could feel Krampus nearby. There's no way I could have taken him down, so I had no choice but to leave you.'

Nick groans as Reve shoves his own sword into his side, driving the blade through his flesh, pinning him to the tree. 'This won't kill you...yet. Once your magic is drained, then you'll die, but it's a sacrifice I'm willing to make.'

Nick looks down, watching the blood ooze from his body, pooling on the ground. 'Where's Scarlett?'

Reve crouches down in front of Nick, running his fingers through the blood surrounding the sword. 'That's the funny part. I have no idea.'

'What?'

'I tried to take her, but Krampus got to her first. I wasn't lying about that. The brute appeared out of nowhere and saved her. Bad timing as usual. No matter.' He straightens and grips the sword, tearing it from Nick's body. 'I'd imagine he's eaten her by now, or whatever he does. I couldn't really give a damn. She was a means to an end. Your end.'

Reve examines the blood trickling down Nicks leg. His frown grows. He holds the sword out in front of him, examining the blade.

'You honestly don't comprehend what's going on,' Nick says, repeating the exact phrase Reve threw at him.

'What did you do?'

'Like I said, I'm not an idiot. I knew it had to be someone from the team who tried to kill me. Then when you woke me after the run, you released some of the memories you hid from me. Your face was still hidden from me, but you were familiar. It just confirmed one of my team wanted me out of the way.'

'What did you do?' Reve asks again.

'That's not my sword.'

Reve looks down at the sword in his hand. 'How did you know?'

'Eve did some research while I was briefing you on the plan to come here. She found out about my sword, and hid the real sword. That's a replica.'

Reve looks at him then screams and rushes him. Nick grips the chains and lifts his legs off the ground, kicking the sword aside before he's stuck with it again.

'Kane!'

Reve pauses when Nick calls out, then makes a run for it, disappearing into the trees. Nick waits, depending on the chains to support him more than he'd like to admit. The wound on his side hurts like a motherfucker, but at least his magic is still intact. In the distance, he can hear the battle with his team and the Púca still raging.

'Kane!' It's only been a few seconds since he called out last, but waiting has never been one of his qualities. Kane stalks out of the forest, dragging an unconscious Reve behind him. 'What the fuck took you so long?'

'I had to collect an old friend on the way.'

'Is he dead?'

Kane shakes his head, dumping Reve on the ground. 'I resisted... just.'

He pulls a set of keys from Reve's pocket, pausing for a second as Damon drops out of the sky in front of him. The Boogeymen folds his wings, then turns to face Nick. 'You okay?'

'He stabbed me in the side, so no. Not really.'

Kane unlocks the chains, helping to support Nick as he gets himself together. 'You believe him about Scarlett?'

Nick presses his hand to his side. The wound is still bleeding but wasn't intended to kill him. Reve hadn't hit anything vital. 'Yeah. He was spilling his guts about everything else. No reason to lie about that.'

Damon draws his blade from his belt, slicing Reve's jacket apart.

He gestures to Nick who lifts his coat out of the way so Damon can bandage the wound with Reve's coat. 'Can I kill him?'

'No. You can't. If anyone is killing him, it'll be me.'

Damon grins, showing his fangs. 'And that's why we're friends.'

Nick takes his real sword from Kane. He needs to help with the Púca situation, then figure out where Scarlett is. 'Damon, bring Reve back to the workshop and lock him up. I'm far from done with him. Kane, let's get back to it.'

Damon nods and crouches over Reve. The two of them disappear in a cloud of black mist, leaving Nick alone in the woods.

His wound is painful, but it doesn't begin to match his worry for Scarlett. Time to spill someone else's blood. After that, Krampus better put his affairs in order. Once he finds the bastard, he'll make sure he is the last thing Krampus ever sees.

Scarlett shivers under the heavy coat Talen gave her. She's not dressed for wandering through the deep snow. The coat is helping but a pair of hiking boots would be a bonus. 'How much further?'

Talen stops and sniffs the air, smiling as he looks down at her. 'Nick is close.'

'You can smell him?'

'His magic.' He crouches down in front of her. 'Climb on my back.'

'I'm fine, really.'

'We need to move faster. We risk the team every minute Nick doesn't know you're okay.'

He's right, so Scarlett wraps her arms around his neck and her legs around his waist. 'Hold tight. I can move at great speed.'

She hangs on and he takes off. Great speed is one hell of an understatement. The landscape rushes by as Talen clears mile after mile in no time at all. He comes to a stop in a forested area, and holds up his hand to stop her from speaking.

Through the trees she hears the sound of fighting. She recognises Púca screeching and screaming. He lowers her to the ground and slowly approaches the clearing. When Scarlett sees the scene in front of her, she has to cover her mouth with her hand to stop herself from shouting aloud.

There must be at least a hundred Púca in the clearing. Bodies are strewn on the ground, their purple blood staining the clean snow. From what she can see, the team is still upright and fighting.

Then she sees Nick. He's fighting like the others, but something isn't right with him.

'He's injured,' Talen says, answering the question before she can voice it. 'Reve and Damon are missing.'

'Do you think it was one of them?'

Talen nods. 'My money would be on Reve. Damon is twisted, but dedicated to Nick.'

Scarlett watches the men fight for another few seconds. 'Why are we still hiding here?'

'How would you suggest we insert ourselves into that battle? You will be killed within seconds. I did not save you to throw you to your death hours later.'

'But I thought you were bringing me here so I could help?'

'I brought you here to keep you safe. The danger has not passed. No one is controlling the Púca. They will fight until they die. Or until there is no one left to fight.' He gets to his feet and shrugs off his coat. 'You must remain hidden until I have the Púca under control.'

'What? You're going out there?'

'I must. There is a chance I can control them. I have more in common with them than I would like to admit. Please promise me you will remain in safety until I call for you?'

Scarlett looks over to Nick. He's flagging, his sword hitting the ground between strikes. 'I promise. He can't last much longer, Talen.'

'Trust me.'

He smiles then turns and steps out of the trees. It takes a few seconds for the team to notice him. Cobh kills a Púca which brings him face to face with Talen. Scarlett stands when Cobh attacks. Then she remembers her promise and ducks down again. Within a few seconds, the Púca are attacking Talen, while Cobh does the same.

When Nick notices Talen, he seems to find a hidden energy reserve. His posture straightens, the sword firmly in his hand as he makes his way towards Talen. Cobh is thrown aside by Talen, landing in a pile of snow near Scarlett. She is about to call out to him when a Púca notices her. It snarls, moving towards her. Focused on Talen, Cobh doesn't see it, or her.

With no choice, Scarlett pushes to her feet and races through the trees around the edge of the clearing. She needs to get away from it, but not from the team.

Behind her, she can hear Talen shouting something in a language she doesn't understand. He keeps speaking loudly, his voice carrying around the clearing.

Then there's silence.

She glances over her shoulder, but the Púca isn't chasing her anymore. The creature is standing a few feet from her, staring ahead blankly.

Scarlett looks through the trees. It's the same in the clearing. Every Púca still alive, is frozen to the spot.

Talen did it. He's controlling the Púca. Then she realises the team are heading in his direction, Nick at the front, sword poised ready to strike.

'Stop!'

Her scream reaches him just in time. He stops with his sword against Talen's neck. She hurries through the trees weaving between the frozen Púca, until she's in Nick's arms.

'You're okay!'

She nods against his neck, then pushes away from him. 'I'm fine. Talen saved my life. Don't hurt him, Nick. Please!'

Nick looks at Talen, his face not giving anything away. 'He saved you? How?'

'The Púca took me from the cottage, but Talen rescued me. He took me back to his home and looked after me.'

'Why?'

Scarlett knew Nick wouldn't be overly keen on thanking Talen, but she didn't think he'd react like this. 'Because, putting it simply, he's not a bad guy. Is that reason enough?'

Nick frowns at her for a long time, and no one interrupts. It's a good few minutes before he looks back at Talen and lifts his sword again. 'Talk. Now.'

Talen clears his throat. 'My magic is still linked to yours. I felt when you were injured in the crash. Scarlett had helped you by the time I got there, but I stayed, watching over you.'

Nick doesn't appreciate the gesture. His eyes whiten and his sword moves closer to Talen.

'Nick, please,' she says, trying to diffuse some of the tension. 'Let him speak.'

'No one's stopping him.'

'I saw the Púca arrive to take Scarlett. Reve went inside the cottage, but some Púca followed. Then they left, with no sign of Reve. But they had Scarlett. So I made sure they didn't get far with her. I brought her back to my house to keep her safe. I knew one of your team must be trying to kill you, but I didn't know who. I thought it would be safest to look after her until you returned.'

'You see!' Scarlett says, moving between Nick and Talen. 'I swear he did nothing to hurt me.'

'I never thought I'd agree that Krampus is on the level, but she's right.' Damon materialises next to Nick and crosses his arms. 'I didn't kill Reve, but we might have had a bit of a heart to heart. He saw Talen here take Scarlett from the Púca. Which he was controlling, by the way. He thought Talen would be the perfect scapegoat. No offence intended by the goat remark. Fuck that! Be offended. I don't actually care.'

Nick lowers his sword and takes a step closer to Talen. 'You've got control of Krampus?'

Talen blinks a few times. Clearly he wasn't expecting Nick to ask him that of all questions. 'Yes. I have for a few decades. My human form is slowly returning.'

Nick glances down at Talen's legs, then at the rest of the team. No one says anything and it's driving Scarlett crazy.

'Nick—'

He holds up his hand, silencing her. Her first reaction is to tell him where he can shove that hand, but she stops herself. This isn't her world after all. As much as she wants to interfere, she's not going to. Not unless Nick decides to kill Talen. Then there will be a whole load of interfering.

'Send the Púca away.'

'We're not going to kill them?' Hunter asks, clearly disappointed.

'No. Reve was controlling them. We're not just going to kill them for no reason.'

Talen nods and utters some bizarre words. The Púca disperse, leaving them alone with the dead bodies.

'Thank you.'

Talen's mouth drops open at Nick's words and Scarlett smiles. Talen may make it out of here in one piece after all.

'I have to sleep, but after we need to talk.'

'I would appreciate that.'

Nick nods. 'We'll take you off our wanted list until then, at least.' He lifts his hand again when someone complains, and they fall silent.

'Again, I would appreciate that.'

'Be here at midnight in three weeks. We'll talk then. Flint, get rid of the bodies. Cobh watch his back. Everyone else, back to the workshop.'

Scarlett stands in front of Talen and smiles up at him. 'Happy?'

He smiles back, showing fangs that put Damon's ones to shame. 'Very much. I just wanted to be left to my own devices. The fact he is willing to talk is more than I could have wished for. Thank you Scarlett.'

She reaches up and hugs him - much to his and Nick's surprise, if the curse from behind her is anything to go by. 'Thank you for saving my neck.'

'Of course. You better go before he changes his mind.'

Scarlett walks back over to Nick, laughing at the confused look on her face. 'What the fuck was that?'

'He's a nice guy, Nick. You'll find that out for yourself when you speak to him.'

Nick takes her hand and leads her back to the rest of the team. 'He brought you back in one piece. Whatever happens in a few weeks time, I owe him. That's a start.'

18

Nick is jolted awake when someone nudges him on the arm. He's so beyond exhausted. What he desperately needs is his bed. Or any bed. Hell, he'll sleep right here and now if he has to.

'Nick. Nick! Are you still with us?'

He shakes himself awake again. 'What? Yeah, sorry. I'm still here.' He smiles at Eve, but she doesn't return it. 'I'm fine.'

'He's injured and exhausted,' Scarlett says, hurrying over to help Eve.

'I don't need you two fussing over me. I'm fine.'

Scarlett takes his arm, helping him up from the workshop floor where Damon left him. 'Stop being a stubborn ass and let us help you.'

He gives in. He honestly doesn't have the energy to argue. While the rest of his team go to get cleaned up or eat, he lets Eve and Scarlett bring him to the infirmary. Scarlett helps him out of his coat and t-shirt while Eve grabs the first aid kit.

'God, Nick! This is nasty.'

He shakes his head, trying to put Scarlett at ease. 'It's not too bad. Trust me. It just needs a bandage. Ouch! Fuck Eve!'

Eve grins at him as she dabs at the wound, cleaning the blood from around it. 'Oh I'm sorry. I thought it wasn't too bad?'

'You're fired!'

'Whatever, Boss. Now shut up and let me see to this.'

Nick winces as she pokes him again, but does his best to ignore her, focusing on Scarlett. Things were so crazy after the fight, he hadn't really taken the time to look at her properly. 'Are you okay?'

She slides onto the edge of the bed next to him. 'Seriously. I'm fine. Talen got to me just in time.'

He nods. That's the part he's still struggling to get his head around. 'Do you believe him?' he asks. He's going to make up his own mind about Talen, but she's the only person who's been close to the legend in centuries. Her input is invaluable.

'Talen?'

Nick nods.

'I do. I know I'm so new to all of this but, from what I saw of him, he's genuine. He's getting his humanity back, Nick. His legs are human again. You must have seen that for yourself.'

He did. In spite of what Reve thinks, Nick is far from being an idiot. He's read up on everyone on his team. And those who used to be on the team. Like Talen. The last report he read on the guy went into great detail about his appearance. Krampus had taken over the man, turning him, twisting him into a monster.

The creature he saw today may have had horns and grey skin, but the man was now visible and that's all that matters to Nick.

'What does he want? He must have told you. Fuck Eve! Will you give it a rest and stop poking me?'

She backs away, hands in the air. 'Relax Boss. I'm done. You know where I am when you're... you know. Whatever.'

He smiles as she leaves the room, moving over in the bed so Scarlett can sit beside him. 'Sorry. So, did he tell you?'

'He just wants to be left alone, Nick. That's all he wants. He's been looking over his shoulder for decades and he's tired.'

Nick lies back against the wall as he processes that. He can hardly blame the guy for wanting a quiet life. Right now that sounds like heaven.

'Nick, what are you going to do with Reve?'

Now that's a great question. He knows what he wants to do but that doesn't mean it's what he will do. 'I don't know. I'll figure it out when I wake up properly.' He shuffles down the bed. It's a foolish thing to do, given that, if he actually does fall asleep, he's not going to wake up again for a few weeks.

He tucks her in beside him and rubs his hand through her hair.

'How did you know? About Reve I mean,' Scarlett asks.

'I didn't. The more I thought about it, the more I kept coming back to the fact it had to be someone from the team. You need to learn how to use the magic. You can't just take it and run. It doesn't work like that. But when I was going to sleep, my fucking headache was irritating me. I'd had it since I woke up with you.

'I thought it was down to the crash, but it felt wrong. I couldn't explain how, until Reve woke me up. It felt familiar. Like he'd been in my head before. He also wasn't as careful the second time. Whatever he was trying to do to my head released some of the memories. I didn't see him, but I knew it was him. That probably doesn't make a lot of sense.'

'No, it makes sense. Talen said he could sense or feel your magic. Is it the same with all of you?'

'Sometimes. We use our magic around each other when we're fighting. It's bound to feel familiar after a while.'

'And was getting yourself stabbed with your own sword part of the plan?'

'It wasn't my sword. That's the whole point. If it was, I'd be drained of magic and dead.'

'I don't like the sound of either of those.' He yawns, so she digs him in the arm. 'You're exhausted.'

'Yeah. Time to get you home.'

She takes a long breath and falls silent. It's unbelievably shite and he feels the same. He doesn't want to let her go. Not again. Saying goodbye to her the first time was horrible. No point putting it off though. If he doesn't get his ass in gear, he's going to fall asleep and she'll be stuck here.

She climbs off the bed and holds out her hand to help him up. He dismisses it, deciding to be all macho and get up himself. Which fails, when his legs buckle and he only stops from landing on his ass, by grabbing onto the bed.

'You can barely stand.'

'I need to get you home.'

Scarlett leaves him hanging on to the bed as she disappears outside. He groans loudly when she reappears with Eve and Damon.

'What the fuck are you doing?' Damon asks, glaring at him.

'I'm trying to get up so I can bring Scarlett home.'

'I'll bring her home,' Damon says, dragging Nick to his feet. 'You can barely stand. Actually, you can't stand. Seriously, Nick. You need to go to bed before you collapse.'

Scarlett gets in on the disapproving looks Damon and Eve are already giving him. 'Let Damon take me home. It's okay. Really.'

He wants to be the one to take her back, but his body isn't on board with that. The way he feels right now, he'd probably crash the fucking sleigh again and kill both of them. 'Fine. You win.'

Damon hits him with a cold glare. 'It wasn't a request. I'm taking her home. You're going to bed. Now, are you going to let me help you back to your room, or should I knock you out and carry you back?'

Scarlett tries to commit the workshop to her memory, as she follows Nick and Damon back to his suite. Damon may have joked about knocking Nick out and carrying him, but it's not too far from the truth. Nick is barely able to put one foot in front of the other.

She can't believe she has to say goodbye to him all over again. It was painful enough the first time.

Damon half carries, half drags Nick to his room, lowering him into one of the chairs by the fire. 'I'll leave you alone. I'll be outside when you're ready, Scarlett.'

Nick pushes himself to his feet, using the back of the chair to help him. 'Talk about déjà vu,' Nick says, pulling her into his arms. 'I hate saying goodbye to you over and over again.'

'Then don't.' She wasn't expecting to just come straight out and say the words to him, but she couldn't help it. But then his eyes lower to the ground and he licks his lips. She's pushed too far, too fast. 'I'm sorry.'

'No. Don't ever be sorry for being honest with me. I just... fuck!'

'You're going to need to go into a little more detail.'

He laughs and nods. 'I would love to spend more time with you. To see where this will go, but I can't see how to do that. I live in Lapland. I have responsibilities there. I have a job to do that takes a hell of a lot of my time. I have a contract to fulfil, and I can't walk away from that. You live in Dublin and have your own life. We've known each other for a few days, Scarlett. I can't ask you to leave everything to be with me. Not after days.'

'I'm not saying I leave my life and move in here. What about dating each other? Meeting up and seeing if we have something, before either of us make a life changing decision.'

Even before he opens his mouth, she knows he's going to shoot down that idea. 'I can't. I'm sorry.'

'Why not? You keep telling me you like me, that you're attracted to me. So why aren't you willing to give this a chance? If I said I wanted to give things a go with you, what would you say?'

'I'd say you're fucking nuts after what happened over the last few days! You've been attacked by Púca, kidnapped by Krampus, and thrown into a world that's dangerous on a good day. It's not just the fact I'm Santa that's causing the problems. It's my other job. You saw a small part of what we all do. We could be fighting like that every few days. It's a constant thing at the moment.

'I'm not bringing you into that life, Scarlett. I won't do it. I'd be freaking out about you being hurt if you stayed with me. I know it's cliched to say we're from different worlds, but we are. My world isn't safe for you. I can't lose anyone...' He stops himself and looks away. 'It's the way it has to be, Scarlett. I'm sorry.'

He's right. She hates to admit it, but everything he said makes sense. She wants to be with him. She knows that, but he kills monsters for a living. She works in recruitment. The two don't generally go together. 'Shit!'

He laughs at her reply. 'Too fucking right it's shit! Damon will make sure you get home safely. And I trust him. No question about that. We won't have a replay of last time.'

Nick tilts her chin up and kisses her. The kiss is slow, a lot more passionate than any other time he's kissed her. How can she possibly feel this way about someone she's known for a few days? It doesn't make any sense. But Nick is Santa, so sense doesn't really enter into the equation.

He leans heavily against the wall, stifling a yawn. 'Sorry, I'm not yawning because of you, I swear.'

She rubs his arm and smiles at him, trying to commit every single detail of his face to memory. She doesn't want to forget him. His pale blue eyes are unfocused. He needs to sleep. 'Thanks for making this one of the most memorable Christmases I've ever had.'

He grins, his gorgeous face lighting up. 'Me too, Scarlett. Me too.'

She hopes next year will be exactly the same as this year, but deep down she fears this will be the last time she sees Nick. 'Goodbye Nick.'

'Take care of yourself, Scarlett.'

She nods, unable to speak as she struggles to hold back the tears.

'Damon!' The door opens and Damon steps inside. 'Can you bring Scarlett home now?'

Damon gives Nick a strange look and sighs before nodding at her. 'Of course.'

Damon holds out his hand and she takes it. Nick smiles at her as a mist envelopes her. The next time she blinks, she's standing in her living room.

'That was quick,' she says, looking around at Damon.

'I'll have to tell Nick you said that. He's actually faster than me when his sleigh is at full speed. Glad to finally beat him at something,' he adds, showing the tips of his fangs when he smiles at her.

Damon opens the door and peers outside for a minute, before closing the door and locking it again. 'I'll check everything is secure.'

She stays standing in the middle of the room for a long time. Now she's home, she hasn't got a clue what to do. Again. Coming back here without Nick the first time was bad enough, without having to do it all over again.

Damon comes back downstairs and crosses his arms. 'You're secure. I can't feel any nasties outside either. With Reve locked up, you'll be safe.'

'Thanks, Damon. I suppose I had better finish packing.' She heads upstairs, but he stops her at the bottom step.

'He's doing this to keep you safe. Nick... he's lost a lot Scarlett. More than I can imagine. What he's doing seems drastic, but you have to believe he's doing it for the right reasons. He's doing it because he cares about you. We live a dangerous life. He wants you far from that.'

'I understand, and I appreciate you telling me all that.

Unfortunately, it doesn't make his decision any easier to accept.' She turns away and goes upstairs to finish packing.

19

Nick adjusts his grip on Atlas' reins as he glares at a rock in front of him. He woke up two days ago, in the worst fucking mood he's ever been in. And it hasn't improved since then. If anything, it's getting worse by the day. It's a self-inflicted bad mood, which isn't helping the situation.

He pulls out his sword when a tall shape emerges from the trees. Talen raises his hands. 'I am unarmed.'

'I'm not.'

Talen nods and comes to a stop a few feet from them, keeping an eye on Atlas as much as Nick. The reindeer isn't taking too kindly to Krampus, snorting loudly at the demon.

'I'm surprised you came. I was convinced I'd be out in the cold, alone.'

Nick swings his leg over the saddle and drops onto the ground. 'I came because I promised someone I'd listen to what you have to say.'

'And I appreciate that. How is Scarlett?'

And there goes Nick's mood, dropping to a new low. 'She's safe. Away from all of this, where she belongs. So, what do you think we can achieve by talking?'

'I want what we all want, Nick. I want to live my life without looking over my shoulder. I had no idea how strong Krampus' contract was. If I'd known I would not have signed. But it's too late to change that. As I said to Scarlett, I've made mistakes. Mistakes I can't undo. All I can do now is make sure Krampus is under control.'

Not for the first time, Nick is grateful he was offered the contract he was. Being stuck with something like Krampus, the Horseman, or the Boogeyman sounds fucking horrible.

At least he's driven to make people happy, if he can. Making kids wishes come true at Christmas is easy, compared to some of what the others have to deal with. The whole going on fire thing that Flint does is freaky as hell. Thirty-five years later, he still hasn't got used to seeing him like that.

'And you're sure you have a hold of it?'

Talen nods. 'My human form is returning. I'd prefer the transformation was progressing a little faster than it is. But I'm happy it's happening at all.'

Nick slides his sword back into the sheath and crosses his arms. Maybe some of that sentimentality Scarlett released is getting to him, but he believes Talen. Not that it helps him figure out what to do next.

'What do you want from me?'

'I would like you to forget I exist.'

Nick frowns and turns to face Talen. 'What?'

'I've spent most of my life being hunted - justifiably so. But I'm tired, Nick. All I want is to become human again. Nothing more. I long for the day I can look at my reflection and see my old self.'

This guy is either really good at lying, or he's one of the saddest guys Nick has ever met. He actually feels sorry for Talen. 'What about the team?'

'I don't understand?'

'Do you want back on the team? Not that I'm offering that right now. I meant, in the future.'

Talen gives him a long look, before he nods. 'Of course I'd like that, but it's not the priority for either of us, is it?'

'No,' Nick admits. 'I wouldn't necessarily rule it out though.'

'I'd appreciate that, but I know I have a long way to go before that is even an option.'

'Where are you living?'

Talen raises his eyebrows, no doubt suspicious about the reason he's asking that question.

'I'm not planning on coming after you. I'm just curious.'

'I have an old cabin.'

Judging by the holes in his clothes and the general unkempt appearance, Nick doubts he's living in lavish conditions. He can't believe what he's about to do, what he thinks he's going to do. And no doubt he'll get it in the neck from everyone else, but he's never cared about stuff like that. He's the boss. He'll use that card if he has to.

'I'm going to make you an offer, and it's just that - an offer. You can refuse or accept. We've just finished a new wing in the workshop, but it's empty. I had it built in case we needed more room. If you want, you can move in to one of the rooms. You'll be left alone and will be free to come and go as you want.'

'Why would you make such an offer?'

'If the end goal is to earn your place on the team, you'll have to do just that - earn it. You can't do that out in the arse end of nowhere by yourself. Might help you to be around people. Help get your humanity back a little faster.'

'I doubt any of the team, or your workers, will appreciate that.'

'That's their tough luck. Once I tell them you're under my

protection they'll have to accept it.'

'And you would offer me your protection?'

'Yes.'

'Why?'

'One of my team tried to kill me. A new Sandman will be brought in, but our numbers are low compared to the fuckers we're fighting. We need all the help we can get. And from what Scarlett said, you're a fan of research. That could come in useful.'

'You really believe Santa and Krampus could fight together again?'

'From what I read, they made a damn formidable team. Who knows? It could happen again.'

Talen smiles, his large fangs gleaming in the moonlight. The demon may have a hold on Krampus, but he'd give Damon a run for his money. Both are as scary as each other.

'I would like that very much.'

'I'll organise everything.' He passes Talen a wristband. 'This will help Eve find you. She's my assistant. Runs the whole workshop for me. You can trust her. She'll also gut you if you piss her off, so try to behave.'

'Thank you for the warning. And thank you for this chance, Nick. I would have been content to be ignored. I never thought anything like this would happen.'

'Don't get too excited yet. It's not going to be easy. I can protect your life, but I can't make people like you.'

'I understand.'

Nick takes hold of the reins and pulls himself back into the saddle. 'One chance Talen. That's all you get with me. See you soon.'

He takes off and heads home to break the news to everyone. They're going to be pissed off with him about it, but he couldn't care less. He's all about second chances. It would be seriously hypocritical if he didn't offer Talen the same second chance he was given.

20

Nick shouts, hurling the plate complete with the half made sandwich across the room into the far wall.

'What did the sandwich do to you?'

He glares over at Eve but, as usual, she's completely unfazed. He leans on the counter, pressing his hands onto the surface, trying to get his temper under control. He's been on edge ever since he woke up, lashing out at anyone who dares to look at him the wrong way. Or even look at him at all. Yeah, his mood has been so far beyond dire.

'What do you want?' She bends down to pick up the remains of his lunch. 'Leave it!'

But again, she ignores him, picking up his mess, dumping it in the bin beside the counter. After washing her hands she takes out a fresh plate and a couple of slices of bread. 'What do you fancy?'

'I can make my own fucking lunch! I don't need you to do it for me.'

She points to the bin and grins. 'All evidence to the contrary. Now I know bread can be troublesome, but it didn't deserve that now, did it?'

He huffs out a breath and smiles. 'Sorry. Ignore me,' he says, rubbing his forehead. He's got another headache. Probably from all the glowering.

'I've just left Talen. I have to say, he's a genius when it comes to data. He's only been here a few weeks, but he's already compiled data on more creatures than I would have been able to in a few years. He's a definite asset.'

'Good. He giving you any trouble?'

'None whatsoever. He's the perfect gentleman. At least, a gentleman with horns and a tail. I owe you an apology.'

'For what?'

'Doubting your sanity when you allowed him to move in. It was the right thing to do.'

He's glad to hear that. He'd been doubting his own sanity on that decision for a while, but from the little time he's spent with Talen, he knows there's goodness somewhere under all that demon. It'll just take time to get it out.

'So,' she says, as she stubbornly makes him the sandwich he was too pissed off to make himself. 'Why are you doing this to yourself?'

'Making lunch?'

She rolls her eyes at him. 'You know what I mean, Nick. With all due respect, Boss. Why are you being an ass?'

'I just apologised for that.'

'I meant why are you being an ass to yourself? There are forty-three people living here, Nick. Including you. Now why is it that forty-two of those people can see how much you miss Scarlett? Even Talen can see it and he barely mixes with you. There's only one stubborn fucker who can't see it. That's you by the way. I'm going to be blunt here.'

'Go for it. Don't hold back just because I'm your boss,' he adds, sarcastically.

'Sometimes you need a kick in the ass. Consider this that very kick. Why did you send her away?'

'Oh can you just leave it, Eve!'

'Just thinking out loud.'

'Yeah, well do me a favour and stop. And what exactly was I supposed to do, huh? I live here. I'm Santa. She's got a job and a life in Ireland. The two don't mix. You know that.'

'And she was in agreement? She was happy to let you send her home?'

'Oh come on Eve. We were together for a week. One fucking week! I wasn't going to ask her to give up her life to move out here with me after one week.'

'Why not?'

He tries to walk away from her, his appetite suddenly gone.

'Don't walk away from me.'

'You don't tell me what to do, Eve. It's the other way around. I'm in charge here. Don't forget that!'

'Oh wind your neck in!'

Nick's mouth opens and closes, partly in shock at what she said, and partly because he hasn't got a fucking clue how to react to that. He's not usually one for pulling rank. He just did it now to shut her up. Looks like she saw right through it, and him.

Eve leans back against the counter and looks him dead in the eye. 'You like her, Nick.'

'Eve—'

'I was making a statement. It didn't need a response.'

'You intentionally trying to put me in a worse mood?'

'I'm your friend and I care about you actually. I'm trying to make you see sense, before it's too late.'

Now he feels like an asshole, but he keeps the glare in place.

'Nick, you've done this job tirelessly for thirty-five years. Apart from the odd one night stand, you've been alone for the majority of that. That's a long time.'

'I can't do it, Eve. Not again,' he adds before he can stop himself. That's what it really boils down to. He lost his family thirty-seven years ago, but the pain is still as fresh today as it was then. He can't do that again.

After Scarlett was taken, it brought it all back to him how fragile life is. Losing his family nearly destroyed him. He doesn't think he'd be able to survive that again.

And there's no fucking way he's going to put her in that kind of danger again. Being connected to him will do just that.

Eve surprises him by taking his hand. And he surprises himself by not pulling away. 'What happened to your family was tragic. I can't imagine what it was like for you. But that doesn't mean it will happen again. You can't hide from love because you're scared.'

'You think I'm hiding?'

'Of course you are. And I'm not blaming you. But nothing in your contract states that you can't fall in love and be happy. You've been hiding behind this job, killing monsters in the dark, for too long. Being Santa doesn't mean you block off all other aspects of your life. That's not what's supposed to happen. You're allowed to have a life, Nick.' She pauses and smiles at him. 'And I'm sure your wife and daughter would want you to live your life to its fullest.'

'It's not that simple, Eve. One week to decide on a lifetime of watching me leave her to fight. A lifetime of having a target on her back. I'm having a hard enough time knowing you're in danger, because you work for me. The same goes for everyone in the workshop. Don't ask me to add anyone else to that list.'

'That's how you feel? I never knew.'

'I'm in charge. It's my job to make sure you're protected.'

'And you do that Nick. You've given each and every one of us an amazing life.' She holds out the plate with a freshly made sandwich. 'Now it's your turn. I hate to think of you walking away from something that could change your life.'

'I'm fine, so drop the fucking subject! Please. Is Jok here yet?'

Eve sighs loudly, then shakes her head. 'No, Boss, but he's on the way.'

'Did he get Reve's replacement?'

'He did. The Sandman's pendant identified a suitable successor. He's accepted the contract.'

That's something at least. They need the extra body back on the team. Now that leaves him with another problem. Once the new Sandman takes over, what is he going to do with Reve? He's been locked in a cell under the workshop since Damon dragged him back here a few weeks ago.

'Are you going to kill him?'

Nick looks up at Eve, but her face is blank. 'I have to. He knows too much and it's not like he's exactly trustworthy. I'll wait until the new contract is signed and his powers transferred.'

'Do you really think he's going to sign his powers over to someone else?'

'Yes. He only needs one unbroken hand to sign the contract. That leaves a lot of bones I can break to convince him.' He takes the plate from her. 'Make sure everything is ready for the new Sandman. He'll be staying here until he's completed his training. We need him ready to go ASAP. We've got a job to do.' He holds up the plate as he walks away. 'Thanks for the food.'

'Nick!'

He stops and looks over his shoulder at Eve.

'Just think about what I said.'

'Will do.' Nick takes his lunch back to his suite and drops the plate on the table. He wasn't really hungry to begin with, he just needed something to do. He gets where Eve is coming from, but it's much more of an issue than she believes it is. He lost the two people who were his entire world. There's no way he's going to drag someone else into this craziness, and risk losing them too. That would make him one shit Santa, as well as a shit human.

He sits on the edge of his bed and stares at his sandwich. As much as he misses Scarlett, she's exactly where she needs to be - away from him. Away from all this.

His selfishness had cost his wife and daughter their lives. He's not going to make that mistake again. Not with Scarlett.

He picks up the sandwich, glares at it, then dumps it back on the plate. He can't afford to think about them, or Scarlett, right now. The new Sandman needs his full attention. And he's got to deal with Reve in the next few days. His time is up. He'll do the deed himself, without involving anyone else. It's his burden as the boss.

Nick takes a few steps back, leaning against the bars of the cell as he catches his breath. He passes the contract through the bars to Eve. 'Get the new recruit to sign this.'

'Will do, Boss.' She glances at Reve, huddled in the corner of the cell, hugging his broken hand to his chest. 'Should I stay or...'

'Leave me alone with him.'

'Nick...'

'I'll deal with him. Get that sorted.'

Eve nods and leaves, shutting the door behind her.

'So, you're actually going to do what needs to be done? Glad to see you're finally growing a backbone. I'd be impressed, if it didn't mean my death.'

'What the fuck is your problem? You were the Sandman. That used to mean something to you. Why would you throw it all away for a little extra power? I don't get it.'

Reve pushes onto the cot, wiping blood from his face. It hadn't take as much persuasion as he thought it would, to get Reve to sign. He put up a fight but it was half-hearted. 'We're losing Nick. I don't need to tell you that. The fight isn't going in our favour. So I thought I'd tip the odds a little.'

'By taking me out?'

'No. By increasing my power. By taking command of the team. By finally using our powers as they were intended. To kill anyone who defies us.'

'That's what all this is about? You want to kill all the other legends?' He wasn't expecting Reve to come out with that. He thought the bastard was power greedy, not downright bloodthirsty.

'Of course! Isn't that what we all want?'

'No, it's not! What the fuck gave you that impression? You've been on the team longer than I have. You know that's not what we do.'

Reve laughs loudly. 'Oh fuck off, Nick! Is that what you really believe? Are you telling me you plan to pick pathetic fights with them every few days? To keep swatting them back, only to have them push harder next time? It's like fucking Groundhog Day! Has been for decades. You had the chance to change things for the first time in decades. You're the youngest Santa we've had. I thought you'd come in with a new way of doing things. But you were such a disappointment.'

'You wanted me to come in and what? Order the team to kill anyone who stood up to us? We don't kill unless we have to.'

'But that's the problem! Our jobs are to kill, Nick. Everything else comes second to that. Instead of killing each and every monster you've come across, you re-home strays and bring them back here. I mean, what the fuck, Nick? Putting Santa in charge of the team was a huge mistake. Always has been. But, it's not your fault. We all live with the traits of our contracts. You can't resist the need to bend over backwards and let everyone fuck you. Damn people pleaser!

'I mean how the hell is someone like you, meant to lead a team like us? We're fucking formidable, Nick! We've got the Boogeyman and Horseman on our side. Do you have any idea what Damon and Flint could do by themselves if you let them loose?'

Nick hadn't been fully up for killing Reve. Not until he started spouting all this crazy shit. The guy has something loose somewhere. 'The second we lose ourselves to our contracts we're no better than the ones we're fighting. It's the end of us and of the balance we maintain. That's the whole point of the team.'

'No, Nick. The whole point of the team is to keep control. We haven't had control of our enemies for decades. If I had managed to combine your magic with mine...' He smiles, and Nick realises Reve is more unhinged than he initially thought. 'Think what I could have achieved! I could have led this team to the victory we've been fighting millennia for. Ended all this creeping around in the shadows. Unless you push Santa aside, and take control again, this team is as good as finished.'

He stands up and faces Nick. 'I don't want to be around to watch you weaken this team. Do me a favour and just get it over with, Nick. Kill me!'

Nick plans to kill Reve either way, but hearing him ask for his death, helps take some of the weight from his decision. He pulls out his sword and holds it up in front of him. 'You're wrong about me, Reve. Yeah, I want to help people. I'm drawn to make people happy, but that's got nothing to do with my contract. I've always been like that. The difference is, since signing the contract I've learned that there's some evil shit in the world. Vile creatures who think of nothing, or no one, but themselves. And it's my job to kill them to keep the rest of the world safe. That's the part I put first. Always has been.'

He quickly swings his sword, separating Reve's head from his body, killing him instantly. Reve slumps to the ground, but Nick has already left the cell. He walks past Eve, not surprised to find her waiting outside. 'It's done. Get Flint down here to burn the body.'

21

Ten months later...

'Scarlett? Hello? Hey!'

She blinks and looks away from her screen. 'Sorry?'

Her co-worker, Dani, smiles as she sits on the chair beside her. 'You were miles away. Again! Why am I getting the impression that report isn't holding your attention?'

Scarlett smiles apologetically. 'I'm sorry. My head is just somewhere else.' In Lapland with Santa.

Just like it has been every single day since she last saw Nick.

Dani stands and hands Scarlett her bag. 'Come on. We're getting an early lunch. No arguments, so just walk.'

She locks her computer and follows Dani out of the building and along the packed street, to their favourite cafe, around the corner from the office. With the weather so good, it seems everyone has come outdoors to get some autumn sunshine. Dani grabs a table and chairs outside the cafe and hands her a menu.

'So, what's on your mind?'

'Nothing. I was just day dreaming.' It's been the same daydream for the last few months, and nothing she tries to distract herself with works.

'About that guy again, huh? Nick?'

She nods. Dani had been told the bare bones of the story. As in the fact she had a holiday fling with a gorgeous guy. That's it. Nothing else. 'I know I must be boring you at this stage. I'm sorry.'

Dani places her menu back on the table and leans forward. 'Stop apologising. You miss him. It's perfectly normal.'

'Yeah, but it's been nearly a year. I'm starting to bore myself.'

'From the snippets I was able to drag out of you, he showed you one hell of a time. It's not going to be easy to find someone who can top that.'

Scarlett nods. She knows that for a fact. She's had countless dates and, as nice as the guys were, none of them could compare to Nick.

'How about I grab our usual? I'll be back in a minute.'

Scarlett watches the crowds pushing past each other and lets her mind wander. Or does, until she spots something at the far side of the street. She pulls off her sun glasses and leans forward. Damon is standing in the alley between two buildings, at the opposite side of the street.

Over the months, she thought she'd caught glimpses of different members of the team, but this is the first time one of them had actually stayed long enough for her to be sure. He crosses the street, the crowd seeming to part for him. The Boogeyman may be wearing unassuming black jeans and a black tank top, no wings or horns in sight, but the menace surrounding him is hard to ignore. He sits on the chair Dani had occupied and stretches out his legs.

'Is he okay?'

Damon nods. 'Yeah. He's okay. Just wanted to make sure you are too.'

'I know you've been keeping an eye on me.'

'You know he likes to be in control of every situation. It's his way of ensuring you're safe.'

'So why are you showing yourself now? Not that I'm complaining. It's good to see you.'

He shrugs and smiles briefly, the tip of a fang visible for a few seconds. 'Are you going to write a letter to Santa this year?'

Scarlett stares over at him, not sure what he's hinting at. 'Excuse me?'

His black eyes lock on hers. 'I want to know if you're planning to ask for something... or someone, in particular this year.'

'You want me to write a letter to Nick?'

'You still like him.' It's a statement rather than a question, so she doesn't answer. Damon leans across the table, his black eyes making her squirm. It's like looking into a black hole. 'Tell him. Write him a letter and burn it, just like you did when you were a kid. Fuck knows he's not listening to any of us. I think the stubborn fucker might need to hear it from you. It's getting tiring watching the two of you ignore what's in front of your fucking faces.'

'You're not watching me? As in, really watching me... are you?'

'Now why would I do that? Your life is your business. If you want to waste your time with Chris, Adam, Philip, Ellis and whoever else you've had endless boring dates with, that's nothing to do with me.'

She stares in horror at Damon. Those were some of her dates. 'Damon! Please tell me you're not listening in on my dates?'

He leans closer, his black eyes seriously freaking her out. He smiles again, showing a very long, very sharp fang. She glances around, convinced someone is going to see him. He's not exactly being subtle. 'Don't worry. People see what I want them to see.'

'Are you spying on my dates?'

He shrugs, not in the slightest bit bothered by her question. 'I go where I want, but I will say one thing. I didn't see anything you wouldn't have wanted me to see.'

'What the hell does that mean?'

'It means Nick is my friend. You're important to him so, that means you're important to the rest of the team. I'm not going to do anything inappropriate.'

She nods, believing him. She doubts the Boogeyman has any reason to lie. 'What do you want me to do, Damon?'

'I already told you. The rest is up to you. You and Nick are as bad as each other! One of you is going to have to stop this fucking charade and speak out, before you drive the rest of us insane.'

He stands and smiles down at her. 'Good luck on your date tonight.'

She opens her mouth to reply, but he's gone. Scarlett looks around, trying to spot him in the crowd.

'Who are you looking for?' Dani asks, as she takes her seat again.

'What? Oh, sorry. No one.'

Dani passes her a coffee and takes a sip before she speaks. 'So, are you looking forward to your date tonight?'

She bites back a smile as Damon's words come back to her. 'You know what? I think I might cancel. I'm just not feeling it.'

'Is that so?'

'What does that mean?'

'It means you're still hung up on this Nick guy, and no one else is going to even come remotely close to him. So what are you going to do about it?'

'What can I do about it. It's over.'

'Yeah. That's exactly what it sounds like. Or, how about this for a crazy idea? How about you try to find him and get in contact? Who knows, Nick could be going through the same date after date scenario you are. What's to say he's not still pining after you, like you are after him?'

'Hey, I'd hardly say I'm pining.'

'I'm sorry, but you are absolutely pining! Think about it, Scarlett. But you know I'm right. You need to get in touch with him.'

Scarlett sips her coffee and glances across the road again. Damon is back at the mouth of the alley. He smiles, then vanishes again.

Seems like the Boogeyman and her friend are on the same page. Maybe she needs to send Santa one last letter.

22

'Do you have everything you need?' Dani asks, helping to load the last of the bags into the back of Scarlett's car.

She quickly double checks the number of bags, then nods. 'I think so. There's no mention of freak snow storms this year, so I don't need to load up with as many provisions.'

'Have you packed enough food for two, just in case Nick does arrive? You wouldn't want to have to get dressed to go and buy food. That would interfere with the plans to stay in bed with him all week,' Dani says, making ridiculous kissy faces at her.

'Oh, knock it off!' Scarlett desperately wishes that part will come true. If Nick shows up at all she'll be over the moon. Spending a week in bed with him would be the cherry on the cake. 'I'm trying not to get carried away, Dani. I don't even know if he'll come. I could go up there and end up with my nose buried in a book the whole time.'

'Exactly! You have no idea either way, so stop assuming he won't show up. Who knows, he could be waiting for you when you get there.'

She closes the boot of her car and shrugs, suddenly not so sure about her plan. 'A year is a long time. He could have met someone else.' Although she hopes Damon would have mentioned if he had. His job is to scare people, not play cruel tricks on them. The Boogeyman hadn't done anything to make her think otherwise, so there's no reason to think he'd start now. And both Nick and Damon had made it clear they're friends.

'Would you just stop over thinking everything!'

'I can't help it. It's what I do.' She checks her phone and wallet are in her bag, then hugs Dani. 'Okay, so wish me luck.'

'You don't need luck. He'll come, then he'll make you come,' she adds, laughing at her own joke.

'Oh you are so funny,' Scarlett says as she climbs into her car. 'I'll let you know what happens.'

'You better,' Dani says, closing the door.

Scarlett pulls out of the car park and heads in the direction of the cabin. She told Dani she'd contacted Nick last week, but in truth, she hadn't. In fact, she hadn't even written the all important letter yet. The dozens of drafts are still in her bag.

She doesn't know why, but she really wants to send it tonight from the cottage. Christmas is still a week away. There's plenty of time for him to get the letter. At least, she hopes there is. Damon hadn't been too forthcoming on the details.

She's going to remain positive though. Or at least as positive as she can be, given she's going to contact a man by burning a letter!

If it was possible to explode with excitement, Scarlett would be splattered all over the walls of her cottage. She's spent dozens of Christmas' here, but this time it's different.

This time she had carefully unpacked all of the decorations Nick created last year, hanging them all over the cottage. While she worked, Christmas music played in the background, and the smell of roasted chestnuts filled the air.

She was going all out, throwing everything but the kitchen sink at the preparations. After what happened last year, it would be a little hypocritical to think there was no point decorating. Three days with Santa had made her see the holiday differently.

And he's also part of the reason she's gone to town this year.

Nick had burst into her life this time last year, and turned it on its head. Or had tomorrow night, last year, to be exact.

There hadn't been any contact between them for the year, but she wasn't expecting there to be.

Okay, so maybe that's not really true. She had hoped he'd reach out to her, but he hadn't.

She had to keep reminding herself he's Santa. It's not like he's a regular guy with a regular job. He was probably up to his neck in demons, or Púca, or whatever else is thrown at the team. And it's not like they had made any plans. Quite the opposite in fact.

They'd said goodbye. As in forever goodbye.

Scarlett pours herself a glass of wine and sits on the floor by the fire. She looks down at the letter in her hands. It's addressed to Santa with Nick's name underneath. She hadn't written a letter to Santa since she was a child. But there was no other way of getting in touch with him. This was the only way of telling him what she wants for

Christmas.

She wants Nick.

Nothing else.

One year without him, and she's never been more sure of anything in her life. She wants to be with him. As completely ridiculous as it sounds, the last year without him had felt empty. Boring. Lonely. She'd dated, or at least tried to. It wasn't their fault, but after being with Nick, how could anyone else even begin to measure up?

And that was before she even considered anything sexual.

But a year is a long time. Nick could have found someone else in that time. Right now he could be sitting by someone else's fire. He could be showing someone else what his hands, his mouth, and other parts of his body could do.

She shakes those thoughts from her mind. Damon wouldn't have come to see her if that were the case. It hadn't stopped months of those thoughts, mixed with more unsettling ones, like him being injured fighting, or worse.

The letter in her hand must be the hundredth draft at least. She lost count of the number of previous versions she'd penned over the last few weeks. She didn't want to say too much, in case one of his workers read the letter, before passing it to him. Maybe he didn't even read the letters himself any longer?

She presses the back of the envelope, making sure the seal is secure, before kissing it and throwing it into the fire. 'I really hope you get this, Nick.' She watches as it burns, the smoke disappearing up the chimney.

As the last banshee falls to the ground, Nick straightens and looks around the room as he catches his breath. He'd taken down twelve banshees. Not too bad.

'We good?' he asks, waiting for the responses from the rest of the team. One by one, they call in. Everyone on their side is alive and still standing. The other side didn't fare so well. But that was the plan.

He spits out a mouthful of blood then wipes his face. 'Would you look at the state of you,' Hunter says as he enters the room. 'I don't even think I'd want to shag you right now. You bathe in their blood or something?'

Nick looks down at his t-shirt and grimaces. Hunter may have a point. 'It wasn't intentional. How the fuck did you manage to stay clean?'

'I don't go into a fight swinging a sword all over the place. I have a bit more finesse.'

'I just wanted the bad guys to die.'

'And that is why I have a clean outfit and you're covered in blood. This is the side of Santa that would give kids nightmares.'

Damon grins widely when he sees Nick. 'You're appealing to my inner darkness, Nick.'

'You're all seriously messed up, you know that?' He smiles as the newest member of their team walks through the doorway, covered in as much blood as he is. 'All good?'

Rocco grins and nods. 'I need a shower, but yeah. All good.'

The new Sandman had slipped into his role like he was born to do it, which could very well be the case. Who knows the way this contract shit works. The tall, sandy haired man was a natural, flying through his weapons and fighting training. Even Damon was impressed, which rarely happened.

Hopefully, he won't follow the same way as his predecessor. 'We ready to go?'

'All set, Boss.'

One of the banshees behind him groans, so he spins around and severs the head, kicking it away from the body. 'Get everyone outside.

Make sure all the heads are removed. We don't want them coming back to life. Or death. Or whatever they do.'

Damon falls into step beside him as they make their way through the building. 'You doing your test run tonight?'

Nick nods, then wipes his face on the bottom of his t-shirt. Banshee blood stinks. 'I always do. Why?'

Damon shrugs but doesn't say anything else.

'Would you just say what you want to say, but don't ruin my good mood.'

'Scarlett.'

Nick was expecting that. If anything, he was expecting one of them to bring her up today. 'What about her?'

Damon just looks at him.

'You think I should stop by her place?'

'Of course I do. We've left you alone for the year, hoping you'd get your head out of your ass and stop being a fucking martyr, but enough is enough.'

'Hey! I'm not a fucking martyr.'

'You've been moping around for the last eleven months. The only time any of us have seen you smile, is when you're fighting. Which I appreciate, but the others are a little worried. Apparently, having a bloodthirsty Santa isn't what they want. I, on the other hand, have no issue with that.'

'I'm not bloodthirsty! What the fuck is wrong with everyone? I'm doing my job. We all are. My private life has nothing to do with that.'

Damon slams him against the wall, holding him in place. 'You don't have a private life, Nick.'

'And you do?'

'More than you do.'

That surprises him. Damon and Eve are the closest friends he has, but he barely knows anything about either of them. The team tend to split, doing their own thing, unless they have to fight. Damon having a private life wasn't something that ever crossed his mind.

'I'm not having a go. You're a damn good leader. But you're losing yourself in the job. And I don't mean the Santa part. We exist to keep the balance. That's what you keep telling us. We walk the line between good and evil. Do what is needed to maintain that.

'The problem is, if you continue like this, you'll be tipping it the other way. We don't go looking for fights, Nick, but lately that's all we're doing. You're existing to fight.' Damon lets him go and takes a step back. 'You can do whatever the fuck you want. All I'm saying is that, you're more than what you are right now. Don't lose yourself to your contract. It's not a fight you want to face, believe me.'

Damon walks away, leaving him surrounded by the aftermath of their fight. Nick looks around him, bodies strewn along the corridor to either side of him. He wipes his face, tasting banshee blood on his tongue. The disgusting stuff is everywhere. He glances down at his sword, the blade covered in thick black blood.

Damon is right. He's picking fights, going from one battle to the next, trying to distract himself.

Trying to take his mind off Scarlett.

If Damon is worried about him, that's one hell of a wake up call. They may be friends, but Damon's fondness for pain and suffering isn't something they have in common. The Boogeyman has a firm hold on Damon. Nick knows that, and has known that for a while, but maybe the situation is worse than he thought.

He wanders outside, decapitating a few more banshee on the way out, then joins the rest of the team. Compared to the others, he's definitely got more than his fair share of blood coating him.

'Are we ready to head?' Jok asks, wiping his bloody staff on his jeans.

'Yeah,' Nick says. 'We're done.'

He stands in front of Damon, closing his eyes, as his friend brings him home. A few days with her, and he's still thinking about her a year later. Maybe Damon has a point. Maybe he's running from something he should be running towards instead.

Nick paces outside the door. He's been pacing for the last ten minutes, but that's as far as he's got. He doesn't even know what he's doing here. He arrived back from the mission and just walked. How he ended up here, he has no idea.

Fucking Damon!

This is his fault.

Everything was going just fine, until he brought up Scarlett. Okay, so maybe that's not entirely true, but he could have done without him mentioning her.

'Nick?'

He comes to a stop and looks over at Talen. Appears he's been caught. 'Hi.'

Krampus stands in the doorway to his room and looks in shock at him. 'What in the world happened to you?'

Nick grimaces, and wipes at his blood stained t-shirt. He didn't even think about getting cleaned up, before he came here. 'Just got back from a job. Sorry, I can go and get changed.'

'Don't be silly.' He smiles, which is slightly unnerving. Damn, his fangs are massive. 'Do you want me for something?'

'No.'

Talen leans on the door frame and just looks at him, which pisses Nick off for no reason. It doesn't take a lot for him to get pissed off lately.

The two of them keep up the weird silence for a ridiculous length of time. Nick came here to talk to him, so why isn't he talking?

Talen steps aside and gestures for Nick to come into his room. He squeezes past Talen and stops in the centre of the room. Talen pulls one of the chairs he brought from his old house nearer to Nick, so he sits down.

Talen sits on the end of the bed and faces him. 'I'm surprised to see you here, Nick.'

'Yeah.' He's a joke. Leader of the team, yet for some reason, he can't string a damn sentence together. Not that he has a clue what he wants to say in the first place. Or even why he's here. Or what he's doing with his life, full stop.

Actually, he's a pathetic joke.

And it's not helping that Talen is just sitting, looking at him.

'Eve gave you records from my predecessors.'

It was meant to be a question, but comes out as an accusation instead.

'She did. Is there something you need to know?' Talen asks, not in the least bit fazed by Nick's tone.

He can't sit still, so gets up again, scrubbing his hand over his hair while he paces. 'Damon thinks... actually, Eve too. Probably everyone, if I know the way this place works. They think I should... that Scarlett and I can... be together.'

Why can't he get the damn words out?

Talen nods as he leans forward, clasping his hands together on his legs. 'Quite a few of your predecessors have managed to fulfil their contract, while also maintaining a romantic relationship with someone not of our world. Is that what you are trying to ask?'

He drops back on the chair. 'Yes, it is. I was doing a fucking dire job at it though.'

'I understand why. It's not an easy topic for you.'

Nick shakes his head. 'I don't know what to do for the best, Talen. And I don't know why the fuck I'm talking to you about it! No offence.'

Talen smiles. 'Perhaps because I'm impartial, or more so, than anyone else here. You are not my boss, or my friend... yet,' he adds, his smile growing.

'Yeah. That's probably it. I just don't want anything to happen to her, because of being with me.'

'What Reve did was an isolated incident.'

'You don't believe that anymore than I do, Talen.'

Krampus nods, his attention falling to his hands for a few moments. 'But surely having Scarlett here with you, would be preferable to leaving her unprotected in the world?'

'She's not unprotected.'

'Sending Damon to keep an eye on her isn't the same, and you know that. You are not a man who gives up control easily. Having her out in the world without you being able to see her, to be with her, is driving you - forgive me - into a foul tempered, rather volatile man.'

Nick levels what he believes is an impressive glare at Talen, but the demon just smiles, so he gives up.

Knowing that he's won that argument, Talen continues. 'Do you want her here with you?'

'What I want doesn't matter.'

Talen laughs, a deep rumble that sounds more demonic than Nick was expecting.

'You fancy telling me what's so funny?'

'You, Nick. Always Santa.'

'What the fuck does that mean?'

'It means that you are becoming your job. You are Nick and you work as Santa.'

Nick is about to put Talen back in his place, but stops when he remembers saying pretty much the same thing to Scarlett, when she first found out who he was. He always thought he kept the two sides of himself separate. Clearly he's doing a lousy job. First Damon, and now Talen, have said roughly the same thing to him, within a few hours of each other. 'You been talking to Damon?'

Talen shakes his head, confused. 'No. Damon... I fear he would be the last person I would have any interaction with.'

Nick straightens, grateful for the change in topic. 'What's he done?'

'Nothing. I foolishly thought we might get a chance to speak to each other. Damon and I are very similar. Our contracts control us more than most. The battle with the darkness inside us is a daily struggle.' Talen narrows his eyes as he looks over at Nick. 'You are already aware he is fighting his contract?'

'I suspected. I'm keeping an eye on him. But, give him time. He might come around.'

'Perhaps. I presume he shares my thoughts about you and your contract?'

'Yeah.' He leans back in the chair and frowns at the ceiling. 'I honestly haven't got a clue what to do for the best. I have a responsibility as Santa. But there's a chance you and Damon might be on to something, with the neglecting myself part. Just a chance. I just haven't got a fucking clue how to satisfy both sides of myself, without messing up everything for her.'

'What makes you think that will happen?'

Nick shrugs. 'I don't know.' Enough of this feeling sorry for himself. He stands up and nods at Talen. 'Thanks for listening. I wasn't planning on loading all this on you. I guess Scarlett was right. You aren't as bad as I thought.'

Talen laughs, pushing to his feet. 'I may be mistaken, but that sounded like a compliment.'

'Yeah, it kind of did, didn't it? I better go and get cleaned up for the run.' He turns and walks over to the door, then stops to look back at Talen. 'You settling in all right?'

'I am. Thank you.'

'Good. Tell Eve if you need anything.'

Talen nods. 'Again, thank you. Stay safe Nick.'

'I'm not planning on having a replay of last year.'

As he walks away from Talen's room, he smiles wryly to himself. Would it be so bad if he did have a replay? He'd take the crash again, if it meant he could do it all over again with her.

23

It takes him a good half hour to wash all the blood off his skin. The stuff is like glue, refusing to wash away easily. He had gone over Damon and Talen's words in the shower. He can't stop replaying their conversations in his mind.

He hadn't realised how far he'd slipped.

Having it pointed out to him by both the Boogeyman and Krampus, made it all the more worrying. He steps out of the shower, wrapping a towel around his waist. One of the banshee had hit him on the side, but the cut doesn't seem too bad. It's still bleeding though, so he quickly bandages it and examines his appearance in the mirror. Apart from a few more scars, he looks exactly the same as last year. And the year before. And before that.

He'll look forty-one, be forty-one, for another few decades if that's what he wants. That's another reason he's not too keen on bringing Scarlett back here. He'd done a lot of research over the year. Anyone he's in a relationship with, would be under the same contract he is. No ageing for them either. And that's an even bigger ask than relocating out here.

Everyone she knows will grow old around her. All her friends will die, before she ages by even a day. It's too much of an ask.

But it's not necessarily something she needs to decide on straight away. She's got to be at least five years younger than him?

Why is he even thinking about details like that?

He drops down on the bed, then opens the top drawer of his nightstand, taking out the letter. Without opening it, he knows it's from Scarlett. No one else would have addressed the letter to Nick. He wasn't expecting it. Hoped for it, but was still surprised when it arrived this morning.

He turns it over.

It's still sealed. He can't bring himself to open it. Scarlett wouldn't have taken the time to write to him, if she wanted nothing to do with him. Unless she didn't want him to even consider dropping in on her, when he does his run?

What if she says she's taken the year to think, and decided it would be best if he stayed away? What if she says the opposite? What if she's thought about it and wants to see how things go between them?

Both decisions terrify him, and that's just ridiculous.

He still cares about her. That hasn't changed or diminished over the year. Not that it helps him make any kind of decision. He runs his fingers over the cut on his stomach. Whatever about the whole Santa thing giving her problems, it's the other side of his job that's giving him the headaches, when it comes to Scarlett.

He turns the letter over in his hands, looking at his name on the front, before placing it back on the nightstand.

He's going to do his trial run tonight as he always does. Kane and some of the others hadn't been too keen on him having a replay of last year, but he needs to go. He always does it. The workshop had been on lock down for the last week, all sleighs checked on a daily basis, and Kane has been stuck to his ass for the month, which is driving him insane.

As he gets dressed, his attention keeps going back to the letter. He gets billions of letters every year, yet this one is scaring the hell out of him.

Someone knocks on the door, so he picks up the letter, stuffing it in his pocket. 'Yeah?'

Eve opens the door and smiles at him. 'That's much better. I definitely prefer you without all the blood.'

He rolls his eyes as he picks up his coat and puts it on. 'You're hilarious, you know that. Is everything ready?'

She nods and falls into step beside him as he leaves his room. 'The reindeer are hitched up and the sleigh checked. You shouldn't blow up this time.'

'Wow! That's put me at ease. Thanks.'

She nudges him in the arm. 'You'll be fine. You nervous?'

He walks through the main workshop floor. Seems everyone has gathered to see him off. 'About what?' he asks, keeping his voice down.

'The run of course.' The look she gives him instantly puts him on edge. 'Why? What else would I be talking about?'

Nick approaches the sleigh, waiting for him in front of giant double doors. He gives each of the reindeer a rub. Their relationship has improved over the last year. Not by much, but at least they don't try to bite him whenever he goes near them. 'Why don't you cut the crap Eve, and just say what you want to say. I've already had a sermon from Damon and Talen, so you might as well add your two cents to the pot.'

'Are you coming straight back, or will you be gone for a bit?'

'It's a practice run. I'll be back by the morning as usual. I'm not planning on any detours like last year.'

He curses when she thumps him full force in the shoulder. 'What the fuck?' He hears a collective gasp, mixed with a few sniggers, from the workers. 'I'd appreciate if you didn't hit me in front of everyone.'

'You're the most frustrating man I've ever met. Have you even opened it yet?'

He walks around the sleigh, checking it for himself. 'Opened what?' he asks, knowing full well what she's talking about.

'Nick...'

He straightens, making sure the sleigh is between himself and Eve. She's got a powerful punch on her. 'Do we really have to do this now? It's a bit public.'

'Oh they all know,' she says, gesturing at the men and women, all with their attention on him.

'They know what exactly?'

'That Scarlett sent you a letter, and that you've probably been too scared to open it. They also know that you genuinely like her, and have been moping around the workshop for the last year, or killing things with a little too much enthusiasm.'

'I don't have time for this.' He tries to step into the sleigh, but the reindeer decide to have their say by taking a few steps forward, pulling it out of the way.

He curses under his breath and crosses his arms, knowing it's making him look defensive, but that's how he feels. He's being ganged up on by the whole fucking workshop. And his bastard reindeer.

He walks away from the sleigh and stands in the centre of the room. 'Okay. Fine! What the hell do you all want me to do? Tell me! I'm all ears. How about I grab a few beers? We could all have a lengthy chat about my private life. It's not like this isn't an important fucking time of year for all of us.'

Eve stands in front of him, the smile on her face seriously rubbing him up the wrong way. But given his current mood, everything would probably piss him off. 'Stop hiding. Open the letter, Nick.'

'What? Now? In front of everyone?'

She leans against the side of the sleigh and smiles over at him. 'We're your family. Why not?'

He doesn't want to open the letter. Doing it while he's alone is bad enough, without the whole workshop watching him get ditched. That thought stops him in his tracks.

You only get ditched by someone you're in a relationship with. He didn't have that with Scarlett. But it's what he wants. For the first time since his wife died, he actually wants something more than just sex. He wants a relationship. Wants to be with someone.

But that still doesn't solve the biggest problem. 'It can't work, Eve. If she wants... me, I don't know how to make it happen. Who I am... what I do... I can't ask her to be a part of that.'

Eve walks over to him and places her hands on his arms. 'We'll all help you find a way to make it work, if that's what you both want. But until you open the letter, you won't know what she wants. It's a fairly important first step, don't you think?'

'If I open it, will you all back off and let me do the run?'

'Maybe.' She squeezes his arms, then winks, before stepping back to lean on the sleigh again.

Looks like he's on a losing streak with this. Even though a part of him would love nothing more than to tell them all to fuck off and storm back to his room, that's not going to help the situation.

He pulls the letter out of his pocket, takes a deep breath, and opens it. Ignoring the fact he's got too many people watching him, he forces himself to read Scarlett's words.

Nick,

I'm going to get straight to the point and leave out all the normal pleasantries you'd usually include when you write a letter. I've spent the last year trying not to think of you. I've tried to forget our time together over those crazy few days. Tried not to think about being with you.

But I can't.

Even if you include all the craziness, it was still the best time I've ever had with someone. I miss you. I've missed you every day.

I know this is a busy time of year for you, but if you find yourself near my cottage again, it would make my Christmas to see you.

Oh, and just in case you haven't figured this part out yet. Santa, for Christmas this year I want you.

Scarlett x

She wants to see him! He reads the letter again, just to make sure he isn't imagining it.

'I'll take that stupid grin to mean she wants to see you?'

'Yeah! She wants me for Christmas.'

He grimaces, as a cheer breaks out from his onlookers.

'Oh fuck off the lot of you!' he responds, unable to stop grinning. 'Still doesn't help me figure—'

'Enough!' Eve shouts, startling him into silence. 'The figuring out bit will happen later. Go! Do the run and see Scarlett. I'll get Kane to meet you there. One of the guys can bring him over. We're not leaving you unguarded this year.'

He pulls Eve into a hug.

'Boss. You're hugging me. In public. Are you okay?'

Nick separates himself from her and straightens his coat. 'Yeah. All good. I'd better go.'

'See you in a few days then. I packed a bag for you just in case. It's in the sleigh already.'

'You packed a bag for me?'

She shrugs. 'I was hedging my bets. Now go!'

He climbs into the sleigh, thankful when the reindeer don't move again, throwing him on his ass. He takes the reins and settles back in the seat as the massive workshop doors open.

He still doesn't have the first clue how he can begin to have a relationship with Scarlett. But they're both on the same page and, right now, that's all that matters.

Scarlett decides against having another glass of wine. It would be a complete waste for Nick to show up and have her off her face, drunk. Unable to sit still, she paces the living room, checking her watch every few minutes. How long does she give him? She's already exhausted, but doesn't want to go to bed and risk missing him.

Which means she's going to have to stay up for the next few days. Not the most intelligent idea she's come up with. She could always sleep during the day. She doubts he'd bring the sleigh near here in the daylight.

If he even comes at all.

But what happens if he does come, and wants her to go back with him? She wants to be with him, or to give it a shot, but would he stay here, or would she go there?

She sits on the couch before getting to her feet again. It's all well and good saying she wants to give things a go with Nick, but the small detail of him being a kick-ass Santa isn't helping. It's not turning her off though. Far from it.

She checks her watch again. It's nearly two in the morning. He's not coming. She tries not to get down about it. He could come tomorrow instead. She makes sure the fire is safe, then turns off the lights and climbs the stairs.

The letter may not have even reached him. Or he got it and decided not to come.

She shakes her head as she pulls the duvet back and climbs into bed. He wouldn't just ignore the letter if he got it. Or at least she hopes he wouldn't.

She turns off the bedside light and closes her eyes.

Then she hears something outside. She jumps out of bed and

hurries over to the window, peering out into the night. Not that she'd be able to see anything out the window. It's pitch black outside.

Scarlett opens the window and leans out. She could swear she heard bells. But there's nothing there. No sleigh. No reindeer. And no Nick. She hangs out of the window for a good five minutes, desperately hoping to hear a bell, or see a massive sleigh in her driveway. But there's nothing.

'You're going to catch a cold.'

Scarlett spins around and screeches when she sees Nick standing by the foot of her bed. She leaps into his arms, wrapping her legs around his waist. So much for remaining cool and dignified.

He holds her against him, the smell of cinnamon instantly hitting her. 'Happy to see me?'

'Eh, yes! How did you get in here? I locked the door.'

'I might have come down the chimney.'

'I love that! I can't believe you came.'

'You asked me to,' he says, before kissing her. He even tastes the same.

When they finally come up for air, he puts her back on her feet and looks at her. 'Still as fucking sexy as ever.'

'Look who's talking.' It's like time has stood still for Nick, which it probably has, considering he doesn't age. He is every bit as gorgeous as he was the last time she saw him.

'Fuck, Scarlett!' He takes a step back and grins at her. 'I missed these Snoopy pyjamas. You're really spoiling me now.'

'You got my letter?'

'Got to admit, I had to convince myself to open it. Thought you were writing to tell me to keep away.'

'Are you kidding me? It's been the longest year ever.' She takes his hands and guides him towards the door. 'I want to show you something.'

She brings him downstairs and turns on the light. His gorgeous smile grows, when he sees the decorations covering every surface of the room. 'Bit different to last year.'

'Getting to know Santa kind of changed things for me. Please tell me the sleigh is in one piece this year?'

He laughs and opens the front door, pointing outside. She walks over to the door and smiles when she sees the huge sleigh complete with intimidating reindeer. 'No more blowing up.'

'Glad to hear it. So, is this a quick visit, or are you able to stay for a bit?'

He gathers her into his arms again, gently brushing her hair behind her ear. 'I guess that depends on one very important question.'

'What question?'

His eyes whiten as she looks at him. She's forgotten how stunning it is when they do that. 'What do you want for Christmas, Scarlett?'

'That one's easy. You, Nick. I want you.'

24

He's worn out and tired, but in the best possible way. It doesn't matter how many times he's with Scarlett, it's never enough. He'd lost count of the number of times they'd had sex over the last few hours, only taking a break when they both fell asleep, exhausted and satisfied.

He scrubs a hand over his face and opens his eyes, wincing as the winter sun hits him through the window. The clock on the bedside table reads three-thirty in the afternoon.

Scarlett climbs back up the stairs, carrying a tray laden with her famous Irish breakfast. 'That smells good.'

'I thought you could do with something to recharge you. You've had a busy night.' She places the tray on the table beside the bed, then climbs in beside him.

'It was quite an impressive evening all right!'

She laughs, passing him a cup of coffee. 'Oh it was way beyond impressive. Nick?'

He swallows his mouthful of bacon before answering. 'Yeah?'

'When I said in my letter that I want you, you know what I meant, right?'

'So it wasn't just my body you were missing?'

She nudges him in the side. 'Not just that, no. I know it makes no sense, but I really like you.'

He frowns at that. 'Charming.'

'No! I meant really, really, like you, after only knowing you for a few days.'

'I'm just kidding. Seriously though, I feel the same. The last year has been a blur of fighting, and pretty much doing whatever I could, to not think about you. Total fail though. The whole fucking workshop knows I was moping about you.'

'You were moping?'

'Apparently.' He turns to face her. 'When I lost my wife and daughter... I didn't think I'd be interested in anything serious again. And I'm still not sure bringing you into my chaotic world is a good thing. But I want to see where this will go.'

'So do I. I tried to get over you the last year. But I failed miserably. I couldn't stop thinking about you. Infuriating man!'

'You know that's the second time I've been called that in as many days.'

'Eve?'

'Who else.'

'So what happens now?'

'What I would like, is to stay here with you until tomorrow. Then, I have to get back to the workshop, or else my magic will go nuts with me again. But, I'm sincerely hoping I won't be going back alone. I'd like you to stay in Lapland with me for a few weeks if you can? Just see how things go. I have to do the run, then I'll be out of it for a week and a bit, but waking up to you there, would be a dream come true.'

'Really? You want me to come back with you?'

'I know it's a bit weird, given that I'll be asleep for a lot of that time, but, I guess I'm hoping it'll give you a bit of insight into what life is like in the workshop. And it's not like I'll be leaving you alone. Eve will look after you. Kane too. It might give you a chance to see what you think, without me in your face confusing things.'

'I'd love to!'

'Really?'

'Of course!'

He wasn't really expecting her to agree so quickly. Maybe if he'd asked the question last year, she would have given the same answer? Could have spared them both a lot of trouble.

'You look a little surprised.'

'I am, but in a good way. It's the answer I was hoping for.'

He can't help but laugh when she claps and gives him a tight hug. 'I can't believe I'm going back to your workshop. This is so freaking exciting!'

Nick couldn't agree more. The thought of doing the Christmas run, then coming home to her, has him nearly as giddy as she is.

Scarlett pulls her woolly hat over her head and walks outside. Nick is finishing loading her bags onto the sleigh, something she still laughs at, when she allows herself to think about it rationally. She's going on holiday with Santa to Lapland in his sleigh! She barely believes it herself.

But when she's faced with the man himself, larger than life beside his even larger than life sleigh, it's hard to be anything other than freaking excited.

'You got everything you need? If you've forgotten something, one of the guys can always pop back.'

'No, I have everything.'

He walks over to her and wraps his arms around her shoulders. 'You sure you want to do this? I won't be offended if you've changed your mind.'

'I'm going on holiday to Lapland with Santa! Why would I change my mind? I wouldn't have written you that letter unless I was sure about you, about all this craziness that accompanies you.'

'I love the way none of this seems to be fazing you.'

'Don't get me wrong. It's completely crazy, but I want to do it.' She runs her hand along the hilt of his sword, tucked into its sheath in the sleigh. She can still remember watching him using his sword, when he was fighting the Púca last year. It's not an image she's going to forget, or one that she wants to forget. Even injured and exhausted, Nick fought like no one she's seen before. Not that she'd witnessed many guys swinging swords around the place too often. 'I want to get to know you better - all sides of you.' She taps the sword. 'Even this one.'

'That's good, cause that's the side of my job that takes up the most time. The Santa gig is just one night.'

'Santa gig! Have you heard yourself?'

'To be honest, I'd prefer we didn't talk about anything to do with my contract. It sounds really stupid when I talk about it out loud to you. Anyway, you ready to head?'

'I'll just lock up, then I'll be all set.'

She quickly rushes around the cottage, making sure everything is secured, then goes back outside to the sleigh. Nick helps her into the seat, while Kane takes one last look around, making sure everything is secure before they leave.

The Nutcracker hasn't so much as said two words to her. She's tried to get him to talk, but gets nothing back. She thought Nick took his job seriously, but Kane is in a whole other league. His attention is on Nick and nothing else.

Knowing he's watching Nick, and her, when she's around him, does help put her at ease. She just wishes the stoic man would talk every now and again.

Nick sits down beside her and takes her hand. 'Thank you for doing this.'

'Thank you for asking me to. Hey, does Kane ever talk?' she asks, keeping her voice low as she looks around for the Nutcracker.

'Rarely. He's more of a seen rather then heard kind of a guy.'

'Sounds like great fun. Is he going to be silent the whole way back to the workshop?'

Nick nods. 'Absolutely. Besides, he hates travelling in the sleigh.'

'He does? Why?'

'Because I'm fucking terrified he'll forget I'm with him and go at full speed, which will leave me in pieces all over the damn globe.'

Nick and Scarlett slowly turn to look at Kane sitting behind them. 'How long have you been there?' Nick asks.

'Just a minute,' Kane replies, glancing at Scarlett.

'Right. And just for the record, I'm not going to forget you're both here, so stop stressing. I'm not planning on killing either of you.'

Kane snorts and crosses his arms, dismissing them.

Nick turns back around to look at Scarlett. 'Okay. So we should get going.'

Nick hits her with one hell of a smile before he turns back to the reindeer. 'Time to go home.'

Scarlett sits up straight as Nick steps out of the dressing room. Now this is an image of Santa she could get used to seeing! There's nothing sweet and jolly about the man standing in front of her. He's sexy and gorgeous in his red trousers and white top with black braces.

'Wow! Would you look at you! You're one hell of a sight, Santa.'

He licks his lips as he looks over at her. 'I can say the same about you. Haven't seen you in a skirt before. What's the occasion?'

'It's Christmas. You don't need an excuse to dress up. And you can dress up like that as often as you like.'

He takes his coat from the end of the bed and slips it on, followed by his gloves. 'You want to fuck Santa, right?'

She grins at the stupid smile on his face. 'That's not quite the sentence I was going for. But yes, I'm only human. How could I resist?'

'Now you're just taking the piss. But I'll let you get away with it, on one condition.' He slowly walks over, stopping right in front of her.

'And what would that condition be?'

He drops to his knees and runs his gloved hands up the front of her legs. He groans, dragging his fingers along her black tights. 'I get to destroy these right now.'

'What! Now? But you have to go! Everyone is waiting for you at the sleigh.'

'I'm the boss. They can wait five more minutes.'

'Oh wow. Five minutes! You really know how to spoil a girl.'

'Are you going to be a good girl and let me fuck you or what?'

'I think I might just be convinced.'

He smiles, then guides her towards the chair behind her. 'Sit down.' He pulls off his gloves, then shoves up her skirt and licks his lips. 'No panties?'

'I know you. I thought I'd remove one layer. Speed things up, just in case.'

Nick spreads her legs, burying his face in her pussy. He sucks and licks the wet material like a starved man. The deep moans and throaty groans doing as much to her, as his mouth is. He runs his fingers over her, rubbing the soaked pantyhose against her. 'So fucking wet.'

Scarlett gasps when he tears the pantyhose apart at the crotch, barely pausing for a second, before he's licking her again. His tongue slides inside, his fingers digging into her thighs, keeping her spread wide for him.

She looks down at him and moans. He's peering up at her as he fucks her with his tongue. His eyes are swirling with white. He sucks on her clit, his attention still focused on her, as she comes loudly. Nick holds her in place, his tongue massaging her until she finally comes down.

But he's far from finished with her.

Nick sits back on his heels, then pushes his coat out to each side so he can unfasten his trousers. Scarlett watches as Nick slips out his cock, his hand wrapping around it as he looks at her, his white eyes swirling.

'So, you going to be a good girl and sit on Santa's lap?'

Scarlett lowers onto his knees, gasping as Nick's dick presses against her, teasing her entrance, before he slowly pushes inside. When his dick fills her, Nick draws out, then thrusts back into her again.

She closes her eyes, but he taps her on the cheek. 'You look at me while I'm fucking you.'

Nick looks her in the eyes, the pale blue irises swirling with the build up of magic in his body. His hands grip her waist, holding her exactly where he wants her, as he thrusts into her.

But then she feels his lips on her neck, and on her breasts at the same time. He keeps his hands on her hips, but she can feel his fingers rubbing against her clit as he drives into her.

Scarlett's head drops back, as he uses his magic touch to kiss her neck, his teeth nipping at her skin, his fingers and mouth on her body, teasing her nipples. brushing against her clit. She has no idea what's real and what is being created by Nick's magic, but she doesn't care.

It all feels real. It all feels so damn amazing.

'Come for me. And make it loud!' When she shouts out, he curses and smiles at her. 'So fucking hot, Scarlett!' He lifts her off him and stands, holding his dick in front of her face.

'Suck me, Scarlett.' Scarlett nearly comes again when he slides his slick cock into her mouth. He grips her hair and holds her head in place, as he fucks her mouth. 'Oh fuck, Scarlett!'

She looks up at the spectacular man in front of her. His white eyes are focused on her as she sucks him. Santa is completely captivated by what she's doing to him.

He tilts his head to the side, a sexy smile on his lips. 'So you like sucking Santa's dick? How about Santa makes you come again while you've got his dick down your throat?'

Before she can answer, she feels his tongue slide into her pussy, his thumb rubbing against her clit as he fucks her. Nick groans and tilts his head back. 'Scarlett...'

He's close. His massive body is trembling, his breaths coming faster. He's a powerful leader, a legend, and she's got him quivering under her touch.

He drops his head to look at her again. 'Too fucking right you do! Make me come, Scarlett.'

He drops his hands to his side, leaving her in control. Keeping her eyes on his, Scarlett takes Nick as deep as she can, his thick dick filling her throat. Nick's stomach clenches, his breath quickening. She's close too. His magic touch still on her pussy, bringing her towards another orgasm.

Nick curses and comes in her mouth. As soon as his cum hits her tongue, Scarlett comes, her moans stifled by his dick.

He slides out of her mouth and pulls her to her feet, holding her against him.

She kisses him and he groans. 'You taste good.'

'I taste of you and me.'

He grins widely. 'Exactly! So, I didn't realise the whole Santa thing was such a turn on for you?'

She takes a step back and gestures to him. 'Have you seen what you look like dressed like that? And with your dick still out it's so much better,' she adds, smirking at him.

'That's not usually part of the Santa look. Except for you of course. You get the inappropriate version.' He pulls her over to him. 'If I was to wear this get-up more regularly, you'd be okay with that?'

She nods slowly, trying to play the whole thing down. 'Yeah. That might be nice.'

Nick laughs loudly. 'Don't try to bullshit me, Scarlett. I can see what you want. And you want to be fucked by Santa a lot. And, just for the record, I'll fuck you as Santa a lot.'

A heavy pounding on the door kills his smile. 'What!'

'If Santa is finished fucking, he's got a job to do.'

'I'll be there in a minute. Go away!'

'Do you think Eve knows what we were doing?' she asks, mortification colouring her cheeks.

Nick shrugs and picks her up. 'Couldn't really care less if she does, and neither should you.' He carries her into the bathroom, and sits her on the edge of the sink so he can remove what's left of her tights. He dumps them in the bin and runs his hands along her legs. 'Was that your last pair?'

'I think I packed another.'

He leans over, kissing from her knee up to her thigh. 'That's good. I enjoyed destroying the last pair. I'll have to do that again.' He gives her pussy one last, long lick before standing and smiling at her. 'You blushing?'

'Eve heard us having sex! That's something to blush about.'

He runs the back of his hand down her face then grips her chin, lifting her face. 'You never get embarrassed about that. Ever. You hear me?'

'I hear you, Santa.'

He grins, his eyes turning white as he kisses her. 'You're a real brat you know that?'

Scarlett grabs Nick's coat, pulling him between her legs. 'Now that is entirely your fault, Santa. You've released my inner brat. I hope you have what it takes to keep her in line.'

Nick's thumb brushes against her bottom lip. When Nick kisses her again, he leaves her with no doubt he can absolutely keep her in line.

He releases her, his hand moving down to rest between her legs again. 'I'm absolutely confident I can keep her in line. And I get the impression I'm going to enjoy every single minute of it.'

She slides off the edge of the sink and attempts to fix her hair in the mirror. 'So I should bring more tights with me next time?'

He wraps his arms around her and kisses the side of her neck. 'Sacks of them.'

Nick groans and glares into his bedroom, when someone beats on the door again.

'I think that's your final call, Santa. Zip up your trousers and get that ass of yours on the sleigh.'

She laughs at the look on his face. For some reason, talking about all the Santa stuff around her, makes him embarrassed. And she loves it.

He slaps her on the ass, then disappears into the bedroom. 'Get some fucking underwear on. No way you're leaving here with your pussy on show.'

Five minutes later, they're both presentable, underwear in place and hair fixed. Scarlett hands him his gloves, and steps back to admire him. 'Definitely the sexiest Santa I've ever seen.'

'And you are stunning.'

'Santa!' This time Eve thumps the door so hard the whole thing shakes. 'Presents. Kids. Now!'

'I'm coming!'

Nick holds out his hand and Scarlett takes it. 'We'd better go, or she'll break the damn door down.' When he opens the door, Eve is leaning against the wall a little further down the corridor. She grins widely and places her hand over her heart. 'Would you look at the two of you. So cute!'

'I'm seriously close to firing you.'

She smirks at him. 'Of course you are, Boss. So, are you ready to do your job, or do you need another few minutes to—'

'Eve...'

'Shutting up. Shall we?' She walks down the corridor, whistling to herself.

'I think she enjoys irritating you.'

Nick laughs, following after Eve. 'Yeah. A little too much. So, you going to be okay for the next day?'

'I think I could probably do with getting some sleep. Someone has kept me up for the last twenty-four hours.'

He winks at her. 'That's all your fault.'

'Of course it is.' They step on to the main floor of the workshop and walk over to the far end, where the sleigh is waiting for him. Unlike the first time she came here, this time she's not aware of as many whispers, or confused looks in her direction. Arriving back with Nick the first time had clearly rubbed some of the workers up the wrong way. Perhaps now, after making his feelings for her clear, she will be accepted. A lot will depend on what happens over the next week or two when he's asleep.

Scarlett smiles when the sleigh comes into view. She knows Nick is Santa, but when she sees things like his sleigh, it hits her again just who he is. She leaves him alone to speak to Eve, as they run through some last minute details. She's also relieved to see Kane checking every single inch of the sleigh - twice. No one wants a replay of last year.

About ten minutes later, with all the checks done, and rechecked again, Nick is ready to leave. 'Eve can track me the whole time.' He holds out his wrist, showing her the band fastened around it. 'It's securely fastened. No one is taking this from me again, without losing their head.'

'What beautiful imagery!'

'I'll be back as soon as I can. Make yourself at home while I'm gone, and don't take any shit from anyone. You're with me. I expect you to be treated like fucking royalty.' He raises his voice for the last part and she has no doubt it was meant to be heard by everyone within earshot.

Nick kisses her, then climbs into the sleigh and takes hold of the reins.

25

Waiting for Nick to come back from the run last year had been exciting. Who wouldn't be excited about witnessing Santa after he delivered all the presents? But last year, knowing that she had to leave him, had dampened the event.

This year is different. This year she's waiting for her gorgeous boyfriend to come home to her. She smiles to herself as she looks around the workshop. The beautiful wooden building is her home. She lives in Lapland with Santa. That'll make her next school reunion interesting!

Eve joins her on the walkway surrounding the landing area. 'We just picked up his tracker. He's five minutes away.'

'That's great.'

Eve glances down at her outfit and grins. 'Snoopy pyjamas?'

'It's kind of a private joke. Nick likes them.'

'Does he now? Funny. I never saw Santa as a Snoopy fan. So, how are you feeling about the fact he's going to be out of it for a bit?'

'Okay, I guess. It'll be a long wait. I might be a little irritating, so I apologise in advance.' Nick had explained it to her, but she's still anxious about him effectively hibernating for up to two weeks. The whole thing scares her, if she's being honest. The workshop will keep him alive while he sleeps, but that doesn't exactly put her at ease. How can a building keep a man alive?

'I've been with him since he signed his contract. He's come out of thirty-five big sleeps with no problem. But I get what you're saying. It's the not knowing when he'll wake up, that's the killer.'

The women look up as the sound of bells carries on the wind. 'Sounds like the Boss is back. Move your asses everyone!'

Scarlett smiles widely when the sleigh comes into view. She leans on the railing, but can't help jumping back a few steps when the monstrous reindeer land right in front of her, the sound of their hooves like thunder on the floor. Some of the team hurry over, taking hold of the first two reindeer, while others unhook them from the sleigh.

But then she sets eyes on Santa himself. Nick stands up and grins at her. He looks tired, but gorgeous. 'Hey Santa.'

He climbs down and lifts her over the railing. 'Hey sexy. Miss me?'

'Not even for a second.'

'Now that is a big fat lie. And those get you on my naughty list.'

Scarlett wraps her arms around his chest and smiles up at him. 'Oh I hope so.'

He groans and picks her up in his arms. 'I could get used to coming home to you.'

'I could get used to you coming home to me, Santa.'

She laughs when he grimaces. 'Nick. Please. Just Nick.'

'Whatever you say, Santa.'

He kisses her, then gives her a wicked look. 'You just like pushing my buttons, don't you?'

'There's a strong chance I do. I like when you punish me.'

'You say all this to me when I'm about to shut off for a week?'

'Just giving you motivation to wake up as fast as you can.'

'I already have that. I've got you. Now, I'm beat. I need you to tuck me into bed.'

'Oh would you two please lay off!' Eve says, as she walks around the back of the sleigh. 'There's a strong chance I'm going to throw up.'

He puts Scarlett back on her feet and shrugs off his coat, passing it to Eve. 'Get used to it.'

Eve grimaces and takes the coat from him. 'I was afraid you'd say that.'

Nick takes Scarlett's hand and walks away from the sleigh, followed by Eve. 'Everything ready as I asked?'

'Yes, Boss. Just like you wanted.'

'Thanks, Eve.'

He stops at the top of the stairs and turns to address the rest of his workers. 'Good job everyone. Eve is in charge while I'm out of it.'

Nick walks around the corner, stopping to hold Scarlett back against the wall so he can kiss her. 'I missed you.'

'It was only a day.'

'Mmm,' he grumbles against her neck. 'Too long.' He grabs her hand and smiles widely. 'I've got something to show you.'

He may still be grinning like a child as he hurries through the building to his suite, but Scarlett knows he's flagging. Every few steps he braces himself against the wall, but tries to hide it from her.

Nick stops in front of his bedroom door and turns to face her. 'No peeking yet.' He covers her eyes with his hand and guides her into the room. After a brief wait, he removes his hands.

'Oh my God! Nick! This is amazing!'

It looks like Nick went to town with the decorations. An enormous tree sits in the corner, the fire is lit in the huge fireplace which is also decorated. But it's the banquet that's laid out on the table that catches her attention.

'What's all this?'

'Christmas dinner. I was thinking that it's a bit shitty of me to drag you back here then leave you without any of this on Christmas Day. So I figured I can stay up for a bit and have Christmas with you.'

'Nick! I love it! Thank you.'

He shrugs, suddenly coming across a little self conscious which is strange to see. He's usually so confident. 'Bit early for a full turkey dinner, but I wanted to share this with you. I'm game, if you are.'

'Oh I'm always on for food - you know me.'

He pulls out her seat and she sits, her mouth watering as she breathes in the incredible aroma. Nick does the honours, piling her plate full of food then pours her a glass of wine. He lifts up his glass to her. 'Merry Christmas, Scarlett.'

She clinks glasses with him. 'Merry Christmas, Nick.'

Even though he's visibly exhausted, the next hour is spent tucking into an incredible Christmas dinner in the company of Santa. The conversation flows easily as it always does with him. He's incredibly easy to talk to, his mischievous sense of humour continuously making her laugh out loud.

She finishes her meal with a large portion of pudding and brandy butter, then settles on his knee by the fire, just enjoying each other's company. 'Oh I nearly forgot. I have a present for you.'

She climbs off his knee and rummages in her bag, pulling out the present. When she turns back to Nick, he's holding a box in his hand with her name on it.

'You got me a present?'

'Why do you sound so surprised? You got me one.'

'I know. I just wasn't expecting one from you.'

'I'd be a pretty terrible Santa if I didn't get you a present.'

They exchange gifts, but Scarlett waits to see his reaction first. Nick tears open the paper and laughs loudly when he sees what's inside. He holds up the Snoopy pyjamas and grins at her. 'It's like you read my fucking mind! How cute are we going to be in our matching pj's!'

'Seriously cute.' She opens his gift, carefully lifting the ornament from the box. She doesn't know how he arranged it, but Nick has somehow found someone to make a wooden carving of Snoopy. The details are incredible. 'I love it Nick! Thank you. Was it made here?'

Nick nods. 'It was indeed. I made it.'

She stares at him for a long few seconds, then down at the wooden carving again. 'You?'

'I'm Santa. It's kind of my thing.'

'Yeah, but this is... I mean wow! You carved this?'

'Yeah. It was kind of a hobby of mine before I signed my contract. It was nice to be able to do it again, to be honest.'

Scarlett slides onto his knee and kisses him. 'Thank you.'

'You're welcome.'

Scarlett cuddles in against his chest as Nick wraps his arms around her and yawns. 'Are you okay?'

'Yeah. Just hit the wall. I hate this part. Better get Eve in here. I need to run through a few things before I go to bed.'

Scarlett tidies away the dishes, piling them on to the trays, so they can be brought back to the kitchen, while Nick contacts Eve. It doesn't take a genius to see he's exhausted. His skin is grey, and she could nearly see the black rings under his eyes, darkening, as they ate.

When Eve arrives a few minutes later, he's barely able to keep his eyes open.

'Is Damon here?' Nick asks, his voice slurred and quieter than usual. He slumps onto the end of his bed. Scarlett tries not to freak out, but she wasn't expecting it to be this bad so fast.

'I'm here.' Damon appears out of the shadows at the side of the room.

'I'm going to hit the sack now. You okay to take over the team?'

'I do every year, Nick. Stop being a control freak and leave me to do my job.'

Scarlett manages to pulls Nick's t-shirt off before he can't hold himself upright any longer. At least with him lying down she can take off his boots and trousers, while he goes through last minute, completely unnecessary, details with Eve and Damon.

'Enough!' Her shout stops the three of them. 'Eve and Damon, thank you, but he needs to get some sleep. Nick, they are perfectly capable of doing their jobs, so stop worrying.'

Nick peers over at her through half closed eyes. 'You're sexy when you're bossy.'

'I think I'm going to be sick,' Damon mutters from the shadows.

'I know,' Eve agrees. 'Too tired to sit up, but he's still coming out with stuff like that.'

'Both of you can fuck off now,' Nick says, gesturing towards the door.

Eve and Damon make their exit while Scarlett tucks Nick into the bed, sliding in beside him. 'I'll be here when you wake up.'

'Talk to me.'

She runs her fingers through his hair as his eyes close. 'About what?'

'Anything. Don't like this part...'

Scarlett only manages two sentences of meaningless work gossip, before he drops off. 'Goodnight, Nick. I love you.'

The words come out before she realises she's saying them. But it's the truth. She's in love with him.

She closes her eyes and snuggles up against him, hoping he doesn't leave her waiting for too long.

26

Scarlett shuts down the laptop and turns to peer into the bedroom next door. Nick is still asleep in the bed behind her. It's the second of January. Nine long days and he hasn't stirred. She's worried sick. He's had no food. No water. Nothing at all.

'Are you sure—'

Damon opens his eyes, but doesn't lift his head off the back of the couch. He'd been taking a power nap as he put it, for the last hour. He's not fooling her for a minute. Damon hasn't left Nick's room for longer than a few hours since his friend fell asleep.

'How many times? This. Is. Normal. He'll wake when he's ready. Then he'll eat like a fucking horse. This damn place is keeping him alive. It needs him as much as he needs it. They're linked.' He goes quiet for a minute, then lifts his head to look at her. 'I promise he'll be fine.'

The new Sandman, Rocco, knocks on the door and steps inside the room, looking at Nick through the bedroom door briefly, before smiling at Scarlett. 'Eve asked me to give you these reports.'

'Thanks. You can pop them on the table. I'll get to them after lunch.' Who knew being Santa involved so much paperwork. After two days here she'd finally said enough is enough, and begged Eve to give her something to do. If she had to sit in his suite and just stare at him asleep, she was quite likely going to drive herself insane.

Rocco does as he's asked, then waves, before leaving the room again. She really likes the new Sandman. Reve's replacement seems to be genuinely lovely. He's taken to his new role like a duck to water. And it's kind of nice to have someone else relatively new to this world, to talk to. He's still coming to grips with certain aspects himself, so they've been helping each other out over the last nine days.

'You should go for a walk. I'll stay with him.'

'I'm fine, Damon.'

'I wasn't making a request. You need fresh air. Now you either walk out yourself, or I'll send you out there, my way.'

'Fine!' She's not really pissed off with him. She could do with a break, but she hates leaving Nick. She doesn't want him to wake up without her here.

'I swear I'll come and get you, if he even begins coming to.'

'Thanks. Make sure you do.' She takes her coat, hat, and scarf from the cupboard and wanders through the workshop, saying hello to anyone she passes. Tensions have certainly dissipated in the last few days. She's Santa's girlfriend. It's up to her to make sure she fits into their world, without disrupting it. Nick had saved a lot of the workers from a life living rough on the streets. This was their home long before she came on the scene. She has no intention of messing things up for anyone.

Scarlett finds Eve in the stables, attaching lead reins to two of the reindeer. 'Hey. Perfect timing. I was about to take these two out for a bit of fresh air. Fancy joining me?'

Scarlett takes one of the reins, guiding the massive reindeer out the door into the snow. While still seriously intimidating, the reindeer had warmed to her, not that she'll be rushing to tell Nick that. He was still struggling to get them onside.

'So, how are you settling in?' Eve asks once they're away from the workshop. 'It's been hectic the last few days. I haven't had a chance to speak to you properly.'

'I'm surprised how settled I actually am. I mean the whole situation is so unbelievable if I stop to think about it long enough, but it feels right. It makes no sense, but it's so right.'

Eve smiles and strokes the reindeer on the side of its face. 'I'm glad to hear that. Nick would be gutted if you didn't like it here. Have you made any decisions about your future?'

What a question! She feels at home here, but is she ready to leave her life behind and come here for good? 'I honestly don't know. I care about him, but it's a big decision.'

'I understand that. He does too. To be honest, I'm just glad he decided to go and see you again. He's been unbelievably foul to live with the last year. For Santa, he can be a miserable fucker at times.'

'I tried to get him to consider a relationship the last time, but he was dead against it.'

'He's wary. Did he tell you about his wife and daughter?'

Scarlett nods.

'He blames himself for what happened to them. He's been beating himself up for thirty-eight years. Punishing himself by fighting non stop. You're the first person who has actually made him stop and consider himself. He cares, Scarlett. He cares about you a lot. But I think he's being too hard on both of you.'

'How so?'

'Okay so he's Santa, but that doesn't mean he can't have a normal life. He's been ignoring Nick for too long, just focusing on the Santa part. I think he's scared something will happen to you, if he's not personally looking out for you every second. He needs to be a little less control freak about you, and just enjoy being with you. If he could just relax, and stop expecting a demon, or monster to jump out and attack the workshop, he might be less inclined to want to lock you away here, so nothing can get to you.'

'I don't suppose you have any ideas how I get him to relax?'

Eve smirks at her. 'Me? No. I've been trying for thirty-six years. The thing is, he's not in love with me.'

Scarlett stumbles, hanging on to the rein to keep herself from landing on her ass. 'He what?'

'Oh come on! It's blatantly obvious. And you love him. It's brilliant! Really. And that will give you the critical missing piece in the Nick puzzle.'

'What piece?'

'Everyone else in his life works for, or with him. He can, and does, ignore what we say to him about his personal life. Too often, if you ask me. But, you're his equal. That means our dear Santa may have finally met his match, in you.'

'So you think it's possible to be with him here, to have a life without interfering with his contract?'

Eve pauses as she considers that one. 'Yes. I do. I've worked with that group of men for decades, and I like them all. Okay, so I would very happily slap some sense into one or two of them, but for the most part, they're a decent bunch. But they all have one massive flaw.'

'What's that?'

'They put their contracts first. And though that's not necessarily a bad thing, there's more to each of them than that. Personally, I think they'd all be far happier, and work together better, if they learned to juggle the two sides better.'

'And they're all like that?'

Eve nods. 'Some more than others. Damon for example, is dangerously close to being controlled by his contract. Flint too, but I think that's because of who they are contracted to be.'

'Like Talen with Krampus?'

'Exactly. So to answer your question, yes. I believe you can have a semi-normal relationship with Nick. In fact, I think it would be an epic shame if you both didn't figure out a way to make this work between you.'

Scarlett ponders that, as they lead the reindeer through the trees. 'What about you?'

'What about me what?' Eve asks.

'Like you said, you've been working with them for decades. You probably know them better than most. Is there no one you have a particular soft spot for?'

Eve's laugh does nothing to throw Scarlett off the scent. If anything, it proves what she's suspected since her holiday began in Lapland. It didn't take a genius to realise Eve tended to show up in Nick's room whenever Damon was there. Initially, Scarlett put it down to timing, but as the days went by, she knew it was much more than mere coincidence.

'You like Damon, don't you?'

Eve's laugh dies away. 'Fuck!' she mutters as she trudges along the track. 'Maybe? I don't know. Possibly. Damn!'

'Does he know?'

Eve throws her a withering look. 'Oh come on. Of course not! And I don't *like* him. I have this strange, incredibly irritating crush on the fucking Boogeyman. But I'll get over it. He's just... God he's just so... hot! Irritating, but really hot!'

Scarlett does see the attraction to Damon. He has something about him that's enticing. 'Do you plan to act on it?'

Eve shakes her head. 'No way! Like I said, his contract has him. He thrives on fear and pain. I think it might be too late for him. Too late for us.'

She falls silent, keeping her attention on the path ahead of them. Scarlett leaves her to her thoughts. Being attracted to someone like

Damon would be far from easy. Her heart goes out to Eve. It must be so difficult to be near him , knowing she probably will never have him.

Just like she thought was the case with Nick. But it doesn't have to be like that for them. Against all the odds, they have been offered another chance to be together. A chance she would be foolish to waste.

'Eve.'

She looks over her shoulder to Scarlett. 'Yeah?'

'I need your help with something.'

For the first time in thirty-six years, he knows he's not waking up alone. Scarlett is in the bed with him, her perfect body pressed against his side.

He thought she'd leave while he was asleep. He hates admitting it to himself, but he was convinced she'd change her mind about him, about being with him, and go back to her life. She groans softly in her sleep, snuggling closer to his side. He doesn't move. He's just happy to stay here like this, enjoying the moment.

He needs to stop expecting things to go wrong for him. She stayed with him. She said she would, and he should have believed that. Ever since his family was killed, he'd had his guard up, expecting to lose anyone he let close to him. He was in for a very long miserable life if he keeps going the way he was.

Unable to stop himself any longer, he wraps his arms around Scarlett. She rests her arm on his stomach. Then she holds her breath, and he knows she's awake.

'Morning.'

She squeals and wraps her arms around his neck. 'At long bloody last! What took you so long?'

He rolls over to face her, propping his head up on his hand. 'How long is long?'

'Ten days. I was getting worried. And I mean seriously worried. They kept telling me it was normal, but what the hell is normal around here?'

He brushes her hair back from her face and it hits him how much he cares for her. He knows how she feels about him. Before he fell asleep, he heard her tell him she loves him. But it might just have been a spur of the moment thing.

'Hey, why are you crying? Did something happen while I was out of it?'

'I'm crying because I'm happy, you oaf! This is all new to me, okay? You were unconscious for ten days. It's all well and good people telling me not to worry. But I was worried, okay? Ten days is a long time.'

'I'm sorry you were worried.'

'It's my fault. You told me what would happen. I guess I just wasn't prepared for it. Are you okay? Are you hungry?'

'I'm fine, and yeah, I'm starving, but I'll get something in a minute. I just want to be here with you for a little longer.'

'I have no complaints about that at all. You know, I've been doing a lot of thinking while you were sleeping.'

He gets a bad feeling. A really bad one. 'Right...'

'I'm leaving. I have to go back to work at the end of the week, and if I ask for any more time off, I'll be fired.'

And there it is. The thing he was dreading. Completely expecting, but still dreading. 'Of course.'

'Hey, don't go all gloomy. I'm not finished. I'm going back to pack my things, get set up to work remotely and collect my work laptop, then I'll be back here to be with you.'

He pushes onto his elbow and scrubs a hand over his face. 'You're staying?'

She nods, the smile on her face the best thing he's seen for a while.

'Too right I am! And I know it may seem foolish as we've known each other for no time at all. And that time has been less than normal, if there's even such a thing when it comes to you, but I think... actually, I'm sure, I love you. I don't want to go back to my quiet life. I want to stay here with you.'

It usually doesn't take him long to get his head straight after he's been asleep, but he's struggling to keep up with this conversation. 'You're going to have to slow down at bit. My brain is still half asleep.'

Scarlett shuffles closer to him. 'I love you, Nick. I want to stay with you. To see a lot more of you. To see where this goes between us. It's like you kept saying when you first told me who you were... forget the Santa part. Can't we just see where things go for Scarlett and Nick?'

'I want that too, Scarlett.' He reaches out and rubs his fingers down the side of her face. 'And I love you.'

'You do?'

'I do, but I was afraid to ask you to be here with me. I thought it would be too much. I didn't want you to have to decide between your life and me.'

'I don't have to decide between you. I can still do my job remotely. We're in Scandinavia. It's hardly another planet. I've already talked this through with Eve. Whenever I need to go back, one of the guys will take me. Or you could drop me back, but arriving on a huge reindeer might get us noticed. It absolutely can work, Nick.'

She climbs out of bed and opens the drawer of the desk. Scarlett gets back into bed and holds up the leather cuff. 'Eve made me a tracker. It's the exact same as yours. When I go back to Ireland, you'll know where I am all the time, and be able to track me.'

He lies back on the pillow and looks at the tracker in her hand. She's doing an impeccable job of squashing his concerns, one at a time. Not completely, but he'll give her ten out of ten for effort. 'I don't know, Scarlett. If anything happened to you because you're with me...'

'You can't keep thinking like that, Nick. And yes, I know saying that to you is a waste of breath. I know you need to protect every single person under your roof, every single member of your team. I don't know if that trait comes from Nick, or from Santa, but it's who you are. It's part of you and I love that about you. But you need to try to let go of a little control. This can work, Nick. Please, just give it some time. I don't want us to miss out on something potentially amazing, because you're scared I'm going to get hurt.'

He wants to give in. To just say to hell with it, and let her pop back and forth between the two worlds. But he's fucking terrified. He fights creatures from nightmares, without a second thought. But, it's because of that he's struggling.

'You really want to do this?'

'More than anything.'

Nick nods and cups the side of her face. 'Me too. I love you Scarlett. I really do.'

'And I love you Nick.' She shrieks and rolls over, lying on top of him. 'We're really doing this?'

'I love you, Scarlett. I want to be with you. I never thought about having something relatively normal with you. I'm really excited about this!'

'As you should be!' She grins and lifts herself off his chest, looking down his body. 'Well, well, well. You are excited aren't you!'

'It's been ten days. That's a fucking lifetime, believe me. So, you going to deal with that, or what?'

She gives him a downright sexy smile that does nothing to calm his dick down. 'It depends.'

'On what?'

'On whether you're going to return the favour?'

'You know I'm going to.'

'Glad to hear it. And Nick?'

'Yeah?'

'I've been really, really, naughty.'

He flashes her a wicked smile. 'Glad to hear it.'

27

Scarlett finishes her coffee and closes the laptop. Dani had sent her some files to work on until she goes back in a few days. The plan is to spend a week at home, before coming back to the workshop and her new life with Nick.

Dani is nearly as excited about the move as Scarlett is. Apparently, she is taking credit for the whole situation. Without her pushing Scarlett to contact Nick, they would never have got back together again. She isn't going to ruin it for her by saying that the Boogeyman had a hand in it too!

Not that Dani would believe her for one second. Just like she wouldn't believe Scarlett is moving in with Santa. Nick lives in Finland and that's where she's moving. Dani and the rest of her friends had accepted that without question.

And it's not like she's leaving her life behind for good. She'll be back and forth between Lapland and Ireland regularly.

She checks the time and stretches. Time for a break. Scarlett closes her office door and walks along the corridor to the main workshop. Nick had given her a room in the new building that she could use for work, and she loves it. It was nice to get back to work again after the break.

She'd spent most of the last week with Nick, taking advantage of the fact that, for the moment, no one seems to want to kill him, or kidnap her. The time was spent in bed mostly. Nearly two weeks of rest had given Nick a ferocious appetite, and she was more than happy to help him satisfy it.

During the brief times they weren't having sex, she'd helped Talen make his living quarters more homely. Nick and Eve had assigned him a room in the new wing, but that was as far as their generosity went. Apart from a bed and a chair, he had nothing except the odd mismatched pieces he brought from his old cabin.

After a bit of convincing and sweet talking, Nick had made sure she was able to spruce up the room with other items from spare rooms. Even though Nick and Eve speak to him, there aren't many others in the workshop who do. Hopefully in time that will change, but he'll have to earn the trust of a lot of people first.

Until then, Scarlett is happy to spend as much time as possible with him. She enjoys his company immensely. He shares his many books with her, and takes the time to explain this new world in a way she understands.

The dining room is occupied by a handful of people, who all greet her when she enters. Nick's workers have accepted her, making her feel like one of the family, which she really appreciates. She hasn't met anyone in the workshop she doesn't get on with.

Scarlett makes herself a sandwich, carrying the plate over to an empty table, so she can check a few emails on her phone. She doesn't know when she'll be seeing Nick today. He was up before her this morning, so he could spend the day training with the rest of the team. It's something they do regularly and, even though she's not thrilled about him going out to fight, the fact they train often, makes her feel a little better about it.

Ten minutes later, her peace is interrupted when the team pile into the dining room, talking noisily as they help themselves to food.

Nick is the last one to enter, his serious expression melting to a smile when he sees her. 'Hey there, sexy,' he says, sitting down opposite her.

'Hey there, Santa.'

Instead of his usual red trousers and white top, he's wearing darker red along with a black top. He's also wearing a leather holster over his shoulders, a gun resting under each arm, and a sheath with his sword hanging on his belt.

He frowns as she takes a few minutes to look at his outfit. 'What?'

'Sorry?'

'You look confused.'

'I just wasn't expecting all that,' she says, pointing to him.

'All what?'

'The clothes and the weapons.'

'I wear black and dark red when I'm fighting. The blood doesn't stand out as much on the darker colours. You have no idea how difficult it is to get demon blood from a white top. It's a real bitch,' he says with a wink.

'I can only imagine. I can't believe I'm about to say this, but the whole getup really suits you. I thought you only used a sword?'

'I prefer my sword, but the guns are quicker sometimes.'

'Right.' While he does look good, the fact this is his demon slaying outfit is slightly unsettling.

'Are you really okay? About me doing this I mean. You don't look overly happy about it.'

'I think it just kind of hit me when I saw you like this, but I'm fine, really. Of course I don't want you putting yourself in danger, but it's part of the deal. I know that. And I know you can take care of yourself.'

'I can, and I swear I'm careful. We all are. I will come back to you.'

She jabs him in the ribs. 'You damn well better! But maybe with less blood than you usually come back covered in? I'm not sure I need to see you like that.'

He narrows his eyes and crosses his arms. 'You been talking to Cobh?'

'You mean, did he mention that Santa likes to swing his sword around and make a mess? No. Not at all.'

'I'm going to kill that fucking fish!'

'What the fuck did I do?' Cobh asks, placing his plate of food on the table.

'Sword swinging Santa making a mess. Sound familiar?'

Cobh grins sheepishly. 'You know, there is a strong possibility I may have mentioned something along those lines.' He grunts when Nick thumps him on the arm. 'Ouch! Easy there, Santa.'

One by one, the rest of the team sit around the table, dwarfing the table with their weapon clad bodies.

'How was work?' Nick asks, as the others tuck into their food.

'Good. It was nice to get back to it. And thank you for the office. I never thought I'd have my own space like that to work in. I'm feeling rather spoiled.'

He pats his knee, so Scarlett gets up and settles onto his lap. Nick wraps his arms around her, then kisses the side of her neck. 'Yeah well, get used to it. I plan to keep spoiling you.'

'Fuck off, Nick! Some of us are eating.'

He glares over at Cupid who just waves, and goes back to his lunch.

'What have you got planned for the rest of the day?' she asks as he continues to glare at Hunter.

'Now I'm planning on putting Hunter through his paces in the training room. See if I can wipe that smile off his face.'

Hunter stops smiling. 'Dammit!'

Nick turns back to her. 'Why? What have you got planned?'

'I was thinking of cooking you dinner.'

'Mmm. And would you be dressed or naked while you cook it?'

'I don't have my Snoopy apron with me.'

'Shame. Add that to the list of stuff to bring back.'

'Will do, Santa.'

'I told you to stop calling me that.'

She smiles at him, loving the way his eyes are whitening. She thought it just happened around Christmas time, but it seems his emotions affect the change too. 'And I told you I like irritating you.'

He leans over to speak in her ear. 'Naughty list all the way.'

'Oh give it a fucking rest, Santa,' Damon mutters from behind them. 'All this lovey dovey shit is making me sick. I need to hit something.'

'Then mind your own fucking business. Eat up! Time to get back to work.'

'So, ready to see who's going to win this bet?' Cobh asks.

'What bet?' Nick asks.

Cobh grins widely. 'Just the bet as to whether being a love-sick puppy will make you soft in the field.'

Scarlett laughs, stopping briefly when Nick glares at her. 'Are you all in on this?'

'Yep,' Jok says. 'Could earn myself a fair bit on this one.'

'I wouldn't count on it. And I wouldn't advise any of you get in my way, or there could be an accident.'

'Play nice, Santa,' Jok says. 'It's not good for team morale if the leader guts the other members.'

'Depends on who the other members are,' he replies.

The others laugh, while Nick turns his attention back to her. 'And I don't need you encouraging them. I've a hard enough time keeping them in line.'

'Just make sure you show them why you're in charge. I could earn myself a fair bit on it, if you do.'

He grins and pulls her close so he can kiss her. 'I'm assuming you bet on me instead of against?'

'Of course.'

'That's a relief!'

Their laughter dies away when Eve hurries into the room. She passes Nick a piece of paper which he reads, his frown deepening as the seconds tick by.

'We're heading out!'

He lifts Scarlett off his knee, then follows Eve back through the workshop, Scarlett's hand firmly in his, while the rest of the team follow behind them. As they walk, Eve tells them about the job, but to Scarlett the whole thing sounds like a foreign language. All she picks up from it, is that something nasty is on the rampage, and Nick's team has to stop it.

When they get to the main workshop floor, Nick turns to the rest of the team. 'We ready to get this done?'

Scarlett steps to the side, as one by one, Nick's team checks in with him. It's quite a sight. A group of intimidating men, loaded with weapons, preparing to go into battle. When you take into account the roles each of these men play, it just makes the scene even more bizarre.

Nick beckons her over and kisses her. 'I'd better go.'

'See you when you get back.'

'It's a date. I'm looking forward to you washing my back for me.'

'I'll be waiting for you to show me why you're in charge.'

He groans softly as his eyes whiten. 'Too right you will.' He leans over to speak in her ear. 'You make sure you're ready. I want your pussy wet for me when I get home.'

'I think I can do that,' she says, already well on the way there.

He grips her chin and kisses her, his tongue pushing into her mouth. 'Good girl,' he whispers in her ear before joining the rest of the team. 'I better let them out to play. I'll see you when I get back.'

The six men stand around Damon so he can transport them using his powers. As she looks at the men, she can't quite believe this is her life now. And she couldn't be happier. Nick winks at her. 'I love you.'

'I love you too.'

And then he disappears.

EPILOGUE

When he signed his contract to be the Boogeyman, Damon hadn't put much thought into what it would mean for him long term. Maybe he should have. Maybe he shouldn't have accepted, just because anything would have been better than the life he was living at the time.

He'd been so desperate to escape, he'd said yes without even listening to half of what the role entailed.

Santa. Jack Frost. The Sandman. Those are contracts you could accept without having to think for too long. Even the Horseman would be a tough gig to pass on. That horse is seriously freaky.

But as he hides in the shadows in Nick's workshop, watching all the happy, carefree humans interacting with each other, he knows he made a mistake he can't undo.

It's not the first time this thought has hit him. Won't be the last either. His job is to scare people, to punish them. There's a lot of other shit he has to do, but that's the core of his existence. Has been for fifty odd years now.

His life improved when Nick signed his contract. The new Santa's stubbornness means he is a fan of doing things his way, instead of how they've always been done.

Which included befriending him.

No one was more surprised about that, than Damon himself. The two men just clicked from the first moment they met.

It wasn't the only thing that changed in his life when Nick took over.

He melts further into the shadows, as Eve walks through the workshop, stopping to speak to a group of women. She laughs with them, as she runs her hand over her pink hair.

Eve is unlike any woman he's interacted with since he became the Boogeyman. She's wary of him. That's not surprising. Everyone is. His appearance is far from approachable. At his core, he is a demon like Krampus. When he's in his true form, he has fangs, horns, and wings. In human form, all the physical traits of the Boogeyman disappear. All except for the thirst for pain. That never leaves him. Not for one second.

Just what every woman wants from a potential mate.

She climbs the stairs and walks towards him. As much as he wants to show himself to her, he stays in the shadows, hiding from her, like he's done so many times before. He reaches out as she passes, desperate to make contact, even though she won't feel it.

Eve stops just opposite him and turns to face him. She can't see him until he takes solid form. Even so, she stares at him through the shadows, like she can see him. His throat dries as she continues to look at him. He shouldn't let her get to him the way she does. He should disappear and go back to his house. Leave her alone and stop watching her from dark corners.

But he doesn't.

She smiles, then her lips part, and she licks her lips. He bites back the groan, the stab of his fangs in his lip travelling straight to his dick. This is what she does to him every time. He wants her. He needs her. Has for decades, and the all-consuming feelings aren't going away as much as he wants them to. Or not. Lately, the human feelings he has for Eve are the only things keeping him from letting the darkness take over completely.

But he can't have her. Can never have her. All he can hope for is to continue like this. Watching.

Pain is the only thing he enjoys. The only thing that excites him.

The only thing that arouses him. It's fucked up. She can't be a part of that. Never will. He won't allow it.

That won't stop him wanting things to be so different. Damon reaches for her, the shadows extending towards her, gently brushing against the side of her face, before he gets a grip of himself again and pulls back.

Eve takes a step back and rubs the side of her face. Then she smiles. It's barely there, but he could swear he sees it. He watches as she walks away from him, towards the living quarters, glancing over her shoulder once, before she turns the corner.

She knew he was there! But that's impossible!

Damon considers going after her. The pull towards her is so strong. Common sense is stronger though. He reforms back in his home, if you could even call it that. The period house had been empty for decades and, for some reason, it was assigned to him.

It's dark, cold, and fucking miserable. But it's off the beaten track, and somewhere he can be himself, without risk of being discovered.

He holds out his hand in front of him and smiles. The tips of his fingers are still warm after the brief contact with Eve.

He has to stop doing this to himself over and over again.

Needing to distance himself from the pathetic self-pity taking over, he allows the other side of himself to take control. He welcomes the pain of his horns and wings tearing out of his body. It helps to soothe him, to steady his thoughts. He stretches his wings, dragging the talons along the walls to either side of him.

As much as he wants what Nick and Scarlett have, it's not in his future. Eve isn't in his future. Not while he's locked into his contract. No one in their right mind would want something like him.

He flies up to the roof of the house, relishing the feel of the cold wind against his wings. He roars into the night sky, but for the first time it's not a shout of anger.

It's of despair.

Thank you for reading **North Bound**.

I hope you enjoyed meeting my new cast of characters. There is plenty more to come!

The next book, **Shadow Bound** is coming soon.

Do you fancy staying updated with news about my books?

• Join my mailing list at: www.kafinn.com/

• Like me on Facebook: www.facebook.com/kafinnauthor

• Follow me on Instagram: www.instagram.com/kafinnauthor/

• Keep up to date with new releases:
https://books2read.com/ap/nE2Kdj/KA-Finn

Also, if you have a moment, I'd appreciate if you could review **North Bound** at the store where you purchased it. The band and I would love to know what you thought of the book.

Thanks for your support!

K.A. Finn

Coming next...

TWISTED LEGENDS # 2

SHADOW BOUND

K.A. FINN

www.ingramcontent.com/pod-product-compliance
Lightning Source LLC
Chambersburg PA
CBHW031201020726
47499CB00002B/440